PRAISE

DOWN WITH THE PRINCE

"*Down With the Prince* is a delight to read. With memorable worldbuilding, Renae paints the picture of a world that feels as delightful and vivid as a Studio Ghibli movie. The characters, too, are lovable and unique. Hollis, Lukxa, and Dagen carry the story with their snappy dialogue and memorable interactions. This is a book that will live rent-free in your head!"

HANNAH CARTER - AUTHOR OF *THE DEPTHS OF ATLANTIS*

"*A lighthearted romance filled with a fresh magic system and unforgettable characters!*"

ALEXANDRA BARBAR

"*Down with the Prince is an enthralling fantasy debut from Xanna Renae, filled with palace intrigue, disability representation, and a flirty budding romance. Hanging over all this is a mysterious curse, a time constraint, and something nagging at the back of our characters' minds.*"

WILLOW WHITEHEAD

Cover Art & Illustrations © 2023 LolloCo
Story © Nightshade Publishing®

First Edition December 2023
Paperback ISBN 979-8-9850823-8-8
Hardback ISBN 979-8-9850823-9-5

Published by Nightshade Publishing®
NightshadePublishing.com

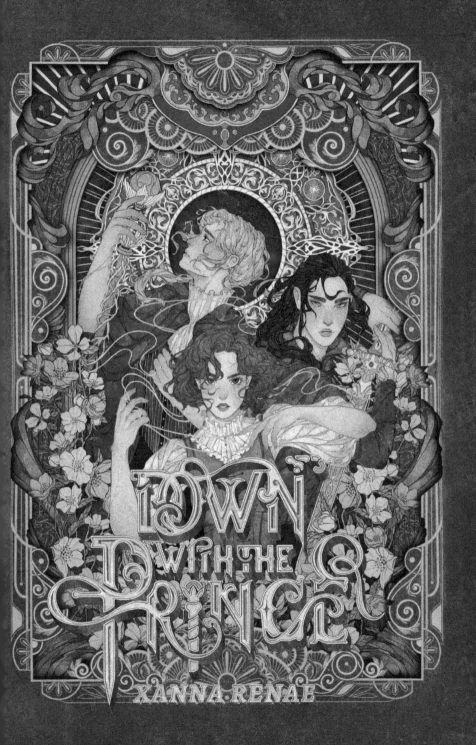

Down with the Prince

Xanna Renae

HOLLIS

LUKXA

DAGEN

Other books by Xanna Renae

Through the Violet Redwoods

Other Books by Nightshade Publishing®

The Willow Tree Swing
Of Ink & Paper
Balloon Children

TABLE OF CONTENTS

To my Dearest Husband, Noah

I once spoke this to you as you fell asleep in the comfort of our conversations: If ever I were to write a happy story, it would be inspired by how you make me feel.

CHAPTER ONE

HOLLIS

There was no recollection in Hollis' mind as to what day it was. She remembered leaving her warm bungalow on the eve of the week's end. Every day since then passed with her camping on the pebbled shores of the Hozen coast, tossing a random assortment of things into the ocean to appease the Seafolk—or rather, trying to. The last of her exuberance drained from her as any ounce of heat left in her bones froze.

At least the coastline was stunning. Little salt-covered shells and pebbles in a range of vivid colors lay scattered all across the waterline.

Hollis turned on her feet. The small hill which had been to her back, where the tall grass swayed in the wind, the sun painting them gold, waved encouragements to her as she stood. Patiently waiting to receive an answer from the folk below the water.

She took in a deep breath of sea air. This part of the world was magical in its own right, all by itself. No trace interference of her people's magic.

Having grown up where bits and pieces of magical traces could be found in everything, Hollis enjoyed finding little traces of the world where the stain of Tablin magic hadn't yet left a botched fingerprint in the fabric of nature.

A gust blew into her face, trapping pieces of hair into her mouth and eyes. Her cane made an unhappy *thunk* on the pebbled ground as it fell, freeing her hands so she could swat at the emerald locks trapped between her teeth.

Once all the salt-coated strands were freed from her mouth, Hollis twisted the side bits of her bangs around her fingers before tucking them tightly behind her ears. Short hair was impossible to deal with. It was a constant torture brought on by a decision that wasn't even hers to begin with.

One moment Hollis was tending to the flu-ridden baker's wife; the next, everyone screamed as the woman's youngest child hacked away at Hollis' braid.

Fortunately, she looked good with short hair. It was no skin off her back. Only long locks off her head. Long, curly locks—

Perhaps she *was* a bit upset about it?

She shifted her posture and ignored the throbs that ran deep in her spine.

Hollis bent to retrieve her wooden cane and plucked a blush conch shell from her leather bag. Her body shook as she straightened and positioned herself against her cane.

This was the last step. If she'd done everything perfectly, sang in the proper tone, procured the right snacks, and made an utter fool of herself, the Seafolk would accept the final gift.

The wind let out a cold breath as the tide crept close to Hollis' bare feet. Another breath. White water drew backward.

Hollis held tight to the conch shell and lobbed it with all her might toward the horizon as the water withdrew. She whistled the obligatory, flowery tune as she twirled her arms in the air, twisting the threads of magic as she danced. She plucked the stands controlling the wind, willing it to circle about in the air. The strands of sunlight were next, pinched in such a way to reflect blinding lights against the water's surface.

By the fields of green, she hoped no one was watching.

She relaxed her hands, allowing the world to return to its unaltered state.

"Well, there's that. I'm—is that my voice?" Her throat cracked as a sound much too like a frog's let from her mouth. Her hands flew to her

cracked lips, hoping to feel that the wretched sound wasn't in fact coming from her.

She spoke again and discovered the sad truth. The days of singing and neglecting her thirst had worn her throat raw.

Now wasn't the time to be vain.

The conch floated on the surface about four yards out, bobbing but staying exactly where it was despite the choppy waters about it. Hollis narrowed her gaze and saw a few little tendrils holding the shell steady. *Finger-like.*

The finger-like shape grew to a full hand gripping the shell. It pulled the shell under the water with a loud *plunk*, water splashed upward and created a prism of light in the mist.

Hollis trapped her lips between her teeth, the skin threatening to break and bleed if she were any more tense.

It wasn't over yet. The Seafolk had shown her they were there—they'd watched her little ritual. The first time Hollis had completed it without the aid of her parents who now lived comfy retired lives traveling the world.

The wind waltzed Hollis' hair around every direction it could. She paid them no heed as she stood, eyes wide, watching. Waiting.

Warmth broke wider along the horizon. The sudden onset of heat reminded her body how frozen it was. She wrapped her arms around herself, under her cloak, to hold the shivering at bay.

Plink, plink, plink.

The conch shell washed over the pebbles and little shells and landed against her frozen toes. The calmed tide no longer threatened to encapsulate the world the Seafolk were wrongly separated from.

A breathy laugh escaped her chest. She'd done it. The duty of peace lay heavy in her hands. She'd needed to extend the sorrows from the Tablins' that created the creatures in their twisted amusement, extending regrets on their behalf. A task she'd completed.

A sharp huff created a cloud of mist in front of her face. Her ancestors

weren't regretful at all considering they went on to merge man and bird next. Since she lived away from the northern parts of the world, though, she didn't have to deal with the Airfolk. Truly a blessing.

But none of that mattered. Sorrow was accepted from the Seafolk. Grace was given.

Now was the time to go home.

Hollis stumbled about the shore in her stiffness. Gathering up her little odds and ends that scattered along the pebble beach.

The wind's blue threads wrapped around her in the salted air, pushing her legs and cane forward. "I understand it's time for me to go; give me a moment of respite. I'm slow." She hated when the wind bullied her around. Acting like she didn't know a soft bed awaited her in her warm little bungalow above the village. As if sensing her desires, the wind's threads kicked up little blades of grass and pebbles to show her way home.

Oh, how her bones ached, but she did not have a care left in her body to mind it. No, every bit of caring had been tossed into the sea. She didn't need to linger about to heal herself for the journey home.

Hollis stumbled about in her walking, shaking out her hands and legs as she went. Trying to bring some feeling and warmth back to her bumped skin.

Harvest had only arrived a few weeks ago, but the mornings along the sea were already frigid beyond reason.

This is why you sleep until noon, Hollis. Wait till it's warm to greet the world.

Her foot slipped.

Quickly she braced her cane deep against her middle to keep her from falling face-first into the dirt path. Her stomach groaned at the impact. A light retching went up her throat.

Oh, she hated herself.

"Miss Hollis!" A deep and hearty voice bellowed from the very top of the hill she now fought. "Glad to see you're coming back up in one piece! If you've got the time, can you come check your enchantments on my shop?"

The old grocer, whose name sat on the tip of her tongue—names were fickle—fretted his hands at his belly.

Wait, had he seen her stumble? Perhaps he was still far enough away that he hadn't seen her little accident. But how many times over the last several days had he come to check on her? How much of the silly ritual had he witnessed?

Her face burned as she shouted her response up to him. "I checked your wards before I left, remember? They're fine." Her voice still sounded scratchy and worn.

She continued her labored climb toward the plump grocer whose tattered hose seemed as if they had had a battle with a sharp nail and lost. Her ankles almost gave out beneath her. The handle of her cane threatened to splinter as she gripped it harder.

The pain radiated from her ankles up to her knees made her want to snap the man across his balding pate with her cane. Instead, Hollis leaned against a large rock and pulled up a corner of her skirt, noting the ghostly skin of her bare leg.

The usual lilac threads woven around her ankles took on an angry violet hue, clustered and tangled as if the pain had gnarled them up that way.

While she could smooth the pain away with a touch, the exhaustion would still persist. Goodness only knew if she would even have the energy to make it home if she paused any longer. It was time to rest.

The Grocer let out a sheep-like bleat of disapproval. He shook his head, cheeks blooming red in the brisk salted air. "I think they've all worn off, my dear. I'm finding things knocked onto the floor in the morning, produce missing!" He wore a thoughtful expression, tapping his finger against his chin. Something he did when formulating a little plan. Hollis leaned and waited to hear what his new idea was. "Wife's made clover cookies. Am I to understand those are still your favorite?" His newly found smile broadened as Hollis hesitated and tucked her lips into her mouth. He'd struck her weak-point. By his grin, he knew that. "I'll meet you back at the shop. Don't worry; take your time. I have to deliver the rest of these papers. I don't want you injuring yourself again on account of me! Oh, I almost forgot." He waved a small tube above his head before tossing it onto the ground toward her feet. "Here is your copy of today's paper. I'll put it on your tab, dearie." Next thing she knew, he turned right around and made his way up the hill toward town.

If only Hollis understood why the majority of the village found it unsettling to hand things directly to her. Always leaving things where she had to go hobbling.

A sigh broke past her lips. She let her shoulders slouch, only to lose her balance as her bag pulled her backward. Perhaps a bit of healing was warranted.

Righting herself, she adjusted the leather satchel and bent down as if to tie her shoes.

This better be worth it.

Focusing her gaze once more, the fabric of her being came into sight. Her fingers ran over the lilac threads that traced her legs, smoothed the frays and eased the tension of formed knots. The pain released from her body as the tired weight grew deeper on her shoulders. Hollis moved her hands up to her throat and realigned everything in her throat so her voice could settle.

She stood and took several measured steps. No sway threatened her frame.

Good enough.

She drew in a deep breath to calm her nerves and let it go in a burst of air, allowing herself to stand still.

Turning on her heels, Hollis slowly took in the world around her one last time. The crashing sea stretched into the horizon, and the blend of pinks and purples had every creature singing blissfully with the coming dawn. The beauty of the Hozen coast kept her living here longer than she'd stayed in any of Catol's other four prefectures.

The prefecture of Rex was fun—plaguing the students of supposed 'forward scientific thinking' never failed to amuse her.

Eargile was never short on money for healers. They tended to hire directly from the Healers Guild. Which she was no longer a part of.

Then Capital prefecture Catol.

The capital city itself was a place she stayed a decent distance from— being that close to the central Tablin Healer's Guild wasn't a *pleasant* feeling. That, and the capital was crawling with those who wouldn't mind revisiting the not-far-off days when those with the same gift of Tablin sight were—

Hollis shook as she banished the memory from her mind. Closing her eyes, she promised she would no longer think of such things.

Currently, there was a grocer who needed appeasing—*again*.

Town broke into view as she crested the hill, having won her battle against the sloping climb.

Rows of terraced shops with ornate hand-painted signs waved in the wind, greeting her. Oil lamps that stood proud and tall were being quelled by some young boys with mischief on their brows.

Her body eased further at the sight.

Hozen was beautiful and safe. And this little village of Quinlin was her favorite place to linger thus far.

Hollis searched around for the newspaper that had been left. She scanned the wheat-colored grass and late blooming flowers, finding it had rolled a few paces down the road toward town. She bent and snatched it from the ground, dusting off the specks of dirt that clung to it.

"Perhaps a reading break is in order? *Hmm?*" She bit her lip as an excited smile broke onto her face.

Once she unfurled the wad of papers, she read as she walked. The balancing act of holding the paper in one hand and walking with her cane in the other was not enough of a struggle to keep her eyes from drinking up the latest gossip—news.

As she sifted through the text in search of juicy tidbits the date landed in view.

"Printed *three weeks ago*." She groaned, letting her head fall backward.

"Typical. All the news is going to be old and boring now." She kicked a rock in her path and sent it soaring.

Tearing her eyes away from the date she settled on the article that graced the front page.

The High Council of Catol announces the theme of the Winter Tournament in celebration of Prince Dagen's coronation and twentieth birthday. A Masquerade Under the Stars!

The event of the season is only two months away.

Knights from every prefecture will be competing for the Champion-of-Winter title and a chance prize of ten-thousand gold. Previous victors include our exotic Captain of the Royal Guard: Sir Lukxa Ryoo, Councilman Dem Eargile, and the late King Trist himself when he was but a knight.

She skimmed over the rest of the article, glancing briefly at the photographs from last year's tournament. It was merely the back of, whom she assumed was, Knight Captain Lukxa Ryoo as he was given a wreath of holly from a thin, but still breathing, King Trist. *May his soul rest in the fields of green.* No mention of Queen Susan, as the photo must have been right after her passing.

Hollis turned the page.

Her eyes went wide as she took in the next headline. What was *this*?

Crown Prince Dagen accused of Harassment of Staff Inside Dukedom Walls. Secret Interviews Prove the Hands of the Crown Have a Mind of Their Own.

Hollis scoffed. It didn't matter that the man was a prince and should act with decorum. Every week a new scandal sat across the newspaper for all to see, in black ink.

Prince Dagen may have been approaching twenty years, but he seemed to act forever below his age and station. Not that Hollis was any better. But, she enjoyed subverting expectations. It gave her the room to breathe and be whatever she wanted.

Hollis froze in her tracks, the paper slipping from her grasp.

Oh, the grocer. She could be whatever she wanted to be *after* payment

sat in her pocket.

The road turned from crushed dirt to a tightly packed stone, a much more pleasant surface to press her cane into.

"Remember, it's the tedious work that pays the best," Hollis muttered to herself until she almost believed it. "Pays the best, Hollis." And she needed the coin. She only had a handful of payments left on her mortgage and she would fully own her home. It would be her own little place to return to whenever she wanted.

Other villagers soon joined the waking world. They trickled out of the various buildings around the heart of the square or in from little paths. Various colors of threads weaved about in her sight.

The pressure they gave and the *clacking* sound of shoes on the stone paths pulsed against her skull.

A few frazzled-looking beings ambled in the square who were likely stressed or tired—a combination of both *wasn't* unlikely, especially from a few of Hollis' regular patrons.

Hollis groaned internally. Come afternoon, she'd be busy with the weight of emotions she could feel swelling about the square.

The world melted away as she closed her eyes, willing the threads to recede into the back of her mind. Accessing her sight needed a strict focus on the world. Releasing that tension didn't rid her vision of the life threads entirely, but it lessened the severity of walking through crowds.

This close to the peak of harvest season had patrons ringing into her shop constantly. She could already feel the migraine that would present itself.

Hollis navigated herself around the square with her eyes closed, keeping her head slightly bowed in the hopes that no one would see what she was doing. A few bodies bade her a good morning as she stepped around them. The central fountain trickled louder as she approached. She opened her eyes when she kicked the side of the basin of water.

At least her reflection didn't look as ratty and worn as she felt.

She continued onward, content that her vanity was intact.

9

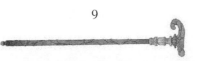

The overwhelming sense of *everything* drove her faster to the old grocer. The bright yellow sign with swirling hand painted letters bade her *enter*. Hollis pushed the dark wooden door open, banging it against the hanging bell inside. She winced at the sharp *chiming*.

Respite came from the warmth that the shop oven lent despite the chill air of the free world. The scent of baking cookies wove about her.

The grocer's wife stood polishing the countertop off to the left by the till, concentration ingrained deep on her wrinkled face as she scrubbed at what Hollis assumed was a stain. Sage threads sat woven over the older woman's skin.

It was a wonder in her mind that so many people throughout history fought to obtain the Tablin sight. While the gift of being able to reweave the fabric of reality around them was tempting, the overwhelming presence of the sight was enough to remind one of the weight that the gift held. The history it branded.

Hollis quickly averted her gaze.

Behind the woman sat half a dozen trays of cooling cookies, the steam wafting off of them dancing in the air.

"Good morning, dearie. What brings you by our shop so early in the day?" She shifted her stance while cleaning as if easing her back. "You usually aren't seen until the afternoon sun has well passed."

The older woman gave a hearty laugh as she returned to her toil. She must have been cleaning and baking for hours to have worked up such a sweat with her bundled and worn threads.

Oh—she'd asked Hollis a question.

"I was out at the Point; ritual business of the Seafolk. Now I'm here checking the wards." Hollis balanced back and forth on her toes.

The matron's laugh continued. "You know, when I was a wee child, I thought I saw Seafolk or what have you." She made a dolphin-like arch motion with her arm. "I'm sure now it was just a large fish of some sort. But I am happy that you're, ah, *taking care of us* in all regards." She turned her

10

head back and forth between Hollis and the counter. "And I'm sure those wards my husband pays you to make are most helpful."

If she was firm in her belief that Hollis' wards did nothing, what was her reason in allowing the old grocer to pad Hollis' pocket?

Pity?

The line people drew in what they believed was an interesting conundrum. The older woman was more than happy to pay Hollis to smooth her tense threads—did her beliefs surrounding what else made up the world stop at what she could sense and feel? Not an unfair notion, but small-minded at heart to carry on with the conversation as though Hollis were insane.

Hollis nodded and took account of the things out on the shop floor. She spied deals on the oils and herbs that were out in large wooden boxes, with a little shelf that held a scoop and glass jars beneath it. A handful of cloth bolts were listed at a discount. A few lighter patterns caught her attention. Hollis could imagine stitching little patches with them on the worn parts of her cardigans or pants.

Flour is cheap now, too. A shipment must be coming in soon. Wouldn't hurt to get a few pounds later.

A fresh loaf of bread sounded so nice.

Fruit looks mouth watering too. Hollis slipped a few ripe strawberries into the pocket of her skirt and a final small one into her mouth as the watchful eye of the old woman stooped under the counter to fetch something.

Extra payment for having to stumble in here again.

"So," the matron continued, poking her head over the counter as she set a few bottles on top of the wooden block. "Have you read the paper this morning? Seems our prince is getting himself into trouble again." Back under the counter she went. "Goodness knows how many heirs he has sired in secret. You have anything like him back in Tablin?"

Hollis choked on the strawberry as she quickly swallowed it.

It didn't matter how many times she explained that she'd never touched

a toe on Tablin soil, everyone expected her to know everything about *every country* that made up the Tablin region.

As a child Hollis dreamed of seeing the magical world beyond the sea. To meet long-lost family, learn magical secrets, eat traditional snacks. . .

Speak graciously to her.

The old woman stood straight again, having arranged all her bottles on the counter.

Hollis needed to respond. "I am not well versed in anything relating to the *different* Tablin royal families. I grew up here, in Catol."

The old woman's face soured.

What could have caused a reaction like that?

The tension melted away from Hollis' jaw as she thought.

Oh.

Had she spoken through clenched teeth? Again?

Her readiness to correct the behavior was cut off by a hand clamping down on her shoulder.

"Ah, you're here! I told you she would come." The old grocer stepped past her to greet his wife by the counter.

He'd been standing behind her for who knew how long. Had he seen her eat anything?

The smile he shone on her didn't let on that he did. She was in the clear.

His wife scoffed. "Where there are cookies and coin—"

"Pay her no heed, Miss Hollis. So, you were out with the Seafolk. What are they like?" His eyes shone with curiosity swimming in the aged blue. "I don't know if I've told you or not, but I was a sailor in my youth and quite a good one at that. Sailed all around Catol, even touched the shore of Tablin once." He pulled a bundle of keys from his pocket and fumbled as he tried each and every one in the lock to the back storeroom.

"No, I don't think you've ever told me. I'd love to hear some of your stories sometime." He had told Hollis those stories, several times over in fact. "As for the Seafolk…" She trailed off. "Well, I would say calming them is

12

as easy as calming a distressed child." Even if she'd never directly spoken or more fully interacted with the Seafolk. When they were upset, it was clear she had to do something until they stopped. Tossing pretty things into the ocean, singing apologies, whatever it took.

"Ah, a labor of love." The grocer let out a warm laugh from his belly as he presented her with the now unlocked and open door to the storeroom.

Hollis furrowed her brow. "I guess? I've never *actually* calmed a child so I would not know. Bet that's what it's like though."

She set her cane against the wall and leaned into the small room as her hands gripped the doorframe of the storeroom. Not able to be bothered to take a step inside.

On the surface, everything appeared normal. Hollis focused past the surface and to the natural weave of the area for any sign that something moved around with her trace on it. She could see the spots where it was clear a human had moved things in the room, adding things to each shelf.

"Well, do you see anything. . . unnatural?" He whispered, his breath creeping over her shoulder. "My jars of beef have been shifting around on the shelf; found one on the floor this morning. I'm convinced it has to be some sort of magical creature—a *ghoul*." She could smell the coffee on his breath, along with the sweat on his forehead.

Holding back a gag proved difficult as her throat bobbed.

"Uh," something flickered to her left, pulling her eye. Tilting her head, Hollis leaned a bit closer to the shelf. Nothing seemed terribly amiss, but it had caught her eye.

A few white whiskers poked out of a small hole behind the jars of canned beef, and then a small pink nose. Any missing stock was going to feed a shrew family. The poor creature was harmless.

The little thing carried bits of her lilac threads over its head, its paws trying to shake the trace off. Animals didn't much like being covered in magic. It would manage to clean it off soon enough.

"Well?" The grocer pushed.

"I'm still checking around, really checking things for you." Hollis threw a smile over her shoulder before turning back to step inside the room.

Her hopeful smile melted into befuddlement.

There was no satisfactory way to answer his questioning. His paranoid mind never relished in her giving him absolutes when it came to things like magical creatures in his storeroom. No matter how many times Hollis attempted to explain to him that the only magical creatures in his world were a few species of blended animals that somehow still lived from the ages when Tablins were once a part of the natural fold and got too creative, he still blamed ghouls and other monsters for everything.

Regardless, Hollis didn't specialize in removing pests when she was most assuredly a pest herself.

Focus, Hollis. He wants an answer; think quickly, think faster.

She couldn't let him see that then she had no idea what to do with this, though. She wanted to be paid.

Her foot tapped against the ground. Her mind churned out ideas faster than she could sift through them.

Perhaps it was best not to scare him with the truth that there was absolutely nothing abnormal in his stockroom? "Aside from the mold on your windowsill? Nothing sticks out to me. But there are some creatures that even slip past me." A total fabrication. Hollis saw everything. "So, if you want to be safe, why don't you pour some. . . rum steeped with leather around the door frames." That sounded reasonable. She spun on her foot and extended her free hand. "Cookies now?"

His mouth hung open a bit, thick brows knit in confusion. "What does the rum do?"

She hadn't a clue, but it was the first thing that sounded like a good thing to her tired mind.

Maybe there's an old Tablin saying about it? Leave your drunk company at the door? That's not right.

It had to have held some benefit she didn't know, but a benefit all the same.

He stared at her, still blinking.

Hollis opened her mouth and hoped something intelligent came out. "Doors are. . . happy when drunk? They stay tight-lipped, unlike people. So, they'll keep any unwanted magic creature from venturing in." *Yes, that makes sense.* She gave him her brightest—and hopefully most convincing—smile.

"Well, many thanks, Miss. Hollis. I'll have my boy run the cookies to your house in a bit."

She forced a grin. "I can't wait." It was physically impossible for her to do so. Waiting required self-control. Of which she had none.

A loud *thunk* came from upstairs. One of their grown children no doubt. Presumably their youngest, and still single, son greeted the world with a hug to his bedroom floor.

Not only was it her second time checking the enchantments this month, but it was the second time the grocer suggested her promised payment to be delivered by the young man.

She didn't know why they continued pushing the boy on her. She was five years his senior at four and twenty.

Hollis gripped her cane with extra care in her right hand, rearranged the heavy leather satchel, and headed out the front door.

Leaving the shop without stomping like a child was a feat in and of itself. But somehow, she retained a regal stature and kept a decent pace through the rest of the village.

Her steps lead her past the small bakery. It was tempting to pop in to grab a fresh bun and look at the baker's son, but the absence of her coin purse pushed her onward. Then again. . . maybe she could persuade him to gift Hollis something if she were sweet enough?

Her ankles cried out once more.

"*Fine, fine fine fine*—I'm going home; happy?"

Her mind calmed as she broke free of the town. Her eyelids grew heavier with each step until she came upon the final stretch to her lovely house.

Her little cottage sat near the Screaming Cliffs, which hadn't screamed

since she struck a deal with the Seafolk living in the waters below.

The door, which had been painted purple by some children the past fall, stood cracked open—which wasn't uncommon. Hollis huffed as she squashed down the jumbled feelings of having to deal with *more* people or creatures this early in the morning.

She noted the horse tied to a tree just the other side of the road. It appeared to be cared for, threads in all the right places as it contently chewed her grass. Her eyes narrowed. She paid good money for that grass to be well-maintained.

Hollis gave into the angry desire and she let herself stomp the rest of the way, doing her best not to trip on the now dirt path.

The door pressed back the brass bell as she shoved it open. It chimed with her arrival.

A *scratching* sound followed the brass bell as she whipped her shoes against the hay-like doormat. Beyond the front landing was the blush-painted office that made up the lower portion of her home. The walls were lined with bookshelves and golden frames. Some of the frame held pieces of art, while others simply hung empty, or had little letters from family nailed to the wall.

Hollis' style was chaotic and timeless. Her home was filled with trinkets and bobbles that brought her joy. Which was nice considering she rarely had people coming to bring such emotions of happiness—aside from her paying clients.

A wave of warmth enveloped her as she scanned the room.

Three plush cream velvet chairs that she'd pawned off an old man sat arranged by an emerald settee and a few side tables, across from which was her arched fireplace—which Hollis had either left burning *several days straight* or the guest clad in the garments of a royal officer had lit.

His uniform was slightly wrinkled, but it still seemingly sparkled with magnificence.

He turned to face her.

The guard was tall, even sitting as he was. His long hair was kept tied back at his neck with a dark red ribbon, contrasting nicely with his beautiful dark, almost navy, color. She suppressed the green feeling of jealousy at the man's long locks. His sharp and angled eyes intrigued her, they looked like the kind of eyes a seer would have. Glossy and pale enough to see into the next realm—typical Omil features.

She doubted this man held that kind of power, but it was an interesting thought to entertain.

It was interesting though. What would someone think seeing an Omilian knight and a Tablin healer together? Hidden away in a remote village, tucked into her cute little bungalow?

That we were going to commit regicide, most likely.

Omil and Tablin shared a bloodied history with Catol—who was a friendly neighbor to neither country.

Hollis shook her head free from the silly thoughts. "Good morning." Hollis smiled at the man. "How can I help you?" She walked adjacent to the sitting area and behind her littered, wood-topped counter, which sat parallel to the door, tucked into the side by the stairs to her living space and stuffed her pack beneath it.

Next, she set her cane in a gilded umbrella stand that was turning green at the bottom and quite possibly had coral growing on the inside. She'd found it on the beach and brought it home one rainy day last spring. It kept filling with water over the course of the journey. To the point, Hollis was so sick of dumping it out that she considered pitching it back into the sea. But it was shiny and golden. Two things she couldn't resist.

She righted her skirt before focusing her attentions left, into the sitting area and onto the strange man.

Emerald threads under his skin, tightly woven, not a single one out of place or fraying. They were a handsome color that lay on his skin. Hollis wondered what they'd feel like under her fingertips. Taut and strong, like they had no give? Would they bend and accept her magical touch?

17

All interesting things she wanted to discover, but the more important matters came first. Why was this man sitting in her house? And how was she going to kick him out?

CHAPTER TWO

HOLLIS

Hollis kept an appearance of calm as the guard stood to greet her. Or she tried to. She shifted her weight between her legs and resisted the urge to twirl her hair around her fingers. Chewing her lips was something she couldn't restrain, though. She'd need to place an order for more lip salve before the season was through if she continued worrying them so.

"Good day." He tilted his head toward her. "I'm here for a Tablin healer, a woman by the name of Hollis." His voice was pleasant. Beyond pleasant. It was low and scraped the bottom of her stomach with warmth. It almost wiped from her mind that guards stopping by her home was never a favorable thing.

If he were a normal knight, she wouldn't bat an eye. But this man's uniform carried the markings of a highly-ranked *palace* knight. A gold-stitched sun marked each of his shoulders.

How was she going to play this?

Hollis openly practiced Tablin Magic and regularly worked for anyone with legit coin. But. . . no matter what any piece of paper said, no matter that some of the people of Catol had '*finally accepted Tablin magic*' and allowed the guild to work freely without harassment in the country, the Royal Family would never make peace with the fact they lost the ability to keep a strangling hold on her people.

"Sadly, no one in this village goes by that name to my knowledge." Hollis stepped past him and the rest of her sitting space, and through the arched doorway into her kitchenette.

Her eyes traced every surface. She needed her kettle and a pain-soothing tea—one that would hopefully give her enough energy to deal with whatever conversation was about to ensue.

Dishes piled up on her little breakfast table—not dirty, thankfully. She never yet found a place in this house to put all the pretty plates and cups she'd collected.

Hollis ran her tongue over the tips of her teeth as she craned her head around.

She didn't spy the kettle on her red countertop. It was filled with various potted plants that spanned the space from underneath her sink to halfway along the counter. The first half of the counter remained clutter-free at all times to have a place to prepare food or herbs.

The open cupboards above and below the counter didn't reveal the hidden kettle either.

Hollis huffed and tapped her feet, her hands resting on her hips.

Where are you? Did you grow legs and leave me?

The handsome guard followed her. "I was told Hollis lived here. Last night the tavern keeper told me that, since they were at capacity and that no one could find her in the village, I could stay here, stating *this* as her residence." He leaned against the doorway, an arm braced above his head.

She was right in her earlier thinking; he stood a good half-head or more taller than her. And he was nicely toned from the looks of his arms. Oh, she liked that. Too bad she couldn't invite him to stay longer.

Hollis *tsked* several times. "You heard wrong, good sir. This house is called the. . . Holly House. Ah, interns of the Institute of Herbal Medicine

stay here. Agricultural projects. If it's tea you need, I'd be happy to help you with that." She gave him the best smile she could muster and went back to her kettle hunt. The words *stupid kettle* escaped her lips in a mutter as she picked up random plants and knicknacks.

She glared at the hand-painted tiles on her walls. *Where was it?*

Anger touched at her. Unaided by the flowers filled the house in an almost dizzying perfume, but she enjoyed the chaoticness of it. They also served as wonderful medicinal herbs both for herself and her patients.

"*Stupid kettle.*" She hissed as she walked past the counter and opened her pantry door.

"If you're in search of the kettle, I do believe it's hiding behind the violets." The knight pointed to the little purple pot under the kitchen window she had nailed shut last winter. Too many little creatures trying to make their way inside and eat all her food.

She stepped around a few boxes that sat on the little multicolored rug on her kitchen floor to reach the counter.

True to the knight's word, the kettle was nestled behind the painted terracotta pot. She plucked the kettle from its spot and filled it with water from the sink before pushing past the guard. She couldn't help but notice the firmness of his chest as she did so. She tried not to dwell on the man's figure as she hung the kettle on the iron hooks by the flames in the hearth.

Afterward, she tossed a few extra logs in. Sparks flew out around her legs, cooling to black before they settled on the ground.

She had a gas stove, but she hated it and fire was aesthetic—Hollis lived for anything of the sort.

Oh, she needed a name. A new name that sounded pretty to match her face.

"I'll pay you back for the wood I used." The knight tapped the coin purse at his side.

Hollis settled herself against the emerald settee. "No need. Simply tell me why you're here and we'll get you on your way. I assume a custom blend of tea? I do specialize in those." She waved her hand toward the chairs in the room.

"I'm not here for tea but something far more important." The knight followed her beckoning and strode back into the room. He sunk into the chair he'd perched himself in when she arrived.

"I see." She sat nestled against the arm of the settee. "Well. . . if you're here for carnal pleasures, you'll have to come back Thursday. Don't know what it is with that day in particular, but it's the only day I ever feel up for it." Her body burned. She chewed on the inside of her cheeks to keep a cough from escaping.

The knight blinked. Then blinked again.

That was a stupid thing to say. She really needed to think more than she spoke.

How could she recover from that?

He furrowed his brow. "You must be aware that prostitution is illegal in Catol. What a ridiculous thing to say, Miss Hollis." He cocked his head and knit his brows together. That was an attractive move from someone chiding her about sexual behavior.

"Again, I believe you have the wrong person. This is the Holly House, and I'm. . . Ivy. And if you're too worried, we'll forget the whole thing and you can pay me in royal secrets instead of gold." Hollis shrugged her shoulders, enjoying the way his pale eyes twitched and his hand gripped the seat.

No, this was all right. Surely he felt uncomfortable enough to leave now? His legs bounced, heels making a dull *tap* on her floor.

A coy smile grew on her face. Perhaps this would be the thing that drove him out her door? If so, she would have to employ this tactic more often.

The knight's face pinched before settling into a smolder. "Well then, I'm so happy that it is, in fact, Thursday. So very happy indeed."

Stones sank in her stomach. Acid crashed up her throat.

The guard stood and then began a slow walk toward her, a slight swing in his hips. Hollis scooched backward against the couch as far as she could,

but there was nowhere else to go.

He planted his hands on either side of her body, a knee wedging between her own as his head leaned down to mingle his breath with hers. The warm scent of sandalwood and musk wafted from him. How she chastised herself for enjoying it.

His eyes bore into hers as if he could search her mind.

Perhaps he did have some sort of magic she wasn't aware of?

"Is it Thursday already? Sadly, though, I don't think you could afford me." She placed a hand flat against his chest and gave a subtle push.

He scoffed. "I easily could afford you. But, dear *Ivy*, that would still be prostitution. Would it not?" He leaned away, ever so slightly, still caging her body against the settee.

"Yes, and you wouldn't want that, being a fancy palace guard and all." Something glinted at his waist, beneath the robe of his uniform. She slipped a hand around his side and pulled the hilt of his sword forward, eyes widening at the glimmering gem. "Fancy sword you have, good sir. Ruby encrusted top, so you're well-ranked. Why hide this from me? I'd never ask payment from such a good-standing knight—no, *Captain*."

He sighed, leaned away, then reached up and mussed his hair. "Where is Hollis? Please let us be done with this charade."

She needed him to leave. Perhaps he would if she doubled down on the prostitution bit. Her arms found their way around his neck, pulling him close again. "So, is payment still an option or is this something we can discuss *after* we're done?" Hollis needed to drive the man into such an uncomfortable state that he would just leave her alone.

The knight chuckled, showing off a set of pearly white teeth. "Of course. Are you wanting to take this upstairs to the bedroom? The one filled with books and journals, all signed *Hollis*? Or is there another room for this type of activity? Perhaps even right here?" He glared down his nose at her.

She resisted the urge to crane her neck away from him. Clearly, he'd spent longer in her house than she thought. What other things had he helped himself to? Were the brownies in her chill box safe? "Are you going to tell me what you'd want with her?" The question slipped out before she could vet the words.

"Are you Hollis?"

"She may be I; I be may she." She blinked. "Wait."

He turned his head and laughed. "Now we are getting somewhere. But I do not have time to continue in this game." He released her and walked around the room, poking at the different items he came across. "The Tablin Healers Guild in Rex told me that I would be able to find Hollis in this area. I was sent to you—*her*—by the people there. Now, please answer me. Are you Hollis, and do you have the sight?" He seemed earnest.

She preened slightly as she spoke. "You're getting closer to being honest about what you want. I appreciate that." If the Guild sent him, then she needed him out of her house quick as possible. There was no love lost between herself and the Guild when she left. Why would they send this knight to her door? What had she done to deserve this?

Perhaps she misremembered her banishment?

"You're welcome. Now, Miss Hollis." She might have known he would see past her ruse, what with eyes like that. "Do you have the sight or not?"

"I never said I was—"

He raised a hand to cut her off. "Miss Hollis, we have need of someone with your ability in the palace."

"A mistake really," she scoffed.

He cocked his head. "What?"

"Oh, nothing." Hollis nodded her head in mock understanding. She'd put words into his mouth. "You want me to find someone for you from *outside* the Guild, I understand now." This would be easy. She'd simply lie and be off before he could discover the truth. A wonderful idea. A perfectly solid plan. Send him westward back toward the Guild and hope he found some other Tablin willing to do whatever it was that he asked.

"The Guild told me to hire a Tablin Healer named Hollis, that they

would. . . assign her to this. They did warn me she was someone who *wasn't* in her right mind—but would do anything for the right price."

Hollis leaned forward, eyes narrowed. "What do you mean I'd do anything for the—" She swallowed her tongue.

He grinned.

Caught.

The plan had failed. Now what could she say to get this man to leave her alone?

Contracts with the Royal Family were taboo amongst most Tablin healers. There was no telling what would be on the other end of signed ink. "Well, how do you know—"

"I had already asked several other healers outside of the guild association for assistance. And stopped by the Herbal Institute—which is in Northern Hozen, far from here. It seems you're the best person for the job. Their words."

The kettle hanging over the fire screamed. Hollis quickly went to the fire to pull it off. She emptied the contents into a small green teapot sitting on an end table near the fireplace. "Well, I'm sorry." Time for a new lie. "But I don't have any kind of Tablin blood. I'm an herbalist." Hollis tossed in the sweet assortment of herbs that would soothe her muscles.

They quickly spun the air with a minty aroma.

His face flattened. "You can try lying about your name, but appearances do not lie. I doubt anyone could color their hair to be as pine as any Tablin. Your eye color screams of your heritage as well—rusty, practically maroon. Just as it would be impossible for me to hide the Omil in my veins, you, dear *Hollis*, are *Tablin*."

She shook her head. "Tablin is the continent of which there are many countries. Some were settled with people from all over the world and have not a lick of magical sight within them. You claiming I look Tablin is baseless—"

He tapped his foot repeatedly. "Do you truly have the sight as I have been told?" He held up a hand. "Please answer me. I grow impatient with this conversation. Besides, you perfectly match your old Guild portrait." He crossed his arms over his broad chest and took a stance like a man who would not be denied.

Hollis sank, finding all warmth had left her body. Not even the burning teacup reached her. There truly was no hiding the fact that she was Tablin. He knew who and what she was—or knew what he hoped she could do.

She swallowed, doing her best to stop digging her nails under each other. "I am Hollis Avyanna—and yes, I do have the sight."

"Thank you for your honesty." He turned from her and then walked back to his chair. He pulled a stack of papers from the satchel he'd stored beside it then handed them to her, before sitting back down. "I am Sir Lukxa Ryoo, a Captain in the Royal Guard. This contract is for your services as a healer in the castle, lasting a month. You'll have quarters while you work in the castle. Pay is thirty-five hundred electrum—"

"—Can't you say *silver?*" Hollis skimmed the pages, finding the numerous clauses annoying to decipher.

"Very well—*silver.*" Sir Lukxa's face, smooth as a river rock, impassive yet warm. The tension had run out of him it would seem. "Your basic needs will be met inside the walls. Three meals a day, along with an allowance of coins paid weekly. You can petition me to get anything else you might need. Again, you will have a single month in which to heal your client. He must be in perfect health by the Tournament and Coronation celebrating Prince Dagen."

Hollis bit her lip, flipping through the pages one last time. "I'll sign the contract—"

"Thank you," he breathed, leaning back into his chair.

"*But* not until you tell me who I'm treating. The contract doesn't say anything about my patient."

He sat forward, back straight as a board, face working as if he were calculating. "That information isn't something I can explain freely—"

Hollis held up a hand, cutting him off. "You're correct, you're not doing

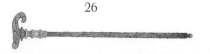

26

this freely." She pointed at the pages. "The payment is almost four months' salary for the average person in this country. The reason you were turned away by every healer is that no Tablin wants to work for the Royal Family. . . They weren't *lying* when they said I'd do anything for the right price. Got me kicked out of the Guild. I don't treat blindly, though. You tell me who I'm treating and I will sign my name." She kept her hand raised, head tilted.

"I'll double your payment if you sign without asking any more questions." His face remained impassive.

This was growing more interesting.

A secret sick person. A *mystery*.

She narrowed her gaze on Sir Lukxa. "If I sign. . . you'll tell me right away?" She leaned forward in her chair, fingers clutching the papers. Her thoughts spun, trying to figure out who in the world he was trying to get her to treat with her sight. And giving her a month? It would be a complicated case if it was something the guild didn't feel comfortable taking on with such a large timeframe.

"No. Not until we reach the castle." Sir Lukxa shifted in his chair as if growing tense.

She was poking cracks in his wall. "How about this? You double my payment and tell me who I'm treating right now, and *then* I'll sign?"

He scoffed and rolled his eyes. "That's not how this works." *Oh*, he had sass. Sbe could work with sass.

"I think it is, Sir Lukxa." She tossed the papers on the table between them and stood to retrieve another teacup. Filling it with tea, she then handed it to him. He accepted the cup. "This doesn't work without trust, and there is a great lack of it in this room. I don't trust the Royal Family all that much, nor their sudden desire to have a Tablin Healer, and you don't want to reveal the name of my patient or patients. I'm not sure we can come to an agreement." She sipped her cup of tea. The mint cleared her senses and grounded her.

Sir Lukxa set his cup on the table after taking an obligatory sip. "What is it that you want?"

Hollis shook a finger. "I thought I made that clear. I want a name."

He leaned back in the chair, a hand cupping his jaw. "Has anyone ever told you that you're very exas—"

"Nothing that comes out of your mouth right now will be new information to my ears unless it's a name." She blinked.

He swallowed, his lips mashed together into a thin line. "You sign, I tell you who you're treating, and then you come back to the castle with me *tonight*. We leave right away. No time for goodbyes to any family or friends in the area."

"I wish I had friends—goodness, that would be nice. Family lives in Rex." Hollis took a long sip of tea and found the pain that plagued her was easing as well.

A line of rationale came into her mind the longer she thought about it.

There wasn't a chance in the world that the Catolian Council was going to trust a Tablin healer with someone as high ranking as a. . . fellow councilor, a high-ranking knight, or let alone Prince Dagen himself—and he was off at finishing school somewhere in Rex anywho.

Most likely this whole situation was that the council wanted to get a watchful eye on how Tablin sight worked.

Or they didn't want to plague any of their royal healers with a tedious task, especially with the tournament and coronation on the horizon.

Hollis gave another cursory glance over the guard. No part of his threads indicated that he was lying or attempting to trick her.

Perhaps she had nothing to fear. She would sign, learn who her patient was, and then if she hated the idea, she would fling herself off her balcony and into the sea to escape.

Yes. She bit her lip to keep herself from grinning like a fool. That was a much better plan.

"All right, Sir Lukxa, I can agree to that. I assume you brought a pen?" She plucked the papers up from the table and thumbed through the stack

until she found a solid line in which to fix her signature.

The captain said nothing as he handed her a pen.

Hollis read over the final paragraph of the paper a few times. Letting the words sink in. She'd live in the castle one month as he said, working as a healer. All her needs were outlined and stated that they'd be met in stride, and she would be paid a healthy salary.

Nothing that screamed trouble.

No, she would be perfectly fine.

The pen had no difficulty gliding over the paper. Soon she signed her name as neatly as her sleep-deprived mind would allow. "I've signed, now it's your turn."

Sir Lukxa took up the pen and signed his name on a line beside her own.

He let out his breath, tossed the pen on the table, and fell back against his chair. Then he ran a hand down his face, giving a small break in his composed façade.

Exhaustion.

He leaned forward in his chair once more. The words he tried to speak seemed to catch in his throat, resulting in odd noises as he opened his mouth like a fish.

Finally, he spoke clearly. "We are hoping that your Tablin magic can give us insight into how we can save Prince Dagen's life."

Oh. *Oh no.*

They were doomed.

CHAPTER THREE

LUKXA

Lukxa watched the thoughts behind the woman's bloodshot eyes scramble as he finished speaking. Hollis rubbed her hands together, chewing on her lip.

If the expression on Hollis' face was anything to go by, she was attempting to formulate a plan, one he was all too willing to entertain now that her signature lay fixed on the paper. Fatigue plagued his being. He had spent days trying to track this woman down along the coast of Hozen.

The length of time Dagen had left in this world dwindled. This was Lukxa's last chance to find a competent healer for the prince.

He finally had someone. The ruse of stating the Healers' Guild had sent him worked well to create some sort of trust with Hollis that he desperately needed. Now that Lukxa had her, right where he wanted her—in his sights—the minor entertainment was deserved.

He thrust out his arm, pulling his sleeve back enough to check his watch. Well, a *few* moments of enjoyment could be taken. They had a handful of hours of riding to make it to their first destination, and they could not be late.

Warmth washed over him once more. His muscles cried in relief as the tension he'd carried seemingly vanished.

Hollis would be the one to help Dagen. Everyone else had all but picked the flowers and polished two gold coins for his burial rites. The council had brought three separate physicians from across the country to try and heal Prince Dagen. All of them left within a week, claiming it was useless. Lukxa had been the one to source and track down a healer this time. Not relying on the council and their picks. No, he thought the council would have made a decent pick of the healers they brought in. At least make it seem like they cared enough about Dagen's health.

Lukxa knew better.

Tension reformed in his jaw, grinding his teeth together. He pressed his tongue up against the roof of his mouth to help relieve some of the pressure. Next, he counted back from twenty, slowly.

He watched as Hollis froze in her machinations. "*Wait.* You said I would be accompanying you to the Castle—isn't Prince Dagen—" She rolled her eyes. "*May the sun shine on his crown*—at finishing school somewhere in Rex?" She clapped her hands together and pointed them at Lukxa, her eyes narrowing. "Not only are you telling me that he's not where people think he is, but he's sick? And that I have a *month* to heal him? To heal our future king." Hollis blinked several times. "Perhaps I missed more in those outdated newspapers than I thought." Her last words were nothing more than a whisper through the cupped hands she put over her mouth. Her eyes opened wide as if outdated papers were the most horrifying thing she could think of.

It almost made Lukxa uncomfortable with how aloof the woman seemed. But when the papers constantly printed slander, Lukxa could not be surprised that care for Prince Dagen was disregarded.

"No," Lukxa bent into what he hoped was her line of vision. "Prince Dagen is residing in the castle right now. It is a well-kept secret, as is his sickness I'm not at liberty to discuss more." Lukxa gripped the fabric of his cloak tight. Answered questions led to people being far more informed than he would like. Once Hollis was inside the castle walls, unable to escape or leave, he would tell her everything he could think of to better her chances of healing Dagen.

Even if bringing Hollis back would paint a larger target on his back.

She rose from the settee and shook her head, her hands raised in front of her chest. "I need to. . . *pack*, but I can't do that if you're following me around like a ghost. I need room to breathe and—and think." She paced about the room and landed near the fireplace.

Lukxa quickly stood and followed suit after carefully packing the now-signed contract back into his satchel. "Have no worries. I won't get in your way while I am here."

Her eyes narrowed. The light from the fireplace illuminated them and made glow. "No, you won't." Hollis' hands were all over him, an attempt to shove him.

It amused him greatly to see the woman try and push him around her home, much like a butterfly attempting to control the gust under its wings. Lukxa side-stepped, trying to dodge a pile of precariously stacked teacups before she all but shoved him into the side of a bookshelf near the front window.

"I believe you have packing to do?" Again, he narrowly missed being pushed over a chair.

The world shifted under him as she grabbed the back of his cloak and *tugged*. Lukxa flailed his arms as he tried to gain purchase on something, finding it on the flat side of the emerald settee he'd caged the woman on earlier. The wooden frame on the top dug uncomfortably on his back.

Far from the smartest idea he'd ever had—pinning a woman against furniture. . . Lukxa would blame it on the lack of sleep the past four days he rode to Quinlin to find her—why she had to live in one of the furthest villages in the farthest prefecture in Catol was beyond him. He slid himself over the back and sat on the settee, then pulled his legs up to curl himself up on the piece of furniture.

Hollis stepped around him and went into the sitting room.

She trailed a finger over a few books from the shelves, grabbing up a few into her arms before dumping them on a desk that was nestled in front of a window.

Her collection of stories spanned several genres. Perusing her literary collection—and home in general—had kept him sane the night before. The ocean outside sounded like it screamed every time it crashed against the cliffs, driving any ability to sleep from him. It was *unnerving* how humanistic the screams sounded. It had kept him awake enough to explore the woman's house and learn more about her, sleep would have been more welcomed.

Dullness brought on by fatigue settled deep in his bones.

Hollis' little burrow was filled with trinkets of all kinds outside of the books. While Hollis wasn't what he expected, her home fit his imagination perfectly. Eclectic and warm. He wondered what her personality would have been if he'd come under less alarming circumstances. He had heard that Hollis was a diligent healer. Her work and skill in medicine could not be topped according to her reputation. Lukxa wished her someone who would not have put up so much resistance to helping the crown.

He stood, ignoring how his muscles ached, and walked over to Hollis by her shelves. "Perhaps instead of thinking of me as something in your way, you could use me to your advantage? I'd be more than happy to help you—"

She turned and crashed into him, eyes wide as a doe's—had she *forgotten* that he was there?

He refused to let the sinking note of regret and dread fill his stomach. She was one of the best Tablin Healers in the country. Her methods so useful and chaotic that the Guild had banished her.

"No need! You see, I'm quite efficient when I work alone. So if you would be so kind as to step outside? I'd hate to be forceful with you." Her voice dropped, sounding much like a child imitating an adult.

"You have already shoved me around your entire sitting space." He let his

head tilt to the side. "And you walked in here using a cane," he deadpanned. "Though it would be remiss of me to ever underestimate someone."

"Exactly!" She beamed. "And you did such a wonderful job finding me. You should take a rest, a breather! Outside." Her hands wrapped around his middle, fingers dug into his back.

The muscles along his spine contracted. He spun around. His legs moved, his arms swinging lightly at his sides. "What the—" His body marched itself up to the door, nerves tingling like they'd been tied to strings and pulled. Hollis followed closely behind him, hands ghosting over the back of his jacket, opened the door, and pushed him outside. Sensation returned as he fumbled over the threshold and chills ran down his spine.

"I'll come out when I'm ready to go!" The door slammed shut behind him with the telltale *click* of a lock. He tried the handle just to be sure, but the brass knob resisted his attempts to turn it. "Why didn't I think of that earlier?" He heard her laugh from inside.

He leaned his head against the odd purple door.

"I will have you know I searched the entire building, there is only one real way out—your kitchen and water closet window screens are nailed shut. I imagine because you get some unwanted guests living around here. Wild animals and whatnot. But I am eager to see what you try and get away with. I will be right here." He would not be *right there* by the door, but that was beside the point.

Lukxa shook his head and trailed a worn path on the grass in front of her house.

The noise around him silenced his mind. He lifted his head toward what lay just beyond Hollis' home.

The waves crashed up against the cliffs the house stood on. Each one sent a cloud of mist through the air.

A dull ache gradually sank in his body, pooling out of his feet and into the earth. Lukxa lifted his head toward the ever-bluing sky. Closing his eyes, he drew in a deep breath.

Soaking in the morning sun was a luxury he wasn't often awarded at the palace—at least a sun with salt on the breeze.

Memories of the warm sandy beaches he tumbled about as a child burst to life. Memories of his home not far from the water, of friends made from every stranger he met. Endless nights of sun spent making little core memories. His knees still wore the scars of sea glass from a most unfortunate incident running away from his friends playing silly hiding games.

I knew I should have hidden in the tea fields that day.

Those fields were long gone by now, covered in ash and the leftover remains of the Catolian conquest.

Despite their regional separation, nothing was too different between his first home and the village that surrounded him. Both were filled to the brim with superstitious minds, many of which plagued him with questions as he'd sat in the tavern the night before.

When the small bits of information Lukxa could give to answer whatever question was asked of him ran dry, the tavern keeper promptly told him there was no bed Lukxa could rent. A helpful older woman pointed him in the direction of Hollis's dwelling with the knowledge that Hollis never minded outsiders barging in.

"*Part of her job is welcoming in strangers with odd requests.*" The older woman laughed as she spoke.

That should have been a blazing red flag, someone else letting Lukxa stay the evening in Hollis' home without her being aware of it. He had been far too tired to care about thinking his actions through. But that was neither here nor there. There was only the here that was now.

Lukxa stopped his pacing and ran a hand down his face, a poor attempt to rub the sleep from his eyes.

This expedition had taken much longer than expected. His dear councilor friends weren't too fond of the idea of bringing a real Tablin Healer into the castle in the first place. Lukxa's excuse of this being a more believable plan could only cover him so long.

The reminder came without fail that if Lukxa had not failed years ago, Dagen would not be suffering as he was.

Lukxa's goal was to make Dagen live now. Dagen had to make it through this and Lukxa would need to expose everything he could without implicating himself.

Lukxa was caught in a game with no winners. If he divulged what he knew, Lukxa would be imprisoned right alongside the ones who hired him. If he said nothing, they continued harming whoever they could step upon.

The unlatching of a door sounded in the air—but not the one located behind him.

He walked around the small cottage, mindful of where he stepped as he came upon a bright bed of flowers that made up the eastern wall. Around the back of her home, Lukxa found himself shivering in the shadow of a balcony that sprouted from the back of the cottage.

Goodness me.

Hollis stood with a pack slung over her shoulder, not more than seven feet between her body on the balcony and the edge of the cliffside.

"Now listen here, you pesky bird—the Seafolk and I are on good terms. I need you to relay a message. *Hey*—don't you peck at me!" Hollis spat venom through her teeth at what he assumed was a small bird fluttering in front of her face. . . He narrowed his gaze at the creature. It was a hummingbird mixed with something else entirely; the tail was all sorts of *wrong*. Like the tail of a. . . *goldfish*?

His eyes went wide. He'd seen some of the odd creatures made by the Tablins of old but had never been lucky enough to see one like *this*.

Intriguing.

Lukxa perched himself against the wall, arms folded tight across his stomach to try and retain some heat that the harsh sea winds worked to sap from him.

Hollis' green hair flew around in the air, doing nothing to aid the crazed expression etched on her face. Her brows furrowed and arched; her cheeks flushed a bright red as her lungs heaved. She'd packed up in quite a hurry.

She swung her leg up on the thick wooden railing, and then the other followed. Giving Lukxa a clear line of sight up her skirt.

He grinned. "Are we discussing payment before or after *this* happens?"

"What are you doing?" she cried.

Her body slumped down, stabilizing herself by gripping the wooden rails much like a cat who miscalculated a leap.

The bird-like creature flew off without a trace.

"Watching what I am sure is going to be a most entertaining moment. I would not have expected you to break our contract right away in such a dramatic matter. But regardless, you are coming with me to Catol—broken bones or not. Go on, Hollis. Jump." He waved his hand in the air. "Do continue; I think I will enjoy this. You plummet, I throw you onto my horse, and we head north." He shrugged his shoulders, letting a grin overtake the expression on his face.

He could see the beams of sunlight wrapping around the cottage, desperately trying to reach his freezing form again.

Hollis glared at him.

He spoke up again. "Can't come up with anything? Come now, I thought we were being honest."

Hollis gave the impression of a drenched cat.

Then, slowly, her shoulders caved in toward her chest. "I'm being honest in saying that *I can't help you.*"

That took him aback. "You have the sight, correct? Can you heal people with it?" Was this why she was cast out of the Guild? Was she secretly a fraud?

A pit grew in his stomach, consuming the bits of hope he had.

Her eyes grew wide with worry. "Yes, I can heal—"

The pit shrunk. "Then you simply refuse to help?"

The light bits of salt he could taste in the air were rapidly replaced with the full weight of seawater. An indescribable taste and smell.

"*No.*" She steadied herself once more as she shifted her feet like a cat ready to leap, her eyes focused outward towards the crashing waves that scattered above the lip of the cliff sides.

Lukxa would not let this last opportunity to clear his name and save Dagen's life slip through his fingers.

Catolian medicine had *failed* time and time again to heal Dagen. The past seven months were a waking nightmare.

If Lukxa couldn't bring Hollis back, it was as good as Lukxa slitting Dagen's throat with his own hand.

"Then what is it? Talk to me—help me understand what's wrong so I can help you." He watched her shuffle until she sat her bottom on the balcony railing and began drumming her fingers along the stained wood. "Are you going to answer me, Hollis?"

Her glare turned piercing. "People get *upset* when their wild wishes can't be fulfilled. I doubt I can be of any help to the Prince, *may the sun shine on his crown*. But still, I will be dragged to the palace, and, by a lack of understanding of what Tablin magic really is and what it can do—or rather can't do—I will be put to death as my ancestors before me." Her voice rose dramatically as she looked down at him through her lashes.

There was no blaming someone trying to save their skin. He was after the same.

Lukxa checked his watch. Time was ticking away.

"Hollis, you have my word that harm will not fall upon you."

Her glare melted to something he felt was curiosity. "That's believable."

He let an exasperated sigh past his lips. "What will it take for you to come willingly with me? I promise you will not be harmed—and if you are unable to figure out what ails the prince, I will bring you back here and then you can *throw yourself into the sea*. Is that better?" His voice held an edge of exasperation.

Lukxa had to think of a way he could get her from the balcony without her causing major harm to either of them. His fingers twitched.

The walls felt sturdy enough, which meant he could scale them without worry; the worry lay in how eager she was to throw herself into the sea or if she'd be able to overtake his body as she'd done earlier. Though now that he knew what the prickling of her control felt like, he could try to resist it.

Lukxa readied his feet. A moment's notice could find him pulling himself onto the balcony and grabbing her. He had to think of something to say.

"What about a Binding ritual? I—I've heard Tablin Bindings are a type of vow that is unbreakable. I'd promise that you would be kept safe from harm during your time spent in the castle. You would not meet the fate of your ancestors by my hands, and I would do my best to keep any others from trying."

Catol's horrible history with Tablin seemed to loom over her mind in a manner it had not when she had signed the contract. The stories she must have grown up hearing were fresh from the mouths of survivors. And here he was, waiting to drag her to the center of a blood-stained kingdom for a crown responsible for slaughter.

"You—" Her gaze melted to something he felt was curiosity. "It's believable that you'd go through with one."

Lukxa nodded his head. "I would. I'm willing to if it means you'll come back and help."

She laughed. "You weren't suggested to me at the Healers Guild, were you? They rejected you outright and somehow you heard my name in the mix."

He trapped his lips between his teeth. She was close enough to the truth, perhaps settling in a half-lie would ease her mind more.

Lukxa nodded his head. "Yes, that's true."

Hollis pulled her bag off her shoulder and set it on the rail beside where she still stood. "Tell me. . . what do you know of Binding rituals?"

He wracked his mind for every detail he could recall. It was more of an off-handed comment made to hopefully build trust. "I know they are unbreakable; once a vow is made it lasts until completion. I could promise my protection over you, you promise to do your best to heal Prince Dagen—I won't even put in a clause about perfectly healing him. Just that you have to try."

Finally, she laughed. "You'd marry me to keep me safe?"

He balked. His lips parted, no sound escaped him. *Marriage?* "Apologies, I—"

"I'll accept your proposal another time. Perhaps when you've treated me to a lovely night and dinner. For now. . . Tell me more about his condition. Prince Dagen. I know you said you wouldn't, but I need to know as his physician."

"Why don't you come down and we can talk?"

Hollis pursed her lips and crossed to the railing above him. "All righty then. Catch." She tossed her bag down into his arms.

The wind was knocked out of him as the bang landed hard against his chest. He craned his head up at her. "What was that for?"

She jumped.

Her skirts fluttered as she descended. Lukxa managed to drop her pack and catch Hollis by her knees, her torso crashing against his shoulders and chin. His legs groaned as his shifted stance kept him from tumbling backward.

"What made you think *that* was a good idea?" His voice came out strangled and stiff.

Hollis climbed off him, patting her skirt and straightening out the dainty blouse tucked into it. "Well, a good sign that you can trust someone is by seeing if they mean what they say." She gave him a blinding smile.

He furrowed his brows. "What? That I promised no harm would come to you?"

"No, when you said you'd enjoy watching me break my bones." There was a twinkle in her eye as she spoke.

She fussed about as she tucked a loose strand of hair behind her ears. Once all the strands were secured, she pushed past him, clapping him on his shoulders. She then scooped up her bag and pulled her cane out of the top of it. "You're a lot stronger than you seem." She grinned back at him, her teeth almost shining in the sunlight. "Nice muscles, Lukxa."

"Please address me as *Sir* Lukxa." He called out as he followed behind her.

"Yes, well, I guess if I'm going to the capital with you, I should grab a few more things from my house."

He smirked. "Do you have your keys buried in that pack somewhere?"

"What are you talking about? I left the balcony door unlocked."

He leaned on one leg, cocking his hip. "Hollis, where are you standing right now?"

Her hands flew to her mouth, eyes wide in horror as her face paled. He could hear her muttering something under her breath.

"Being that you are on the ground, you had better hope we can get whatever else you need in the citadel. I'm sure it would not be too difficult."

"No, no I have my keys. I have to have them." Hollis dropped the pack to the ground and shuffled through its various pouches.

He sighed.

The sleeve of his shirt pulled back as he extended his arm to check the time.

Perhaps there were a few more moments to spare? Could he afford it? Her little stunt had put them back considerably. Any planned breaks he'd formulated would need to be eliminated.

She likely needed to pack Tablin medical supplies. If she had anything unique in that manner, it would be tricky to find in Catol without requesting it from the Guild.

"If you can further promise not to run off, I'll unlock the door from the inside."

"How do you plan on doing that?" She pointed an accusatory finger in his nose. "Did you swipe my extra key when you went snooping around my house?"

Her hand was soft in his as he pushed it out of his face. "No, I did not steal anything of yours. I mean I can get onto your balcony. It does not appear that hard to scale." He gave another once over the path he could take up to her balcony.

Hollis' face melted into something that looked akin to uncomfortableness. She shifted in her standing, hands twiddling. "Then why didn't you do that earlier? I'm sure you could have scaled it without me realizing and grabbed me." Her arms wrapped lightly around her sides.

Another breeze swept around the house, whipping their hair around and roaring in his ears.

Lukxa did his best to speak over the wind. "Because I want you to trust me. I need your help, Hollis."

She *huffed*. "You know, leading with *I need your help* would have been much easier than acting like you were sent after my head by the Guild."

"*I did!*" A laugh burst from his chest. "Are you telling me there's a reason I should be hunting your head instead of seeking your help?"

Her eyes went wide, mouth hung slack. "Why don't you break into my house again and let me finish my packing?" Her squeaks hardly registered in his ears over the harsh wind.

Hollis' laughter continued as he turned to the balcony.

Taking a few steps back, he ran toward the wall, gaining height as he jumped and flung himself toward the balcony, catching the bottom ledge with his hands.

Pulling himself up the wooden rails without them snapping was a miracle. The muscles in his arms tensed as he pulled himself up to a place where he could use his legs.

He swung himself over the banister and checked on Hollis.

Hollis sitting on the ground and *not* running away was the second.

"Do you think you could do that again sometime? I found that incredibly attractive."

He wiped a hand over his forehead. "Maybe if you're lucky."

The blush that stretched across her face was intoxicating. "I wouldn't mind getting lucky."

Lukxa ducked into the balcony doors, finding himself in Hollis' bedroom once more.

It was organized far less chaotically than the downstairs office was.

The sage walls on this level were neatly filled with frames of dried flowers and a random assortment of paintings. The wooden floors were covered in different textured cream rugs, while a rainbow of colors painted them from the hung stained glass pieces around the windows.

This perfectly fits your owner.

Pushing past any other thoughts he left the room and made his way down the stairs. He could hear her muffled voice coming from the other side.

Lukxa turned the lock and pulled it open.

Hollis' face lit up as she held a brass key. "Found it! I always pack a spare."

"You are too late, Hollis."

Hollis screamed and jumped back, hand over her heart and heaving chest, as she took him in. "Goodness. All right, well, I best get to it."

"How much *more* do you need to pack?" He eyed the satchel at her side. It didn't look like it held much, but he'd been surprised by the people in his academy and their packing skills.

"Well, that depends. I have no idea what sorts of things to pack to treat the prince so any information about that would be—"

"You won't be receiving any information detailing his highnesses' condition until we're *in* the castle. This is a matter that we've kept close to our chest, and it won't be straying any further than needed. Pack whatever you think you'll need that the Crown would not be able to supply." He settled himself back into the plush velvet chair.

Hollis climbed the stairs, hand holding fast to the railings to pull herself upward.

A knock sounded on the door.

"Sir Captain Captor, could you get that for me?" Hollis' voice called down, accompanied by a few large *thunks* and a resounding *oww*.

"It would be my pleasure." He shook his head and internally groaned as he rose from the comfortable chair and stalked over to the door.

Standing on the other side was a young man with blazing copper hair and a build no stronger than a bundle of straw. The young man leaned from foot to foot as he made no effort to hide his sizing up of Lukxa. "*Um*, who are you?" The young man asked, his thin face filled with confusion.

Lukxa shook his head. "That doesn't matter. What do you want?"

"I'm supposed to deliver this package to Hollis. Do you know where she is?" The red-headed young man leaned about, trying to see behind Lukxa and into the house.

"Hollis is busy at the moment and asked me to get the door. I can accept that on her behalf and I promise it will make its way to her." Lukxa extended one arm out, gesturing at the small box the red-headed man held.

The young man scowled. "Who are you to her? What's a knight doing here?"

Lukxa jutted his arm out and snatched the box out of his grip. "Thank you; have a good day. So you know, Hollis will be gone for the foreseeable future, just as a note." Lukxa shut the door and peeked out the window curtains until the young man stomped back off toward town.

Opening the box, Lukxa found a few dozen cookies nestled inside. The treats were cool to the touch, and the warm scent of vanilla and clover filled the air. Finding no harm in the goodies, Lukxa quickly popped one in his mouth, delighting in the sweetness.

"Who was that?"

He almost choked as he quickly chewed and swallowed the treat. "Some red-headed man with a package for you. No idea what's in it." He closed the lid to the treat box.

"I hope you scared him off well and good!" Hollis' voice sounded incredibly chipper.

A few moments later he heard Hollis' footsteps padding down the stairs. The satchel on her side had grown, and the addition of a pack on her back welcomed him. She had changed her shoes out for a dark green pair of walking boots.

He handed the small box of cookies to her. "I take it you have everything you need now?"

"Almost. I just need to pack a few things from my kitchen and then I'll be ready. Feel free to take a seat again." She smiled as he did just that. Then she took the box and walked into the kitchen behind him. He could hear her rustling about a handful of minutes before it went silent.

The nerves along his neck tingled, the world slowly fuzzing. The same feeling from earlier.

He let himself curse, albeit internally.

Lukxa spun and caught her by the wrists, her eyes wide with surprise, a gasp letting from her lips.

"Sorry! It was worth one final shot." Hollis squeaked.

"No, no it wasn't." He inched forward until his nose brushed against hers. "I'm letting you out of my sight again."

CHAPTER FOUR

HOLLIS

While Hollis didn't mind traveling by horse, the *cheap* rented double-saddle failed to protect her bum from reaching the point of bruising. There was balm in her pack she'd be able to apply come evening, but she wasn't happy about the need arising at all.

Sir Lukxa seemed unfazed by the horse's movements as he sat behind her. Hollis could feel his body raise every now and again, likely to bring relief to his own well-rounded bottom. She'd do the same, but her balance on the creature would likely falter and she'd end up with her own bottom in Sir Lukxa's face—something she doubted he'd care for.

The landscape around them glittered with light. The sun melted any drips of dew that lingered on late-blooming flowers and grass. The sight was breathtaking.

If only she could fully enjoy it.

A shock ran up her spine as the horse continued. Whipping freezing air across her face.

She shuddered.

"Are you quite all right, Miss Hollis?" Sir Lukxa's voice reverberated against her back, something she thought only happened in romance novels.

Hollis nodded her head, not wanting to crane her head to meet his face. "I'm all right, just a bit sore. Are you sure we can't take a break?"

He *sighed*. "Quite sure, I am sorry. You could post if that would be of any help."

Context, Hollis. You can figure out what that is. Perhaps that was the official word for standing whilst one rode a horse? That would make sense. "Thank you, but I would hate to make you uncomfortable."

"I've posted several times as we've ridden. Has it been making you uncomfortable? If it has, I will apologize." His grip around her lessened, as if he were trying to bring some degree of separation to their glued bodies.

"No, it hasn't bothered me," she answered truthfully.

"I assure you that you will feel much better. I will hold you steady so you will not fall off." One of his hands left the reins in front of her and settled tight on her waist, giving a slight lift to aid her in standing on her set of stirrups.

Relief flooded her legs as she raised off the saddle the slightest bit. Hollis drew in a deep breath and slowly released it, trying not to groan.

The further inland they rode, the less the air tasted of salt. Now it lent more floral and spice. Harvest lingered best it could in Hozen. Truly it portrayed the beauty of the prefecture in a way no other season was able to. Spring was a close contender in Hollis' mind. The vivid fields were a sight to behold.

One attribute of their journey she could live without would be the frozen wind. She'd have to do something about that soon. Tremors ran down her spine, making it most awkward in her mind.

"I take it there's a reason you have not used your magic to aid in your recovery? Of being sore, that is." Sir Lukxa's voice snapped Hollis out of her musings, drawing her attention back to the fact that her legs were now shaking. She sat down. Sir Lukxa's hands kept her steady as he settled her back against him.

"I've exhausted myself already with work the past several days. I'm not

sure how much more I could add to my body before I simply collapse." Her ribs tightened every time she drew in a breath.

She felt Sir Lukxa's arms tense the slightest bit. "Is that something I need to worry over?" The tension laced into his voice.

"Have no fears, Sir Lukxa. After a decent night's sleep, I'll be fully recovered." She ran her hands down her face. Goodness, she hated riding on a horse. "Besides, healing myself will only wear me down. It tends to double the load on my person. Working on others, or the world around me, is far less taxing." An idea came to mind. "For example. . . " Hollis stuck her hands in front of them, focusing her gaze until she could pluck the slowed threads of air that surrounded them. She spun them with her forefinger and thumb until they sped up.

A warm breeze swept over their faces. She could feel the Capitan shiver behind her.

"That is a nifty trick. There a reason you couldn't have done *that* an hour ago?"

Hollis took some of his hair to her face as she assumed Sir Lukxa shook his head.

She laughed and leaned against him, her eyes drooping shut. "I didn't think about it, truthfully." She sighed. The warmth brought a sense of peace to her body. A comfort.

He jostled her shoulder. "Do not fall asleep on me yet. I assume we'll be arriving in Sagin soon enough, Hollis. But before we get there, I do want to apologize for how brashly I treated you inside of your home. It's a matter of great importance that I bring you with me, but lack of sleep and energy had me acting in an. . . uncouth manner. I hope you can forgive me for taking your bait and reeling it." Again his voice reverberated down her spine.

An unexpected turn of events, truly so. "Pay it no heed, Sir Lukxa. I'm simply impressed that nothing I did faltered your resolve. Perhaps my own lack of sleep and energy had me giving less than my best efforts. We'll have to try another time." She relaxed further, giving him more of her weight to bear.

"Consider it done. Will you be needing to eat when we reach Sagin, or do you think you'll be able to wait until we reach Catol?"

She straightened. "In what manner of travel are we taking that you think I'd be able to last a three-day journey *without* food?"

He laughed. "I think our manner of travel will have us in the capital by the end of the afternoon."

Her eyes opened wide, her mind spinning with possibilities. The best warhorses weren't bred anywhere near them—if he'd even deigned to pull them from training in the first place. Even *if* he had, they wouldn't have been able to make the journey there and *back* to Catol in that timeframe.

It hit her amongst the musings. "You intend for us to ride the *military train?*"

The air around the station was thick with the taste of smoke. The train itself was smaller than she'd expected. It was no secret that Hozen wasn't blessed with the grandest of things from the Capital or Rex. No one cared all too much for sharing with an entire prefecture where most people didn't attend schooling past the age of fifteen in lieu of continuing a family business. Not to mention Hozen's station of knights and guards was far smaller than anywhere else in the country.

Still, the train itself was a magnificent thing to see. It was able to carry fifty knights from here to any capital in the better part of a day. The train offered open carriages wherein several bodies were lumped in together with no privacy, and secluded carriages where that wasn't the case. Hollis assumed their purpose was to appease high-ranked officers' or for the sharing of private information.

Sir Lukxa's rank and coin from the crown got them a private carriage in the middle of the train. An odd spot for one to find privacy, at the center of everything.

Nothing seemed to connect the different carriages. They all sat like

little capsules strung together. Bodies jostled Hollis around. She hated being pushed around. Pressing forward, she caught up with Sir Lukxa who stood in front of the private cart he'd booked. It was far smaller than she imagined it would be. They'd both be able to sit facing each other with space for their legs to stretch out. Hardly comfortable if traveling with more than a handful of companions.

But it was private.

Sir Lukxa tossed their things inside and stepped up himself.

He turned back to her. "Wait. Do you need help?" Sir Lukxa turned back to face her from the step into the train cart, a hand halfway down to her.

Hollis nodded. "Thank you." Soon, her hand was within his grip.

Sir Lukxa stepped off of the cart and placed his other hand around her waist. He gripped her and vaulted her into the air. Hollis tripped over their bags and fell haphazardly onto the cushioned seat.

"Apologies. I didn't mean to *fling* you inside, Hollis." He stepped into the carriage and shut the door behind him.

Hollis took a minute to breathe, letting her lungs fill with air to expand her ribs to be sure none were injured in her less-than-perfect landing. She could add them to the list of injuries she'd sustained since leaving with the knight captain. The muscles running along her spine and legs burned. Pushing up against the cushions to right herself she found the air to respond. "I think I'll be fine. Thank you. Now that we're settled down, do you think you can finally tell me of his highnesses condition?"

His face fell flat. "We have been over this *several times* over the last few hours. Security measures—I'm sure you understand."

"I don't, I really don't and I don't care. What *can* you tell me? Not as a knight captain but I'm assuming as. . . a friend? I want to know what I'm walking into." Hollis slightly stuck out her lower lip.

Sir Lukxa tilted his head down and raised his brows at her.

What's that face supposed to mean? Annoyance? Rude.

She raised her chin in defiance and refused to relent.

Both his hands ran down his face, rubbing his cheeks red. "You're not going to stop pestering me until I give you something, I assume. He fell sick just a few months ago. It wasn't bad at first, nothing the council felt we needed to announce to a kingdom that just lost its previous king and queen to illness. Over the past. . ." He trailed off, mouthing something. "The last six months, it has gotten worse, quickly. And so has his reputation as the country's future ruler. Prince Dagen is not able to eat or drink well on his own. He fevers and has an unshakable cough. Anything else you will have to learn yourself when you see him. That is the end of this conversation. You have broken my resolve enough. I gave you something. Hopefully, it can be useful for you to start thinking." He nodded his head. "Why don't you try and get some sleep? You've been claiming exhaustion the past few hours of riding, and it'll be a long ride. We won't arrive until close to mid-evening. You'll wake in time to have dinner at the castle."

The thought was sound.

"Fair. Thank you. It is the start of something. Already crossed several things off of my list with that time frame and few symptoms." Hollis nestled herself down against the small, cushioned bench and took in the sight of the carriage as she let herself doze.

The walls were chilled, likely metal with a somewhat in-fashion fabric plastered to them. The carpeted floors were a nice touch, decently plush and somewhat clean from shoe marks. The deeper brown color hid much of the dirt from sight. The benches themselves were comfortable the more she sank into them, the crushed velvet-like fabric felt nice against her skin as the visual world faded from view first, leaving only the threads of the world around her, constantly moving and reweaving as the train ripped through the air.

And then, nothing at all.

Her body jostled and then flew to the side, her shoulder colliding with the wall of the carriage. Her head never made contact, held tight by something warm.

"Are you all right?" Sir Lukxa's voice coaxed her eyes open, finding his own not far from her own. His body was precariously balanced in the carriage, legs braced, and an arm spared for holding her head upright.

"Yes, quite. Thank you for saving my head from the most unfortunate ache it would have had. What happened?" Hollis stretched her joints, wincing as they *cracked* and *groaned*.

She saw a small cloud of smoke trailing past the window, coming from the front of the train.

Sir Lukxa made no move to leave the caging position he held her in.

"Are you quite all right?" She asked him, sizing him up and down.

"Yes, I, ah. . ." He grimaced. "I jumped forward to keep your head from splitting and. . ." He groaned. "*Cramp*. In my leg—there's a cramp in my leg." He blew out a steady stream of air from his lips.

Hollis smickered. "My, what a hardened knight you are."

He grunted and shifted his weight. "A cramp is a cramp no matter who you are." He let out another sigh, the force of it ruffling her hair. "All right. I do think I've recovered."

Muffled shouts came through the closed glass. Hollis twisted at the latch holding the window locked shut. It wouldn't budge.

Sir Lukxa's hand replaced hers. His face twisted as he wrenched the latch open and slid the window up, the sides of it grinding as it slowly rose. He craned his head outside, blocking her view.

His body did nothing to block the foul smells from entering the carriage.

"I think the front of the train hit something or fell off the rails." He shut the window, trapping the scent of burning coal inside their once lovely, smoke-free, carriage.

"That's terrifying!" She could feel her body start to shake. Every possible thought and situation ran through her mind faster than the train claimed to go. "Why are you saying that with such a straight face? Do we need to move away from the train? Is it going to explode—"

Sir Lukxa pushed a few fingers against her mouth. "It will be fine. The smoke is likely from the engineers quelling the fire or some grass set ablaze. Trains are stocked with water to ensure nothing terrible happens from anything that would happen to catch fire. This sort of thing happens with the older trains."

"It's a pity we don't get any of the fancy machines the rest of the country does." Hollis sighed and leaned back against the bench. She wasn't totally convinced that nothing terrible was going to happen to them, but, at the same time, she didn't want to leave the carriage.

They now sat opposite each other in the cabin while the voices outside their cabin rose in intensity.

"I hope no one's injured. Maybe this can be fixed soon." She wrapped her arms around herself to provide a sense of warmth that the carriage suddenly didn't have.

A sharp cry pierced through the air, followed by several more. She straightened, eyes wide as she darted her eyes around their carriage.

Don't let yourself get too weighed down by it. She took a steadying breath and tucked her chin to her chest. She couldn't block out the sounds.

Sir Lukxa flung open the door and hopped down to the ground. "Let's go help."

Hollis cracked an eye open, watching him hold his hand out to her. "I'm sure there's a proper medic on this train somewhere. I'll leave it to them." There was no telling what would happen if she was dragged out of there. She was exhausted.

"If there's not, I'm coming back for you." Sir Lukxa shut the door and quickly jogged out of view before she could speak.

She hoped he wouldn't return.

Tucking her chin into the dip of her clavicle she let her eyes sink closed once more, hoping sleep would quickly claim her once more.

The door swung open as her first dream dissipated into nothingness.

Sir Lukxa gave her a sheepish expression that Hollis instantly knew as one of breaking bad news. "I am afraid I might have made mention of your presence here while the medical officer was working. They want you to come help to get the operators patched up quicker." He extended a hand.

Hollis narrowed her eyes. "You didn't let it slip accidentally, did you?"

Sir Lukxa smacked his lips in an awkward response. "I'm not answering that."

"I am tired, Sir Lukxa. Please do not make me,"

"It will be added to your pay."

Stretching out her body and cracking as many joints as she could, Hollis let him take her hand and lift her out of the carriage.

"I'll fetch you your cane and bag, no worries." He disappeared into the carriage before reappearing with her cane. "The ground isn't the most even out here. Do keep a hold on me until we're to the front." He kept her satchel slung over his shoulder. She wrapped her arm around the crook of his elbow.

She took in her surroundings. While she couldn't recognize the exact location of where they were, it would seem they were already inside the prefecture of Catol. The capital that shared the name likely wasn't more than a few hours north.

The sun didn't sit low on the horizon, but it wouldn't be long before it sank. How many hours had she slept? No feelings of refreshment soothed her.

The trees took on a maroon and golden hue. Autumn had shown its colors in fuller bloom. She could almost imagine how the air would smell were it not contaminated with smoke. Like fallen leaves, the sun roasting little acorns and pinecones, and dew.

Yes, Hollis would keep thinking of these things instead of basking in the reality that the air truly stunk.

She tripped, ankle twisting in a hole in the ground. She shoved her cane forward to lean on it and keep from eating the grass and pebbles they walked upon. Sir Lukxa's grip tightened on her arm as he helped right her.

Heat flushed her neck. Neither spoke as they continued walking.

A crowd of knights gathered around the front of the train. Some worked on tying ropes around the engine that had fallen off the track and lay on the edge of the wheel while others sat on the ground with soot marring their faces. A few bodies lay on the ground in the middle of the circle.

Her breath hitched in her throat as she more clearly saw the damage done. Burn marks scorched three prone bodies. Nothing life-threatening, but the injuries would require a great time to heal.

"This will be added to your overall payment. I'll be helping the rest of the knights get the train back onto the tracks. Hopefully, we can get this settled quickly. If you need anything, holler and I'll fetch it." Before she could respond, Sir Lukxa was running back toward the engine, rolling the sleeves of his shirt up before tying his hair into a knot on his head.

"Hello!" The sudden voice startled Hollis. "I'm Medical Officer Jones. I was told that you'd be able to get these men as good as new." Jones stuck his hand out to shake hers with great vigor. She couldn't place his accent.

"I'm not sure who told you that it'd be perfect—"

"It's common knowledge that Tablin Healers are quite gifted." The medical officer interrupted her. He led her toward the bodies on the ground.

Hollis gave a side-eye to the man standing beside her. "I'm not sure how much help I can give. Truly. Do you not have a burn salve in your bag? Or any ointment?" She stepped closer to the medic as she spoke, hoping to keep their conversation somewhat private. "I can lend you some of mine."

"I do have some, yes. But if these men cannot help operate the train, it would only be running on two people. And there's far too much to ask of them. We need the wounded healed *now* if we're to make it to the capital today, *safely*." Officer Jones, still gripping her hand far too tightly, tugged her forward until she tripped. "All right, we've a healer who can fix you right as rain."

The man on the ground where she stopped said nothing, only groaned in protest as Officer Jones resettled his body against the ground.

Half the threads in his body were singed to the point of snapping. It wasn't something that time *couldn't* heal. . .

Truly if the man is given ointment and rest, possibly a graft, his body would reweave itself to a living state. Of course that couldn't be done here.

His skin wouldn't look as it once did if she didn't interfere, but it would be healed eventually.

Everyone else here didn't have time, apparently.

It's fine. You can manage three people, Hollis. You're exhausted and on the brink of throwing up all over them—which would most assuredly end in infection, but. . .

She clapped her hands in front of her face, at a loss of words.

The ground threatened to *squelch* as she crouched and unwillingly set her bottom in the bloodied grass. The stench filled her mind. She gagged.

Control yourself, Hollis. You're a professional.

The strings under her fingers grew tense between her forefingers and thumbs as she rolled them. She'd need something to supplement the bulk of the threads to reinforce them.

Hollis ripped up blades of grass from the root and sifted through the little pile she'd made for the greenest ones. Once she had five or so pieces, she held them against the man's body. Green threads slowly revealed themselves as she focused. She grabbed at the grass' threads and rolled them and the man's threads together.

Whispers broke around her.

"*What's she think she's doing?*"

"*How is grass going to heal him?*"

"*Is she insane?*"

She could feel a presence looming over her, likely the medic ready to pull her away and chastise her.

"Be quiet, all of you! His burns are. . . they are vanishing?" Medical Officer Jones's voice was a mix of startled and joyful. "How are you able to do such a thing?" He crouched beside her, watching her every move with eyes wide.

"The sharing of Tablin sight magic is forbidden; surely you know this." It wasn't, but she didn't feel like explaining it to the man. Not when she had bodies to heal.

Orders shouted over the chaos drew her attention to where Sir Lukxa was with a few other highly ranking officers. It seemed most of the knights on the train now stood around with the operators—she'd ask someone later what train workers were actually called—to pull the giant beast of metal up and on the tracks.

Their sounds of effort were hard to block from her mind as she slowly worked her way over the bodies of the burned knights and. . . attendants? Was that their name? People who controlled and drove a train.

That didn't matter.

She continually added extra fibers until the threads of his body felt supple and taught under her fingers—no fraying, singeing, or risk of snapping felt. Using the clothes around the man's burns for healing was a temptation that grew in the back of her mind. The weaving of living things versus something long dead such as fabric was always fun to play with. But if she played seamstress to anything but the knight's bodies, she would be working all night.

Hollis closed her eyes and relaxed the focusing required to access her Tablin sight. After a breath, she opened them and nodded her head. "This man is healed. You can move him back to the train and wait for him to wake. You'll be able to put him right back to work as you wish. He might feel like death though."

Hollis' vision doubled. She belched as acid swam in her stomach.

She wasn't built to heal like this.

"Can you not do anything about that?" Jones asked. Hope thickly laced in his words.

Hollis did her best to control the glare that wanted to escape her. "I *salvaged* him; his body is going to feel that soon. Mayhaps not today, but he *will* feel the pain of being put back together eventually." She spoke pointedly.

The expectation for *more* circled around her like a hawk. She'd strike it down before it could dive at her.

"Now, let me continue working on the other *two* people you need me to save."

The other burned man lying on the ground groaned and grunted with every movement she made; their female companion suffered in a deafening silence. Hollis' vision doubled as she finished tucking the threads of the dark-skinned women back into a proper weave. All the workers would have minor scarring but would be able to feel and move around with little to no problems. A miracle in-and-of-itself.

"I've done all I can for them. Get them to the shade and give them some water once they wake up." Hollis gestured to Officer Jones, who in turn had a few knights that surrounded them to pick up the woman's body and carried her over to the shade of the train. Jones walked with them.

Hollis had been left with the small crowd that had gathered to watch her heal.

"You know, I think I landed on my shoulder in an odd manner when the train twisted. Do you think you'd be able to heal it too?" A man's voice drew her attention skyward to see that she'd once more been surrounded by a crowd of people.

"Get in line, I'm closer to her."

"Wait your turn!"

"I'm—"

"Me next! My ankle is always giving me trouble!"

The complaints filled her mind, and she was unable to get a word in as bodies plopped themselves in front of her, pointing to their aches and pains. Medical Officer Jones was nowhere to be seen.

The man complaining of his ankle grabbed her hands and placed them on his injuries with some "encouragements" to hurry up so more people could be patched up and board the train again.

The group blocked out most of the sun; some even crouched and shoved their aching limbs in her face.

"No, I—" Hollis' throat closed as a man ripped her hands away from the other man's ankle and put her shaking hands on his arm.

Nerves overwhelmed her. Her hands moved mechanically to soothe threads and knots in every form that sat across her, hoping the crowd would quickly leave. There were only a handful of people. Perhaps it would be better to heal them and make her escape.

A haze fell over her vision as people continued grabbing at her, demanding healing and fixing. She moved along with the motions of everyone surrounding her. More bodies joined the crowd.

Hollis could feel herself sagging, her energy all but spent.

Threads blended together in her mind until they were all she could see.

Vague sentences of wonder floated about overhead. People spoke in awe as they were healed.

Another body plopped down in front of her. Bright pink threads coursed under his skin. The threads in his hands were frazzled. Far from the worst thing she'd seen from the group.

"So, as long as I can remember, I've had this awful crick in my neck." *His neck?* His hands were what called to her. "I must have slept wrong ages ago. . ."

Hollis stopped listening as she reassessed the man, ignoring his hands entirely.

Oh my. The threads at the base of his neck had turned black, far from the bright pink the rest of his body held. Those threads had rotted inside of him.

"It seems to be a problem you were born with, manifesting at a later age. There's nothing I can do for this."

His brows knitted together in confusion, bordering the line of anger. "What? You've got to be kidding me."

Her voice sounded lifeless as she spoke. "It's as I said, there are limitations to what can be done—"

"Now listen—I've been standing here for a good while. I've seen you heal everyone who you lay hands on. Give me my miracle. It's my turn."

Hollis' eyes snapped up at him, soul fully reuniting with her body. "It's as I said." Her voice sounded stronger as she responded. "There are limitations to what I can and cannot do. The pain you get in your thumb, I can see the threads are worn and tired. I can soothe that, but the pain in your neck is something that was with you when you came into this world. It will grow with you until you die. I'm sorry." She shook her head and made to stand.

The man yanked her back down. "*No!*" His voice roared.

"*She's joking, right?* You're just tired, aren't you? You don't want to heal us anymore." A voice grew from a whisper to an angry accusation at her side, which one she couldn't tell anymore. The world grew heavier on her shoulders and eyes.

How had she let this come? Her mind had gone still and silent as the voices rose earlier. The healing was automatic.

She shook her hands in front of her face. "No, I'm sorry. There's only so much I can do."

She hated this moment. The moment when healings stopped and feelings burned. Expectations unmet fueled by indignation.

The crowd seemed to grow tighter around her; the warmth of the sun disappeared from her scalp. The shouts grew louder. Her mind reeled as the man sitting across from her gripped her shirt and shook her.

"I want my neck *fixed!*" The man's shout bounced in her ears. His hands gripped her shoulders and shook her. A jolt ran down her spine as her own neck *cracked* at the force.

"*Enough!*" A loud cry ripped through the air, silencing all of them. "What is going on here?" Sir Lukxa's voice cut through the crowd, which now stood frozen, every pair of eyes wide and filled with shock.

A trembling voice answered. "Sir, we—she won't heal us—"

Sir Lukxa's hands cut his hand through the air as he spoke. "She wasn't

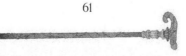

asked to heal you by anyone with the authority to do so! While you all were hovering, we finished setting the train." His voice fell low, scraping against the earth. "I want everyone here to sit in the back carriages until we reach Catol. Your reward for letting your fellow crew do all the work will be decided when we see the—"

"But with her healing us, we could help! Isn't that what Tablins do? They fix the mortals they screwed over. She should be healing us so we can work better." The crowd seemed to agree with the sentiment.

"You lot aren't owed anything. I have memorized your faces. Expect *great* things when we return. Miss Hollis, I'm sorry I dragged you outside. Let's be back to our carriage. The train is leaving soon as it's ready." Sir Lukxa reached an arm down to help pull her to her feet. The ground swayed underfoot.

Shadows at the edge of her vision rushed to engulf herself and Sir Lukxa as the group of knights swarmed back to their own compartment upon the train.

"Sir Lukxa," she whispered, "if you move me, I'm going to vomit." Her throat shook with the threat as the world spun behind her closed eyes. She took several deep breaths, steadying herself. The bile in her stomach settled as she rubbed her hand over her stomach, calming the storm inside.

"Okay, now we can go." Her voice rose just above a whisper.

His arm wrapped around her middle as he half carried her back to the carriage against his side, her feet dragging behind her as she attempted to walk.

The bench felt comforting under her bum and soothing to her spine. The ache that pulsed through her body came in waves as her body ceased to move against the cushion.

"I'm sorry." He said nothing else, only kept his head bowed and hands resting lightly upon his knees. The folded-up sleeves of his uniform were covered in soil of some kind.

She watched the guilt on Sir Lukxa's face, how he wrung his hands

against his legs.

"This, Sir Lukxa, is why I do not do big cities, large clinics. People want, and they crave, and they think they deserve."

CHAPTER FIVE

HOLLIS

Hollis could *almost* call the gates of the citadel impressive. They cast a long shadow over herself and Sir Lukxa on the now cobbled road that wound from the military station outside to the tall stone walls lined with guards.

Historically, the citadel was a place where a mortal man would have fought tooth and nail to enter. Now, all manner of people were bundled up within the walls. No battles were won to make their way inside, no secret tunnels used: people simply waited in the check line and were ushered inside once they were deemed safe.

She and Sir Lukxa passed through the check line without being stopped. Lukxa's menacing glare and imposing aura must have been unmistakable to the young workers sitting at the tables at the gate. That, and his uniform signified his high rank.

A strand of hair fell in front of her face. Hollis quickly tucked it back into its place under her maroon headwrap. If one stared at her face long enough to see her eyes, there would be the possibility of recognizing her Tablin features—but her hair would be a giveaway the moment the sun touched it. Thus, she kept it under wraps.

Nothing good would come from being recognized as a potential healer from the Guild, or being discovered inside the walls by the Guild themselves.

Lead lined her bones as they continued walking through the crowded area, exhausting her further than she already was.

There was also the possibility of arousing fear. The captain of the royal guard escorting a sick-looking Tablin woman into the heart of the country— into the castle itself—history wasn't fond of that action.

She would do her best to pass as Catolian for the time being, which meant her current mission was to stay undetected. Thankfully, she was good at that.

Sir Lukxa bumped into her side as he stepped around a horse pulling a cart of laughing children and some furniture. The wrap on her head unraveled a tad. Her hands made quick work at retucking and reforming it upon her head.

Not good enough apparently. It was a string of bad luck, and even worse luck for the prince she was required to heal. Either way, she would do her best to get something out of this trip.

The capital was a breath of stale air—which she appreciated from time to time. She enjoyed being secluded away in tiny little villages and cities, slowly moving from place to place in a world she only half belonged to. Quinlin hadn't grown tired of her yet. Hollis couldn't remember how long it had been since she arrived and solved a handful of people's problems. It wouldn't be much longer until they grew too comfortable with her and became lax in their belief that she was doing anything at all for them.

Which, *to be fair*, she wasn't doing anything half the time.

She wanted to linger in Quinlin a while. And would most assuredly return to her home there after any long quests.

"When do I get to see His Royal Sickness?" she stated, swinging her cane every few steps.

The owner of a glass-blowing stall gave her a side-eyed glance as she

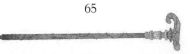

passed by. While the smell of heat and coal pushed out past him and the sand he stood upon. She gave him a light, flirty smile and kept walking.

Sir Lukxa glared at her. "Yes, please say it *louder* so all of Catol can hear you."

"I still do not understand why you don't just tell the people he's sick. All those nasty rumors would clear right up if they knew the prince—" she sighed internally, speaking before she forgot, "—*may the sun shine on his crown*, wasn't actually acting out, but bedridden and ill. It'd be great for everyone to fawn over." A chuckle broke free of her chest, and she pressed a hand to her lips to try and stop the sounds.

"You do not have to say that every time you speak his name or title." His jaw ground shut as he spoke, his eyes darting around at every stranger's face to make sure they had not heard her. "And you will see him tonight."

"Fine, fine." She wondered at what sort of illness plagued His Majesty.

Her money was on a disease of the frisky variety. His reputation being the main thing supporting her theory. After his parent's death, the perfectly poised prince broke free a bit. At least that's what the rumors said, and if the Council wasn't wanting to dispel the rumors, and they were everywhere, there had to be a hint of truth to them. He wasn't seen often, but his name was everywhere. From the tongue of every harlot to the winds of despair in the farthest reaches of the country where skirmishes were a daily occurrence. If it weren't for the council, she was sure the country would be in ruins. With the death of his parents, Prince Dagen simply stopped caring.

But money was money, so she would care enough for the both of them.

She let her eyes roam over the buildings that surrounded her. They were far taller than anything in Quinlin. These houses and apartments seemed to touch the sky. They had to be at least six stories tall. It reminded her of where she'd grown up near the border of the Hozen and Rex prefecture. The buildings there had always towered over her frame as a child. It was a drastic shift from where she lived now, where the tallest building had three stories, and most homes had only one. Hollis herself was lucky to have a home with two stories. It gave a nice separation from a working space to a cozy area to relax.

A small boy in worn linen overalls stood on a wooden crate, shouting. He waved a newspaper wildly above his head. Her eyes almost dried out from how wide they'd opened. *Freshly printed gossip.* She moved closer to hear what it was that he was calling out over the noise of the crowd.

Sir Lukxa clamped a hand down on the back of her neck. "Hollis, have you forgotten what we're here for?" His tone was patronizing. Of course she didn't need to be reminded.

She threw a smile over her shoulder. "I just want a copy of the paper. It will only take me a few moments." Her cane was the only thing that kept her from being knocked to the ground in the clamoring group of people, all wanting their own copies of the daily news.

Hollis side-stepped away from Sir Lukxa's side and reached at the coin purse on her waist.

The news that made it into the papers back home was either weeks behind current events or all the articles consisted of fishing updates. This was *Capital* news. The wonders that could be printed inside the pages were neverending. She bounced on her toes as she approached the line to claim a spot. The smile that grew on her face was almost painful. A fresh paper with hot, capital, gossip would count as the first win of this trip.

"Tensions rising with Tablin as ruling clans rumored to plan barbaric sieges against the Catolian Royal Family! Will we have to wage war again? *And!* Prince Dagen caught in a nefarious affair with capital funds! All this and more in today's paper! Won't be here tomorrow." The young boy's toothy grin seemed to shine as he shouted all the words properly over the bustling crowd.

Her heart stopped beating. The little boy handed out papers to the crowd. He slid the little coins handed to him in a metal bucket behind the box he stood on—stuffing a few into the front pocket of his pants.

"Rotten creatures, those Tablins." A crackling voice startled her, and she spun to see an old man batting the back of his hand against the paper. His face was dried like a leather saddle and looked to be just as worn. "I don't know why King Trist left them alone so long—may his soul rest in the fields of green. They're dangerous people. Always have been. Why'd he have ta die and leave us with his worthless son?"

How rude. Insulting both her people and the prince at the same time for completely unrelated reasons. Or perhaps enough stories had been woven about both Tablins and Prince Dagen, *may the sun shine on his crown.*

Besides, most Catolian's have a good relationship with Tablins. In regard to the Tablins of the Healers Guild or other healers. . . doing work for them. . . Either way, she stood firm in the resolve that this man was simply a dullard with nothing better to do than snatch up the cheapest gossip he could get his hands on. Hollis doubted that this was a reputable press either. This story was built to dredge up old fears of her people.

Most of Catol was fine with Tablin healers now.

Perhaps that was the caveat? They only liked the ones who served as healers.

She stuck up her nose away from the boy on the paper stand. No longer willing to spend her hard earned coin on such filth. Such, fresh and gossip filled. . . okay, she wanted to *peek* at a paper.

"At least he can't get the crown 'til he's twenty. We have got a just over a month left with the council holding the reins. And if the boy knows what's good for 'im, he'll let them keep ruling while he's off being whatever. Honestly, he's almost as bad for this country as those Tablins across the sea are." A second man, who looked much like the first, chimed in.

Hollis shook her head, mindful to not let the wrap slip and fall to the ground. It would be quite the revealing moment, perfect comedic timing.

A plump woman to the mens left came and peered over his shoulder to catch a glimpse at the fresh paper. Hollis tried not to gag at her obnoxious perfume and the ridiculous dyed and dried flowers she'd stuffed in her hair. She gave a hoot as she fanned herself with a discarded sheet from the paper. "Tablin has been nothing but a magical thorn in our side for generations.

Article says we've intercepted *secret communications* between, uh, their country names are so hard to say. Those countries need to keep to their own and leave us alone. Honestly, even the Healers Guilds aren't all that good. Who knows what they're really doing to us when they claim to be fixing us."

"Perhaps we should go around keeping tabs on them all. I know, it sounds outrageous, but what if they're here, spying on *us*?" The men spoke in agreement.

Hollis' free hand reached out to tap the first man on the shoulder, a slight tremble spreading in her fingers. She clenched her jaw, trying to regain a sense of balance through her body. "Excuse me, but can I take a peek at that paper? Sounds quite interesting." Her cane shook next.

The older man gave her a rotten scowl, which matched the state of his putrid orange threads. "Buy your own paper. Trying to take from an old man's hard-earned wages." He gave Hollis a once-over, eyes glossing over her own but stopping at her cane. "That isn't a fashion piece either—it's for people who need it." His leg jerked out towards her cane.

A hand clamped down onto her shoulder and pulled her back. Sir Lukxa moved in front of her, blocking the man from advancing towards her. "Excuse me, sir, but brawling isn't allowed in the citadel. I'm going to have to ask you to leave. Ma'am, I hope you're all right." Sir Lukxa said with a level-headed tone. The image in her mind of his hair and the pins on his lapel glistening in the sunlight, hand on the pommel of his sword and a menacing glare on his face, put her shoulders at ease.

The old men blabbered on with some half-hearted *sorry* before he rushed out of the area. The woman simply turned, scoffed, and walked toward a nearby shop with a multitude of expensive shoes in the window, her frazzled periwinkle threads fizzing even more.

"Thanks." Hollis graced Sir Lukxa with a smile.

He raised his brows before turning his head past her to the boy on the box, who had begun repeating his headlines to the market. The bucket's metallic twang had lessened, replaced with the sound of bouncing coins.

Sir Lukxa sighed. "Pay them no heed. Those papers aren't even fit to be used for bathroom cleanings." His face bore a heated glare. "They are only helpful in spreading ridiculous rumors about the prince."

"Why not shut them down or run them out of town?" It was a humorous picture in her mind. A group of shady people being tossed out of town with their printing press loaded on their shoulders, spilled ink trailing behind them, telling of their sad tale. The amusement brought on by the idea did nothing to aid the building headache that pounded against her skull.

Now that she thought about it, her stomach churned with the desire to consume food. Had she eaten *anything* today? Yes, she ate the entire box of clover cookies she'd packed on the train.

"Because if we did shut them down, it would only fuel the suspicions that the people have. People are allowed to think what they want. No matter how stupid it may be."

Confusion knit her brows together. "But this is directly harming the crown. Treasonous, is it not?"

"I'm sure most of them will forget everything they read by tomorrow, eager to consume whatever is being told them next." Sir Lukxa shrugged his broad shoulders and pushed his way through the crowd, setting his pace slow enough that the people surrounding the press could get a good look at him.

That was a ridiculously sexy move. Able to part a group of people like that simply by walking through them. The surrounding crowd gawked at the captain but kept pushing papers onto passersby who happily gave up coin for the freshly printed drama.

Hollis pushed through to catch up to him, her far less imposing presence not aiding her in any way.

A few whispers of *Sir Lukxa* met her ears, tied with his title and race. It seemed his being spotted drove up sales as the sound of *clinking* coins met her ears at a faster rate until they'd walked far enough she couldn't hear it anymore.

Sir Lukxa spoke once she matched his stride, his voice just loud enough for Hollis to hear. "Their words may tarnish the crown, muddle it a bit. But the crown will always shine in the light of the sun on the head of its ruler." He lifted his head, toward the looming spires of the castle. "Come now, we've got better, more important, things to worry about." He scratched at his neck as he walked.

They broke into what she assumed was another village market, nestled into the heart of the citadel square. The buildings surrounding them didn't seem much different than the ones in Hozen: cream facades with dark wooden bracings along the sides. Even the hand-painted signs were done in a similar enough style.

"I wonder if they designed most of Hozen to resemble this square?" Hollis turned her eyes to capture every little detail. Each shop had their windows open, sending a wave of different scents to all the people. Roasting meats, soaps, confectionaries—a far wider variety than she'd ever found holed up in the small villages she preferred.

"If my understanding is correct, the square is decorated to now look like Hozen. Brings in a soft charm." Sir Lukxa said, pointing out several areas where one could see the flaws in building designs, cracked seams that hadn't quite been patched to cover the rough stone beneath.

"Can we stop for a quick treat?" Even with the fatigue that grew heavier upon her body, frazzling her threads beyond belief, the possibility of food was sure to aid in her recovery. Her stomach sounded and joined in the group of minor aches that were sure to grow worse if she didn't eat soon. The second nap she'd had on the train did nothing to aid her.

Sir Lukxa shook his head. "I can get whatever you want after we get inside the castle. I do not feel like paying for a full meal out when there's a lovely free one inside. And I do not want to chance anything happening to you before we get to my apartments. I promise I'll get you food as soon as we're settled."

Hollis mulled it over, finding that Sir Lukxa's words made too much sense.

71

It would be quite something if she were pulled away from the castle even longer, and the derailment of the train already ate into their time. Sir Lukxa had said she was set to meet Prince Dagen tonight.

The better part of the day had already folded down on them. The sun sat behind the castle, sending blinding rays of light around the edges.

Nodding, she followed behind the captain. Hopefully there *would* be a hot meal inside just waiting for them—mainly *her*. She was starving.

Each step away from the lovely bakery brought them closer to the looming shadow of the castle. It became hard to swallow the stupid amount of nervous spit her body kept producing—as if she were some poisonous frog preparing to win a fight. She thought a moment on if there had ever been records of Tablins being poisonous.

Her thoughts ceased as the shadows hit the ground in front of her.

"We aren't going in the front gate, do not worry. Follow me around back, where we'll be entering by the stables and servants entrances." Sir Lukxa waved a hand and she followed him around the outer wall, stepping around the shadow it cast. "I do not want any pomp and circumstance with my arrival."

The castle stood fierce against the blue sky. The chill air from the surrounding mountains washed over the perfectly even gray stone walls. They made up the outer gate and partially obscured the rounded spires and walls of the main building. The body of the castle itself was an impossible shape, jutting out and standing at odd angles with additions that defied the laws of the world. The windows were encased in iron, aging the building by centuries. A handful of the windows were painted in brilliant colors. She'd have to track down those rooms eventually to see what painting they cast along the floor.

Hollis stood in awe of the castle for several beats of her heart: this building, which was at least a hundred times the size of her home in Hozen, had stood the test of time and war over and over as anger and pride crashed against it—willing it to the ground.

She scoffed and walked onward again, remembering the words of her grandmother. *Nothing will bring the reign of Catol to the roots of weeds; Catol is a weed itself.*

Her cane sent a small pebble soaring. She watched it fumble on the ground as it landed, rolling around until it found a new home near the stables. The smell grew putrid as they approached, the grounds seemed surprisingly sparse in the midday sun. In fact, there wasn't a soul in sight within the stable. A few horses grazed in the gated area, but no bodies accompanied them.

"Why is there no one working?" Hollis craned her head to survey the surrounding area. She could make out what seemed to be an entrance to a garden, perhaps there were people elsewhere inside the castle grounds to place the voices she could hear. Otherwise, the side courtyard was empty.

"The castle has run on a surprisingly small outdoor staff since the king and queen passed and Prince Dagen fell ill. All the stable crew, kitchen hands, and gardeners take dinner together once all duties are finished—no worries, there will be hot food for us. Most dine in the halls on the far side of the castle, but a good some enjoy frequenting the bakeries you were eyeing."

"Ah." She drew out the word. "You could have said that earlier when you told me *no*. Are you ignoring your coworkers?"

Sir Lukxa turned over his shoulder, no response on his lips as he led her toward the wooden door.

Hollis quickly followed behind.

Her body seized as she broke the line of shadows. The darkness froze against her leg. She leaned back on her other leg, which was still in the sun, and pulled herself out of the dark.

"Hollis?" Her vision came into focus on Sir Lukxa. He jogged back towards her, a calm expression on his face. "Nothing is going to happen to you." His face held strong.

"Something doesn't feel right." The words tumbled out of her mouth.

He gave her a look of confusion. "What do you mean?"

"I'm not entirely sure. I just—something isn't right here." She pushed forward into the cast shadow, enduring the cold feeling that pulled at her marrow.

Sir Lukxa quickly came up beside her, standing tall.

Obviously whatever this is, he doesn't feel it.

Hollis stumbled. He quickly caught her elbow. The closer they got to the castle, the harder it became to stand without the world spinning. The grip Sir Lukxa had on her elbow to keep her upright cut off the flow of blood to her hand, freezing it even further.

Was she having a flare? Perhaps she should have eaten more on the train instead of sleeping?

He bent his head and whispered in her ear. "Is this exhaustion from earlier?"

"Possibly? It doesn't feel like my typical spells, but my body is always surprising me." Hollis peered around the stone walls of the castle, at every spire and iron window, every inch of roof she could spy as she approached, desperately checking for some magical trace that something was wrong.

Nothing stuck out to her. A quick glance backward showed the same nothingness surrounding the outer wall. Her stomach tumbled in her throat, burning with bile.

Something weighed in her skull, pulling her to the ground. Darkness muffled the sounds of the world around her.

"What are you doing to me?" The words felt like sludge pooling out of her lungs.

"I am not doing anything." His grip tightened as he continued to walk her toward the castle. "We are almost there. Can you make it?"

Hollis shrugged her shoulders best she could. "Maybe?" Her words were slow to leave her lips. The grip she held on her cane went slack.

Her heart screamed against her rib cage. A haze, thick and scratchy, settled on her mind. Every feeling was new and terrifying.

"We are almost in. The servants' entrance is just ahead—make it 'til

there and I will carry you to the clinic." Lukxa's grip on her arm continued to tighten continually to a degree Hollis knew would bruise.

The threads in her arm twisted to a nasty purple shade.

Again she looked around, trying to spy the different threads that made up the natural world in the courtyard. The little wispy strings of the paperwhites, the thick bands across the stone walls, and the dead brown of the doorframe.

She did her best to glare up at him as his words registered. "Don't insult me so. I know my body better than any doctor could dream of knowing a patient. I'm difficult to treat." She noted the concern knit between his dark brows. "Besides, I thought you wanted to keep our arrival a bit more concealed?"

"Yes, well, plans can change. Watch your step—right foot." Her toes grazed the surface of something feeling very much like a rock. "All right, three more steps and we are there."

"No doctors; I'll be fine. We've got to stick to the plan."

"We do not have a plan yet," he deadpanned.

"Exactly." She smiled and braced both hands against her cane. The threads grazed her fingertips, hardly noticeable considering this wood was dead in its use. "I have to be completely drained from earlier and didn't realize how bad it had become. Nerves are getting the best of me. It's like I'm waiting for some monster to jump out and catch me here by the castle." She stopped herself before finishing the thought aloud, *I didn't think I was afraid of coming here. Maybe I am?*

"That sounds reasonable. Wait here. I need to make sure the kitchen is empty before I bring you in; otherwise, I'll have to find another solution. I do not fancy dragging you inside like this." Sir Lukxa stabilized her before quickly jogging the rest of the way to the small wooden door they'd been working toward.

She leaned hard into her cane and turned her head, afraid of emptying her acidic stomach. A ripple of fabric caught her attention. Hollis spotted a man in a light cloak who stood a handful of paces away from both herself and Sir Lukxa. He couldn't have been more than a few yards down the side wall. His hair was the color of midnight and sat tousled above a set of amber glaring eyes.

Sir Lukxa hadn't seemed to notice the stranger. She tried calling out for Sir Lukxa's attentions but found the ordeal too strenuous. The man's face tightened as he met her gaze, but she couldn't place the expression. His lips moved as he lifted a hand to steeple under his mouth. The moment he stopped speaking, he flicked his fingers forward and stalked away around the far corner of the castle wall.

Sir Lukxa peered past the door, closed it, and quickly made his way back to her. "Looks like everyone is still gone. Let's get you inside." His arm took the place of her cane as he shuffled her forward.

Any attempt to tell Sir Lukxa of the man she saw brought a pounding in her skull. The words refused to let from her mouth.

Why can't I speak? Mouth, open please.

She pushed at the wooden door. Hinges protested at their use as light flooded against her body in rays of color and a host of warm scents accompanied it as the servants' door to the castle opened in front of her. A few servants bustled about from place to place. Sit Lukxa helped her up the small step and into the promise of warmth inside.

Air flooded her lungs as her jaw went slack. Her vision became speckled with black. Words came as the world spun. "Sir Lukxa?"

"Yes?"

Her throat clenched, a sour feeling building underneath her tongue. "I can't see anything."

CHAPTER SIX

LUKXA

Hollis lay prone on Lukxa's bed. Her chest slowly raised and sank. Her breathing sounds scratched against his skull. Three cream blankets piled up to her shoulders, and pale fingers clutched the hems. Occasionally her hands would find some semblance of strength as they pulled the sheets to her forehead to wipe off the gathered beads of sweat. A subconscious notion of her unconscious mind.

Lukxa sank further into the plush chair he had dragged to the side of the bed and ran a hand down his face, hoping to clear his own exhaustion that was setting in as he watched over Hollis.

Only a few hours had passed since she had fallen by the servant's entrance. Lukxa tapped his foot against the floor. He could not leave and run any errands with her like this. Without knowing when she would wake up, or what she would do once she woke.

Once he had piled Hollis up on his bed, he had done the only thing he could think to do: he summoned a page and sent a few notes out into the castle. One to each of the nine council members: informing them of his successful return and one to the kitchens to have two meals sent up to his apartments. Lukxa had eaten his own meal of roasted bird and mashed potatoes with greens as quickly as it arrived. Hollis' sat untouched, resting in the small oven in his own kitchenette so it would not spoil from being left out.

His visit to Dagen would have to wait until he was certain Hollis was all right.

There was not a thought in his head that made sense at how to deal with this. Bringing in one of the court doctors could leave them as baffled—Hollis said it was unlikely that they would know how to treat her. Lukxa knew the ruse the council had built for her, so it would not be strange to be inside the castle walls with her. And, as Hollis said, the court doctors may not know how to treat her.

Tablins were interesting creatures—

No. His face tensed several moments. It was wrong to think of Tablins as a different breed of people. The only difference was that they had a more magical ancestry, and it wasn't enough of one to get hung up on as people in the past had.

Sickness seems to be spreading everywhere around me.

His thoughts wandered from Hollis to his ward.

Most of the medics brought in assumed that Dagen caught a lingering bit of illness carried over from his parents. It didn't matter that he'd deteriorated in an entirely different manner than the late king and queen. Perhaps it didn't matter, considering no one had been able to heal them either.

He rolled his neck, *cracking* it a few times. His gaze landed back on Hollis. "Well, Hollis, you said you'd need sleep. I should not be worrying too much." He gave his face another pull before standing and returning the chair to the area behind his bed that he designated as his study. The area was lined with bookshelves framing the windows that peppered the space.

Lukxa paced the room. To the left of the study was a kitchenette, cupboards filled with little odds and ends so he could prepare his own meals at *his* convenience if the kitchens were closed. Walking down the room, parallel to his bed, was the door to the water closet and his dressing area. Every exterior wall of his room was peppered with windows, all letting moonlight drift along the floor.

He did several more laps of his room. Dressing area, bed, study, kitchenette, washroom door. Five laps later had him settling down in his chair at his mahogany desk.

Lying on his desk was a pile of papers that had not been there when he had left on his journey.

He thumbed through the stack as he replanted himself in his chair, finding reports from the different stations he presided over in the country. Councilor Dem seemed to pen an extra copy or two of reports from his own men, scribbled notes of '*I thought you'd enjoy reading these*' with a smiling face beside them. Lukxa grinned back at the little ink smile and set to reading.

Let us see what was dealt with while I was gone. Art thief was captured; drills run as I specified; three knights up for promotion—Dem heavily considered two of them to be rising powers in the ranks, the other was an unknown to Lukxa, likely pulled from Councilor Kleo's ranks. She trained her knights in entirely different manners, but her methods provided results.

The next bundle of papers that were tied together was discovered to be all the everything the council passed in Lukxa's two-week absence. The note taped to the top of the pile gave an index. The contents included proposed ideas by the people and council alike. It would not be a load of light reading: the script upon it was smaller than Lukxa's pinky's fingernail. *Joy.*

He trailed his eyes down the page. First came the overly pompous budgets, then proposed ideas on changing up different systems—things that would never change but people always spoke about needing to change.

Several pages in had him reading through what his own weapons order count and stock were. Tension grew between his brows. The numbers were skewed. On paper it was written that he had twice the amount of weapons ordered than he should.

A letter with a wax seal slipped out of the stack, landing neatly in

Lukxa's lap. His throat bobbed.

It was as if they had heard his thoughts.

Pushing everything else aside on his desk, Lukxa set about opening the letter, carefully pulling at the green-yellow tab until the chilled thing gave way. He scanned through the lines thrice before grabbing an extra piece of paper and a pen to decode the gibberish in front of him. He mused his thumbnail with his teeth as he scribbled out possible translations until he settled on the most likely decipher.

Saturday, Quarter till Midnight: It's time for a chat.

A date, time, and brief threat. Far from a respectful way to ask for a meeting but he could not complain. He had put himself into this situation. And things were in fact taking far too long to get himself out.

"My goodness, what did you do?" A voice pierced through the silence of his room.

He snapped back to see Hollis sitting up and clutching her head while groaning as loudly as he imagined she could. Her hands raked through her hair as she massaged at her scalp until tremors slowly took over her movements.

"I didn't do any—" Lukxa began.

"Why's it so hot in here? Who needs this many blankets to sleep?" she grumbled as she pushed the blankets off her, untucking them from the tight, neat folds in the wooden bed frame. "Oh, wait. Now it's freezing in here." She hurriedly gathered up a sheet or two back to her shoulders. The shaking in her body grew worse.

Lukxa stood and burned the letter and his translated note in the fireplace while he gave Hollis the time to gather herself. She blinked and looked around the room, her eyes squinting when her gaze landed anywhere near the fireplace.

Deciding she was conscious enough, he made his way over to the bed and sat beside her on the plush blankets. His landing jostled her as the bed bounced slightly.

"How are you doing?" he asked.

"Where am I?" Hollis ran her hands over the sheets once more.

"These are my apartments. I figured they would be a safe place to watch over you for now. *Again*, how are you doing?" He pressed his hand against her forehead. She was clammy, but not truly feverish. That was a good sign. He trailed his hand to her cheek in good measure.

"Everything's fuzzy. Like. . ." She wet her lips. "Like I'm seeing things through a strip of cotton fluff." She did another glance around the room, stopping when she made eye contact with him. Hollis tilted her head to the side and scooted closer to where he sat on the bed.

He became acutely aware of the chill of her hands resting close to his legs, nose dangerously close to his own. Her eyes shook as she checked him over before she sat back.

Faint traces of tea and other herbs under the train smoke lay over her skin. "You look different, much clearer—like I'm seeing through you without seeing your insides." Her eyes shook again, and then she gripped her head, her teeth clenching as she let out a low hiss of pain.

Lukxa waited until the wave of pain had passed and her face returned to normal before starting up their conversation again. "What do I normally look like?"

"Well, just like *you*, but I see everything else too—that wouldn't make any sense to you. I see the world, every fiber of someone's being, like a tapestry made up of colorful strings. You're usually all woven uptight and handsome. Now, you're just handsome." She reached a hand out and traced a trembling finger down his jaw. He steeled himself and waited to see if she was going to pull at her magic and manipulate him.

The tingling sensations never came. Only the faint feeling of her nail lightly dragging over his face and neck. "I can't even feel the strings. . . My sight is *gone*?" Her head dropped close to her shoulder, eyes lining with tears before she blinked them away and righted herself. It didn't seem to stop the frantic muttering under her breath. He couldn't make out half the words she spoke. The other half he knew were loan words in his mother tongue of Omil.

A Tablin language?

Panic churned in his stomach as the room seemed to drop several degrees. "But you just said you could see me?" That was not good. If she could not access her sight, she could not heal Dagen. Lukxa did not want to further entertain the thoughts he had about what would happen when Dagen passed. He swallowed. Those thoughts had plagued him long enough.

He had to work toward a solution.

"Yes, as I assume a normal person would—but my magic seems to have just stopped. I can sense it still. . ." Hollis smiled. "It's nice and warm, bubbling up inside of me. I just can't see or feel it anywhere else." She blinked several more times as a paleness set into her face. Her eyes unfocused.

Lukxa lurched forward and managed to wrap his hands around her shoulders, steadying her as she fell back against the stack of pillows.

"What could cause something like this?" Lukxa asked.

Hollis burrowed deeper into his pillows as he withdrew his support.

"I haven't the slightest clue." Her voice came out no louder than a whisper. "I've never heard of anything like this happening before—but I didn't grow up in Tablin." She trapped her bottom lip between her teeth. "There are other forms of magic people have dug their fingers into. I don't know what it would have to do with my situation, though. And it's quite complicated and hurts my head just thinking about it. It's always best to go with the simple answer, that I'm fatigued and exhausted. I've run myself sick into the ground and will need time to recover." She paused in her ruminations, and her eyes lit up. "I do remember it happening once—when I was a child. Only lasted a day or three. I had a horrible cold. That has to be the answer. I just need more sleep. I'll sleep more and my sight will be back."

Hollis curled further into his bedding, acting rather comfortable with her wild hair sprawled across his pillows. The look on her face was anything but comfortable though. Her eyes sat wide, pupils dilated.

Lukxa nodded. Unable to afford the ability to lose control of himself in his fear.

Hollis spoke nothing else as he retrieved her dinner. She finished the meal and tucked herself back into his bed and drifted off.

A few hours later found all the reports read and signed off on. Out the window, the moon sat against the crest of the mountains. He turned over his shoulder to find color returned to Hollis' sleeping face, the tip of her nose rather rosy. Her lips still seemed dry and all the veins in her face and neck stood as dark rivers against her skin.

Lukxa could not remember the last time they had stopped for any food or drink before riding the train. She had eaten a snack packed away in the seemingly never-ending bag she wore. Even stronger was the memory of hearing how her stomach had *growled* at the sight of the bakeries. The way her stomach sounded as she ate her dinner.

He had been the one that pushed her to her limits. This was the consequence.

That could be rectified. He had already fed her; next was watering.

A scoff broke free of Lukxa's chest. He was speaking like she was a house plant.

He stood, shaking off the grim smile, and made his way over to his small kitchenette to fill two cups of water. There was no stopping his shoes from making light *clacking* sounds against the wooden floors. Hopefully they were not loud enough as to wake his sleeping guest.

The chill of the glass was refreshing set against his hands as moonlight washed over him from the window above the sink, bringing him back to reality in a sense.

Lukxa slowly tipped open the tap. The water slowly drizzled from the faucet into the cups. He enjoyed the sound of dripping water filling the silence as he surveyed the empty training grounds below his kitchen window. No one lingered or loitered outside, so his gaze drifted back into his dwelling.

Aside from the reports Dem brought, nothing had moved since

Lukxa had left.

If anyone had come snooping, they put things back exactly as they were. Books were lined up by author's last name in his shelves, their spines still coated in a thin layer of dust; the chest that held his training and ceremonial swords was locked tight, traps seemingly untripped.

The lingering scent of dried eucalyptus filled the kitchen. Dried bundles of leaves, free of mold and decay. Thankfully he had not left anything fresh in his cabinets or pantry, else the whole room would be rancid.

Lukxa ran through what Hollis said as he returned to her side and lightly pressed a hand against her shoulder, stirring her awake. He waited until her eyes found focus on him to hand her one of the cups.

"You need sleep, but I think you may need water a bit more." He handed her one of the two glasses he held.

"Thank you, Sir Lukxa." She slowly sipped at the water.

He drank from his own cup. The water washed away some of the dry, stale feeling in his mouth. "I have a question. . . about what you said earlier. I did not know there were other types of magic."

Her eyes peered over the rim of the cup as she drained the rest of the contents in three large gulps. "You're joking, right?"

She seemed to have regained some of her sass and strength.

"Why would I be?" Lukxa tapped his finger against the rim of his glass. "I was brought to Catol when I was young, and even then as an orphan I grew up in the Knight Academy in Eargile. They do not teach a lot about magic there." No, the western province of Eargile was a cold place, settled into the walls of mountains. A place where you learned how to survive in the cold with the warmth of strength, brothership, and wit.

Hollis raised her brows, giving him an incredulous expression. "You're *Omil*."

His mind was drawing a blank on what his race had to do with anything. "Yes, but I grew up here after the war with Catol and Omil—"

"Which was fought over Omilian magic."

An uncomfortable feeling settled in his stomach.

She blinked. "Goodness, you don't know? The Omil people developed magic very similar to Tablinian—except for the fact that we're born with magic and the Omilian people just. . . tapped into it and made it their own. Catol wasn't happy they wouldn't share the secret of unlocking magic in mortal men. Don't you know Catol has a history of changing the subject of war to fit their—"

Bile rose in Lukxa's throat with memories of burning wood. "I'd be careful with your words, Hollis. They're borderline treasonous." His knuckles turned white as he gripped the sheets.

He sighed. Power was an unfortunate cause of war, and he'd long dealt with those feelings. So why did they keep returning when he least expected them? He counted backward from a randomly chosen number. Once he hit zero, he looked up.

Hollis' face sat frozen. Upon meeting his gaze it morphed as her lips pursed and her brows furrowed. "So sorry to bring up the other side of a rusted coin. History isn't as pleasant as the victors like to gild it. Ask the newspapers we saw earlier."

Lukxa bit his lip. "Why don't we change the subject. Do you want to walk around before going back to bed? I know I can get restless after a. . . nap? If you are feeling steady enough by the end of it, I can fulfill my promise to you and introduce you to Prince Dagen." It was growing late into the night, he would not assume many would be awake except for the occasional knight. And if he stuck to the areas near his own wing there would not be a soul in sight wandering the halls.

Hollis wrapped the sheets around herself tighter. She fussed with her lips as she seemingly thought about his proposal. "That doesn't sound too terrible."

Lukxa clasped his hands together. "Wonderful." He hoped he wasn't going to regret this.

CHAPTER SEVEN

HOLLIS

The crushed velvet cushioned each achy step Hollis took down the neverending hall. The image of her threads running up her legs carried frays and thorns that dug into her skull shone clearly in her mind. She only wished she could see it outside her imagination.

The overwhelming perfume from bouquets of flowers placed every few windows did nothing to help the pain radiating in her skull. Even though lilacs matched the color of her being, she wasn't always keen on the scent they lent.

Hollis wouldn't say anything about her discomfort though, no. That would lead to Sir Lukxa dragging her back to his apartments and depositing her on his bed the rest of the evening—a thought that sounded much more appealing when phrased in such a manner but would surely lead to a long night of boredom.

Besides, she had to meet the Crowned Prince of Catol himself. *Dagen Alder Catol.*

Hollis wondered at what the prince would look like. What he would act like. Was he anything like the papers claimed? Any ounce of truth in the ink published would be interesting.

Sir Lukxa's voice interrupted her thoughts. "If you're one to care about historical builds, you'll note that the stones used on these few top floors of the castle are actually older than the stones right under us," Sir Lukxa said in a tone that reminded Hollis of a stuffy teacher. "When it was decided to add on to the castle, they wanted to build up, each new addition adding to the legacy the crown holds, now bearing down thousands of pounds of weight onto the old. Poetic in a sense. It only lasted a few additions before the castle became too heavy to lift from the foundation."

Oh goodness, he's deeply into ancient history.

She raised her brows at him and tucked chin to chest.

"Hey. Do not look at me like I am one of those insane scholars; it is one of the things they taught us in the Knights Academy. A theorized true meaning being that the newer construction would be impenetrable, solid." A ray of moonlight traced across his face, reflecting the pale shine of Sir Lukxa's eyes.

Sir Lukxa was stunning enough that the historical talk didn't matter. His long hair was in pristine condition. It bounced around as he moved, flowing like shimmering water from where it was tied with a red ribbon. She liked the ribbon.

"I can see the points in both being true, good sir. Sometimes it's nice to preserve what was while caring for what is now." She'd now seen a good portion of the wing that Sir Lukxa resided in, the *Royal Guard Wing* as he called it. A wing entirely of his own with rooms to spare for any additions to his family. Being that he was unmarried and had no children, that she knew of, the wing was supposed to be empty sans himself.

'Supposed to' and 'are' are two entirely different things, Hollis.

Now they'd wandered out of his sanctioned space and into the main portion of the castle. The halls were silent as they walked, broken only by their small pieces of conversation. The wall to her left had a small crack that ran diagonally halfway up the wall. She wanted to trail a finger along the fracture, to poke at its weak points and see how the wall would react. To see if she could feel the snapped threads and will them back together.

While Hollis had only seen a portion of the castle, she was confident that she could find a story everywhere she laid her eyes. Every precious vase or painting had a story she wanted to investigate. It redoubled her longing for her sight; she yearned to see the fibers of paint left in the brushstrokes on portraits and scrolling landscapes. To feel the age and memories of the wooden plans used in various little hutches.

Another ray of moonlight cast along the floor.

"Where are we heading now?" she asked.

Sir Lukxa turned around, walking backward. "I figured we would—"

The ground pitched underneath Hollis, sending her tumbling forward. Sir Lukxa took a sharp step forward and caught her by her sides before she could acquaint her face with the carpet. He pulled her up into the air and braced her body flush against his. His grip locked tight behind her knees.

Hollis gripped his shoulders tighter as a wave of nausea overcame her. It bore down on her body as an oppressive weight, willing her to the ground. She turned her face away from his. When her stomach settled she looked back at him through her lashes.

"You're considerably flushed. Are you feeling faint again?" Sir Lukxa's face was scrunched up in the light of the oil lanterns. The flames danced along his face, shining bright against his pale eyes. She could feel his breath across her face.

Her fingers tightened their grip on his shoulder.

Warmth that crept up behind her ears and spread to her face. It was quite possibly caused by the fact that Sir Lukxa's hands, which gripped her steady, held close to her bum as he held her off the ground, pressed against himself. Not that she minded. "I hadn't noticed. I think I just tripped over my own two feet."

"Do you want me to run back to my room and fetch your cane?"

She shook her head. "No, I'll be fine. It's good to walk without it at times, to make sure my muscles don't become too dependent on it." While that was true, she wouldn't make mention of the fact that she routinely forgot to set her cane in hand, including when she left his room earlier.

Despise and hatred grew deep for the inanimate object. Something she so often needed, a part of her identity she both cherished and resented.

"If you say so."

"I do. Now, as much as I like being cradled against you, I don't think it would be wise to continue on like this. What if someone were to see you?" She tapped her fingers against his shoulders as realization set in his widened eyes.

Sir Lukxa slowly set her back on her feet and steadied her. He made no effort to move from his spot in front of her though, instead he traced her up and down with his eyes. "I think I have shown you around as best I can tonight. I will arrange Wilfrin to show you the rest of the castle some other day when I'm occupied. It has escaped me to make mention of this." He drew in a deep breath. "Your *cover* while here, considering we cannot exactly tell people the truth, is that you are a close friend who has come to visit me. That you will be working as a medic in the area for the tournament in the meantime."

She nodded in response. No idea in her mind as to who Wilfrin was, and knowing she would need to be told her cover again—several times.

Sir Lukxa opened his mouth and acted like he had something else he wanted to say to her; he pursed his lips and furrowed his brows. "Now it's time for our final destination this evening." His voice just above a whisper.

She cocked her head, which sent a few strands of hair down into her face. "Prince Dagen, correct?"

"Yes." Sir Lukxa brushed past her and back down the hall. They turned down the way they'd come from, quickly taking a passage on the left that she'd overlooked in their first adventure. The hall was unlike the others she'd seen. It was lined with portraits in gilded frames filling the red-papered walls. She couldn't put names to the faces but understood that at some point these people were powerful. It didn't seem that anyone here would hang the portrait of anyone who wasn't deserving.

As they walked further down the hall, the portraits lost the luster of gems and gold, filled with people sitting in a leather chair with a few plush furs. The lack of scent in the air gave the hall a cold and sterile feeling.

"Are all of these still Catolian rulers?" Her fingers hovered over the last frame in the darkened hall. It seemed the lanterns in this hall weren't often attended to. Though, now that she looked, there were no lanterns in this hall at all. Only sconces with candles lined the walls between the frames.

She turned her attention back to the picture where she stood. It was a thin silver frame, though it may once have been leafed with gold. Painted in oils was a simple man and woman sitting on a settee, with a few children scattered in front of them. A forest grew strong in the background, bright and verdant.

"Indeed, stretching to before the country was unified and territories with clans led the way. Not the first Catolian ruling family, though. Perhaps the fourth? I cannot remember off the top of my head if the portraits of the first three reside in the castle or if they have been stored away in some library in Rex." Sir Lukxa rattled off the answer.

Hollis stared at the portrait in an attempt to see what regalness could come from the family. Their hair was mousy, cheeks plump and red, clothes not too different than the style she wore now. *Interesting, the ways that time flows, what lasts and what decays.*

Sir Lukxa tucked his hand behind a tapestry that hung down from the ceiling. A moment later a soft *click* registered in Hollis's mind.

"While there's an easier way to come upon His Majesty's chambers in my wing, this is one of the few hidden halls." Sir Lukxa's voice was just above a whisper. Why, she didn't know. There was no one around. They hadn't seen a single other soul this night.

Hollis cocked her head to the side. "Why are you showing me this? Surely you wouldn't want me knowing all your secrets."

He pushed back the tapestry with his arm and stared at her. "You mentioned honesty and truth were important to you." He shrugged his shoulders and set back to fussing with the door. "I figured the best way to further earn your trust would be keeping my hand—and tricks—open."

She didn't have a response for that. He disappeared behind the woven fabric, and she followed.

A few windows in the ceiling lit the small cobblestone hallway as they entered. The night sky was brilliant above them.

Stars shone in the crisp air, it sent a shiver over her skin. It had been warm through their entire journey, and the sudden chill was shocking. Despite the open aspect of the ceiling the hall remained dry.

Hollis reached a hand up, unable to reach the openings.

"There is actually glass there, no worries. It is so thin that it does not keep out much of the chill the night brings. An old technique—folding the glass over itself, stretching it thin. Of course, I could be remembering wrong." Sir Lukxa reached up. His hands were able to graze the panes of glass. His fingers left trails on the condensation lined windows.

His knowledge warmed her. His dedication to the castle and crown. "You seem quite knowledgeable for a knight, even a captain."

Sir Lukxa nodded. "When I became the prince's right-hand it was imperative that I study beyond the knowledge given me by the academy of Eargile. I was assigned tutors while Councilor Dem oversaw the duties I would later inherit."

"Why were you chosen?"

He stopped moving. "That is a story for another time." His voice had lost its warmth.

"What happened to trust?"

He turned to face her. "Trust is slowly built. If I placed every burden of knowledge I have on you right away, you'd crumble under the pressure of either oversharing yourself or of my secrets. If I share pieces slowly, you'll

grow used to the weight they bear."

A beam of light broke into the dim hall, illuminating the walls around her and bringing a wave of fresh air. While the city was bustling and filled with people, the night air showed no sign of being tainted by human hand.

Hollis trailed her fingers in a small stream of blue light. She could only imagine what the air felt like as threads. Smooth, slowly rippling through the fabric of the world until the sun would rise and with it bring a heat that would seize the thread and add a torrent of movement from them.

She let her hand fall at her side and made to catch up with the captain. *Just another night's rest and you'll see again.*

Stepping into the light found them in the same hallway of Sir Lukxa's apartments. The door they emerged from was tucked behind a small alcove in the wall that she hadn't noticed when they'd left Sir Lukxa's rooms.

"Is it even faster to take the passage?" She'd enjoyed the little trip. The intimacy of the space and secrets.

"You find it surprising that a clean cut passage would be a faster way to get to this side of the wing from the entrance than wandering the entire way I took you?" Sir Lukxa laughed.

She bit her lip, greatly enjoying how the sound of his laughter bounced against the walls. "You could have answered that in a simpler manner. What I find more interesting is that Prince Dagen would reside so close to you. I would have thought he'd be in a wing all on his own?" Hollis clasped her hands in front of her, kicking her legs as she walked.

It didn't quite make sense in her mind that someone in the Royal Family wouldn't be in a grand wing of their own, but instead lived in what was likely a modest room near their guard.

Hollis remembered being told that the prince had returned to the castle in secret. Perhaps that was part of the reasoning he was here? "I remember—"

Sir Lukxa gave a tense smile, freezing the words in her mouth. "When it takes more than the beat of your heart to come to someone's aid, you've taken too long."

There was a lot to unpack in that statement, but now wasn't the time to go digging into his tragic backstory.

"Prince Dagen's room is the one at the very end of the hall. The room to the right will be filled when he takes a queen, to the left houses his manservant—a knight from a noble house. I promised I would visit Prince Dagen when I returned, if he heard I arrived and *did not*. . ." He trailed off. "That does not matter. I suggest we. . . refrain from telling him that you are temporarily without magic. You can use tonight to acquaint yourself with him and whatever else you can provide without your sight. And, I will tell you now, Prince Dagen is not in the best of conditions. His demeanor may be cheerful, but do not let it fool you into thinking him in a state better than he is. Any comments made—"

"I'm not foolish enough to insult a royal to their face or yours, have no fears." Hollis waved her hand, wanting him to hurry.

Sir Lukxa spoke as he walked. "I was not insinuating that you would. Your speech is rather brash at times, Miss Hollis."

She tilted her head as she followed. "I'll give you that. I need to work on my thinking before speaking."

"I believe you think just fine." He snorted as he came upon the door and rapped against it a few times. When no answer came, he pulled a key from his pocket and unlocked the door. A gentle push opened it. "Prince Dagen, I've returned. I hope the interruption is not seen as untoward." An oppressive stench rushed out the door, followed by a weak cough and mumbled words.

Hollis pushed the door shut behind her as she followed Sir Lukxa into the room. The moment the lock clicked, miasma coated her skin. A gag burned in her chest. Sir Lukxa didn't appear to be bothered by it, or perhaps he'd grown used to it.

Or men are gross and the smell just doesn't bother him.

Lukxa settled in on a chair he pulled up to the prince's bedside, a cup of water in the captain's hands. A pitcher sat on a small table beside the bed, a dark oak color which matched all the furniture in the ornate room.

This was not the face Hollis was expecting. She was prepared to face a womanizing grin and aura of someone who didn't care.

The person lying in the bed was far from that.

Prince Dagen's face now showed he was gaunt and starting to yellow around his eyes, and his golden-wheat colored hair pooled around his head like oil. His face still held a touch of fat on his cheeks, the only good sign about him—that, and the slight glint in his eyes. How she noticed it with the sunken degree his eyes were was a mystery, but there it was amid the dark brown.

Hollis trailed her eyes over Prince Dagen's blanketed form. His face held a kind smile as he spoke to Sir Lukxa. No immediate trace of anything venomous could be found upon Prince Dagen.

She rubbed her mouth a few times to cover a small retching from her stomach, wincing as she ripped off a bit of dried skin from her lips. A quick look around the room didn't reveal a used chamber pot anywhere, nor piles of anything unpleasant upon the dark floors.

She blocked out Prince Dagen and Sir Lukxa's conversation as she took a turn along the perimeter of the room. Picking up the vases of flowers, fresh and dead alike, peeking behind the thick cream curtains that covered the windows. Every drawer in the desk and dresser were checked, taking care to not throw or rumple the prince's clothes. A fine silk dressing shirt caught her eye. It was beautiful. The temptation to slip it into her pack growing. It was so pretty.

"Hollis, what are you doing?" Sir Lukxa's harsh voice shocked her.

She squeaked and spun around, silk shirt still clutched in her hands.

Sir Lukxa blocked most of her view of the prince from his position on the chair. She could make out a vague outline from underneath the many furs and duvets laid upon him.

"I'm checking for anything. . . suspicious in the room while you catch the prince up on whatever it is you're catching him up on."

"Did you find anything in my shirts that is worrisome?" Prince Dagen's voice was frail as it tried cracking out each word.

Hollis blushed and tucked the shirt back into its drawer and pushed it shut. The rich wood gilded under her fingertips.

"Thankfully not, Your Highness." She quickly made her way to the prince's bedside. The air hung on to her with each step she took towards the prince, filling her lungs with the heavy feeling.

Whatever was causing the smell wasn't far from the bed itself. When was the last time an attendant bathed him?

Was he truly lying in a pool of his own filth?

A layer of sweat plastered a cream, lightweight shirt to his skin. "Not often I have a woman grappling at my clothes. You can keep the shirt if you want it, truly." Prince Dagen gave her a slight smile, showing off the blackening bits around his gums.

"No worries. I was simply inspecting your drawers as normal, seeing if there was anything in there that could be making you sick." A weak half-truth. She was now debating if she would have been able to lift anything pretty from his room.

Hollis pointed to the chair Sir Lukxa was sitting in and flicked her hand at him to vacate it. Sir Lukxa stood, a frown forming on his face as he offered the seat to her.

She happily accepted the chair and settled herself down onto the cushion. Relief ran up her spine as she settled down, finally off her aching legs.

"Can you tell me what you first noticed with your illness?"

Prince Dagen's face turned to Sir Lukxa, a confused crease in his brows. "I thought you were to have told her of my condition—"

She jumped to Sir Lukxa's defense, not wanting to stand in any possible tension between the two men. "He has." A total lie. "But I want to hear it from you. There's a chance you remember something or thought you'd told someone but hadn't. For instance, do you have a rash?" She rested her face in the palm of her hand, arm propped up by her knee. Why she was lying to aid the captain she didn't know. But Hollis wasn't a large fan of conflict, and did not want to be caught between it.

The faster she got information, the faster she could get away from the gag-worthy room.

The prince lifted his covers and pulled at his clothes. She caught a glimpse of his stomach—rather the sharp floating ribs poking down towards it. Any muscle the prince once claimed had atrophied.

"I don't see any rashes, nor has my manservant made mention of any. I thought it was mourning, to be honest. I was sick every time I ate a meal without my parents." The prince swallowed. "Things never got better as I healed from the loss. The first thing I really noticed was that the headaches never stopped. I drank more water. Figured they'd go away. But they didn't. Then came nausea, diarrhea, double vision—all manner of unpleasant things." His voice cracked the longer he spoke, sending him into another coughing fit.

"Here. You need to drink more water." Sir Lukxa handed him the glass of water once more.

"You've become more of a pesky nanny than a friend as of late, Sir Lukxa. Whatever happened to you and your going three days without drinking a drop of water? I thought you were fun." The prince took small sips, holding the glass to his lips before resting it on his chest. Simply holding it up seemed to bring a sweat to his forehead.

"Oh yes, it is so fun to watch you turn to dust because you refuse to drink an adequate amount of water." Sir Lukxa turned to face Hollis. "Hydration is vital to health, is it not?"

She nodded her head in agreement. "I would certainly say so."

Sir Lukxa snapped his fingers and pointed at the prince. "You heard her say it. You need to keep drinking water."

"Such a good attendant you are." The prince's face soured before he swallowed the rest of the water and handed the glass back to Sir Lukxa.

Hollis could hear Prince Dagen's stomach protesting the water, it

seemed to fight its way back up his throat. The prince tried sitting up but seemed to find difficulty in moving with the blankets atop him.

"Here. You don't need all of these piled up on you, right?" Hollis said, pulling the covers down past his knees, revealing his drawers—which were as soaked as his shirt. "Goodness, are you always sweating this much?" The question slipped out with a surprised and slightly disgusted tone before she could filter it.

Prince Dagen grimaced and ran the edge of his sleeve across his face, drying it off a bit more. "Occasionally, I think it's just the heat. Thank you." He moved to sit up further against his pillows.

Hollis' stomach churned once more as another wave of the smell rolled onto her. How she hadn't thrown up on the crowned prince was something she'd have to ask a higher power. "Apologies, my prince. If it's all right with you, I want to begin your care with a physical examination. I find it useful to start with the most basic level and then move upward."

"Pardon my interruption, but you're Tablin, correct? Lukxa told me he was leaving to get a Tablin healer. Why can't you just. . . magic?" Prince Dagen's voice pitched, face looking rather unsure with pitched brows and a tense smile.

Hollis ran her tongue across her teeth, musing in thought. "I think it best to start here. I can see the makeup of a person, everything that forms or goes against their being, but one symptom can be caused by several different ailments. Examinations help me filter my thoughts." She wouldn't explain much further; instead, she'd let him fill in any gaps and hope he would answer his own questions about her abilities. She would answer later if needed, when she had more than half a brain.

"Tell me what I need to do for you." Prince Dagen asked, his fingers drumming along his stomach.

Sir Lukxa gave a small chuckle. "I do not think she'll struggle with that."

Hollis shot the captain a quick glare before speaking to the prince. "Firstly, I'll feel for anything that I would deem dramatically out of place or frozen, the body works as one functioning unit. When one part stops operating at full capacity, the rest of it starts falling apart." She rubbed her hands together in an effort to warm them before placing them on the top of Prince Dagen's head. The oil from his hair coated her fingertips and clogged under her nails as she carefully pressed around his skull, dragging her fingers down behind his ears and spine.

Nothing out of sorts here.

"Are you able to move so your back is facing me?" Hollis motioned with her hand to the prince.

Prince Dagen glowered then opened his mouth to reply.

She raised a hand and decided to spare him the trouble of moving around. "Never mind that, it's fine. I'll just wiggle in behind you." She kicked off her walking boots, a challenge in-and-of-itself, and tossed aside the numerous fluffy pillows that were tucked behind him. Both men made awkward noises of protest but she paid them no heed as she sat herself down on the damp bed behind the prince—*may the sun shine on his crown forever for this.*

His back was a landmass of ridges and bones. It was a wonder the prince hadn't simply ceased to be. While he was yet a dead man walking, he wasn't too far from wandering into that territory.

"Are you able to do any physical activity? Maintaining the little muscle you have now is important. You don't want it all atrophying— essentially, dying."

"No," he coughed. The straight seated position she'd put him in, with her sitting awkwardly behind his board straight spine, was likely awkward for his body. "I was told that I should not move from bed unless necessary."

"The others before you said he needed to *save his strength.*" Sir Lukxa gestured to Prince Dagen as he spoke. His clipped words didn't sound pleased at the other medics suggestions. Hollis would agree with that feeling.

Hollis wanted to scoff but composed herself somehow. "Save your energy for what? Wasting away in bed? I'm rescinding that order. You need to move around as much as you possibly can. Keep your body working. Stop when you feel terribly winded or aching, but push through as best you can."

"You're confident that I'm going to recover? You'll be able to heal me, Lady. . . *um*. . ." Prince Dagen blushed and wiped at the sweat on his brow. "I know Lukxa said your name earlier, but I can't remember it right now. My mind is foggy so often." She could hear the sorrow dripping in his voice.

"Hollis. I'm Hollis Avayana. How long has your memory been affected?"

"Do you think that's a part of the illness?" Sir Lukxa asked, not having moved from his position behind the chair she had forced him out of earlier. He stood close to the side of the bed as if he were waiting for something to happen.

"It could be a side-effect of whatever is going on. Can you remember when this all began?" She climbed out from behind Prince Dagen.

Sir Lukxa extended her a hand as she climbed off the bed. The front of her shirt was damp with sweat.

She took a calming breath to keep herself from pitching a fit. It was fine.

Prince Dagen mused his lips. His brows knit tightly together as he seemed deep in thought. "I think it started. . ." He tapped his hands together. "I'm, I'm not sure. I'm sorry." His head hung low as his body slumped forward, sending another wave of stench against her.

"That's all right." Hollis took a step away from the entirely too-plush bed to be away from the foul scent for a moment. After she composed herself, *again*, she decided on the next course of action for the exam. "I'll examine your arms and legs next, and then I'll feel and listen to your chest and stomach."

Standing beside the bed, Hollis ran her hands over the rest of Prince Dagen's body, doing her best not to think too heavily about the sweat that now coated her hands.

It was odd, feeling over someone's person without any texture of thread upon her fingertips. There was some time spent in her life learning the art of holistic medicine—it hadn't been a long stretch of time, but it existed.

She'd have to rely on that knowledge for the time being in figuring out what was—*wait*.

The skin just over his heart felt *wrong*. The scent of smoke and anix filled her mind.

He's not. . . No, she couldn't say anything yet. There was study and research to do—she needed her magic back before she could let loose her lips with thoughts and ideas.

Think before you speak, Hollis. She chewed on her lip.

That's what she would do. She would think twice before telling the prince and captain.

Sir Lukxa's mouth pressed against her ear. "What's that look of terror in your eyes, Hollis?"

She moved her head away from his and met his intense gaze. She followed Sir Lukxa's eyes down to her hands, which rested over Prince Dagen's heart. She could feel its struggle to beat evenly, how sluggish it had become in an effort to live.

"I have no idea what you're talking about, Sir Lukxa." Hollis didn't raise her voice above a whisper.

Prince Dagen's paper hands enveloped hers. "If there's something you know, please tell me. I trust the magic you have, I really do." His eyes were wide, his lower lip dropped below his bottom teeth.

Think, think, think. You know how to think. Pause before you open your mouth, Hollis!

"I've felt what's making you ill, but I'm not exactly sure as to what all it. . . completely is?" *Oh goodness*, she was a terrible liar. Her parents always caught her in her little white-lies and schemes. But she had pulled off a few decent lies in her time.

Prince Dagen leaned back against his pillows, the fat he still had in his face relaxing.

Sir Luxka set a hand, warm and strong, on her shoulder. He leaned his face a hair closer to her. "What type of illness is it?"

"Not an illness per se. . ." She clamped her mouth shut.

"What do you mean, it is not an *illness*?" Sir Lukxa's face melted into something unreadable by her eyes. His grip on her shoulder tightened.

Prince Dagen's mouth opened and shut like a fish gasping for water. The sounds his body made were closer to dry heaving.

"I mean. . ." She wracked her brain, trying to come up with a suitable answer. "Sir Lukxa, you know I don't want to jump to any hasty *conclusions*—"

Sir Lukxa's face didn't lend to any sort of reaction. "I am open to hearing whatever it is that plagues your mind. *Now*." His voice graveled low, almost threatening.

She turned her gaze between the Prince and Captain, unsure of how to lie with both of them boring holes into her skull with their eyes.

Finally, she settled on looking Prince Dagen in the eyes. A misplaced speck of hope shone in the deep brown color. Her lips trembled as she formulated the words.

She hated crushing hope.

Her words cracked as she spoke, like her voice didn't want to raise to meet the awaiting ears of the men before her. "I'm not sure where the root of it lay, or from whom, but. . . Prince, you are being cursed."

CHAPTER EIGHT

LUKXA

Steam wafted in the air of the water closet as Lukxa took a long swallow of gin from his glass. His feet hung over the edge of his soaking tub. He kicked them lightly on occasion, sending water up his legs. The once hot water he soaked in had grown tepid. A shiver ran up his spine as he forced a swallow.

In-between stages were tormentive. No matter what the substance, once things grew muddled it was hard to tell what direction things would continue to go. Lukxa leaned his head back over the edge of the tub.

It did not matter. The aches in his shoulders and back had melted like morning frost off a window pane. The remaining gin in his glass was quickly downed, flooding his senses with pine as the liquor slid down his throat.

He let himself breathe a few moments more before he pulled himself out of the tub.

"*Dry off yourself and the floor; don't want Hollis slipping and breaking her neck.*" Speaking to himself in his mother tongue was a habit he managed to shake most of the time when working. It had others sending long unreadable looks in his direction—or it had in Eargile. He had not slipped up around anyone within the castle to gauge their reactions to him speaking a language which may be on its way to earning the title of dead.

Early in his friendship with Dagen, the young boy had asked Lukxa for the translation of everyday items, and the occasional expletive. Much to Dagen's chagrin, Lukxa had not quite learned all the vulgar words Omil had to offer before coming to Catol. Or that was what he'd told the then young prince.

Lukxa ran his free hand through his hair, shaking out the long length of it.

After having it tied the majority of the day, it cried in relief at being let free. It reached down past his shoulder blades now that he was finally allowed to grow it out past his ears. There were a few dried and split ends he would have to trim soon. But it had taken ages for his hair to grow this long again. The joy pushed back the needed maintenance.

Padding along the moonlit bathroom floor, body dry and clothed, Lukxa braced himself to enter his now shared bedroom. His original plans of placing Hollis in one of his guest rooms had been scratched from his mind the moment she uttered the word *curse*.

Curses meant someone was actively wishing harm. It meant there was a level of danger in or around the castle that he had not felt already. Something worse than Lukxa himself.

It also meant that he had not had quite enough gin yet to forget the stomach-wrenching thought of it all. Another glass was needed. Lukxa took the back of his hand that held the glass and lightly pushed on the bathroom door until it was wide open enough for him to slip out of.

The room was far colder than the steam-filled washroom. The chill pulled at his marrow. Begged him to curl up by the fire or in his sheets. He turned his attentions toward the bed.

Hollis was still curled up in the same spot she had been in when Lukxa went for his evening wash. This time, her head lay at the foot with a few pillows. The sheets were now only tucked around the side edges of the bed frame creating a tube of sorts, with an additional few blankets piled on top.

Hollis' new sleeping arrangements for the foreseeable future.

Lukxa needed to keep her close and safe.

A quick venture to the kitchenette refilled his glass. The cold floors were shards of ice digging into his nerves.

Wood *cracked* in the fireplace on the far side of the room, the flames eagerly licking up the dried ash wood. Lukxa crossed his room again. His free hand gripped another piece of wood from the small bundle of firewood he kept in his room. Gripping the dried piece tightly without getting splinters in any of his fingers was a difficult task with the one hand he had free, but the other was still appointed the important task of holding his glass of gin.

Lukxa did his best to add the additional piece to the fire without causing too much noise. Waking Hollis was something he was trying his best not to do this evening. The desire for some time to himself needed to be fulfilled.

Sparks scattered into the air as the fresh wood *cracked* and *popped*.

He sipped from his glass and watched the sparks slowly disappear from sight as they cooled into black nothingness. Once they were all gone, he turned his back on the growing warmth and padded his way back to his kitchenette, instantly missing the warmth of the rug and fireplace.

The nights and mornings grew ever deep in their chill.

Lukxa tapped his finger against the rim of his cup at half the speed his mind raced. His nails created a light *clink*ing sound. He'd now filled the crystal glass thrice with gin and four times with water. Maintaining a delicate balance of the two for relaxation and keeping wit. Several things lined up in his mind and he didn't like that. Not one bit.

He contemplated the choices that were before him as he swallowed the remaining liquid in the glass. Pine gin brought a sharp freshness to the back of his throat. He had decided a glass or two had been earned, and that quota had been filled. His hand found its way to the neck of the textured glass, his fingers running up and down the ridged sides of it, contemplating if *another* glass was something he could slip past his morals.

Something to chisel away at the memory of hearing the word *cursed*.

He had seen terror flash across Hollis' eyes. Brief, but there. He had no choice but to believe her.

She's sightless at the moment. There's a chance she could be wrong—do not forget about that little detail.

Hopefully her lack of sight would be remedied *quickly*. Perhaps when it was, she would realize that she had made a simple mistake. That Dagen was not actually cursed, but simply sick.

Guilt weighed heavily atop all his heart, settling itself deep amongst the veins and flesh.

Lukxa leaned his hip against the countertop and looked down at the training yard. It was bathed in moonlight. The fence posts accumulated frost that shimmered along the aged wood.

He stopped tapping his fingers.

The knights of the castle were good people, at least, every man and woman in his company was smart and loyal. Squires were too stupid to be able to pull off something like a curse, and no one he could think of attached to them would have cause for finishing off the royal family like this.

King Trist had no relatives and Queen Susan had two sisters who both only bore daughters, both of whom were married off to crowned princes. No one to contend with the throne on either side.

It was something he had given great thought to—the '*what ifs*' surrounding the throne.

The three family council seats would be up in arms on who would sit on the throne if Dagen died without producing an heir. The same power struggle from generations ago come full circle.

Which seat holds the most leverage?

Hozen tended to stay out of any disputes. Eargile overflowed with military prowess and was extremely loyal to the crown. And Rex only cared about advancing technology and their own minds. All of which was reflected in the council members—but the members having some sort of involvement was the only thing that made sense.

Lukxa knew what the mission he had been bought for entailed. Failure had not yet come; he made a half-hearted bargain to keep his head whilst buying himself more time to figure out who all he sold his sword to. He knew some who sat hidden within the castle walls. Their wicked grins as they spoke of purification and the right of ruling a country. And while he knew their faces and had slowly gathered evidence of their other crimes, Lukxa could not be sure they were the only ones acting upon the desires that bought him.

But, perhaps it was good enough to strike at the ones that made themselves visible? He could disrupt the core and scatter the rest of their followers.

All he needed was proof of some other wrongdoings.

"Are your eyes the shiver I feel up my spine?" Hollis' voice was dripping with sleep. "What's this? You're drinking and didn't even offer me a glass? Such a rude host you are."

Lukxa turned back to see her sitting up on the bed, rubbing her eyes before hiding a yawn with her hand.

"I did not think alcohol best for your current state." He turned the cold tap of his sink, filling his glass with water once more.

"Oh, but I've earned it. For the most part." Hollis pushed herself from the bed and joined him in his kitchenette, propping herself onto the wooden countertop. "By the way, I forgot to ask if you had a bit of salve handy? I would be most appreciative, as I don't feel like digging around in search of mine." She scratched at her head, sending her curls flying around her face.

Hollis wore a light pair of half pants and a long shirt that had to be stained with paint and plants alike. He followed the length of her legs as she finished perching her bottom on his counter.

She had asked him a question; what was it? *Salve. She needs your salve.* "Yes, I do have some. I will fetch it for you. Right now." He set his glass down with a bit more force than necessary and turned to the cabinet he kept stocked with different medical supplies. He fumbled the small jar of rose salve he had been given by one of the nurses in the castle ages ago. Knights were in constant need of salves, Lukxa knew he had a nasty habit of worrying his lips dry when training.

He turned back to see Hollis dumping out his water and filling the glass with more than a fair share of his gin.

"Do you have *any* boundaries?" He did not know if his words were clipped or simply confused sounding.

"Oh, plenty. But I trust that you aren't carrying any diseases that would be passed to me. You only have to wash one glass in the morning this way." She lifted the glass a tiny bit, giving him a toothy grin, and took a sip.

"Wait." He leaned forward and caught the glass, not taking it from her grasp. Simply holding it fast. "Are you even old enough to drink?" The scent of pine melted with the sandalwood of his soap and lotion filled his mind—she'd used a hearty amount of his things when washing earlier it would seem.

Hollis' face grew concerned, almost offended. "Goodness, you went hunting for me across half the Hozen prefecture and you don't even know how old I am?" She pulled the glass free and took another sip. "Four and twenty. How old are you dear, knight captain?" She spun the glass around in her hand, reflecting the moonlight from the window onto the floor.

"Five and twenty. Though. . ." He swallowed. "I will be six and twenty just after Prince Dagen's birthday." Lukxa's voice graveled as he responded. He felt better about his tipped mind knowing he was only just two years her senior.

He plucked the glass from her hand and replaced it with the jar of salve in its place. Her hand felt soft against his, and, though her fingers were frigid, they still felt nice against the fire beneath his skin. He let his gaze linger on their hands together. His weren't swallowing hers whole, but they still enveloped hers nicely.

Goodness, what was wrong with him? Ogling the woman brought here to heal his friend. His *cursed* and *dying* friend.

Had so much time elapsed since his last late-night enjoyment of gin or any other drink that his tolerance had plummeted through the floor?

Hollis rolled the jar between her two hands.

Or, a simpler thought—he could stop blaming the drink and acknowledge that he found the woman sitting across from him to be absolutely chaotic and beautiful.

Perhaps there was no harm in allowing himself to realize the obvious?

She gave a huff and rubbed the salve all over her lips, then pressed them together a few times to ensure she'd fully covered them. "So, what is it that's keeping you up this late into the night? Thought you would have been ready to sleep an entire week with everything we've been through."

He brought the glass to his lips, being mindful to avoid where she had drank from as he did. "I am just thinking." He tapped his finger against the rim, his gaze winding out the kitchen window. Caught on the few lingering lights in the city.

"Generally? Specifically? About all this that's been happening or something long past?" She hooked a finger around his cheek and turned his head so she was the focal point of his gaze.

His lungs froze. He forgot how to breathe.

Hollis was ethereal in the moonlight. The light both highlighted the green of her hair and muted it to a sage color. Perhaps he was wrong in his earlier thoughts? Tablins *were* different from the rest of mankind—descended from the creators of the world. It was the only explanation for the beauty she held. Even with the veins that crept around her body, giving her eyes an especially tired, blue cast, she looked every bit the ethereal being her people once were.

He let out a shuddered breath.

Lukxa blinked several times, righting himself. "Are you sure that you felt Prince Dagen being cursed?" He peered over the rim of the glass, keeping eye contact with her as he took a deliberately long drag of gin. Some part of him hoped the expression was intimidating enough that she would give him a straight answer.

Perhaps he had had more than enough drink to cast aside most of his professionalism.

Or this is just what speaking with her does to me. Her wit is enjoyable.

She pursed her lips, mulling through thoughts that he could see spinning behind her eyes. "I've been thinking about who would be motivated to harm the prince. Who's set to take the throne if he were to pass?" She slipped the glass from his hands and took another sip.

That was not an answer.

"It is a thought I have given much attention to as of late. Truly, Hollis, I am not sure." Another sip. He wiped his mouth with the back of his hand. "It would be up to the council and some scholars to find out where the lineage last produced someone to take the throne. Most likely some duke within the Catol prefecture would have the most claim." He bit his lips, trying to recall conversations he had with the prince. "Prince Dagen has a few *distant* cousins who brag rather loudly at parties with their close ties to the inheritance of the crown. I am not sure how valid their claims are." He *scoffed*. "I know I seemed endless in my knowledge earlier, but there are a few things that I seem to *conveniently* not know the answer to."

Hollis' brows furrowed.

He let out a slow drag of air from his lips, steadying his mind before asking the obvious question lingering about them. "So, Miss *Healer* Hollis, you believe someone here is causing Prince Dagen's illness— curse, whatever it is?"

Her eyes went wide. "I didn't say that," she spoke hurriedly. "I'm trying to *think* before I speak; give me some credit. I simply wanted to know what hands I'd fall into should the prince's illness progress any further than it has." She trailed her eyes away from him, pursing her lips.

Lukxa's body burned. Downing the rest of the gin seemed to fuel it. He scoffed, rolling his head. "You seem rather confident in his passing?"

Hollis frowned. "I'm not, but it never hurts to be prepared. Remember what I said about people getting their hopes set far too high?"

A sharp burst of air let from his mouth. "Yes. . . I think the Council has been tracing the line the past few months on their own, not that I'm privy to everything they do." Lukxa bit his lip, doing his best to keep back his more *negative* thoughts.

Hollis hooked a finger under his chin, pulling his gaze to meet hers. "That's a rather interesting look there, Sir Lukxa. What sits behind that rage?" The skin around her eyes was rimmed in veins and shadow, deepening the maroon of her iris.

He quirked a brow. "What gave you the idea that what I feel is rage?"

Hollis grinned and tilted her head back. "Because it's a far cry from the devouring expression you just had. This is sharp, burning." She dropped her hand and swiped the glass once more and filled it before downing it just as quickly. "Hypothetically speaking, if it isn't someone outside the castle reaching in, it'd have to be someone inside the castle reaching above their station. You've spoken highly of your knights and the people you work with. No one here outside of the Council could even obtain a drop of power without them and the crown agreeing. . ." she trailed off, musing her bottom lip. "I don't buy it. The council has done nothing but watch out for the people of Catol while the prince has been sick. They did a great job after the passing of the king and queen. I can see why you'd think it was them, but I don't think it's a strong enough answer."

The muscles in Lukxa's jaw tensed, grinding his teeth together. "Which is why I didn't say anything."

"*But. . .* if you have some suspicions, I wouldn't cast them out. It's always the ones who watch out for the weak that slip into the lust for more power over them. More of a grip to have against us *poor plebeians.*" Hollis gave her voice a pitched sing-song tone, playing with the glass as she spoke.

He took the divergence of topic. "Speaking from experience there, Hollis?"

She met his gaze, her eyes brimming with some sort of angsty and sorrowful expression. "It's why the Tablins that were cast out of our realm in the beautiful weave of reality and were put down with all of you on this. My ancestors twisted too much power for nature to allow. They were put into their place. Thankfully, with most of our magic still intact. Don't know what I'd do without it—" She froze, her teeth set against each other with a loud *snap*.

Lukxa set a hand on her shoulder. "I am sure your sight will return. We can stop by one of the bakeries come afternoon if you would like?" Breakfast would have been a more appropriate time to have a bakery visit were it not for his earlier commitments.

She shook her head. "I'm not sure leaving the castle is something I want to do right now. I'm exhausted."

"Well then," He tilted his head. "I will pick something up while I am out. Any requests?"

Hollis' spine straightened. She peered quite keenly at him. "If you're taking them. I like clover and chocolate. And really salty things—I eat a lot of salt. Keeps me upright. Tea is a must." She glared at him. "Don't give me that *look*—you can lower your brows and rid yourself of your. . . whatever you would call that smile. Most of the teas I packed are *medicinal*, for your information. I left my normal blends at home. If there's an apothecary in the citadel, I will need some medication in a few weeks. I realized I'm almost out of some of my medications. And I'll need those if I'm to work without being a wreck the whole time." Hollis kicked her legs and let her head lull side to side as she spoke.

Lukxa went to take another sip—or would have, if the glass still contained anything to drink.

Hollis offered up the gin so he could refill his glass. The expensive bottle which had been full at the start of the evening and now dwindled towards the middle of the label. He held the glass out, allowing her to fill it.

"I never did ask what it is that ails you. Is it proper for me to ask?" Lukxa let his eyes trail over Hollis. Searching for what could be the obvious source of her maladies. He could not find anything out of ordinary on her person that he could see. Her earlier explanation had not solidified in his mind.

Hollis sighed loudly as she set the glass bottle down. "Yes, *why I'm sick and walk with a cane* and *haven't healed myself* and everything everyone always asks about. I guess when part of you is tied into the fold of nature your body gets strained. My body wears down easily, I'm tired. My joints and muscles ache and groan every chance they get and slip right out of their sockets. Other than that, I do not have a string out of place. Perfectly healthy. Some Tablins have the sight and are perfectly healthy. I fell into the group who have the sight and are cursed by it." She stole a sip of gin. "It's why Catol thought we'd be so easy to take over." Her voice had taken on a sarcastic quality he had not heard before—a bitterness. "A country filled with magical sick people would be easy to enslave and conquer. But we aren't that easy to get rid of. Just as we were not able to control that which we came from, others cannot own nature." Hollis tapped her fingers against the glass, her nails making a soft *clicking* sound.

This was *new*. The ethereal glow that circled her had turned gray and ashy. Perhaps a bit of prying was necessary. "Are you all right?"

Her head shot up, her eyes glazed. "Yes, I'm fine. Drinking too much loosens the mind to memories best forgotten."

"Ah," he spoke. His mind tried to think of a way to spin the conversation away from her poor memories. "Some Tablins really do not have the sight?"

Goodness, Lukxa, asking about the sight again? Have you no brain behind your pretty face?

"That's what you keyed in on?" Hollis laughed. Oh. . . He liked that sound. "It's one of the reasons my parents said the wars happened. Too many Tablins concerned with breeding out our magic, combined with too many outsiders wanting access to it. Attacked on all sides." She leaned forward and took a sip from the glass, not even bothering to take it from his hands. He tipped it upward to allow for a decent swallow. "Such a depressing topic we've ventured into." Hollis made a sour face as she took another sip.

"We started our conversation debating who was hypothetically committing regicide, so I'm not sure we've strayed too far." Lukxa took a large pull of his own, feeling a slight haze over his mind as warmth grew from deep in his stomach. "Can you tell me more about the Omil wars and their magic? You seem to know quite a lot about the topic." He looked out the study window, past the crest of the mountains where Omil lay—or whatever was left of it.

No one ever spoke much in the way of a relationship between Omil and Catol. If there was any country left lying there, he was none the wiser on the topic. Felt better not to ask if he still had a country and family. Lukxa preferred to bask in ignorance.

He was a surrendered child. There was no guarantee when he and thousands of other Omilian children were surrendered to Catol by their parents that their little lives would be anything more than torturous. No promise that Catol would raise them as their own.

Lukxa was one of several that were conveniently given to the Knight Academy to be trained up to protect Catol. He had hated this country for years. Let his rage boil and burn to the point of no return.

Until someone had extended a hand of grace.

Oh, wonderful. You're melancholic and *drunk now.*

"Several drinks in, and now you believe me about your lineage's magic? Let's see." Hollis *hummed* several moments, eyes squinting as she drummed her fingers against her knee. "From what I understand, Omil magic was first created with the same principles as the Tablin sight, but as an exchange of power: wilt a flower to heal a wound. Some magicians got to the point they could memorize a symbolic pattern and cast what was known as a spell— which goes beyond what Tablin magic can do. It's amazing to think about, really. They tapped into nature and bent it to their will, but we just move along with it. Lots of people died in the discovery and practice of the magic. And when Catol came knocking for the information, Omil left them out in the cold. So, Catol being the country they were, burned them to the ground. That's all I know of it—seems like a lot but really isn't. I couldn't tell you more even if I wanted to, though." She took the glass from his grasp once more and downed it in its entirety before she shoved it under the tap and filled it with water.

Perhaps the first time this evening he had seen her drink any.

"How do you just know the most random of things? I imagine that no one outside of you and a handful of people knows that Omil magic existed— *exists*?" The idea that his people had once used magic was fascinating. The image of learning magic himself was intoxicating. Power, magic, control. Things he lacked greatly inside the castle walls. He had the facade of power as captain of the royal guard. But his position was built on rotted ground. And it groaned and threatened to crumble beneath him.

"It's not my fault you never got a proper education on the matters." Hollis downed the water as quickly as the gin that had come before it. "I may not know a lot of things, but I am an expert in all things magical—and the dealings of Catolian conquests." She gave him a pitying smile. "Besides, you likely don't know of it because it was small in practice and Omil wanted it kept secret. You were a child. I doubt those kinds of things are told to someone so young. My parents are fascinated with magic and history. Taught me everything they knew before they sent me off on my own adventures."

There was a lot to unpack in that statement, but he didn't feel like digging into her personal stories lest she start prying into his.

Hollis ran a hand down her face. "It's late. *Early*? I want to sleep."

"Give me a second," Lukxa said. A tension grew deep in his stomach.

It was time for him to crawl into his bed with her. To feel her legs and have his mind filled with the sounds of her breathing.

He placed his hand on the other side of her body, effectively holding her on the counter as he quickly filled the glass with water, downed it in a swift motion, and all but slammed it against the counter *without* breaking it.

Lukxa met her gaze as stepped between her legs, grabbed her arms, and slung them over his shoulders before picking her up in his arms by her thighs. "I do not want you breaking your head open on my floor when you eventually trip and fall."

"How rude to assume I'd perish from a few drinks." She gripped his shoulders. A groan built in her throat. "Move slower, please." She tucked her head under his chin.

"I haven't taken a step yet. Your constitution is terrible." He took pause for several seconds and repositioned Hollis in his arms so only her side was pressed up against his chest. Carrying her as a prince would a princess. Lukxa shifted his feet until he'd turned and faced his bed. It was only a few long strides away.

The room grew hazy in his sight as he slowly approached the bed, pausing every time Hollis grunted, or groaned, or hugged him tighter.

"I'm going to have to move you again." He whispered in her ear before pulling her chest flush against himself, freeing an arm to pull back the covers of the bed to crawl under.

Hollis' body bounced as she leaned herself out of his grip to lay back against the bed. Her arms still wrapped tightly around his body, his hands trapped under her legs.

"The top is my side of the bed. We agreed upon this, Hollis. Remember?"

Her arms tightened around his neck, tugging him down with force.

He dropped his grip on her legs, catching himself on the bed.

"We shared a glass; can't we share this tonight? I don't wanna move." Her glazed eyes tried focusing on him, catching a few specks of moonlight in her shaking irises.

He kept his gaze locked on her eyes, not allowing himself to stare too intently at her parted lips. He would not look again. *Could not.*

Lukxa swallowed. "All right. You can sleep at this side. I'll sleep down at the foot." He grabbed at her hands locked behind his neck.

Hollis shook her head which sent blood booming into her cheeks, giving her a heavy flush. Then she tugged him closer until their chests were almost touching. "No. You're so warm."

He was too drunk for this. Too far gone to care about the appropriateness of the situation. His vision spun, face burning every time he turned down and caught her gaze. They were already sharing the bed; sleeping at opposite ends of it seemed the best he could make of the situation.

His abdomen burned.

Long hair spilled over his shoulders as his head dropped, blocking his view of her.

Perhaps it would not be the end of the world for one night? Justification could be found in one drunken night.

He lifted his head, eyes trained on the ceiling. "You need to let me go, Hollis. I have to grab your pillow."

"No," the word fell long out of her mouth, her head falling to its side. "Don't move me. You'll do fine."

He blinked a few times, swearing in his mother tongue. "Your neck is going to hurt in the morning." The bed *creaked* as he laid himself down on his side. His free arm shot out to pull the covers over their shoulders. Hollis tightened her grip around him, burrowing her face deeper into the crook of his neck.

Her fingers wove and lightly pulled through his hair. He pictured the actions she had done several times over of manipulating the threads visible only to her.

She muttered something incoherent against his neck, quickly followed by a lulling pattern of deep breaths.

The pillow was soft under his head as he made himself comfortable without moving Hollis around in his arms too much. He couldn't find a shred of caring about propriety in the world as he tightened his grip around her waist, pulling her cold frame flush against himself.

He was going to hate himself in the morning.

CHAPTER NINE

HOLLIS

Something warm held Hollis captive. The world spun as her eyes blinked. A groan forced its way out of her dry throat as she attempted to push herself up into a seated position upon the sturdy warm bed.

"You're crushing my lungs." Sir Lukxa's voice rasped.

She blinked again, her vision spinning as the form of Sir Lukxa grew solid under her body. Her hands were planted firmly on his chest. "Goodness, I'm sorry." She pulled her hands free from his person. Rubbing the fogged sleep from her eyes brought the world into clarity.

It was too clear. She focused her gaze downward at the man on the plush bed. Swatched in a silken blanket. Nothing.

The threads of life still missing.

Hollis' lungs did their best not to explode her ribs outward. Nerves lit, sending fire through the layers of muscle and fascia.

Perhaps she was still recovering? Her sight would return once her hangover was cured.

A cough broke free of her lungs, shaking her frame, sending her back down on the bed beside the captain. Hollis took a deep breath and exhaled until her body was a block of lead against the cushion of Sir Lukxa's bed.

Waves of nausea crashed up her throat. Panic edged in her mind.

She clenched her eyes shut and bit her lips.

Fingers trailed over her right cheek. "My, had you consumed *that* much gin last night?" Sir Lukxa's voice was warm against the chill of the morning air. It sounded closer to her head than she thought he was and had her ears throbbing. The sound of Sir Lukxa's sleep laden voice grounded her though, pulling her out of spinning thoughts.

She twisted her head away from his voice. The world spun behind closed eyes. Even though she remained motionless her body seemed to rock and sway as if she floated on turbulent waters. This was what death felt like. "I think it's likely a combination of *that* and finally resting. I've done a lot the last few days, you know." She nuzzled back down onto the pillow that she shared with the captain.

Shared with Sir Lukxa. She was. . .

Fire burned up her neck, her eyes shooting open. "Where's my pillow? What am I doing up here?" The world spun as she turned her head once more. Her head dropped back onto the bed.

Sir Lukxa rolled onto his back, laughing lightly. "Oh, goodness. You do not remember anything from last night?" He slapped a hand over his eyes.

That did nothing to help. "I remember everything aside from falling asleep. I don't tend to remember what I do right before I crawl into bed. If I did anything untoward. . . my only regret is that I do not remember it." Despite her words, shame clawed her stomach to shreds. Hollis checked downward under the small tent she pulled up in the covers, being sure that the pair of them were still clothed.

They were.

Sir Lukxa turned his gaze back to her. "If I was truly uncomfortable, I would have done something." There was an edge of embarrassment in his own voice. "You were cold and tispy—if not drunk—and did not want to

let me go. It is understandable." His eyes turned down toward the bottom of the bed before snapping back to hers. The pale blue irises vibrated before he spoke. "As for your pillow, I vaguely remember you attempting to strangle me when I tried to fetch it. How is your neck?"

Hollis trailed a hand up from the warm sheets, traced her clavicle, and rubbed at the base of her skull. Nothing felt terribly out of place, no bones jutting out sideways and in need of *cracking*. "I think it's fine. You must have done a decent job serving as a makeshift."

Sir Lukxa sat up, giving her the perfect opportunity to pull the full length of his pillow under her head. Which, despite her also sleeping on, smelled only of the knight. A slight musk mixed with an earthy tree smell. She liked it.

"If you're awake now, would you mind freeing me?" Sir Lukxa asked.

Wait, free him?

Hollis took a moment to register the rest of her body. Pressure grew on her legs. Looking down she could see a mass of tangled something underneath the sheets. Attempting to pull at her legs proved no results. How had they stayed so entangled with all the moving she'd just done?

"I think they're numb." Hollis trapped her lips between her teeth and met Sir Lukxa's gaze, catching a hint of pink around the edges of his face.

"Do you mind if I move them for you then?" His voice was filled with uncertainty and tentativeness.

"If you're asking to manhandle me, please, go ahead." Oh, that came out differently than she expected.

His face flushed before he awkwardly threw the covers off of them, revealing their quite tangled limbs. Carefully his hands picked up her leg which was bent around his own, her ankle having locked itself around his other leg in an effective trap.

She threw her head back against the bed, hard. "*Ow ow ow*, that hurts." Her legs screamed as he moved them, her foot hanging limp at an odd angle. Pins and needles running along her flesh.

Finally freed, Sir Lukxa stood from the bed and towered over her.

"I am sorry. Do you need me to fetch you something?" Gone was any possible trace of embarrassment on his face. It was replaced with the firm expression of a captain.

"No, I just need to move around some." Hollis picked up her leg from her knee and bent and stretched her limbs. Rolling her ankles and twisting her legs as a whole. "I'll be right as rain soon enough." She situated herself upright, taking in the captain in all his morning glory.

Dawn trickled in from the windows, forming a halo of light against Sir Lukxa's dark hair. The navy color shone brilliantly, lending him a appearance of a celestial warrior. It was interesting seeing him with his hair untied. Seeing it loose and hanging to his chest softened his face. . . the softness could be attributed to morning bloating. She could appreciate a healthy bloat in the morning. It was attractive on him. But it was likely that everything would.

Past him, the light to the far right side of the room—which she was finally able to see with lighting *other* than dim candle light was his study. Furniture sat in a square shape in the area just past the bed by several feet. A few high-winged chairs, an impressive desk, and a settee that looked terribly unloved in front of the fireplace that struggled to keep the apartment warm.

Perhaps she should sleep on that? Closer to the fire. But also closer to the window.

Hmmm. She'd take the bed with the warm captain.

The whole sitting study area rivaled the size of her own back home. With the kitchenette and wash room, it was likely that Sir Lukxa's apartment was larger than the first floor of Hollis' home. This place was filled with far less things. Practical decoration on the walls, sconces with candles at various levels of burned, dried flowers and herbs, and the occasional framed picture.

The bed itself had its right side pressed up against a wall. Four posters sprouted up from the base, it had no elaborate silk covering floating down as Prince Dagen's did. Its positioning lent to the fact that only one person would really sleep in it. It would be a pain for a second person to try and climb off the bed without disturbing the main occupant. Hollis wondered if, for the next month she was here and sleeping in this bed alongside Sir Lukxa, it could be turned so the head was against the wall.

Walls surrounding the room looked more a neutral blue in the morning light, rather than the deep gray she'd thought they were the night before.

A clock *ticked* softly somewhere hidden from her immediate sight. Hollis remembered it chiming a few times the night before when they had first discussed her sleeping arrangements for the foreseeable future.

The size of his one room rivals my home itself.

Even his baths had been an impressive sight. Hollis hadn't the time for a proper soak in the large tub his room held, but she would make the time.

She could hear Sir Lukxa in it the night before. At one point she watched a little cloud of steam waft under the door to the washroom. It had sent a shiver down her spine. Despite the fireplace, the room had been quite chill.

Now freed from her legs, Sir Lukxa moved from the bed to the dressing area that sat on the parallel wall the bed was on. It had a tall dark wood chest of drawers, or dresser, whatever the proper word was, a maroon chest, a folding screen that covered the area both from the door to the left, and the prying position from the bed. Lastly the area had a long golden mirror. Hollis could see herself in it if she turned her head enough.

"What are you doing today? What am *I* doing today," she asked.

Sir Lukxa glanced over his shoulder as he discarded his sleeping shirt and pulled on a black, high-necked shirt—without giving her enough time to study some of the marks she saw against his ribs. "I have a meeting, and then I will run down to the market to grab you some food, remember? Clover bread, chocolate, and you asked for tea. Though, I would be remiss if I did not tell you I have an extensive collection of non-medicinal teas already. In fact, you seem like you could use a nice black tea to wake up." He grinned and pulled his hair from the neck of the shirt, gave it a quick brush, and tied it with a red ribbon. His hair now sat neatly tied between his shoulder blades while the length ran down mid spine.

Next, an olive-colored pair of loosely-fitted pants were pulled from the lower drawer of his dresser. It didn't look like his captain's uniform at all, she noted.

"Are you going to ask me not to watch you change?" Hollis asked.

"I figured that if I asked, you would ignore me. You tend to favor that." Sir Lukxa glanced over his shoulder as he made to remove his pants.

She returned her gaze to the study and found that the small library, which lay nestled near the windows of his room, most fascinating.

A light laugh came from the direction Sir Lukxa changed in. "Interesting response."

"You have a lot of books," Hollis commented. There were four bookshelves in this room, each tightly packed with books on either side of the black-iron, rounded window. The leather and cloth spines had some traces of dust from what she could see. She'd take a rag to them later. Books shouldn't be left in such a state.

"I think I have an appropriate amount of books for someone who likes to read."

"With all the dust on them? Hard to tell you enjoy reading them." She grinned and laughed. "What is it that captured your fancy in words?"

Sir Lukxa scoffed. "They're dusty for a specific reason. Why don't you investigate them while I'm away? Maybe you'll find a new favorite. Do be careful of the third shelf though, that one is rigged."

"Rigged with what?"

"Don't find out."

Hollis nuzzled her jaw further into the pillow and blanket. She missed her own library tucked into the walls by her bed back in her cottage. It was one of the trickier things to pack when she moved around the kingdom, but being that she was able to warp the contents of a few boxes, it made it possible to lug the books around Hozen all the easier when she decided to up and move about to someplace new.

Another chill overtook her, it pulled a shiver from her bones.

"Did you pack anything warm with you?" Sir Lukxa asked. At the metal

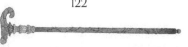

sound of a buckle, she assumed it safe to look back towards him. She turned her head and found him fastening a scabbard to his person, his attention wholly engulfed on his task. He'd tucked the black highneck into the waist of his pants and put on a pair of boots that covered his ankles.

She shook her head, though he couldn't see her. "I do not own much *warm* clothing. It doesn't snow in Quinlin—or most of Hozen for that matter. We get lots of rain, though. Southern areas like Quinlin get terrible rainy seasons." Hollis never had to worry about flooding from the storms. Her house sat high on a hill overlooking the ocean. Nerves did come with the fear of the ground simply crumbling back into the sea, taking her house with it, but Hollis inspected the threads of the earth during those storms, and found it to be solid.

"I'll lend you a few items until I can get you some warmer things." Sir Lukxa finished fastening the tie and squatted. He pulled open the bottom drawer of his dresser and pulled out an assortment of clothes that seemed to be made of wool and thicker materials. They were quickly tossed into a chair by his dresser—a little wrinkled pile.

Hollis wanted to march over to the brick fireplace and throw several logs upon the small fire until it grew so large that the room had no choice but to be warm. If she was going to survive through mornings such as this, she needed the room to be far warmer than Sir Lukxa seemed to keep it. "It was warm yesterday. How is it suddenly so cold?" She pulled her hands up to her mouth and blew warm air into her palms.

"The afternoons here are warm, but mornings and evenings are much chillier. Oh, I forgot I had this." Sir Lukxa grabbed a dark knitted sweater and pulled it on over his high neck. "You'll have to change midday, but that's a survivable event. Come evening you'll have to add a few layers back on."

"That sounds ridiculous." She huffed, pulling the covers closer to her face. The ache in the back of her skull resounded. Her vision doubled as her hangover reminded her of its presence.

"It takes the sun much longer to climb past the mountains and warm us up. The mountains are kind enough to give us a good chill. Check for yourself. We've got frost." Sir Lukxa grinned and pointed toward the windows in his study as he made his way to the kitchenette and set a kettle on the stove.

Hollis willed herself out of bed, leaving the warm blanket behind. Her feet just shy of freezing to the floor as she made her way to the windows.

True to his word a delicate trail of frost covered the edges of the panes. She could almost see her breath as she stood close to them despite the fire that crackled not more than a handful of feet away. "How do you live in such weather?"

He crossed back over to his dressing area. "*Easily*. You grow accustomed to it." Sir Lukxa studied the pile of clothes, a finger against his lips as he plucked up different pieces of clothing. "I do not think my old pants are going to fit you." He tossed them back into the drawer. "You will have to make do with your own skirts and pants. The shirts should not be a problem. They're worn, but not threadbare. Do note that there are training ranks on the collar of these that would identify these as mine, but your hair should be able to hide them." He held the shirt up against his person. It didn't reach across his shoulders. "I cannot believe I used to fit into these."

The kettle hissed from the water that beaded down the enamel siding.

Hollis glared over her shoulder, walking closer to the center of the room. "Are you saying I have the figure of a young boy?"

He made a sound she struggled to decipher. A laugh mixed with something deep in his chest? "I would not say *that* at all. You are much more petite than I. That cannot be denied." He pointed at her and moved into the kitchenette, standing in front of his gas stove.

Hollis chewed her lip and stared down at her figure. She had a good handful on her chest and hips. Nothing extravagant. Besides, if her bust were any larger she'd have even more back problems.

"Do not look too deep into my jest, dear Hollis." Sir Lukxa's voice held a hint of humor she wasn't quite accustomed to. He was almost acting the same way she saw him with the prince.

The prince.

The thought of his curse filled her throat with acid. It felt horrible—her insides tried to claw through her skin.

She wrung her hands. "Sir Lukxa, how long do you expect you'll be gone?"

He fussed about his apartments, grabbing a few things and stuffing them inside a leather satchel not too unlike her own. "I'll return much before lunch, so you should not worry too much about that."

The kettle screamed, filling the air with a fine layer of mist. He removed the kettle from the heated surface. A mug was quickly found and then he tossed in a satchel of tea from a blue tin decorated with gold lines. It smelled divine from where she stood, enthralling her to step closer. She would obey.

As she stepped closer to retrieve the mug Sir Lukxa put the tin of tea back in the same cabinet he'd gotten her salve from and went back to muddling around his apartments.

"If you are ever hankering for tea, you will find it here." He tapped the door of the cupboard.

She nodded in response.

An idea crossed through her mind. "Would you be willing to wait for me to finish this and walk me to the library then? I'd like to get some reading done while you're away. I doubt your collection has the sort of books I'm wanting." The mug had a rough texture, it was pleasant set in her hand—and warm. Hollis inhaled the steam, delighting in the scent of the black tea.

He paused in his twiddling. His tongue ran over his teeth. "I do not think that such a great idea. I would feel much better if you stayed here." His gaze seemed forever away.

"But—" she began.

"If someone is causing Prince Dagen harm and wishes him dead, then I can only assume they'd want a similar fate to one who was capable of breaking whatever has been laid upon him. *If* that's something you're able to do?" His pale eyes pierced her.

The mug lost a touch of warmth in her grasp.

Hollis cleared her throat. "I can disentangle the curse from his being once I regain my access to his woven body. But I would feel much better if I could research. I assume there would be books here on Tablin magic, some sort of baseline I can think through." She'd never been one to research things of magical merit. Then again, she'd never had the access to the books that she was *sure* lay in this castle.

Rare books. The idea of them made her bounce on her toes.

"What makes you think the castle library has anything that would be of use to you?"

"Catol has tried for ages to capture an understanding of how Tablin magic works." Hollis drummed her fingers on the mug. Pursing her lips "And I know for a fact that they've raided more than a fair share of libraries during the wars. I could only assume the books were stored here somewhere."

Sir Lukxa sighed, seemingly fighting himself. "I know. *But,* I do not feel I can risk your safety while I'm gone. I will take you later and I will even help you search. Besides, any books that cover magic and curses and *whatever else* you need would be tucked away under lock and key. We will need permission from one of the Rex Council members to gain access, specifically the keeper—Councilor Shad. I do not have time to get that right now. So, *stay.* Read through my books, find something hidden in my cupboards—if anything feels like it is rigged to be a trap it likely is, so stay out of the chests and half of the drawers on my desk lest you want to lose a finger." He pointed to each space as he listed them.

She straightened her spine. "My oh my, how exciting."

He glared. "I mean it."

"I guess you've plenty of things to entertain myself with." Hollis gestured to the shelves of books.

With a nod of his head, Sir Lukxa grabbed a dark cloak that hung beside his door, fastened it, and left. Giving her time to explore however she wished. She'd simply wait a few good moments—long enough to finish her tea—and find her way to the library.

She set the mug down and dashed over to the door. If she left and returned *before* he did, he'd never know that she'd left.

The door *clicked* before she made it.

Her jaw dropped. He'd *locked* her in. Or perhaps it was more habit than conscious action?

No, he most definitely locked her in. If anyone was stupid enough to break in they'd likely leave with less than they carelessly waltzed in with.

She gripped the handle and twisted it. The door refused to budge. There was no bolt on the inside that she could turn. It seemed the door could only be locked and unlocked, on either side, by using a key.

"Maybe there's an extra somewhere around here?" Hollis first searched in the area that was likely safest for her fingers.

Sir Lukxa's dressing area was simple. There was a mirror, a dresser, and a traveling chest.

The chest was locked, she turned her attention to the dresser. A few pieces of paper and some small portraits lay strewn atop it. The little pictures showed off a few groups of who she assumed were knights he'd trained alongside. Each wore the same clothes and young faces. Sir Lukxa stood even with most of the men in the group, along with a few women. His hair wasn't as long as it currently was, brushing past his ears at most. She preferred it at the length it was now.

A small jewelry box revealed no secrets, or at least, no *key*. She did succeed in finding one of the many traps he'd warned her about. She had lifted a small box and a metal wire swung down in an arch to snap her finger. Thankfully she was quick at pulling her hand away.

You don't get to keep my finger today, little box.

She drummed her fingers against her thighs while deciding what drawer to start with.

A wave of pain thrummed behind her eyes. She could almost *feel* the world. She could feel the tension and how the fibers of her being were woven. Then skin.

"You're still there—*here*. I don't know how much longer you need to rest, but I will drag you to the surface myself if I have to." A dizzy spell overtook her once more, sending her off-kilter. She stumbled blindly back to the bed. Her body collapsed upon the top of it, clutching Sir Lukxa's pillow to her chest.

She waited to move until the bed solidified under her.

"Maybe I'll just wait here. Oh, my tea. Just out of reach." Her mouth moved best it could to speak while being squished against the bed.

A quick nap was needed, and then she would break out of the room and find something *interesting* to do until Sir Lukxa came and found her again. Yes, that sounded like a nice plan indeed.

The bed was comfortable enough.

Sleep lay just beyond her grasp, leaving her in the annoyed state of consciousness. But the dizziness had subsided.

"I can't stand this. Okay, Hollis. Let's *think*." She rose from the bed, grabbed her tea, and paced the warming room. "Doors aren't the only way in and out of the room. How else do people sneak about?" She took a large gulp of the now cold drink. Sir Lukxa had been correct, the black tea was doing wonders for her mind.

A beam of sunlight shot across the floor.

Hollis cocked her head. "I can work with that."

She downed the tea, dressed herself, and unlatched the lock on the window.

CHAPTER TEN

HOLLIS

Watching the prince sleep was far more boring of an idea than Hollis had thought. Prince Dagen didn't snore or move about. He lay there giving the impression that he was dead—if not for the slight lift of his chest with every shallow, wheezy, breath he took. His complexion had a hint of warmth to it, strongly contrasting the frozen look he'd had the night before.

Perhaps the promise of something being found has given him a touch of hope. She wanted to laugh. Finding hope in a curse.

Visiting Prince Dagen seemed to be the safest option she could entertain considering she didn't quite know where anything else she wanted to explore was. Sir Lukxa was less likely to reprimand her if he found her safe and sound inside Prince Dagen's room. Hopefully.

Hollis shuddered. It wasn't a pleasant conversation in her mind.

Though, perhaps he would let it lie considering she'd done an excellent job of escaping out his window and walking across the side of the castle until she found another open window to crawl back into.

Hollis took another turn around his room, basking in the golden light the space offered. The late morning sun reflected off the gilded pattern of the wallpaper and ornate mirrors, sending prisms dancing across the beautiful hardwoods.

She had even snooped through Prince Dagen's washroom when she first entered and he hadn't woken. She smelled all the vials of soap and perfumes. None gave a hint of holding a curse within. It would have been an extravagant idea to curse him with washing soaps and oils, but not something she would want to hate herself for overlooking.

With the sheer variety he had organized in the glass cabinet, she was sure the prince wouldn't miss a few of the more floral scents she slipped into her bag.

A mirror in the corner of the room drew her attention. She trailed her hands along the window-filled walls and paused at it. Her reflection showed back at her. No matter how hard she focused, she wouldn't will her threads to become visible to herself.

I guess I can see myself without threads now too.

It wasn't as if *everything* in her life held the texture of woven cloth—every living thing a breathing fabric. The threads lay *underneath* it all. Something she could look to, while still seeing everything that was.

The mirror was cold against her fingertips—almost too chill as she trailed her fingers around the reflection of her face.

"How long have you been in my room?" Prince Dagen's voice squeaked.

Hollis jumped and spun around, landing awkwardly on her ankle.

Prince Dagen's eyes were wide with alarm as he took in the sight of her hovering by one of his mirrors. He clutched his blanket to his chest as he breathed heavily.

"Not too terribly long. Sir Lukxa is gone on some errands," Hollis explained.

Prince Dagen narrowed his eyes. "Are you wearing his *clothes?*"

She watched him blink several times as he looked over her outfit. "Just his shirt. Is that a problem?" Sir Lukxa's gray wool high neck with little

black marks around the neck fit her nicely. She'd paired the high neck with a nice maroon skirt and her usual black stockings and walking boots—not minding that the green of her boots would possibly clash with her skirt in the eyes of others. She didn't mind the mixing of colors and patterns. This was a rather well-put-together, and warm, outfit.

And not boyish—*no*, she looked womanly.

Prince Dagen shook his head. "No, not a problem at all. Just surprised to see you wearing part of the uniform of a knight-in-training." His face flushed as he continued staring at the shirt.

"I needed something warm to wear. The captain assured me I wouldn't be pulled into training exercises whilst I wore it. I think the skirt helps hide the training aspect of the shirt. Looks normal. And my hair, too." She twirled the bits of hair around her face.

Prince Dagen's hands mused at the sheets surrounding him and his lips did a weird thing Hollis noted people often did when they felt awkward. "Not that that would matter. Each class wears different markings. No one would suspect, or treat, you as a recruit. You won't be forced to do any labor while wearing it. If anyone realized whose shirt it was you may get a few, um. . . Anyways. So, you've chosen to occupy yourself by going through my things again?" His face flushed.

She wasn't going to respond to his embarrassed mumbling. The redness on his face was quite amusing. "I was unable to have the most in-depth search yesterday. For instance, there's a hallway behind that mirror, but you've a room on the outer wall. I'd be interested to see where it leads to or how it even works." She trailed a finger around the lip of the mirror, feeling the subtle suck of air.

He chuckled, then coughed. "I'm surprised you noticed that. Then again, maybe I should not be? It leads to a cupboard in the kitchens. Quick way out of the castle."

She turned back at him. "Or a quick way to get a snack."

"Yes. Though I doubt your intentions in coming here are purely for

entertainment in searching my chambers, what are you really here for?"

Thoughts spun like a swarm of birds in her mind. "Sir Lukxa told me to stay in his rooms and I don't fancy sitting in one place *or* listening. And I refused to go back." She felt safer in the presence of another person, even if Prince Dagen wouldn't be able to defend her in his condition. There was solidarity in numbers.

"If he locked you in, I think the only best place that Lukxa could find you would be in his chambers." Prince Dagen laughed, still twiddling his fingers. "I cannot believe he locked you in his room. Are you a princess in a tower?" He swallowed, face twitching.

"For the next month I am—at least according to the contract I signed. Anyway the door to his room is locked and I've not a key."

"I can give you one." Prince Dagen smiled.

"I'll take it." Hollis returned the gesture. "I suppose he'd confiscate it if he discovered I had one—" she cut herself off with a sharp inhale. "Now is a good time to spend creating a story for the council. I don't think Sir Lukxa would want us telling them I think you've a curse placed upon you. But I need a legitimate reason in being able to stay. People assume Tablin magic can work miracles. If I don't have one right away, they may send me away despite what the contract says." Hollis tapped her fingers together as she thought.

A cross expression grew on the prince's face. "Being that I know the council has something up their sleeves against me, yes, we'll likely need to keep the information about the curse to you, Sir Lukxa, and myself. I agree, we should come up with a way for you to stay longer than those who came before you. A cover indeed." Prince Dagen drummed his fingers against his cheek.

Hollis liked the sharpness in his eye.

He sat up, vigor set in his face. "So we need to figure out what you can do when you're brought to treat me. I doubt you'd have unfettered access to myself. Some council members would be likely to tag alongside to watch you heal me. What can we fake to convince the council that you should stay?" He gave her a wide grin, wiggling his eyebrows a few times in a comedic manner.

Even though Prince Dagen was approaching twenty, he was not more than a boy born into a situation he couldn't control. Strings for a puppetmaster to play with attached to his every part.

"Yes!" Hollis clapped her hands, until a chill overtook her body. "*Wait a moment.* You said you know the council has something up their sleeve. What are *you* talking about?"

Confusion swam in her mind.

Sir Lukxa and Prince Dagen both seemed to have something against the current ruling group.

Prince Dagen's eyes went wide as he swallowed. "Ah, forget I said anything in that aspect."

"I find it hard to forget when someone says something so suspect," Hollis said with a smirk "I could concoct some awful-tasting *potion* and make you drink it as our cover."

Prince Dagen's eyes widened. "You know, you're much more entertaining than any other doctor who's tried helping me."

"Flattery will get you far, nicely done. I pride myself on not caring, so it helps." Hollis swept her hands across her skirt. Straightening the wrinkled fabric. "How are you feeling today?"

He grimaced, running a hand over his chest. "I feel pressure in my lungs. Like my ribs aren't giving me room to breathe. I'm sweaty, too, which is great."

She could see the dampness gathering on his pale brows. No matter how often he wiped his forehead, the beads accumulated once more.

"Is it as bad as other pains have been?"

"No, but it's not far from feeling like it."

Every possible curse that this could be ran through her mind. The wickedness it gave was unmistakable. The wrongness it sets in one's being.

She'd hoped to never come across another curse in her life. Never to deal with the knowledge that someone had cursed another being. Never to bear the physical toll it took as the curse was removed.

If only she could figure out what curse it was based on the few notes she had gathered. Smoky, consuming, filled with hatred. She'd take to reading some books later and hope someone else had already put the information together. If the castle had any books she needed.

"What will you do when the council asks you how you intend to heal me?"

She paused, mulling over his question. Blood *thrummed* in her ears. "I'm sure I'll do what I do best."

"What's that?" Prince Dagen leaned forward, arms propped on his knees to hold himself upright. He became all the more eager.

"Lie through my teeth and hope it works."

His eyes widened. "Can we come up with some type of story? A little play to put on so they believe you more?"

"Such as what, my prince?"

"I can try and fake being able to breathe easier. It's not too hard to mimic normal breathing." Prince Dagen coughed, convincing Hollis *completely*. "I can just start vomiting at some point. It makes people uncomfortable so they leave faster. I can give you a demonstration now if you'd like?"

She appreciated the helpful spirit he had. "Oh, most definitely, Prince."

CHAPTER ELEVEN

LUKXA

The roofs overhead blocked the sunlight in the alleyway, trapping the stench and rats in the surrounding darkness.

The stone walls of the alleyway scraped against Lukxa's back. He was thankful he had found the extra sweater tucked into the bottom drawer of his dresser. Even with the wool cloak, he could still feel the edges of unrefined brick and stone making little marks on his body. Combined with the frosted morning air, Lukxa was far from pleased.

The stench of waste buckets from the less than savory *businesses* run in this area of the capital city clogged his nose. He scrunched his face, let out a sharp breath, and scooted around a barrel of trash—the insides of which had been reduced to glowing cinders. Sadly, the little crisp things lent no heat.

Not that he could stick around. Lukxa had a scent to follow. A trail bounding from person to person. Evidence of the finest kind.

Well. . . he would have evidence if this worked out.

He paused as he reached the edge of the alley. His hands braced low on the corner as he crouched down. Lukxa spied the open area that the path poured into.

The Jasmine District was a nuisance to Lukxa—and the rest of the castle guard. Lukxa himself hated coming here, be it information or to obtain smuggled goods.

While Lukxa understood the reasons why someone needed to work in an area such as this, he wished there was a different way for those who were suffering under the thumbs of the greedy and lustful to make a living. Half the shops were filled with young men and women with no other method of money outside of themselves.

The early morning hour meant the district was hushed. Sleep was gained in these hours, hangovers recovered from, and aches and pains nursed.

The base of Lukxa's skull throbbed with the reminder of his own overconsumption. He would drink a pitcher of water at breakfast to compensate.

Breakfast. A wave of nausea crashed over him. Food both appealed to his mind and brought it to ruin.

He clutched his head, his cold hands relieving some of the sick feeling. Perhaps he would need two pitchers of water.

An umber-skinned man in a blue cloak stepped out from one of the nearby pathways and ducked toward a dilapidated building with three candles lit in the window. Lukxa hunched his back and lowered himself further to the ground. A leather satchel hung at the man's side, nearly bursting at the buckles from what Lukxa could tell.

The cloaked man held the bag tight to his side and knocked a rhythmic pattern against the door. He lightly bounced on his feet as he jerked his head in different directions and waited for an answer to his knocking. Clearly, he checked his surroundings for if he was being tracked.

The cloaked man was doing a terrible job, considering he had not noticed Lukxa in across the way. All the cloaked man was doing was drawing attention to himself from the few patrons who could be loitering around this early in the morning.

Lukxa narrowed his gaze, trying to get a better look at the man's face under the hood. He recognized the cloak, but Lukxa knew better than to assume only one person could own a type of garment.

A buckle on the man's satchel *popped*, sending a strap soaring upward in a high arc before smacking into the man's side. The cloaked man quickly dropped to his knees to right the strap.

A beam of sunlight cut through the sky, helping further illuminate the figure.

Lukxa's vision focused, his eyes growing wide as he took in every feature of the man's face that he could.

Caught you.

Lukxa's grip tightened on the corner of the wall. The stone scraped against his nails and the flesh of his palm.

He drew his hand back, a hiss of pain caught in his throat. The damage was minimal as he inspected his hand. A few bits of loose, grainy bits of stone had embedded themselves under his fingernails. His palms had stone burn on them, scrapes that only took off a few bits of surface skin. Nothing terrible. The little wounds would need cleaning though.

Lukxa spat on his hand and wiped it on his pants just up from the ankle of his right boot. While he knew better, the idea that there was such filth on his hands was unsettling.

He shook out his hand and reset his gaze on the cloaked man, who had secured his bag and returned to his bouncing. He rapped the same pattern on the door again.

Now it was time to wait.

Lukxa sat back on his haunches, straightened his spine, and prayed that no puddles of fluids resided anywhere near his bum. He was grateful he could fully sit on his feet and he did not have to place his perfectly clean bottom on the ground. A useful skill he had mastered.

He peered further out around the corner and took in the sights.

The Jasmine District changed every time Lukxa was forced to enter it.

The pathways of entry wound throughout the Catol Citadel. Lukxa's chosen path took him past three herbalist shops, an elementary school, and a church before he would break into the maze of darkness.

The opening in front of him between all the different buildings was no larger than his apartments. Truly the fact such a wide opening existed in the Jasmine District was a sight to behold. Space was heavily capitalized here. The open area surely had its use when the sun set and coin was spent.

A shudder ran through him. As it ran through Lukxa's nerves, his hangover decided to remind him that it had not quite left. His stomach soured as another wave of stench came rushing past on the cold morning wind.

How he did not vomit was a miracle.

Stretching out his shoulders gave Lukxa no relief. Hollis had clung to him through the night, and he had happily obliged. His mind had buzzed with the warmth of gin while Hollis' frozen legs continually found a way to slide up against him while she slept. Though it tormented his mind endlessly, it was not terrible. Lukxa could still feel her breath ghosting over his collarbone.

Truly an experience he would not mind repeating.

Hopefully he could get more sleep this coming evening. Every bone in his body cried with exhaustion. His travels had him sleeping in less than stellar conditions.

Lukxa had spent two weeks searching for Hollis. Two weeks spent in crummy inns and camping out when the nights grew long on the stretch of road between villages.

Tension built in his body again. His neck *cracked.* Thankfully, there wasn't a chance that he had to leave the castle anytime soon. He could get used to sharing his bed with Hollis on her rightful end of it. No more camping out, tracking someone down across the countryside.

Never again.

He ran a hand down his face once more, hoping to wipe away his thoughts while he was at it.

This was not the place to be thinking about Hollis. Amidst the filthy alleyways and corrupted shops. Lukxa did not want to guess at what the shop the cloaked man waited at dealt with. Lukxa did not have to, though. He would find out soon enough.

The door cracked open. The cloaked man—Councilor Sypher's head peeked around the area before he stepped inside, giving Lukxa another full view of Sypher's face. He turned left and right several times.

Lukxa followed after him, his leather shoes *squelching* as he stepped into a puddle of something he refused to put thought to.

Lukxa's hand twisted the handle. He pulled the door open the slightest bit and turned his ear into the crack.

"And you're sure these are legitimate?" an unknown voice asked.

Sypher gave a noise of acknowledgement. "Straight from the desk of Councilor Shad. It's everything you'll need to know on prices. Now, once you sell this information, you all can raise your prices before the purchase order goes out, and, uh," Sypher chuckled, "you'll make back what you owe me for this information quickly." Lukxa could hear the grin in the man's voice.

"Wait! While you're here, I'm starting to remember something. Perhaps we could make a trade. Information in lieu of coin?"

The shopkeeper's voice took on a high, worried pitch.

"Oh, depending on what it is, I might be interested in listening. You've my attention, but time is ticking. I've got somewhere to be."

Lukxa checked his watch. There were five minutes left before *his* next *meeting*. He would have to move quickly if he wanted to make it there on time. While he wanted to hear more of whatever information was being revealed here, he likely would not have to wait long.

Lukxa hoped he seemed refreshed. When he had washed his face this morning his eyes had been rimmed with ashy purple and blue circles. He stifled a yawn. The little beanery he waited in was covered in a thin layer of coffee powder. Patrons sat at the small round tables littered along the unfinished floor. Some seemed to be perky morning risers, while others as if sleep had not quite come and gone peacefully.

He had arrived ten minutes prior, just making it a few minutes shy of the arranged meeting time. Enough time to order a coffee and morning snack. A flaky pastry with a whipped cheese and chocolate drizzle. The thing did not survive to see the table. Lukxa had scarfed it down the moment the warm thing was set in his hand.

Movement out of the corner of his eye pulled his head left. A table of young girls sat giggling and pointing at him. *Joy.* One girl rose from her seat, goaded on by the rest of her party.

Before the girl could attempt to cross over to Lukxa, Councilor Sypher, now dressed in a white cloak sat down across from him. "It's good to see you back in one piece, Captain Lukxa." Sypher rested his elbows on the square table. Sypher's chest heaved as he breathed through his mouth, giving evidence of his run through the Jasmine District to make it here.

The girl who had stood, presumably ready to talk with Lukxa, sat down at her table, deflatedly talking to her companions.

Lukxa turned his full attention back to Councilor Sypher. His brown hair was pulled back into braids along his dark scalp today. Lukxa could spot the blue fabric peeking out underneath the white councilors' robe. The councilor had not brought any cup or plate in his hand indicating that he would not be staying longer than what it took to speak with him. *Business only.*

It reminded him of his meeting this coming Saturday in which he would see Councilor Sypher again, sitting across from himself just as he did now. But Lukxa was ready for that—and ready to use what he needed to today.

"I didn't know there was a question as to if I would return in multiple pieces?" Lukxa gave a chuckle before picking up his cup of coffee, which, when lifted, left a nice clean ring on the table.

The coffee itself tasted burnt and felt like sludge sliding down his throat, but was filled with the energy he needed for the day. And hopefully wash away the small feeling of alcohol that still hung deep in his muscles. Lukxa needed to check the numbers on the bottle when he returned to his apartments.

Sypher nodded his head wistfully. "I've heard some Tablins can strike a man dead before they have even seen them coming." Sypher's voice was thick with jest. He picked up the fork that lay on the table and spun it around in his fingers. "Your idea of bringing in a Tablin Healer to better the cause was quite ingenious, I must say."

"That is ridiculous to assume she would so easily strike me dead." Hollis had no reason to strike him dead; her brashness seemed to throw people off their guard when around her. That was a weapon enough for her to wield. And she had managed to waltz him right out her front door.

Lukxa furrowed his brows. Perhaps she could strike a man dead before they had the chance to realize what had happened to them?

Sypher *hummed*. "I see. I have all the papers you need to read by the next council meeting ready." Sypher opened the leather satchel at his side and pulled out stacks of papers held together with little clips. It seemed the bag held more than Lukxa ever thought it could.

Lukxa's stomach soured, and it wasn't the coffee this time. "What are all of those?" He prayed that all that was needed of him were a few signatures.

"Oh. *These?*" Sypher pointed to the stack, sarcasm dripping from his mouth. "Everything we passed in your two-week absence, along with any proposed ideas by the people and council alike." Sypher handed Lukxa the papers. It would not be a load of light reading: the script upon it was smaller than Lukxa's pinky's fingernail. *Joy.* At least Lukxa enjoyed looking at words on paper.

"I guess that can be managed in time for the meeting. I will do my best." Lukxa felt a tense grin form on his face.

"Yes, you always do tell us *you'll do your best*. But that isn't true, is it?"

Sypher's voice grew stale.

"To what are you inferring?" Lukxa cocked his head, letting a slightly confused expression grow over his features.

Sypher scrunched up his face. "Stalling like this has not done anyone any favors, *Captain Lukxa*." He spoke in a hushed, venomous tone. As Sypher always did. It used to scare Lukxa, truthfully.

"You do not have to flaunt my acquired rank in my face to get your point across. It would have been far too suspicious if things had gone the way they were originally planned." Lukxa drummed his fingers along the table. "This was our best bet. The best for all of you. It is clear that the original plan was one that would have intense growing pains to pull off." Lukxa leaned back in his chair, arms crossed over his chest. Tilting back his head, he glared down his nose at Councilor Sypher. The man did not appear pleased. Or solid.

"Yes. . . You'd better be right about things working out this way. The others are starting to grow suspicious of you." Sypher leaned back in his chair, folding his hands over his stomach. His thumbs swirled around each over. "I do not blame them. I do not blame you. Covering your own skin is the most important thing you can do, because they will absolutely crucify you should they discover anything. But now, you've given us our perfect Tablin scape-goat. No need to make one up with this, whoever you've brought into the castle." Sypher pointed his hand forward, tensing it for emphasis as he spoke. His lips flattened as fear crossed his eyes.

Lukxa nodded. This was his chance. "You know, speaking of the castle, I was almost late this morning." He tilted his head to the side further, still looking down his nose at Sypher.

Sypher blinked. "What does that have to do with anything?"

Lukxa then faced the man straight on, brows raised. "Apparently, someone broke into Councilor Shad's office. Moved some papers around, spilled a bottle of ink. Shad dragged me around for half an hour demanding I find who did that before he finally let me go so I would not be late for meeting you. Of course, he did not know that letting me go to come here fulfilled his wishes too. Isn't that right?"

Sypher narrowed his eyes and swallowed, his lips twitching. "I don't know what you're talking about."

It was time to act. "No, *really*?" Lukxa grinned. "I was under the impression that you broke into his office, stole the stock orders for the tournament, and sold them off to what I assume the highest bidder in the Jamine District is."

Sypher's face fell and a curse slipped through his lips.

"Come on, that is the *least* of our crimes. Of course, I only know my part. But now, I know a bit about you." Lukxa leaned forward and folded his arms on the table. "I do not feel inclined to tell Councilor Shad, or anyone else, what you are doing. It dose not bother me. But, that does not mean it isn't useful to me. Information." He smiled.

Sypher's face morphed into a scowl. "What do you wanna know?"

"The past few weeks, *my* order sheets have been screwed with. Someone is messing with *my* numbers. I wanna know who is doing it. I guarantee it's to pin this whole debacle on me once everything is done and over with. I would seem quite the shady character with stock numbers like that after the death."

Sypher's face pulled taut. "That's it? You stalked me and decided to blackmail me so I'd correct your stock numbers?"

"Well." Lukxa leaned back again, taking another sip of his coffee. "For now."

An annoyed growl let from Sypher as he evened out the pages on the table. "You could have done that in office." He rolled his eyes. "As long as you read my reports and notes you should be fine for today's meeting. Do be sure to return them to me after—I need to keep them for accounting reasons." Sypher rolled his eyes.

"Of course." Lukxa would have to read nonstop until the council meeting in order to finish the documents. And he had so many other things to do.

"Make sure you and the Tablin woman arrive on time for council. It's been moved up an hour. We cannot have any distractions taking us off the docket. There's a time for everything and everything has its time. There's no messing with that." Sypher gathered his things up into his bag. "And next time, don't pick such a run-down place to meet. You can afford better. There's no reason to drag me to a place like this to give you papers in person. Or, *or*, better yet, *untrap your room sometime* so I can feel better about sending any of my scribes to deliver papers." Sypher smiled. It didn't appear to be a very happy one.

Lukxa reached out to shake his hand. "You had errands out this morning too, do not forget. *But.*" Lukxa punctuated the word. "Thank you for coming *all this way*. I happen to like getting out of the walls every now and again for fresh air and refreshments. Small places like this help remind me of the people I serve." He smiled as Sypher's face grew flushed. Sypher gave a curt nod of his head, and stalked out of the beanery—nodding to a few of the classier patrons as he left.

Lukxa stood, plucking his cup from the table. He downed the remaining bitter contents, which brought back memories from the night before. Hollis' arms around him, pulling him close, her breath upon his neck. Lukxa shook his head to rid himself of them and refocus on the present.

He quickly set the cup on the wooden counter where a slew of other empty cups sat. Then promptly left the building himself.

Making his way through the market was difficult with the information he now carried on his shoulders. He had noticed a discrepancy in the accounting books several months prior when going through his own budget for the training hall. While it was true, a large number of weapons had been added to his order forms, what really drew Lukxa's attention was a small blip that stuck out in a random councilor fund.

The closer Lukxa read, the more he saw the blip appear through different accounts. A large sum moved from one account, then an even amount showing up across three, back to the original and others in smaller increments until it disappeared as small spendings.

And now he confirmed that Sypher was involved in changing records. Lukxa would not take advantage of that quite yet. Would not show his hand and what all he actually knew.

Lukxa shook his head and ducked into the building at the far edge of the square.

The little bakery had fresh stock of clover loaves. Chocolate was slightly harder to find but was bought nevertheless. Unsure of the type Hollis preferred, he ventured to get a few small selections with a promise on the tip of his tongue to buy a larger quantity once she picked her favorite out. He needed to keep her on his side. And temper some of her anger she surely would possess after being locked in his apartments.

It felt odd walking back into the castle with a bag filled with treats for a woman who had slept in his bed the night before. The thought alone almost froze him in his tracks. It was an interesting situation.

Hollis didn't take up too much space on his bed. Not to mention, by having her there, he could keep her close enough to not worry about her sneaking out or someone obtaining access to her while she was alone in her own chambers without a guard.

The walk from the market to the castle was an uninterrupted one. Lukxa waved to a few acquaintances, traded pleasantries with the castle staff he encountered, and finally arrived at his door. Behind it, he expected Hollis to be armed with fire in her eyes and a mouth full of stabbing words.

Lukxa reached into his pants pocket and plucked out his key, ready to unlock his door and hear her wrath at being locked inside.

It was for her own good, a last-minute decision he didn't feel like arguing about.

The key slid into the lock and spun with a *click*.

His room was empty.

The bag almost slid from his grasp. Shutting the door behind him, he quickly deposited the bag on his counter and took in his room. There was no sign of a struggle anywhere. No clothes amiss or items sprawled about on the floor. His washroom was empty. Nothing had moved since he had used it this morning. His heart began to pick up pace as he thought through every situation possible.

A frigid breeze swept over his shoulder.

He turned towards his small study area, the window next to his desk was ajar. No one had mentioned anything of a human-like splattering on the grounds below, so the fear of her falling out wasn't a worry at least.

After sliding the window closed and relocking it, Lukxa left his rooms in a storm. Rushing down the hall he unlocked Dagen's door, afraid to find an equally empty room.

He swung into the room and shut the door behind him, his back pressed against the door.

A shuddery breath ripped free from his lungs as Hollis came into sight. "What are you doing in here?" His voice shook with the rage his body would not.

"Oh goodness, you're back already." Hollis' face scrunched with what appeared to be annoyance.

"We were just coming up with a plan on what to do when the Council brings her to see me. She's been taking note over my condition, trying to figure out what type of curse it could be." Dagen's face was bright with curiosity. The young man had a keen interest in learning about whatever he could. Tablin magic seemed to be a new fixation as Lukxa and Dagen spoke through bits and pieces of a plan the last few months.

An odd prick of anger settled in Lukxa's stomach. Dagen and Hollis were safe, though. That's all that mattered at the moment.

Grinding his jaw shut as to keep any furious comments at bay, Lukxa stalked over to the side of the bed where Hollis and Dagen sat.

Lukxa trailed his gaze between the two, both of whom sat with wide eyes as they waited for Lukxa to speak. "It's time for lunch, both of you. Hollis, we'll be formally introducing you to the Council soon. Then, tonight, in the mess hall, we will have dinner with some other knights in the castle I know. You will pose as a long standing friend of mine. So before that happens, we need to nail down our story." He turned to face Dagen. "Dagen, someone will be by soon with your afternoon meal. We will speak more later—I caught a rat. Hollis, if you will follow me, I have your lunch in the apartments and I need to change into my uniform."

Hollis and Dagen nodded as Lukxa spoke. Then Hollis stood, bade the prince farewell, and followed Lukxa to his own apartments.

Lukxa turned on her as soon as the door to his rooms sank shut and caged Hollis against the door. His mouth against her ear. "If you sneak out of my chambers again when you know you're supposed to *stay*, I'll secure you to the underside of the bed frame. Understood?" He pulled back.

Hollis' face was filled with mirth. "That's a weird thing to tell me, but it means I do have one more escape allowed." She smiled. "And don't expect me to not find a way out of that either."

Lukxa leaned his nose against hers, the threat burning in his eyes. His voice graveled out of his throat. "*Try me.*"

CHAPTER TWELVE

LUKXA

A burst of warm air crashed against Lukxa's face as he opened the grand set of hand carved doors and strode into the council meeting room. The light from the glass ceiling shone on the large dark table in the center of the room. Nine bodies sat peppered around the table, with the same amount of empty chairs as filled.

The room itself was large enough to fit the table, somehow. Lukxa could not imagine how the workers managed to fit such a large feature piece and the twenty chairs that surrounded it into such a tight space.

Lukxa spoke his greetings to everyone on the council as he made his way to an open chair by Councilor Dem, his fellow knight captain. Lukxa rubbed his hands along his arms in an attempt to warm them as he sank into his chosen chair. Sitting under the gaze of those who knew what else took place in this room. The filling underneath the velvet fittings had been worn flat. His back and bottom were sure to be sore after the meeting finished. It only added to the uncomfortable feeling in the room.

Extra stretchings required before evening training later. Extra time taken and wasted.

"Not in your full Councilors uniform today, Sir Lukxa?" Councilor

Muse's plump and rosy cheeks appled out with a smile. Little auburn curls sat tight against her face, framing honey-gold eyes. She was the perfect picture of a Catolian mother. Her calm attitude was always pleasant, and she handled any arguments within the council itself in a perfectly fair manner. Something Lukxa could use and strive for. Fairness made Muse the perfect mediator on the council. Lukxa had great respect for the woman.

Lukxa returned Muse' smile with a small grin. He hoped his lack of *formal* dress would not cause complications. "I figured since I am not staying the *entirety* of our meeting—and with my training duties—it would make sense to wear my captain's uniform." Lukxa brushed his hands down the white cloak he had thrown on at the last minute before leaving his apartments. He did not button it up, though. That would be far too restrictive for his liking. "I donned the overcoat just so I would not get ushered out right away. I figured it would buy me some time."

"A fair decision, child." Councilor Dem grabbed Lukxa by the shoulder and shook him a few times, a bright grin on his dark and scarred face. Lukxa *knew* Dem would skip the formal dress himself if possible. Dem hated the fact that, more often than not, he worked most days in the capacity of a councilor in the proper dress rather than in the captain's uniform he had tucked away. Lukxa would admit that Dem's rich black skin made the councilor's uniform look striking. It was fashionable on Dem.

Lukxa did not *hate* the ensemble, but it was quite cumbersome to wear in full. The councilor's uniform as a whole consisted of a textured white jacket that hung down to each member's knees. A stripe of color down the chest signified which prefecture the wearer presided over. The yellow of Hozen's marked Collin, Muse, and Sypher; red of Eargile on Dem, Kleo, and Cane; Rex's purple decorated the youngest, but likely the most cutthroat members of Sophy, Aphi, and Shad. The Royal color of green was hung on Lukxa himself and Dagen.

And buried deep with the king and queen.

The meeting began off without a hitch. Lukxa felt odd sitting alone while Hollis stood outside, acquainting herself with one of the younger knights in Lukxa's employment, Wilfrin. Lukxa had given the knight the small, informal, order of keeping Hollis company when she would have to wait outside while Lukxa sat in for the first part of the meeting.

Later Lukxa would have the knight give Hollis a more formal tour of the castle grounds.

Lukxa sank deeper into his stiff chair and contemplated his choices in life. It was the only interesting thing he could think up while the council members brawled over festival budgets and crop rotations. His tournament budget had been decided months ago. There was nothing for him to talk about on today's docket.

He trailed his eyes around the room. Trying to figure if anything had changed in the two weeks he was gone.

The council chambers were ornate, designed in such a way to reflect the modesty that the council should hold, all while showing off the wealth of the nation at the same time. Lukxa found the rooms to be entirely too much, with the gilded wallpaper and marble flooring. It was not entirely. . . cohesive? The glass ceiling let in far too much heat during the summer and let it all out in the winter. And the walls held portraits of the current council members—sans Lukxa.

It was laughable how Lukxa would meet here with the seldom few vying for the throne, surrounded by the portraits of those who swore to uphold the country—and meant it.

Lukxa was not much better. He had not meant his vows when he first took them either.

Perhaps he just hated being in meetings so much that every tiny inconvenience about the room drove him mad?

Lukxa eyed Councior Dem, who sat in a similar position as he did. The man appeared equally as disinterested as Lukxa until someone's voice would raise in pitch or anger.

"Last quarter the Hozen region brought in sixteen-hundred electrum

and three-thousand gold. I think it's safe to say they've had a tough year."
Councilor Collin's voice deepened with sorrow. It pulled at his pale bushy-
brows. "The reports being passed around will reflect these numbers."

A fluttering of papers went around the desk as councilors handing each
other a few pages before passing them along. Lukxa was the last to receive
any of the reports.

"How many are there?" Lukxa leaned to whisper into Dem's ear.

He quickly counted his stack. "Seven pages. Couldn't they just read
from one? Why do we have to—"

"Councilors Dem and Lukxa, please refrain from speaking while we're
giving reports." Collin's voice would shake the table if it the wooden thing
were not practically mounted to the floor.

Lukxa sank back in his chair once more, recounting the papers in
his hands.

Five pieces. I'm missing two. Great.

Councilor Collin continued. "As I was saying, Hozen has only brought
in a fraction of what we have in previous years." His deep voice drawled on
and on.

Lukxa tuned out the man as he spoke, running the numbers through
his head.

Sixteen-hundred gold? The report Sypher gave me said twenty? Or had
he misunderstood his earlier meeting with Councilor Sypher? Did Lukxa
actually know how to read?

Lukxa pulled the documents from his own bag and skimmed down the
lines, having a hard time finding the budget numbers in the tiny script.

Something *smacked* against the large table, drawing everyone's attention.

Councilor Sophy leaned forward in her chair, her right hand planted
firmly on the table in front of her. "I still think we need to draw evenly from
each prefecture. It would not be fair for others to contribute more simply
because they worked harder." She cocked her head and raised the pitch of her
voice. "Or are you saying your prefecture deserves special treatment?" Sophy's

amber eyes glowed in the bright light from the glass ceiling overhead. She raised her hand up from the table. Lukxa could see how red her palm had grown from the harsh impact, and cupped her chin to lean on. Her fingers drummed on her pale cheek.

Councilor Shad, who sat across from Lukxa, tilted his head side to side, the brown curls of his hair flopping to follow. "I think, perhaps, instead of *monetary amounts*, Hozen could donate more food for the festivals? That way the rest of the people aren't feeling *as* cheated if they read the published reports, and other prefectures still feel as though they are contributing in a greater sense. It might even have other vendors feeling more generous with their donations to the winter solstice. Especially as Prince Dagen takes the throne. A final celebration of young life and moving forward." Councilor Shad spoke, dragging a pen over a piece of paper. Lukxa could see several sets of numbers scrawled along the sides but couldn't make out exactly what madness the councilor had written.

The room was filled with murmuring as everyone mulled over the proposal. Bodies leaned over to another, pointing and tapping random points on different pages.

Lukxa had no one to confer with as he reread the notes from earlier. The only thing Dem hated more than wearing his councilor uniform was being made to talk about numbers. Which was odd, considering the man was great in mathematics.

Councilor Aphi nodded and spoke, a soft tone in their voice. "That works. Rex, as stated earlier, brought in what eighteen-thousand electrum silver and fifty-two hundred gold. From that, we can contribute the standard four percent for winter festivities and an ample supply of medicine for any accidents in the tournament—as we all know there will be an abundance of. I feel that would be standard." Aphi leaned back into a slightly cushier chair. Lukxa was jealous.

No, there was no time to be envious of anything.

Lukxa returned his attentions to the papers in his hands.

He poured over the numbers Sypher had given him earlier, searching for the taxes from the previous quarter. Lukxa *knew* this number didn't match up with the numbers here on this paper. The papers rattled in his hands.

Found it!

The numbers were off, way off from what was written with Sypher's perfect script. All relating to information from Councilor Collin. It would seem Sypher gave Lukxa more information for blackmail than he had intended to. A giddy feeling rose up inside of Lukxa's chest.

Feeling a pair of eyes on him, Lukxa turned back up to catch Sypher quickly turning his face away in the opposite direction that Lukxa was sitting.

Perfect. Sypher knew he'd been caught. It was time to needle that feeling under Sypher's skin.

Lukxa raised his hand.

Councilor Muse clapped her hands. "Now that these numbers have been approved, I believe it's time that we bring in the healer. She's still waiting outside, correct, Lukxa?" Councilor Muse asked him directly as she gestured to the thick wooden doors with her folded hands. A tired smile on her face.

Lukxa nodded. "Yes, I assigned Wilfrin to watch her during the meeting. I'm actually hoping the council can talk about—"

Muse spoke again. "That's perfect. Why don't you fetch her while we finish up some Council business—*official* Council business. Do you understand?"

He was being thrown out of the room. Just as he had the ability to terrify Sypher even more.

"Actually, I have something—"

"Sorry, Captain Lukxa. Your budget was approved months ago. You've no time to make changes. Now again, we'll have to ask you to leave. Just for a few moments." Collin seemed all too happy with the arrangement.

Muse, who sat to Collin's left, swatted at his shoulder. Collin narrowed his eyes at Muse in return.

Councilor Muse had spoken out several times in the past against Lukxa's exclusion from council events before, but she was never able to overrule the majority vote of Lukxa's position on the council merely being a figurehead position.

Lukxa smiled and stood, making sure to gather the papers into his bag. "It's no imposition."

"Actually, Sir Lukxa, I need those copies back now." Sypher stood and reached across the table to him, a glare engrained on his face.

"I haven't finished going through them quite yet—"

Sypher shook his head in a tizzy. "I need them back *now*. Record keeping is tedious and these must be submitted by the end of the night. You have my only copy" Sypher's gaze was unwavering as he motioned his hand toward the paper.

Lukxa was not sure what to do, several impatient stares and tapping fingers. "Of course." As soon as he extended his hand, the papers were yanked away, straightened into a nice stack, and delicately placed inside of Sypher's leather bag. Hopefully he could find another copy of the papers to use against Sypher. Lukxa would bet good money that Councilor Shad would have a copy.

Councilor Collin coughed and then spoke. "You're excused. We'll come to get you as soon as we're ready for the both of you."

"Of course." Lukxa pulled a smile to his face, gave a slight nod, and walked out the doors.

They sealed behind him with a loud *thunk*.

He let a deep sigh free from his lungs in an effort to keep from banging his head against the door.

"Are you quite all right?" Hollis' voice pulled him from the minor bit of rage that grew in the pit of his stomach. She stood by a window, the light illuminating her hair with a halo. Wilfrin stood at her side.

"Yes, I'm fine." Lukxa smiled at Wilfrin. "Thank you for your help. You're free to yourself until training this afternoon."

"Pleasure's all mine, sir." Wilfrin stared at Hollis with a goofy grin and strode off.

He *would not* be asking Wilfrin to give Hollis a tour of the castle.

Lukxa waited until Wilfrin disappeared down another hall before speaking. "What did you do to him?" His eyes trailed back to Hollis, who now sat on a small bench beneath the window, picking at her nails.

"Oh, him? Nothing truly; he seemed to find anything I did a pleasure to listen to. Had a great deal to say about the hidden inner workings of the castle staff. Gossip of the best kind." She grinned. "Are we going in now?"

"No, not yet. The council has a few other matters to speak on." Lukxa took off the white council jacket, tucked it into his bag, and smoothed a hand down his captain's uniform jacket.

His watch continued letting a soft *tick-tick* as they waited for the large council doors to swing open. He scratched at his neck.

The four gold-stitched tally marks at his neck straightened his slouched spine. He needed to act the part of a captain. There was no telling who could walk down the grand halls next. Lukxa would hate to be caught slouching when he so often chided lower ranked knights for doing the same.

The uniform held honor. The black coat was thick enough to keep the morning cold out but woven in such a way as to keep him from ever overheating. Trustworthy in almost any environment. His captain's uniform was completed with a pair of straight fitted black pants and a pair of boots that were comfortable enough for walking and training in while maintaining a regal air. The ruby encrusted sword at his side made little noises as Lukxa paced along the floors. His boots made an occasional *squeak*.

"How much longer are they going to keep us waiting?" Hollis whispered, running her hands down her middle.

Lukxa took in what she had dressed herself in for the meeting. One of his older wool high necks from his training days. The little tally marks on her own neck were subtly hidden by her hair to try and cover the fact she was still dressed in *his* clothing. It was tucked into a maroon skirt that flowed just past her knees. Hollis tapped her feet, the soles of her emerald boots filling the air with an almost annoying *clack* telling of times passing alongside his watch.

"The council is allowed to meet to discuss their own affairs. I'm not privy to everything or allowed to hear everything. We're going last in today's meeting."

"What all do you think they'll ask me? How should I respond?" The words felt aimed at herself, as if she were wondering aloud. A bad habit she had around him. Hollis picked at her skirt, searching for more pieces of lint to leave about in her pile on the grand marble floors.

"Stick to the facts and nothing else. No mention of what you *discovered*. And especially do not mention your lack of sight." His voice took an edge he had not meant to sharpen at her.

Hollis' eyes were wide. The gray powder she'd lined them with as he redressed himself after he returned from fetching her food made her eye color especially rusty. "I know I'm a bit brash and blunt, but I'm far from stupid. No need to worry." She preened. "Though, correct me if I'm wrong, but don't you hold a seat on the council? Technically? Why can't you hear everything?" Her voice sounded more a statement than a question.

Lukxa thought through how to answer the question. "By technical means, *yes*, I do have a seat. As the king and queen are deceased—may their souls rest in the fields of green—Prince Dagen holds the royal chair. Because he's unmarried, the second royal seat goes to me as his chosen right hand, a position he appointed me. I aid him in ruling over the prefecture of Catol as an attendant would a king. Being that the prince is underage, however, his seat is null, as is mine. I sit in merely as a figurehead, giving advice where applicable and listening in."

Hollis cocked her head. "You aren't over all matters of the knights in the kingdom?"

Lukxa shook his head. "Dem, who holds the family seat of Eargile, and I oversee those matters together no matter what. Again, by all means, it is odd that I even have a seat on the council, and again, it is not one that holds true power. Once Prince Dagen ascends to the throne and marries, my position will be given to his chosen queen." Lukxa shrugged his shoulders.

"It feels rather stupid to exclude you just to hold over your head that you aren't *actually* a council member. Honestly, perhaps these meetings should be open door—welcoming anyone who wants to listen." Hollis stretched her arms wide, a rather fed up look on her face.

Lukxa turned his attention back to the tall door, remembering when he used to be just as upset as she was that there were things going on behind these closed doors.

"Can you tell me a bit more about the council? You drilled into my head information on the knights we'll be eating with at dinner, but nothing concerning the council."

Lukxa's face scrunched up. "You do not know who sits on the council?"

Hollis gave him a flat expression. "I know like. . . the representatives from Hozen—outside of the family seat they're appointed by a vote. So, I know the names Collin, Muse, and. . . What, Siphon?"

"*Sypher*." Lukxa corrected.

The large doors swung open before Lukxa had the chance to continue his lecture on why Hollis should better pay attention to those in power over her. They were ushered in by Cane and Kleo, the two other council members from Eargile. Lukxa watched as Hollis looked them both up and down, subtly as she could. Her first time meeting anyone from the council, he gathered.

"Welcome, Tablin Healer, to Catol. I trust that your travels were well and safe?" Muse spoke to Hollis, extending her hands in some sort of kind flourish.

Hollis gave a slight bend of her head toward the woman as she spoke. "It was exceptionally ordinary. I am eager to serve." She straightened, rearranging the bag on her shoulders before righting herself and pressing her cane firmly into the ground. The large bag didn't house everything she'd brought with her, but a majority of her strange odds and ends—an assortment of bottles and jars of herbs. Several books and different kinds of metal pieces. Lukxa wasn't sure if they had any purpose or if Hollis was more like a crow in her knack of lifting shiny and pretty things.

Muse spoke again. "You can hand your bag to Councilor Cane—the man next to you with pale hair." She gestured.

"Oh, I am capable of holding it myself." The smile on Hollis' face was so poised, Lukxa wasn't even sure he was standing next to the same woman. Her ability to pull personality from the air was impressive.

Councilor Collin's deep voice rang out in the room. "It's not to help you hold it—Councilor Cane has to *go through it.*" Collin's voice was gruff as he spoke, a sharp comparison to Muse's compassionate tone.

"I can assure you, the matter has been taken care of," Lukxa spoke. His face tensed up. *Why would someone else have to go through her things?*

Collin grinned. "That's all right, boy. We must make our own search of anyone."

"You do not trust my judgment?" Lukxa quipped, keeping his voice level and raised in pitch.

Collin had a knack for stabbing at him.

"It's not a matter of *not trusting you*; it's a matter of making sure that we're being safe with who we're bringing around Prince Dagen—may the sun shine upon his crown—who, as you know, is. . ." Collin trailed off, not revealing the information of the prince's illness to Hollis yet. It was a matter kept close to chest. Only a few people within the castle walls knew Dagen had returned early from finishing school, the majority of which were in this room. "You've made your assessment of the woman, Sir Lukxa; now it is time we make ours. She must be searched appropriately by a Councilor from Eargile." The man shifted his gaze to Hollis and waved his hand toward Cane and Kleo, who stood impassively at Hollis' side. Cane reached a hand out for Hollis' bag.

Was Collin hoping that Hollis had something of ill-will on her? As if she had brought a weapon to stab the prince first chance she got? Lukxa knew Collin was getting impatient, but this was a bit much.

"*Come*, Collin, Sir Lukxa has said he's gone through it, I trust his judgment," Dem spoke, keeping a lighthearted tone as he leaned toward the balding councilor.

"Procedure is procedure. We should not be making exceptions." Councilor Sophy spoke this time, amber eyes shining underneath her brunette hair. "Shows that we care, wouldn't you agree?" She smiled, showing off most of her teeth. Lukxa was never sure what to make of her smiles.

Hollis raised her free hand. "Oh, it is no imposition to me. You may check me and my things if you must." Hollis handed the bag to Cane, almost dropping it into the pale arms poking out from the white robes. "We have more important details to be speaking about, and I don't want to waste your precious time by delaying the search of myself and things." Hollis turned to Kleo, a mischievous glint in her eye as she grinned at the darker woman. "And you're to search myself?"

"Yes, ma'am," Kleo spoke, giving a slight nod of her head as she stretched an arm out behind her, gesturing for Hollis to step to the side and be searched. Hollis followed, leaving Lukxa to reclaim his seat by Dem. The open chair to Lukxa's right, or any of the four that lay empty, would be where he would direct Hollis to sit once the search by Kleo was finished.

He did not like this.

Cane took Hollis' bag to the bare end of the dark table and pulled items out, placing them in categories of his own design.

Kleo pressed her hands lightly along Hollis' waist where his shirt met her skirt.

"Oh, let me help." Hollis pulled the hem of his high neck shirt free from her skirt.

It flew over her head in one swift motion. Hollis' hair puffed up as the high neck left her, ruining the calming of her curly hair she had done when she applied her makeup earlier.

Lukxa sat, mortified, as Hollis shook the shirt out before dropping it to the ground at Kleo's feet. Every mouth hung agape as Hollis unfastened the clip at the back of her skirts, let it fall, and stepped out of it, leaving her standing in a pale brassiere and underwear. Hollis shook the skirt a few times before turning it in on itself and dropping it to the ground.

She reached for the back of her brassiere—

"I do believe that's enough, madam! What are you *thinking*?" Collin shouted from his seat, eyes blinking as he seemed to refrain from staring at Hollis' figure, something Lukxa found himself looking back to in shock. Lukxa wasn't a stranger to a woman's figure; knights didn't care about gender or propriety when washing up after training or when out on an expedition. There was nothing sexual about it—there was *nothing* sexual about this situation either. But still, it was unnerving.

Hollis laughed. It twinkled in the room. "You mentioned that a search must be conducted. I'm simply allowing you all to make a *thorough* search to be sure that I carry nothing of ill-intent upon me." Hollis' grin was all teeth. "After all, you said it was quite important. Who am I to disagree with safety?"

In a matter of moments where no one seemed able to speak, she was skin.

Lukxa was surprised at how pale the rest of her was, which made the rivers of veins upon her skin stand out all the darker. He was right in his earlier assessment—her figure was not boyish. He couldn't tear his eyes away from her, his mind drinking in every detail that traced her skin, documenting every bruise and scar—of which there were many—every hair and freckle. Every inch of her was made known in his mind.

Kleo's tawny face held a touch of mirth as she did a quick search of Hollis' clothes on her own before instructing Hollis to turn around *slowly*. Hollis complied, chin held level and a single brow raised.

"There's nothing of worry in her belongings," Cane's voice wavered as he placed all the items on the table back into the leather bag with more care than Lukxa would have imagined. Then again, it served as a wonderful distraction from Hollis' naked form.

"Her clothes and person have nothing of note either. Lovely shirt, dear."

Kleo's eyes slid to Lukxa's as she handed his old shirt back to Hollis.

"Thank you. I'm happy that Sir Lukxa's check earlier was correct, but I am happier that you've concluded that yourself. Always best to make sure things are good in your own eyes before trusting the words of others." Hollis gave another coy smile before dressing herself—*slowly* dressing herself. Making a small show to shake out her shirt and skirt before pulling them back on.

Goodness, he had to share a bed with this woman tonight.

No. He would sleep on the settee—even if it didn't fit him.

Gathering up her stockings and shoes, Hollis walked to the large table and promptly sat herself into a chair with more grace than he had ever seen from the woman and delicately pulled the dark stockings up her legs and tied her green shoes.

Hollis cleared her throat. "You said I've been brought for a matter of great importance?" No one else spoke. Some eyes shifted through the room, while others were wide and fixated upon her. Hollis shook her head slightly, giving a *'hello?'* look and motion. "I assume we haven't all day. Do hurry; I have a patient to tend to, if I understood the contract Sir Lukxa presented me, correct? Month to heal them. Perfect condition before Prince Dagen's coronation."

"Yes," Dem spoke, but a pitched cough overtook his words, along with a flush against his dark cheeks. He covered his mouth with his hand and gestured for someone else to finish speaking.

"Miss Healer, have you been informed of the *full* reasoning behind your being here?" Collin asked. His face managed to remain impassive as he locked gazes with Hollis, who refused to lower her chin from its slightly raised position.

Lukxa pressed lightly against her foot, now keeping his gaze locked on Dem.

"I've been informed that there is someone, or *someones*, in the castle in need of Tablinian healing." Hollis' voice shone with confidence. "That's it.

You will have to fill in the rest for me."

With one, extremely foolish action she'd managed to assert herself as the most in-control person in the room.

Dem straightened himself, finally finished with his coughing fit. "In addition to what we're about to tell you, I'm afraid we will be revoking your ability to come and go into the castle as you please. You will be with Sir Lukxa at all times, and when that is not possible, another guard or councilor will be assigned to you. If you're found speaking of anything you learn in this room today there will be. . . unfortunate consequences." Dem sighed and leaned his head side to side.

"What type of consequences?" Hollis asked, leaning her elbows on the table and setting her face in her cupped palms. "I find that, depending on the consequence, one could merely face it and walk away. So tell me, how would you keep me from speaking or walking away?"

Lukxa would burst out laughing if he could. Every other healer that had come through those doors simply shut their mouths the entirety of their stay. Examining Prince Dagen with the least amount of words possible. Besides, it didn't matter what the council threatened Hollis with. Lukxa would do whatever it took to protect her from their grasp.

What had happened to the physicians that failed to heal Dagen?

Lukxa's brows furrowed as he blinked several times. A slight throb formed at the base of his skull.

It is fine. I do not need to remember right now.

Lukxa shook his head, clearing his thoughts to focus on what was happening around him, catching the end of the conversation about the consequences should Hollis fail to abide by their rules.

Hollis' face was pulled tight, slightly green in the cheeks. "That answers my question. I assure you, you have my word that I won't let a single word from my lips. I have nothing to fear or hide by garnering this information. Now, please let's get through this. I don't like keeping someone in need waiting for medical attention. It's rather cruel—wouldn't you agree?"

Several faces in the room turned red.

Councilor Muse picked up the conversation. "Crown Prince Dagen has fallen ill during his time at finishing school. When they weren't able to treat him there, he was brought back to the castle for treatment. This ended up being an unintentional secret we've been keeping. When our physicians couldn't find the root cause, the Tablin Healers Guild sent us *you* to help with your. . . otherworldly sight." Muse' voice held the tone of hopefulness, rising in pitch and uncertainty.

Lukxa would not mention to the council that, technically, Hollis was not a part of the Tablin Healers Guild. He would take solace in the fact that he *was* directed to her by someone within the guild itself, though.

So, technically, I would not be lying about it. Hollis was sent to me by someone in the guild, or I was sent to her. He furrowed his brows as he thought through his lie.

"My goodness." Hollis threw a hand to her chest in mock horror. "I would be *blessed* to use my ancestors' sight to aid the Catolian crown in such a way." She gave a bow of her head. "I assume since I've been checked through quite thoroughly that I may see him right away? No further questions?"

Councilor Aphi spoke up, her voice light and uneasy. Her emotions shone on her golden-olive face, green eyes squinted while her mouth made an awkward shape. "We wouldn't wish to disturb Prince Dagen with you seeing him right away unannounced. Our head physician said he was quite ill this morning. We ask—"

"And keep Prince Dagen waiting for care? I would be remiss letting someone wait, as I've said. I am perfectly fine and ready to see him now."

Collin coughed. "You must be feeling fatigued since entering the castle—"

"Why would I be feeling tired?" She smiled.

Lukxa saw Collin's already pinkish face flush, a tinge of anger in his eyes. "All right. When our meeting is. . . adjourned, we will accompany you to the prince's chambers. There are a few more things to discuss which may take a while. Please feel free to accompany Captain Lukxa to his training.

When it's concluded, you will be sent for so we can escort you to the prince."

Lukxa interrupted him. "I thought we were the final item of today's docket—"

"You're both dismissed." Collin spoke, his words final.

Lukxa sighed and stood up from his chair. "Thank you, councilors. We will hopefully see you shortly." He gave the council a slight bow of his head before extending his arm to Hollis.

"Yes, have a good day Miss—" Muse stopped herself, a hand pressed against her chest. "What should we call you Miss Healer?"

Hollis took up his arm and stood, repeating his nod. "My name is Hollis. *Hollis Avayana*. So pleased to be able to introduce myself."

"Yes." Muse interrupted, nodding her head. "We should have asked your name sooner."

Hollis gave another twinkling laugh. "It would have been polite. Understandably you had other priorities than just being courteous."

"We have business." Collin's voice hinted that he was losing his temper. "In fact, Councilor Shad, your numbers are done, why don't you take this time and show Miss Hollis to a guest room—"

"I've actually requested that she be placed in my apartments," Lukxa spoke. He did his best to ignore the shock on different council member's faces. He swallowed, finding his throat suddenly dry. "It gives me the ability to attend to her needs and those of the prince. That and with Prince Dagen residing in my personal wing of the castle, this means Hollis would not have to traverse far to treat him. No chance of anyone needlessly seeing her outside of her 'visits' to me with her cover. Ease of *security*." That word gave way to Lukxa's actual power in the room.

Collin's face grew hard. While the Council was over matters in the kingdom, *Lukxa* held the final sway in what was done in keeping it safe. Lukxa turned to face Hollis, doing his best at keeping his face stable and not show the range of emotions that bubbled against his insides. He tucked Collin's willingness to throw Shad out of the room into the back of his mind.

Lukxa gave a final nod of his head, wondering what had caused his head to throb so painfully again, before extending a bent arm to escort Hollis from the room.

Hushed words filled the chilled air as the door sank closed once more.

CHAPTER THIRTEEN

HOLLIS

The training yard held the putrid essence of sweat, body odor, and the surrounding pine trees in a horrendous blend. In moderation, the scent was sure to smell manly on a chiseled neck; however, with it being the only smell, it was suffocating.

Hollis lifted her head to try and clear her thoughts of the stench. The few clouds that peppered the sky gave warning to a larger storm that brushed against the horizon, yet the little white wisps did nothing to provide her shade.

She sat on a patch of itchy dry grass as close to the wall as she could, doing her best to keep out of the way of the knights training around her. The blades, no matter how many times Hollis resituated her skirt, kept poking at her legs. How she wished to go sit on the fence or possibly on one of the wooden stages the knights weren't even using.

But no, she had to remain right where Sir Lukxa seated her. She couldn't stray too far from the castle *or* Sir Lukxa's glare. Which was all she'd received from him since leaving the council room. His pale eyes stayed on her form no matter where on the training grounds he went, always smoldering. At least the heat of it kept her from freezing.

The training area surrounding her was just off of the stables and still attached to the castle rearwall. Close enough in location to the gardens that Hollis could spy some lilac bushes blooming—against all odds of the season. If only she could smell them from here too.

A group of younger knights ran past on another lap around the training yard, bringing another fresh wave of stench with them. The cloth at the wrist of the high neck she borrowed from Sir Lukxa wasn't loose enough as to allow her to stretch the cuff and fully cover her mouth and nose. A tragedy of the greatest kind.

Hollis couldn't believe the orders that she was to be monitored at all times.

A scoff broke free in a misty cloud from her mouth. No matter how much it made sense. The council was trying to keep Prince Dagen's—*may the sun shine upon his crown*—illness a secret to keep the people from being worried about losing another ruler and being left with next to no one. So, she was to hide who she was and why she was here.

That didn't mean she had to like being watched at all times. No, not one bit. She'd much rather that the council come clean to the country that Prince Dagen was ill and not off impregnating whoever he could get his hands on in finishing school, or whatever the newspaper said this morning. Prince Dagen was a *busy* man if the numbers were correct. Hollis was astonished at what they printed—and what people believed.

Sir Lukxa's voice rang out over all the clamoring of the field. "Pair off! I want to see everyone working hard. The tournament might be a fortnight away, but that does not mean we can slack off. I expect one of you to win this year in my stead!"

Cheers went up after he spoke. Men and women clapped each other on their leather-clad shoulders, grins etched on their sweating faces.

Hollis knew of a handful of festivals and tournaments that were set to happen in the capital this winter. The main event this year being Prince Dagen's coronation, which would be celebrated with a tournament of knights from not only this kingdom, but a few neighboring countries that

Catol had seemingly good ties with, coming together to fight for the title of Winter Champion. . . Or something.

Hollis never attended any of the festivals in Catol. She found herself quite content to stay in Hozen during any large events. Or, technically, staying *away* from large events. Large crowds were a pain when you stood out in people's minds as some magical lunatic. Plus, the absolute cacophony of threads that came with the masses kept her from attending anything major. They did lend the possibility of earning good coin, though. Hollis could make a fortune operating some sort of kooky booth selling snake oil and swearing it was something beneficial.

"Who is that? The woman over there against the wall?" A whisper came from her left. A short, dark-haired knight.

"She's so exotic." His partner answered. "Is that a training shirt? Is she a knight?"

Another knight chimed in, doing nothing to keep her voice down. "I heard Sir Lukxa is courting her. If you look closely at the neck, it belongs to *his training group from the academy.* Jamison saw her in the hall earlier and she moved her hair some. It was *definitely* there."

Hollis let her eyes slide towards them, catching how their movements seemed lacking and unrehearsed. Her little side-eye turned to a glower and the knights stopped looking her way.

The moment Sir Lukxa was able, Hollis would make him send someone to get her a few sweaters that wouldn't mark her as his. Oh wait, no maybe she liked that?

A shadow of a man with long hair loomed over her, pulling her attention skyward.

"Hello there, captain." Hollis smiled up at Sir Lukxa.

Sir Lukxa stood above her. He grabbed at the hem of his shirt to wipe at his face, giving her a split second to marvel at his toned middle. "Training will last another hour or so. Are you doing all right?" He pulled his hair high in a tied knot upon his head. More beads of sweat formed upon his forehead

before dripping down his neck and disappearing under the high collar of his own shirt. She traced the moisture rather contently. He fared far better than most of the knights, who looked like puddles of people.

Hollis batted her eyelashes a few times. "I'll be fine, thank you."

Sir Lukxa said nothing in response, his face cold and collected as he walked back to the center of the training yard.

Hollis let her attention drift inward. Pulling at her magic and that of the world around her, trying to assess what was going on so she could even hope to snap whatever was restraining her. Her sight felt closer to the surface the more she pulled at it, coaxing it out. Something lay over her sight like a sheet of ice on a lake.

If only she could crack it.

A sharp pain in her chest sent her head dropping backward against the castle wall. Her head throbbed as it made contact with the stone. Deep breaths pushed against her ribs.

Her hands clawed at the grass, pulling it up by the roots as she steadied her breaths and dropped her head to her chest.

The terror of her magic never returning brewed under the surface of her control. She wouldn't relent to it, she wouldn't give it control. Her magic would return.

It had to.

Another shadow passed overhead. She could see Sir Lukxa standing across the yard. Whoever tried garnering her attention was not worthy of her attentions right now. So she ignored them.

The shadow gave a stern *ahem*.

Councilor Shad stood by her side. His mousy hair sat in waves upon his head, framing his round golden glasses, green eyes, and pale—but chill flushed—cheeks. The white councilor's robe drifted open in the breeze, pressing against his thin frame and revealing a gray high neck tucked into a pair of fitted pants beneath them.

"There's been a change of plans. You'll see Prince Dagen now and

reconvene with Sir Lukxa later." Councilor Shad's voice was warm honey.

"Are you sure?" Hollis looked around the training yard. No one was paying Hollis or Councilor Shad any attention.

Sir Lukxa spoke with a small group. His face was pulled tight with focus as he swung his practice blade about, and the knights copied him as he went.

Councilor Shad grimaced. "Yes, you are to see the prince now—*not keep him waiting* as you said?"

Hollis nodded. "I'll let Sir Lukxa know—"

Councilor Shad raised a hand, cutting her off. "I've already sent a page to inform him of this change. Now, I'm to bring you right away. Please come with me." He extended a slender hand down and beckoned for her to join him.

Hollis held back a grimace of her own and set her hand in his. The councilor was right. She wouldn't want to bother Sir Lukxa too greatly as he worked. While she could see lines of exhaustion on Sir Lukxa's face, she could see a strong glint of happiness in his eyes as he moved about. Hollis spied a young girl in a page's uniform standing on the other side of the fence, bouncing on her heels.

Councilor Shad's hand was warm against her palm, almost burning in a sense. It pulled at her middle. Her brows knit together as he tugged her up with more strength than she would have guessed from how he appeared his robes and fitted clothing.

Hidden strength. *Sexy and dangerous.*

Councilor Shad settled her hand in the crook of his elbow and guided her along the wall towards the servant's door. He stood a good half-head taller than Hollis.

Entering the castle again put a slight pressure on her eyes, stopping her for several seconds in the blistering kitchens, which smelled of stew and bread.

Bodies bustled throughout the area. The sound of chopping, tools hitting the sides of bowls, and a great oven roaring was all too much for her mind to process.

The councilor continued to lead Hollis throughout the castle—
seemingly the long way around—to the prince's chambers. The whole
time, Councilor Shad's unnaturally warm hand kept hers tightly in place
upon his elbow.

A person shouldn't be this warm.

"Are you all right, Healer Hollis?" Councilor Shad's face was closer to
her own now, tilted to rest fully in her sight.

His dashing facade were almost enough to pull a blush to her face—but
she was sleeping in the same bed as Sir Lukxa. There was no besting that man
in anything he did—this was a decided fact.

Oh. That sounded quite something.

Hollis reminded herself of her actions the night before. The looks
the captain had given her as she drank from his glass. The bobbing of his
throat and dilation of his eyes. That should have been enough to keep
her warm this morning.

No one had ever looked at Hollis in such a manner. Usually the ones
she got were of fascination for her sight or shock from the words that slipped
out of her mouth. And while she'd been complimented on her appearance
numerous times in her life, none of the pretty words went beyond the surface
of knowing her. And once anyone paying her an ounce of attention heard
her speak, the fevered gazes reverted to one of the previous group.

Sir Lukxa had heard her speak nonsense and still had the ability to lay
his eyes upon her as though he were *starving.*

Hollis liked that.

Hollis put a smile on her face, remembering that Councilor Shad had
asked her a question, *if she was all right.* "I'm just taking it all in; I'm sorry."
The desire to ask Councilor Shad if *he* was all right burnt away in her mind.
Perhaps he was feverish? It would explain the warmth under his skin.

The expression on his face was impassive, but like her magic, something
lay under the surface. *Curiosity?*

"I want to let you know that if there's anything at all bothering you, do

feel free to let me know. I'll do my best to help you in whatever way I can. I'm quite useful." Councilor Shad smiled, showing off a set of perfect teeth.

"Thank you, councilor." Hollis smiled up at him. "I'll be sure to remember that. Now, which way to the prince's chambers from here? I'm afraid I do not know my way around."

"Ah, yes. You haven't been given a proper tour. I can fix that on our way." He slowed his pace as he walked her out of the hall from the kitchen and gestured with his free hand. "Past the kitchens, this wing belongs to the staff. If you ever have a need for a councilor or servant, they'll be this way. Servants closer to the front entries, Councilors on the floor above. The area was first constructed during King Haven's reign. Renovations have happened a few times since to accommodate the growing staff and make the interior more comfortable with the changing seasons." He turned and peered down at her, stopping their walking. "I should make mention that, during the day, the councilors work in their own offices. Mine resides inside the library.

"I'll show you there later so if you ever have questions you know where to find me—or us. I have a full staff working there most of the day. But if you're in search of a specific book it'd be me you'd want to ask. I've read just about every single one in this castle. It never hurts to consult a tome before someone ends up in a tomb, you know. That's what the lead healers in the clinic always spout to younger healers who are too stubborn to ask for help." He nodded to himself and continued strolling her down the halls.

Hollis wasn't going to interrupt his tour and tell him Sir Lukxa had already covered much of this area in the castle. The wandering thought of just how *urgently* he needed to pull her away to see the prince drifted in and out of her thoughts between Councilor Shad's storytelling covering the history and makeup of the castle.

They walked through a pool of sunlight let in by one of the grand windows lining the hall. It breathed some life into her skin as she trudged alongside Councilor Shad. Doing her best to act like she was paying attention to his words as she felt his eyes on her skin once more.

Her cane caught on a small bump in the carpet. A small yelp burst from her chest and she stumbled. Councilor Shad turned and caught her, holding her body up against his arms. She could smell a type of lemongrass soap on his skin and clothes. Clearly he enjoyed the southernmost exports from Tablin. A glowy dew rested on his skin. His hair was perfectly styled, jaw shaved. It was a nice jawline.

"Careful, healer. I'm taking you to fix someone. I cannot have you waltzing into the prince's chambers injured, now can I?" He smiled and righted her on her feet. "Are you all right?" His teeth were perfect.

Hollis nodded and continued onward.

They soon arrived in a familiar hallway housing Sir Lukxa's and the prince's chambers. The scent of unopened rooms somehow filled the whole hallway this afternoon. Perhaps opening some of the thick curtains would give aid to the stagnant feeling.

"Is there anything from your things that you require from Captain Luxka's apartments?" Councilor Shad paused and nodded at Sir Lukxa's door.

Hollis pondered on it a long moment, wondering what all she might need to pull off her little game with the Council. "Just a few things; I'll grab them," she said quickly.

"No problem. Let's gather them promptly." He released her hand to pull a key from his pocket and unlocked the door. He gestured for her to enter the room before following after her himself. It was intriguing how the councilor had a key to Sir Lukxa's room. . . perhaps that was standard. Maybe councilors had keys to every room?

The door sank closed behind them.

"Excu—" Hollis began.

"Open doors invite trouble. Surely you know this? It's an old Tablin saying." His face wore an impassive expression, his head tilted slightly backward. The green of Councilor Shad's eyes was striking in the low light of the room.

The fireplace was barren, unlit during the afternoon. Chill air flitted about, brushing against the raised hairs on her arms.

He raised a brow. "Are you going to gather your things?"

"Yes." She spoke quickly and set about rummaging through her bag. Several long moments passed.

"How do you hope to heal him?"

Hollis paused, a jar of ribbons held fast in her hand. "What?"

Councilor Shad took a step closer to her. "How do you hope to heal the prince? I assume you'll use your Tablin sight, but I'm curious if you're trained in any other methods of healing?" His gaze was steady, but not unkind. "Sorry—coming from the universities in Rex we spend a lot of time going through the sciences of medicine. They never touched on Tablin magic, which is a shame. It's so interesting." His voice took on a silken quality.

Hollis swallowed. "Healing depends on the person. Sometimes I can heal without needing my sight. Other times I use it in conjunction with whatever I find necessary. So I guess it all. . . depends."

He nodded, no words passing his lips outside of his *humm*ing.

Hollis turned her attentions back to her bag. She grabbed a few random matches and small jars of herbs, along with Sir Lukxa's rose salve, and tucked them into a small cloth bag.

"Is that all?" Councilor Shad stood unmoving, leaning against a wall by the door. She couldn't read him; couldn't garner what his mind was doing, and it infuriated her.

Not being able to read someone was annoying. At times, Hollis could get a read on a person by the tension in their threads. Happy people often had relaxed threads in their face, anger pulled them taught. Disgust or annoyance had threads fraying and bunching in an amusing manner.

Hollis patted the glass jar she picked up. Dried mint leaves bounced around as she added them to the ever growing bag. "Until I know for certain what ails him, I think these will do. They generally help."

Councilor Shad smiled, showing off his teeth. Her insides squirmed like

prey being stared down by some sort of predator. She was unsure of what type of consumption his gaze meant.

He licked his lips before speaking. "Wonderful. Then I think it's time we go meet Prince Dagen." His hand curled around the handle of the door before pausing. "Just remember, do not show you've nothing in your palms, healer."

CHAPTER FOURTEEN

HOLLIS

The walk down the hallway and to the prince's chambers was tense. Once more Councilor Shad had settled Hollis' hand into the crook of his arm while he led the way.

They turned the corner and three more councilors came into sight.

Councilor Muse had changed into what Hollis assumed was a more casual attire of a floor-length yellow skirt, a white blouse tucked into the waist, and a golden pin sitting over her heart. She stood wagging her finger at the man next to her.

Councilor Collin was dressed in a fitted pair of black pants and a yellow linen shirt. Contrary to her initial opinion, he wasn't fat; he was built with huge muscles upon his bones. Earlier, the white councilor's uniform had made him resemble an uncooked potato more than a man. It seemed several councilors had something to reveal.

And finally, Councilor Sophy wore a set of clothing under her councilor's uniform similar to Councilor Shad's.

"I've brought her," Councilor Shad announced as they came upon the party.

"Yes, we can see that. Doesn't take years of fancy schooling to find the obvious, dear." Muse chuckled. "So nice to see you again Miss Hollis. We're eager for your visit with the prince. Everyone, behave yourselves." After gracing Hollis with a warm smile, Muse moved to open the door.

"Do remember that nothing in this room reaches the ears of outsiders." Councilor Collin spoke with a chilling threat to his voice. Hollis could have sworn he'd called her something vulgar under his breath, but being that she wasn't entirely sure, she let it slide. No need to dig herself deeper into someone's bad side.

"Oh, calm down. I'm sure Miss Hollis knows what she's doing. We have no reason to fear her twittering our secrets. She's no reason to." Councilor Muse waved a hand at her council-mate and opened the door.

The moment an inch of light breached the hallway the sound of vomiting filled their ears.

The councilors recoiled before righting themselves.

"It seems he isn't feeling the best—perhaps we should come back later?" Councilor Collin said, his face tinged with green.

"Oh, but it's in the moments of illness that examinations are most important," Hollis responded, trying to give her voice the air of confidence.

No one moved.

Ladies first. She swallowed, walked past everyone, and entered the room.

The curse was obvious now as Hollis stepped past the threshold. It coiled around her neck far greater than it had when she first entered Prince Dagen's room. The darkness seemed to revel in the presence of outsiders. With each person that followed behind her, the putrid miasma grew thicker in her lungs. Futile attempts of lavender wafted in the air, but it couldn't cover the stench of bodily fluids and the ever-present curse.

Prince Dagen sat in his bed with an ornate iron bucket on his lap. He met her gaze with a mischievous glint before loudly vomiting into the bucket once more. A grimace pulled on his face as the rest of the Council members flooded in behind her. The prince's brows twisted together for a moment; he seemed like he was in pain. His throat bobbed as he swallowed and pulled a mask of emotions on his face.

"Hello, Prince Dagen." Hollis grabbed the hem of her skirt and sank into a low curtsey—or her best attempt at one. "My name is Hollis Avayana. I'm a Tablin healer from your prefecture of Hozen, sent by the Tablin Healers Guild."

"*Audacity*," someone mumbled behind her. Another few whispers of *his prefecture* filled her ears.

A small peal of thunder sounded outside.

The sun still shone light in through the window. Hollis wondered how long that would last.

A storm was the last thing she needed today. She had hoped the clouds she'd glimpsed far upon the horizon earlier in the day would stay that way. A quick peek out the window proved that they had slunk closer, hanging low and dark in the sky. A sharp contrast to the few splotches of blue remaining.

The rest of the room was just as ornate as it was when she left it earlier. Fresh bundles of flowers sat in a few of the vases. The room had grown warmer, likely heating with the rising day.

"Welcome to Catol, Healer Hollis. I'm pleased to meet you. I wish it were under better circumstances. This is the best welcome I can give you." Prince Dagen nodded his head, apparently doing his best to hold back a smile. He was enjoying this far too much.

"As you can see, Healer Hollis, the boy is quite ill." Councilor Collin spoke pointedly.

"The prince," Hollis chided, albeit with a light tone. "Yes, you told me he was ill. I was prepared for something much worse than this." She walked over to his bedside, arms swinging at her side. She set her bag on the floor beside Prince Dagen's bedside. It landed with a large *thunk*, and Hollis prayed she hadn't broken anything inside it.

"What do you mean, worse than this? The boy—*prince* is quite ill. And has been for months. No other healer or man of science has been able to figure out what was wrong with him." Councilor Collin spoke the words loud and true, his spine straightening and chest puffing with every word.

Hollis didn't like that. If he were a part of whatever group was cursing the prince, he was making his role far too obvious. That was something Sir Lukxa would think. He would listen for little details in people's voices and watch how they moved. Hollis would emulate him to better report what happened here. If he had his suspicions about the council, Hollis would either put them to rest or bring them to light.

Do not show your palms. Councilor Shad's words trickled in her mind, almost as if he whispered in her ear.

"Yes, but they weren't a Tablin healer." A few of the councilors glared at Councilor Shad as he spoke.

Hollis gave a bright smile. "It's true. I'm much more skilled in the areas of the world than they could hope to be—speaking with modesty of course. I trust I will be allowed to start my examination now?" She turned her gaze in all directions of the room.

"You may." Prince Dagen spoke.

"Anything you do to the prince must go through us first." Councilor Sophy's voice was soft in timbre, but her amber gaze was sharp.

"I'm afraid, councilors, that I've already given her permission. And as the prince, I believe my word is law?" Prince Dagen spoke, his tone harsher than it had been earlier.

Councilor Sophy drew back as if wounded. "Apologies, Prince Dagen." She bowed her head.

Prince Dagen's face went green again as he puffed out his cheeks and vomited into the bucket once more.

Subtly peering over his shoulder, Hollis found it wasn't filled with vomit at all. Merely a mix of water and. . . vegetables? Moving it around in his hands to cause the contents inside to splash as if he was truly vomiting. *Clever.* Oh, she *liked* this boy.

Prince Dagen bent his head toward the group. "I would appreciate haste, Lady Healer Hollis." He set the bucket on the ground beside his bed.

She rolled her neck, *cracking* it a few times, and set about trailing her hands over Prince Dagen's body as she had done before.

Magic screamed from inside her core, it begged to be let out and be made useful. Hollis wished she could pull upon it and truly find the root of whatever was making him ill.

Continuing on with a normal physical exam seemed fruitless, but it was something to do while she thought about what to tell the councilors. She listened to Prince Dagen's heart and lungs, tapped and pulled at his joints.

An idea formed in her mind. "Now, you mentioned you've been vomiting quite a deal recently?"

Prince Dagen nodded his head, still wearing the expression of someone in pain. "Yes, quite so."

Hollis *hummed* and nodded in response. "May I see it?" She could hear shifting bodies behind her.

Prince Dagen bent and retrieved the pot from his bedside. She quickly took the cold iron pot in her hands, swirling it around.

She stuck her head into the opening of it and made as exaggerated an inhale as she could. The vegetables carried a delightful smell. The sudden craving for stew grew deep in her stomach.

Faint clamoring came from behind. "*I'm going to be sick.*"

Excellent.

"Are you quite finished yet? I thought Tablin healers had some sort of magic where they could heal someone in an instant and be done with it." Councilor Collin gagged as he spoke.

"Yes, I just wanted to be sure of my findings before I said anything." Why was she speaking? Hollis had no ideas at all but solidified that she did.

Oh, *think, think, think.*

No. Now *wasn't* the time to pause and think; she had to speak, speak, *speak.* "Prince Dagen. . . seems to have caught an interesting variation of the Tablin flu. The stiffness of his joints, the smell of his vomit. Yes, it all makes

sense." All the faces around her drew blank.

That could have been worse. At least this is a real illness.

"The. . . *Tablin* flu? How would he have caught that?" Councilor Sophy asked, her fingers tapping at her berry-toned lips. The woman seemed sharp as a knife

Hollis tried coming up with a quick answer.

"Ah, I wonder why no one had thought of that before." Councilor Shad clasped his hands together. "It all makes sense now." He raised a brow in her direction. What was he trying to do, will her to speak? Was he. . . backing her up? She didn't know how to feel with this hot and cold dynamic of his.

"How is it that he's the only one sick with it? If childhood reminds me of anything, it's that the flu transferred quite terribly. Shouldn't more of us have it?" Councilor Muse asked, taking a small step backward and covering her mouth and nose slightly.

"Well," Hollis started, "it could be that you're healthy enough to have not caught it or you've been exposed to it in some fashion. You, my prince, may not have ever been exposed. Or you've recently come into contact with someone who carried a newer strand of the illness."

"I'll have to think back. I've been sick so long that it's hard to remember those things in exact detail." Prince Dagen touched his forehead and swayed slightly—his dedication to the ruse was truly admirable.

"So, if it is the Tablin flu, what treatment will he need?" Councilor Collin asked.

"Due to the magical nature of the illness, he'll need to be attended by a Tablin healer until the sickness is properly purged. His treatment will include several days of repeated healing sessions with breaks in between."

"I agree. All my research during university on the topic of contagious illnesses aligns with what she has said. And you are most welcome to study in the library to find if anyone says differently." Councilor Shad clapped a hand onto her shoulder, giving it a light squeeze.

Councilor Collin stepped forward, standing rather close to Hollis, as he

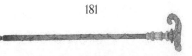

nodded his head, both hands behind his back. "If you'll excuse me, I have a meeting I need to attend to, but do carry on. I assume you'll be able to start treatment on him right away?"

"Certainly. I'll need time to gather a few supplies, but that should only take a day or two. Unless I need something imported." Hollis spoke, her voice calm and collected.

"Aren't we lucky to have found you, *Healer Hollis*?" Councilor Collin whispered through his teeth. "Prince Dagen should be healed just in time for his coronation next month." She could smell his stale breath.

"Yes," Hollis' voice took on a confident edge. "He will be healed in time to wear his crown as King."

CHAPTER FİFTEEN

LUKXA

T he familiar walls of the mess hall reverberated the endless chatter from the occupants.

Lukxa's back quivered with the tension as he guided Hollis into the mess halls. He had yet to relax after introducing Hollis to the council. The looks from those on the council that *knew his nature* were seared into his mind. His training session did nothing to release his nerves either. Everyone in the yard had buzzed with gossip concerning the woman there watching them, wondering who she was, and what her attachment to Lukxa was.

Questions were hurled at him. He did his best to evade them with quick clipped answers to return to training.

And his own thinking.

Goodness. Lukxa was running out of time.

And now he was thrust into another unknown.

The ruse of Hollis being inside the castle as a visiting friend to Lukxa and a healer for the tournament needed to be made known before her presence roused any suspicions amongst anyone else in the castle.

The firelight flickered overhead as a small draft from the door brushed by. The lanterns dangled a few feet down from the ceiling from brass chains. They were lit before every meal by an apprentice in the kitchens standing on the tables, who then would wash the wood top down and set out the necessary plates and bowls and cups.

Occasionally the mess hall tables were decorated with bouquets of flowers and greenery from the ever blooming gardens. Today, a few white flowers peppered the fifteen or so long tables. Each table seated ten persons, give or take if it had a bench or chairs. And every meal saw a few people who pulled chairs from the tables over to the tall iron-work windows that lined the far walls, enjoying conversation as they ate.

Lukxa chose a bench table toward the center of the room. It gave them the best chance of being seen by the other occupants. And that was what they wanted now: for her to be seen.

Lukxa could name every face belonging to a knight that sat in the room. In fact, he'd spent the time between his midday training and the evening meal drilling Hollis with the photos of each knight in the castle. He had even told her a handful of stories about each knight. He mainly focused on the knights Lukxa had personally worked with in Eargile, should any come round and speak with him and Hollis. Only a handful of knights that had been in the same group as him currently served at the castle. Perhaps ten? Hopefully none would be here tonight. None came into vision as he studied the room again.

Hollis had taken fast to the challenge. Her memory was something for him to marvel at.

"Tell us how you and Captain Lukxa met," Wilfrin asked from across the table. The young man grinned and nodded to the brunette woman who quickly took up the empty spot on Wilfrin's side of the bench.

Lukxa took a quick glance around him, eyes wide, not having realized that all the other spots beside himself and Hollis had been taken already. Lukxa hadn't even taken a bite of his dinner and Hollis was already starting to weave a story to life for a now full table.

Better than her stripping naked in front of everyone.

Oh goodness, the images flooded back. He could feel her left side pressed against him, he knew the crescent line of freckles that lined her left hip.

Think of something else.

He could feel a flush creeping up his neck. His throat refused to swallow. The cup of water he grabbed slowly trickled down his throat.

Wilfrin sat across from Lukxa, grinning at every story Hollis told. The woman at his side blinked sweetly at Wilfrin, who would then openly return her affectionate gaze. An endearing sight. To Lukxa's left sat Squire Morgan. Morgan's sharp jaw and red hair was flecked with dirt—he had gotten into another minor scrape at training, it would seem. To Wilfrin's other side, and directly across from Morgan, sat Councilor Dem—freed from his councilor's uniform. Beside Dem sat a blonde woman, who Lukxa guessed worked in the laundering rooms by the state of her red chapped hands.

At the other end of the far table sat a few knights who Lukxa had seldom more than a few interactions with. He did not train with them in Eargile, nor did he work with them inside the castle walls. They seemingly ignored the rest of the table and ate their food at an adequate pace.

Hollis sat to his right, her body situated as close to Lukxa's on the bench as possible. On her far side—

"Councilor Shad, I did not see you sit down. My apologies." Lukxa pushed a smile on his face as the mousy haired councilor turned and gave Lukxa a sharp grin of his own.

"It's quite all right, Captain Lukxa. Your friend Hollis has been keeping us all company while you've been off in your own little world." Councilor Shad gave Lukxa a quick tilt of the head before returning his attention to Hollis, who, now that she was no longer interrupted, continued spinning the story that she and Lukxa had come up with.

"As I was saying, before you two rudely interrupted me," Hollis gave Lukxa a playful jab to the ribs with her elbow. "Lukxa and I met in Eargile. I trained as a healer there for several weeks. Lukxa seemed to find his way into the infirmary quite often—but not for what you would think. No, this man would absolutely *pulverize* his sparring partners and then personally carry them to the clinic." Each of Hollis' words were carefully punctuated. She then took a small bite of her food, her table manners impeccable.

Lukxa jumped in, hoping to add in the perfect amount of friendly flavor. "Pulverize is a strong word, Hollis." He butted his shoulder against hers as he took another long drag of water to wet his throat. "Perhaps your healing skills were not as good then as they are now. You simply thought I tore them apart." He picked up a piece of his own pheasant with his fork and tore off a bit of meat with his teeth. It wasn't terrible tasting by any sense of the means, but it had grown slightly dry while he'd ignored it.

Most all the plates and bowls surrounding the settings of Lukxa's table-mates were half eaten. People slowly picked at their food as they conversed with Hollis.

Lukxa took in the room again as he swallowed down the piece of dry bird with some water. Now that his mind was more present, he could smell the char-roasted birds that sat on most plates in the hall, and a rich fatty smell from the gravy served with it.

Oh, there was gravy to save his throat from the dry bird. He quickly took another bite, wiping the piece around in the thickened sauce and stabbing a few carrot coins on his fork for good measure.

"Don't underestimate your strength. I still don't know if Lukxa was just showing off to prove he wasn't someone to be messed with, or if he just liked presenting me with bloodied knights to heal. It kept me busy, that is for certain." Hollis gave another bright smile.

Everyone around at the table laughed as they fed off her story.

Dem made a large show as he kicked Lukxa's leg underneath the table. His laugh snuffed out the other occupants' voices as Dem managed to speak through bouts of laughter. "I remember you telling me that you were the strongest in your training unit!" Thankfully, this was a true statement in the story. "To think all your hard work was to impress a girl. I would do the same in your shoes, though. Healer Hollis, you are quite a *sight* to take in." Dem's insinuations of romance between Lukxa and Hollis dropped several jaws at the table. Or perhaps it was the subtle reference to Hollis' stunt in the council room that Lukxa was doing his best to push to the back of his mind as her body was snuggled up to his side. Not that anyone else at the table knew of that, aside from Councilor Shad. No, the glint in his eyes proved he *fondly* remembered.

"Why haven't you been able to visit the captain since his post here? It sounds like you two are quite close." The woman at Wilfrin's side gave a modest smile. Wilfrin nodded at her as she finished asking her question. Clearly pleased she had inserted herself into the conversation.

Hollis rolled her eyes. "It's been a nightmare trying to find a time we were both free. Lukxa loves to keep himself busy, and it seems like I go out to a new remote village to work the clinics just before his letters arrive. So, we finally planned ahead." She spread her fingers out on the table, drumming them. "I got permission from the guild to be transferred to a nearby clinic for the duration of tournament plans and fulfillment. I may play at being his personal healer again—if anyone can land a scratch on him." Again she turned up at Lukxa, a wide grin on her face. "Hopefully he doesn't drop any more dead birds at me, or I'll never end up leaving."

Lukxa swallowed, then put a grin on his own face and bent his head down until their noses almost touched. "Now would that be such a bad thing?" His voice rumbled, low and breathy.

The flush that overtook Hollis' face burned brighter than the lanterns above them.

Before he could open his mouth a hand clapped Lukxa on the shoulder. "Goodness gracious, boy! Save that for your private times together." Again, Councilor Dem gave Lukxa a wolfish grin as he sat back down, having reached over the table to pat him.

Lukxa was going to punch him the first chance he got in their next training session.

"Councilor Dem, why are we beating up on our good captain?" A feminine voice to Lukxa's left drew his attention. Standing at the edge of the table was a knight Lukxa *had* trained with in Eargile, Lydia Fowl. When had she arrived in the dining hall?

"Lydia! Too bad you couldn't sit with us tonight," Wilfrin spoke, a wild grin on his face. "Captain Lukxa is introducing us to his good friend, Hollis. Maybe you knew her, too? You and Captain Lukxa were training together in Eargile, right?" Wilfrin gestured to Hollis as he spoke.

Hollis' face had mostly returned to its normal coloring, save a light bit of flushing that covered her neck and behind her ears. Hollis scratched her hand through her hair and stole a sideways glance at himself. Her lips trembled as she met his gaze and quickly turned her face away.

Lukxa furrowed his brows.

"You were at the knights academy with us? As a knight?" Lydia asked. She leaned to one side, cocking her hip out as she crossed her arms. Confusion was drawn on her face.

A knight from another table turned around to join the conversation— also someone Lukxa had trained with in Eargile. And then *another* body or three went silent and narrowed in on their conversation.

Why is everyone so interested in our conversation all of the sudden? When did they all get here?

"No," Hollis answered. Her voice chimed as she smiled up at the woman. "I was there as an intern with the Tablin Healers Guild for a handful of weeks during Lukxa's third year. We stayed in contact all these years." Hollis mused her lower lip with her tongue before smiling again.

Somehow, Hollis gave off the air of being entirely comfortable and confident.

"Uh-huh," Lydia sighed. Her eyes narrowed in on Hollis. "Is that the year when Ethan cut off three of Jacob's fingers during a mock trial?"

Lukxa quickly tapped three times against Hollis' foot under the table. *False.* He didn't feel good about Lydia's attempts to catch himself and Hollis in a lie.

Hollis shook her head. "I don't recall that happening in my time there, doesn't mean it didn't happen though." Lukxa gave a patterned tap of twos and fours on her foot. "I remember helping the lead healers with the surgery on, who was it, Lukxa? Eydis Sycle. Her appendix ruptured in the middle of doing. . ." Hollis trailed off. Like she was racking her brain for the false memory. ". . . Something to do with training. But she waited the rest of the day before coming to us. She was almost septic at that point, I swear." Hollis delivered a convincing version of the story. She tucked her chin down as she raised her brows and stared at everyone sitting at the table who was paying attention to their conversation.

"Indeed," Lukxa followed her up. "I remember you telling me about it when we went down to Arni's pub that weekend for our free weekend from training."

Lydia stomped her foot and snapped her fingers. "That's where you snuck off to!" Her eyes were wide in realization. "Everyone else in the company helped with Eydis' chores that weekend except *you.*" Lydia turned her gaze back to Hollis, now significantly softer. "I'm sorry I didn't remember you right away. I can see you now, in the clinic. Always smiling, right? You relocated my middle finger, like, three times." Lydia gave Hollis an awkward smile.

False memories were surprisingly easy to implant. Lukxa would have to try this more often.

Hollis laughed. "I likely did, yeah. And, it's no worries if you didn't remember me right away. You had to focus on your job, and I mine. The healers on rotation from the guild didn't much interact with the knights. We're easily forgotten." Hollis leaned back against Lukxa, making a show of their 'connection'. "It's a wonder Lukxa and I hit it off as we did!" Another smile, another nudge against his person. Hollis rested a hand on his bicep before she turned and drank more water.

"That's cute. I'm happy you two worked out in the end. Nice to see little flings grow into something more. I'll see the lot of you at evening training tonight." Lydia pointed to the knights at the table and barked a laugh before continuing back on her way to her own table. Lukxa could see her turn over her shoulder and point in their direction as she spoke with the occupants sitting there.

That was all right. Rumors could be faced.

Conversation swelled once more. Stories of Lukxa and Hollis' time at the academy, hearing tales of Dem's time serving as a teacher, and other conversational odds and ends flowed from mouths between stolen bites of food.

The lights in the room grew dim, and the flames flickering as their supply of oil dwindled. Hollis and himself would only need to stay a bit longer before retiring—well, Hollis would. Lukxa still had evening training. If the storms could hold off a little while longer. The thunder that sounded in the late afternoon had ceased an hour before.

Once training was finished it would finally allow Lukxa a sense of privacy to unload the stress of his day. Of course, he would have to wait for *actual* privacy until Hollis slept. Though her being asleep had not stopped her the night they had discussed Dagen's curse. No, instead she drank half his gin and had him feeling emotions he was not quite prepared to feel toward someone.

He trailed his gaze down toward her.

Hollis looked back up at him through her lashes, she held his gaze this time instead of looking away. She sucked in her lower lip with tongue and teeth.

Lukxa could feel his lips part as he bent to whisper in her ear. "Is everything all right, Hollis?" His voice spoke deep and graveled from his chest.

Hollis' spine tensed as she turned to whisper back.

"Excuse me. You said you're with the Tablin Healers' Guild, is that right?" Another knight stood at the edge of the table.

Was his table to receive every spare knight in the room this night?

"Yes," Hollis answered.

The knight mused his lips. "You see, I have this ache deep in my arm and—"

"She is not working" Lukxa cut him off. "I know it is a tempting ask, but you can see someone at the clinic here to deal with your pains." He gave the man a pointed glare.

The man opened his mouth to speak again. "But—"

"*No*. Hollis is not here to be some magical healer for everyone. She is here. . . as my companion." Lukxa settled an arm about her waist, pulling her closer to him on the bench.

The man flushed. "Right. I'm sorry." He nodded his head several times before scurrying off.

Councilor Shad wiped at his mouth with a napkin before he folded it on the table beside his empty plate and drank the rest of his water. "I think I'll be getting back to my books this evening." He bent his head at everyone as he stood and stepped around the bench.

"Before you go, Councilor Shad." Hollis raised a hand at him.

"Yes?" Shad bent his arms on the free edge of the table where he had sat and leaned down to eye-level with Hollis. He gave her a smile that rivaled a slivered moon.

Hollis let out a breathy sound before she spoke. "I'm wanting to pay a visit to the library soon. Is there a specific time I should do so?"

Councilor Shad cocked his head as he continued to grin at Hollis which read like he wanted to eat her alive. "Send me a note, name the time, and I will be sure to have my doors open to you." With that, he straightened his spine, gave a light pat to the back of Hollis' shoulder, and left the hall.

"I'd be careful, Captain Lukxa. It seems like others here want to *make friends* with our Hollis here." Wilfrin laughed as he tore off a large chunk of meat from his plate and ate it.

Lukxa's gut burned as he pushed a smile onto his face again. "No worries, Wilfrin. What you should be worried about is the fact you have not introduced us to your lovely friend." Lukxa steered the conversation away from himself and Hollis. As he did the rest of the evening meal.

Lukxa had woven Hollis into everyone's minds as a natural thing to have at his side here in the castle for the next several weeks. They spoke of vague plans they made on Lukxa's next day off in the calendar, as well as notes that she would likely be busied away as she worked in a nearby clinic in the Citadel. The perfect cover to have her seen seldomly in the castle.

If Lukxa were ever asked about Hollis' whereabouts, he would claim she was off working, and when she was seen around him, it was obvious that she was off duty and chose to spend her time stitched to his side.

Lukxa's jaw quivered as he continued listening in on the conversations around him. The more he thought about it, the more the idea of having Hollis permanently within reach sullied his mind.

CHAPTER SIXTEEN

HOLLIS

Thunder rolled off the walls of the castle. From inside Sir Lukxa's baths it hid itself into every crack of the stone wall. His baths were simple, neat and orderly enough for belonging to a knight—a captain of knights. All Hollis could find truly interesting was the large, copper soaking tub near the far wall with a sitting window. A curtain covered the alcove from the outside world, giving privacy and darkness within the room.

She pulled the window's curtain aside. A shred of light was more important than supposed privacy. Sir Lukxa's apartments were three floors up. Hollis doubted anyone would see her as she bathed from the ground. Next, she turned the taps to the bath. Next she added in a sizable amount of the sandalwood-scented soap to the stream of water.

Hollis had discovered the wooden shelf of soaps nestled in a cabinet near the bath and quite liked mixing them with some of the pretty oil she had found, and rescued, from the prince's baths.

The final ingredient in her bath would be a healthy amount of the soaking salts she had brought with her from home. The salts had been used in drying several batches of herbs, and so carried the perfume they'd lent.

If Hollis felt like it, she'd use the straight razor she'd found in the cabinet here and shave her legs and underarms. Having never seen a grace of shadow cross alongside Sir Lukxa's jaw, she felt it safe to assume that the blade never touched his skin. It had likely been given to him ages ago when he'd arrived in the castle. Hollis happily helped herself to the little tool.

As the water poured into the tub, Hollis twisted the metal ring off the glass jar that held her salts. She reached her hand inside and pulled up a handful of salt. The coarse ground salt stuck to her fingers and crawled under her nails as she sprinkled it in the water. Hollis shook her hands in the steaming water to try and dissolve the salt best she could, through the water stung the skin of her hands until they turned pink.

Just how I like it. Piping hot.

She usually made way with her sight to keep herself from overheating in such temperatures. She turned the knob labeled *hot* back slightly, just in case.

Finding it boring to watch the tub fill with pearlescent bubbles, she turned her attentions to below the window but kept a hand on the bath's inner side to tell when it was filled to the top. Trails of knotted muscles ran down her back as she shifted from leg to leg.

Being at such a great length up from the ground, she could spy the training yards she'd seen out the kitchenette windows. The now soaked knights sat under a grouping of trees or a small shelter that housed training supplies and whatever else she couldn't spy from her vantage point. They were probably waiting for the rain to stop so they could make their way inside. Hollis searched through the men for Sir Lukxa's navy hair or tall stature. He was nowhere to be found.

A few knights made a break toward the castle in the downpour, slipping in the brown puddles across the training yard and further drenching their dark uniforms. It was a humorous sight to behold.

The hand she'd kept flat on the inside of the tub brushed against water. Hollis walked to the far end of the tub and turned the tap closed.

Seated in the small wooden chair she'd pulled in from Sir Lukxa's dining set, she peeled off her boots and stockings. Her feet had swollen to a deep reddish-purple, pain screamed in anger up her legs. Hollis rubbed them, fingers *cracking* as she squeezed at her swollen toes.

She growled.

It wasn't fair. Her sight would have her plucking at a few threads and the swelling would vanish as she rested the entirety of the evening. Now, she would suffer through this pain.

Hollis rubbed her hands up her legs, doing their best to make an impact on the fire beneath her skin.

She stood, stepped out of her skirt, and dropped it to the floor. Angry marks showed along her waist. Her body had swollen much more than she thought it was even capable of.

Stupid rain and pressure. Stupid magic.

Hollis shook her head, sending her hair flying as she attempted to try and free her mind from the building thoughts regarding her sight.

The key in regaining her sight was in the fact that she never truly relaxed since she passed out. Her body was under great strain, and relieving it would allow her sight to return. The bath would cure her. It had to.

Hollis avoided looking at herself in the ornate mirror as she continued on undressing.

Her left shoulder cracked as she tried removing the high neck shirt, ripping a small cry from her throat. Another roar of thunder filled the air as a shock of pain had her falling against the tub, being stopped from plunging in only by her knees pressing firmly against its hot sides.

Holding back another cry of pain and panic was difficult as the shirt tangled and became stuck over her head. Hollis scrambled, knees *cracking*, as she managed to lower herself to the ground. The scent of the bath gathered in the fabric of the shirt and perfumed her lungs. It was suffocating. The shirt pressed into her mouth as she tried breathing in.

Wiggling her arms around gave her no avail; the action only served to grind her shoulder against the socket it sought freedom from. The straps of her brassiere added to the pressure on the offending limb.

The high neck seemed to get tighter each time she moved, she couldn't breathe.

This is how she would go, tangled up in a man's training shirt next to a hot bath filled with oils she'd stolen from the Crowned Prince.

Cries finally escaped her lips as she slid and fell onto her side with the subluxed shoulder. Tears and spit covered the fabric in front of her face, her hot breath clouding her vision.

"No, *no*." Breath came and left her lungs faster than Hollis could absorb the air she so desperately needed.

She needed to move, to right the joint and get this stupid shirt off her body. After several rapid breaths, she pushed up with her legs until she hooked her arm against the lip of the tub. The copper siding grew hot against her person and the water drenched her forearm.

Hollis bit her lip to hold back a scream she tried to tense the muscles in her back, willing her shoulder to move back into its rightful place.

It wasn't enough.

She pushed her free hand back out of the sleeve until she could move it enough to grasp the bend of her slipped shoulder. Taking a deep breath she shoved her body hard against the tub and pulled her throbbing limb forward.

A *crack* filled the air. She cried as her shoulder moved closer to home while not making it fully.

"Hollis? Are you all right?" The door to the bath swung open. Sir Lukxa's steps on the hard floor were drums in her ears. When had he arrived back in the apartments? "My goodness. Let me help you." His hands gripped her sides. They sent a wave of pain up her body.

"*No!* Don't touch me," she sobbed. "I've almost got it." Snot ran down her face as her body shook. Tremors ran through her body. Her throat bobbed.

She was going to vomit.

Sir Lukxa's hands rested over her skin. Not fully touching her, but close enough she could feel the cold his skin let off. "There's no shame in getting help." He lightly rested his hands against her spine again.

No convulsions followed.

Hollis stayed silent a moment, allowing reason to cover her embarrassment.

"I can't get the shirt off."

"I can see that. What can I do?" Sir Lukxa's voice was soft, still laced with worry.

Hollis turned her body away from the tub and leaned down against the ground. "My shoulder needs setting before I can get the shirt off, I think. Do you," her lungs heaved as her stomach tried to upheave. She swallowed the acid back down. "Do you know how to set a shoulder?"

"Thankfully, yes."

Hollis' upper body burned as it made contact with the cool floor. Using the leverage of her position and the fact her shoulder was mostly righted, she leaned hard on the floor as Lukxa's hands gripped her shoulder and applied pressure until a second *crack* filled the air, and a burst of fire ran down her arm.

Her body went slack against the floor as she bit her lips to keep a scream from ripping out of her chest.

Sir Lukxa carefully pulled her body upright and settled her against his own.

Once she was still, Sir Lukxa slipped the offending garment from her body. The actions only pulled light *cracks* from the rest of the joints on her arm. He tossed the high neck outside the room through the still open bath door.

She watched the steam float away through the doorway. "You're letting all the heat of my bath out."

"I. . ." He seemed to be at a loss for words. Which was fine by her. She realized he was soaking wet now that the rest of her body started to feel again. Splotches of mud danced around his face and now decorated her arms. Sir Lukxa blinked rapidly as he swallowed a few times. His hands tightened their hold on the flesh of her back. The ran over a long rope knot that spanned the length of her spine.

Hollis attempted to bring the captain back to reality, his eyes seeming forever away. "Though, if I'm being honest, you look like you may need the bath more than I do right now."

The magic inside of her pulsed against her being, only to be pushed down within her core. The aches of her sight being sapped from her intensified the rest of the torment under her skin. The stinging in her shoulder grew even more as a dull throb formed in her mind with the growing storm outside.

"No, I can wash up at the sink if I really needed to. Which I do not. Are you going to be all right bathing on your own?" His eyes trailed down to meet her own. The pale blue seemed much cloudier in the dim lighting. They took on a gray color.

A bolt of lightning shone in the window, filling the room soon after with a loud *roar* of thunder. The light illuminated Sir Lukxa's face further, shone on his parted lips, how his face was tilted downward toward her own.

Hollis turned her head to face the sink on the far side of the room just in from the door. She could feel her hair brush against his face as she did so. Which keenly reminded her of the fact that she sat in his lap, clothed in nothing but her underthings. She further tucked her chin to her clavicle. "If you're offering to bathe me, I'll politely decline." A tremor set in her jaw.

Sir Lukxa's voice lowered. "I can easily call a maid to help."

"I'm not an infant." Her voice was sharp, the words hissed through her teeth. A sense of anger bubbled up inside of her.

That was new. She hadn't experienced a true anger like this in quite some time. No, Hollis didn't like the red feeling. It left her stomach sour and her heart sorrowful. She much preferred to ignore issues.

The issue of her lack of healing magic was something she couldn't avoid in this moment.

But she could control how she reacted to it. She didn't need to take her anger out on anyone. This could be contained.

She took a shaky breath through her lips, held it, and slowly blew it out. Sir Lukxa's scent invaded her mind as she did so.

"Hollis, I wasn't insinuating that you were, only that you seemed to have just injured—"

Hollis turned back to face Sir Lukxa. The concern on his face hadn't left.

"It's fine now, see?" She lifted her arm, which still burned and felt like it was being both ripped apart and crushed, and wiggled her fingers.

He gave a slow incline of his head, his brows raised. "I take it that happens often for you to know how to deftly deal with it."

"I've told you, being that my body isn't wholly here, it has some problems. My joints doing whatever they please is one of them."

"All of you does whatever pleases you." His eyes darkened, and she knew that her ears would be flooded with reprimands for this morning's incident with the council. His grip on her waist tightened a hair.

"I did what was necessary. Now, I haven't fully figured out what I want to say to you, so again, I'd like to bathe in peace." She leaned away from his chest, still seated on his lap. The pain made its way through her body once more, the sorrow of her magic being gone. The ache in her bones from the storm which continued rolling outside. Everything came crashing down, and all she needed to do to hold herself together in this moment was soak.

How much more could her body take of this? It continued to build against her skin, ready to burst out of her facia.

Sir Lukxa's face was now set in something between discomfort and understanding. His hands slid down from her waist to land on her hips. "If you would allow me a moment to grab myself a towel so I may dry off in my rooms, I will leave you—"

"Thank you—"

He held a hand up. "The door remains open."

Hollis blinked. "What?"

The discomfort melted off of his face. "You have just injured yourself and I do not know if you have even realized that you are shaking."

He was right; she hadn't noticed the small tremors that racked against her skin.

"It's because I'm close to bare and cold." The muscles in her jaw tensed.

"Nevertheless, I want to be able to hear you in case you're in need of any more help. I will be reading in the meantime." Sir Lukxa glowered when Hollis opened her mouth to protest. It looked good on his face. "No, Hollis. This is *nonnegotiable*. If you want a bath, you listen. This isn't me infantilizing you; I want to watch out for you so you have the liberty *to* relax." He raised his brows.

She shook her head in agreement, tremors having seized her throat.

He walked to the cabinet where she'd found the soaps and razor and removed a sizable towel from a stack. He paused before stepping too far from her. "Do you need any more assistance with. . . undressing? You've still several garments on."

She shook her head *no*.

He gave a curt nod of his head in response and left the room, leaving the door cracked in the illusion of privacy.

Standing was a challenge she hadn't been ready for, but met all the same. She pulled her brassiere off, not caring if she broke the clasp, and deposited the rest of her clothes in a similar fashion along the floor. Without any ceremony, she slunk into the tub.

The fragrant hot water burned against her skin and turned her hands red. It was a welcome, almost soothing pain.

Small groans passed her lips as she leaned her head back to hook on the edge of the tub and hold herself up in the water. She practically floated on the surface of bubbles. The tension washed out of her.

"Are you all right?"

She flushed. "Yes, I'm fine. . . The water feels nice?" She didn't know why she was talking past *fine*. Her words were weak and timid.

Sir Lukxa gave no response.

After several minutes of simply floating and soaking, she grabbed the bottle of soap and a washing rag and set about scrubbing herself. She hadn't truly bathed since entering the castle, only wiped at her creases and lathered herself in lotions. She desperately needed to remove a layer of skin.

Not that her body was caked in dirt or dust. And she hadn't started to smell—but the need to be clean was strong. As if the act of washing would somehow rid the curse of the prince, free her trapped magic, and heal.

Hollis held her breath and dunked her head into the water. Her fingers raked through her hair.

She emerged from the water with a gasp, finding Sir Lukxa standing in the doorway, his pale eyes wide, a blush burned onto his face. He'd dried himself off and was dressed once more in his own high-neck shirt and dark pants.

Bubbles ran down her face and chest, joining the cloud of them which now grew past the brim of the tub.

"What are you doing?" The words fell simply from her mouth.

His face grew even redder. "I heard a *splash*. . . I thought you'd slipped under."

She blinked a few times before answering. "No, just wetting my hair to wash it." A few bubbles slid down from her hair and onto her face. She swatted them away before they could land in her eyes and blind her. There was no reason for her to lose another one of her senses.

"All right." Sir Lukxa nodded his head, hands still frozen against the doorframe and opened door. "I'll be ready to speak when you're done."

"I don't think it's going to come back on its own." The words were out of her mouth as quickly as she remembered them in her mind.

"What?" He blinked several times. His position slacked, as if forgetting the entire situation they were in.

"I don't know why I sputtered that all out. My brain is so filled with fog."

"You mean your magic?" He cocked his hip against the doorframe.

She splashed her hands into the water, sending a few bubbles flying back into the tub. "I can feel it reaching out to me, but I can't grasp it. I. . . I'm starting to think that there could be something wrong." Her eyes burned.

The knot in Sir Lukxa's throat bobbed. "Right. We can speak more on it when you're—"

"Done being naked, yes. You've seen quite a bit of me today—"

"*All of you.* I've seen all of you." His eyes were wide as he turned to face the floor.

No more words passed between them as he turned and left. The sound of him sliding into a chair soon followed by another peel of thunder.

She slowly sank into the water until it reached her nose. The flush on her face and heat in her stomach were from the heat of the bath. Really. *Truly.*

Her laughter bubbled up to the surface. Sir Lukxa was correct, she was a terrible liar.

The best thing to do in the moment was push all thoughts out of her mind. She had to relax if she wanted her sight back.

Washing her hair brought great enjoyment to her scalp. Her nails scraped at any bits of dirt or oil that coated the emerald strands in preparation for the perfumed oil. The heat of the bath leaked out as the storm grew stronger outside the window.

Finally the water grew tepid—forcing her to stand.

Water rained from her body into the tub. Hollis ran her hands down her person, wiping as much water off of herself as she could.

Her joints gave no protests as she fluttered around the room and dried herself. The matter of shaving her legs and beneath her arms was quickly done, revealing smooth skin she was excited to feel under the sheets. There was nothing like the feeling of freshly shaven legs in a freshly made bed.

She spied the bottle of oil she had lifted from the prince's room and decided that after the entire day she'd had, her skin deserved even more of the luxury.

The oil was light as the drops pooled in her palm, smelling nice against the sandalwood scent Lukxa's soap filled the room with. The notes melded together on her skin, which drank in the oil as she rubbed it against her arms, legs, and middle.

Hollis ran the remaining oil on her hands through her hair, hoping it would give it a nice shine, and possibly lay more controlled against her head, rather than looking constantly windblown. Then again, she liked when her hair was slightly wild. She did miss the length she'd had, wavy locks which fell to her stomach. But the short and choppy style suited her just as well.

Eventually she would believe that.

She stared at it in the mirror and tried to remember exactly how her hair had been before. It covered her chest, which was always a fun feeling, like the seafolk. She appeared more like a crazed person of the air now. Except, to the best of her knowledge, they didn't have dark veins pushing out against their skin as she did. Her usually poofy hair only added to the wild expression she wore, which she was fine with.

Biting her lip, she turned away from the mirror and set about dressing herself in the fresh set of clothes she'd brought into the room, a set that didn't include a high neck shirt. Simply a set of under garments, a pair of half pants, and a thick shirt Sir Lukxa lent her to sleep in while she was here.

Sir Lukxa's rooms were colder than the washroom had been, but not by much. The fire in the hearth roared as loud as the thunder outside. Glancing around, Hollis found Sir Lukxa settled in the plush chair of his study, a book in his hands.

Thunder still *roared* outside the windows, accompanied by the constant pelting of rain against the windows.

"You're so fascinating," she said as she approached the study area.

"What do you mean by that?" he asked, not looking up from the pages.

"You can read upside down."

Heat rushed up his neck and quickly overtook his ears. He flipped the book upright as she plopped into the chair across from him, curling up against the cushions.

Sir Lukxa sniffed the air as she settled down and pulled a small throw around herself. "Did you use perfume?" He sniffed at her.

She preened a bit. "Perhaps. Do you like it?"

His eyes narrowed. "You smell like Prince Dagen at his coming of age ceremony."

"So I smell royal?" She hoped he would stick to complimenting her and wouldn't realize she had lifted the perfumed oil.

"You smell like a thief." His voice was flat, but his face held a raised brow.

She deflated a bit, pulling the covers around herself. "I don't think he'll mind. It seemed old and unused."

"Ah, he did hate that one. I guess you were lucky with what you decided to steal from the *royal prince*."

She huffed, to which he grinned in response.

"Speaking of which, I borrowed your razor. Considering you don't seem to grow facial hair, I didn't think it'd hurt to use it. But I wanted to let you know because I left it hanging about somewhere in the water closet."

His expression fell. "I don't use it on my face."

Her stomach sank and she could feel herself blushing profusely. "What are you talking about—*where do you use it?*" Horror bloomed in her soul. Her hands cupped over her mouth.

Maybe she didn't want him to answer her question.

The grin that crept onto the Captain's face was unsettling. "Come back Thursday to find out." He peered at her over the top of his book, his face rather amused. "I'm kidding. I assume things went well after Councilor Shad so rudely dragged you away from me? The council placed you in my charge and then ripped you away the next moment. It's like they cannot make up their minds. I am sorry I did not get the chance to talk about it before dinner" He slowly turned to the next page in the book he was reading. As if he was now reading each word on the page and waiting to turn it until the last moment before the next page started.

"Councilor Shad took me to meet with the other councilors—"

Sir Lukxa's brows knit together. "*Again?*"

She licked her lips. "They took me to see Prince Dagen."

The captain didn't speak for several moments.

Finally, he blinked, gathered himself, and turned another page. "That makes sense. And how did your meeting with Prince Dagen and the rest of the council go?" The tension in Sir Lukxa's voice easily showed his displeasure at being excluded.

"Oh, it was fine. Prince Dagen did a fantastic job of pretending to be sick, though it might not have been an act the whole time. I examined him and ended up spewing some nonsense about the Tablin flu."

His face drew tight with concern. "So now you think he also has the Tablin flu?"

A flash of light filled the room.

"No." Hollis shook her head. "Not in the slightest." The rumble of thunder that followed was comforting. While the storms brought pressure to her joints and swelling beyond belief, the sounds were peaceful.

"I see. Do you think they bought it?"

"Prince Dagen pretend-vomited so much when I entered the room I don't even think they took notice of my actions after he stopped." She paused, fondly remembering the green faces everyone held. "Councilor Shad seemed keen on puffing up my story to them all." Hollis took another pause, reflecting on the whole ordeal. "Prince Dagen is nothing like the rumors I've heard."

Sir Lukxa nodded, a solemn expression on his face. "I'm happy you realize that."

"He is just a boy." Hollis wouldn't mention that she had chastised someone for addressing him as such. This was different.

Sir Lukxa faced her. "Yes, he is."

"Interesting how maternal instincts creep up on you when you see such a young face so sick and frail." She let out an awkward laugh. It was true of every patient she'd had with a babyish face.

"Tell me." Sir Lukxa set the book aside and held her gaze. "You said in the bath that your magic is being suppressed? Not just. . . gone due to stress or sickness?" His fingers drummed against his thighs.

"Yes." Her body felt like a snake wound its way down her throat. "It's the only option at this point. I feel it creep inside of me for a few moments, and then it's squashed back down."

"How often is this happening?" He hunched his back and leaned toward her, hands now tapping against each other at the fingertips.

She blew out a breath. "A handful of times? I get faint when it happens. Thankfully, I tend to be able to catch myself. It happened when we entered the councilors' chambers. Though I managed the rest of my encounter with them just fine."

"Yes, your *encounter*," Sir Lukxa said wearily.

Images of everyone's faces as she peeled off her clothes filled her mind once more. Mostly shocked expressions and several blushing faces. Hollis remembered feeling a prickle of disgust against her skin as she sassed them— an activity she usually enjoyed greatly. Sir Lukxa's face had turned pink. His eyes held something she could not decipher or cast aside.

Hollis turned her face away and spoke. "It's hard for someone to break me down and embarrass me if I can't be embarrassed."

Thunder sounded in the room again. Both their attentions turned to the windows at her right, in the kitchen and by the bookshelves behind her. Several flashes of lightning lit up the room. Neither spoke until the storm calmed down. Soon, heavy rain was the only thing they heard.

Sir Lukxa let out a breathy laugh. "So you did it as a power play?"

"I don't know why I did it, to be honest." She shrugged her shoulders as she turned back to him. "I trust the thoughts my mind comes up with. I see an action or string of words in my head and I do or speak. I move how my body wills—"

He smacked his hands down against his legs and leaned back harshly against his chair. "And if your body willed you to do something dangerous—"

"It never has." Hollis grinned at him. "Never once has my mind failed me. Even if I can't think of something in the moment, it acts on its own. I may be cut off from my magic, but nature is still a part of me. I move with the world, and the world itself is good."

Sir Lukxa rubbed at his temple. "I think you're insane."

Hollis' grin grew. "There was never a question in anyone's mind about that. But there is in this: what do we do with the council? I want to find out if they're behind this because I trust you, and at the moment I still trust *them*. Most of them at least. Besides, you've yet to tell me yourself the full reason you don't trust them, so I've the need to discover a reason for myself. Unless you want to be honest?"

He squirmed in his chair. He curled his lips up in what Hollis could only assume was disdain or disgust. "I suppose we'll have to figure out who has the most to gain from anything happening to Dagen—*Prince* Dagen."

"*May the sun shine on his crown.*" She waved her hand around in the air around her head a few times. "That old man Collin seemed angry most of the meeting and was incredibly pushy during my time with the prince. Tried to get everyone else to look down on me, too. Is he always like that?" Hollis didn't want to think back to their encounters in the prince's chambers. Having lived through it was enough.

Sir Lukxa let out a long groan. "Yes. He holds a family seat, meaning his position is true until an heir from the Hozen line is able to claim it from him. So far, no one has tried. He likes flaunting his power and reminding anyone who doesn't have it of their circumstances." His head rolled backward. Hollis suddenly realized that his hair wasn't tied anymore. It was down and pooled behind him.

"Sounds like you two get along great," she remarked dryly.

He flashed her an unappreciative glare. "Not to mention that he and Councilor Sypher are moving funds around in a manner I do not like. Something I need to look closer into."

"Is that what you were off finding out this morning?"

"Among other things, yes." A little grin formed on Sir Lukxa's face. As quickly as she noticed it, it was gone.

Hollis pursed her lips, trying to connect everything in her mind. "So. . . We know Councilor Collin and Councilor Sypher moving funds around in a way they should not and that Councilor Collin was nervous and angry at my seeming *fine* while I examined Prince Dagen. Seems like they are a likely candidate at being behind all of this."

"No."

"*No?*" She was confused.

He shook his head and leaned forward in his seat. "Not all of it. Involved, yes. That I can be certain of by listening to my own gut, but I do not think either of them are the one in control. Councilor Collin is one to flaunt power and bully outside of his council position. But he doesn't have enough brains to do this all on his own. Councilor Sypher walks about like he's the most in charge person to have ever been born, but one can push him over with the slightest inconvenience." A flash of light filled the room, making the darkness that had crept in all the more noticeable. The storm had grown and consumed the sky. The taste of lightning danced in the air.

"He is like a puppet. Dancing on a set of. . . *glowing strings.*" It was an interesting picture in her mind. But it seemed to fit the feeling in her gut.

"Glowing?" He quirked a brow at her.

"Makes him obvious enough that we wouldn't look up to see whose holding them. So, dear Lukxa, it's time to *look up.*"

CHAPTER SEVENTEEN

LUKXA

The library, though filled with papers and shelves serving as insulation, *boomed* with the sound of thunder. The unexpected storm that exploded the night before had ruined the entire day of training Lukxa had meticulously planned. It lingered all through the night and still plagued them through to the next evening.

He groaned internally. All the indoor training areas were already booked. There was no space large enough for Lukxa to finish the training session with his men that had been interrupted. Being unable to burn out his own energy was frustrating.

The rain did not seem eager to let up either.

Lukxa made sure to pen his group's names in the next available indoor slot he could.

While both last night and this evening had gone as far from hoped as possible, it gave Lukxa the perfect situation to retreat into the library. Giving him a chance to try and find a copy of Sypher's report where he listed the wrong numbers.

Lukxa paused, blinking slowly. The accounting ledger. The numbers were likely recorded there.

Yes, the library was far more useful than simply quenching Hollis' curiosity,

The woman he'd seen as skin twice. Unabashed, endless, skin.

Lukxa's face burned, his eyes wide as he ducked around another shelf in an attempt to clear his thoughts. He just needed a moment to right himself. A deep breath helped clear his mind of her.

Hollis trailed not far behind him. "This is more wonderful than I thought." Her shoes *clacked* on the ground.

He turned to find Hollis dragging her fingers along the spines of books held on the shelves the two of them walked past.

Her eyes glowed in wonder as she took in the books that surrounded her, seemingly cataloging them in her own mind.

She waltzed past him, off to a different row. "Since we're here while the library is closed, I take it you spoke with someone about obtaining that special key you mentioned before?"

Lukxa nodded. "Yes." His voice shook slightly. He chewed the inside of his cheek and swallowed before speaking again. "Councilor Shad lent me one of his keys to the top floor. That's where more restricted books are kept, only accessible by the Council and those with a permit." His voice was far more stable this time.

He stepped past the edge of the row and found Hollis in the long aisle.

Hollis gave a tinkling laugh, her head still swirling around to take in at all the books that surrounded her. "Councilor Shad seems to have keys to a lot of different places. And the rest of the council was all right with that? You being allowed access?" She traced a hand against the metal organizational placard nailed to the shelf she stood at. She ducked into the row, out of his sight.

Lukxa scoffed. "It is Councilor Shad's key to do with however he wishes. He does not need the council's permission to give it to *me*, a fellow councilor."

A flash of light filled the room from the glass ceiling above, which amplified the intense *pittering* sound of rain falling.

"It's so beautiful here." Hollis' words carried over the the light tapping of her cane, which gave away her position in the room as she trailed amongst the towering shelves of the library.

Lukxa quickly followed behind her and stopped short as he caught sight of her. Another bolt of lightning struck nearby.

She was beautiful amid the stacks and piles of books.

He swallowed, motionless as she ducked behind another shelf. She was moving quickly tonight.

Lukxa ran a hand down his face, letting it settle deep on his stomach where an uncomfortable heat pooled. He let his head fall back and stifled a groan that built in his throat.

Please, stop thinking about her.

"I couldn't even see there was a third floor up there." She was behind him suddenly, he turned to find her head craned upward, trying to find evidence of what he said.

His throat went dry. A quick swallow of spit fixed that. "The third floor was designed to be private. The second floor eclipses it entirely. The only way to access the third floor is through a, *slightly*, hidden passage in the keeps office." He blinked, her previous words sinking in. "Wait, what do you mean he seems to have—"

"He has a key to your apartments, used it the other day before I *met* Prince Dagen to let me inside."

Oh. That was right. "Yes, he would have a key. He is the master of the keep, keeping one of everything, gathering and hoarding items he deems useful. I am not surprised that he has a master key. Only a bit that he used it for entry to *my apartments.*" His eyes widened as the last bit of shock ran out of him. "Everyone knows how trapped my room is."

Hollis nodded, wetting her lips. "Yes. A kleptomaniac in his finest form, that Councilor Shad." Hollis plucked up a book to her left, read a few pages, then put it back on the shelf. She repeated the process several times over.

"Careful with Councilor Shad. He may find you useful in some manner and steal you from right under my nose," Lukxa joked, tapping his nose a few times.

"And I do so like being under you, *Sir Lukxa*." Hollis' grin twisted and warmed Lukxa's gut more than he thought possible.

"Let us get back to the matter at hand, Hollis." Lukxa diverted. "Do a quick pass on this floor for anything useful. I do not know what you will be able to find down here that can help you with your situation. I would hate to realize the answer to our problems was here all along. Once you have finished with that we will move up to the top floor."

"Right." Hollis drew out the word, a glare settling in her eyes. "So, I'm going to be searching through what has to be several ten-thousands of books, and you'll be doing what again?"

"I'm going to search through the ledgers in the keeps' office." He pointed a finger to the far side of the library where a small door sat tucked between two windows on a protruding wall.

"I guess I'll see you once I've finished my sleuthing. Good luck." Hollis gave him a bitter smile and vanished around the shelves as another clap of thunder rattled the room.

Lukxa wasted no time in marching to the far end of the room and slipped the key to the office he had borrowed from Shad inside of the keyhole. The keeps' office was a medium-sized room built inside the library walls. It butted up against the bottom of the second floor. There were a few windows on the front wall that allowed those who worked inside to see out into the main floor. They were heavily tinted though, to keep the inner workings of the room private.

The door wasn't locked.

Lukxa froze. There was a subtle glow stretching out from underneath the door as he cracked it open.

Lukxa crouched and pulled the door open wide enough to slip through.

Once inside, he quietly shut the door behind him.

Whispers filled Lukxa's ears, he could tell words were being exchanged but couldn't solidify their meaning.

The room was dark, save the small lantern held by two bodies down the center aisle of the room. On either side of the long center aisle were two rows of desks, four in total. Each wall beside the desks was filled with shelves and cabinets. Lukxa crawled to the left side of the room with his arms on his stomach toward them, tucking himself between the row of desks so he wasn't quite beside the shelves, but still had some obscurity from the first set. He needed to get a good look at whoever was in here.

Lukxa craned his head over a few of the small, pale wood, accountants desks to try and pin who the voices belonged to.

One man rummaged around on Councilor Shad's wide desk, his back toward Lukxa; the other rifled through the shelves and drawers that lined the wall behind the desk.

"I still don't know what we're here for." A gruff-sounding voice filled the air as another wave of thunder shook the room.

A loud sigh filled the room. "The. *Ledger*. He said he might have left it out instead of bringing it back with him. If he did, it would have been *put back*."

"Right. *I knew that*. I just don't know what it looks like."

"You quite literally said that you didn't."

Lukxa could not make out their faces with their heads downcast. They were both blond, though, he could tell that much—that didn't narrow down the list of suspects. Wait. . . One may have been a brunette?

"Councilor Sypher said the ledger would be in Councilor Shad's office, but it clearly isn't because *we* can't find it. . . Maybe he left it on the third floor?"

The blood in Lukxa's veins ran hot. Sypher was trying to cover his tracks. His teeth ground against each other.

"There's a third floor to the library?" The gruff voice asked, craning his head back toward the door. Lukxa ducked his head to avoid being spotted.

Though, he was as a worm against the ground. He likely did not have to worry much.

"It's not very visible from the first floor, you dolt. Not with how the room bends toward the center or whatever. The third floor is special. It holds special documents and books. Copies from conquered nations, books on magic, and private council business."

"Wow, you've learned a lot since becoming a paper pusher. Wait, there's magic books in here? Can we learn it?" The man gasped.

"With your brain, Charles, it isn't likely."

Charles—a name Lukxa could put voice to face. A slightly older squire who had not quite made it to knighthood. Often seen training with his cousin Edwin, who had moved from knighthood to more clerical work. But under which councilor, Lukxa couldn't remember. When both men came to the castle they had been placed in Lukxa's guard. Neither lasted long.

Paper pushers hiding papers. Not a happy thought.

"Let's go up there then," Charles spoke.

"We can't access it." Edwin sounded less than enthused.

"Why not?" Charles' voice took on a whiny quality that was unbefitting of a knight.

"I don't have a key to the door. We'll have to come back tomorrow night after getting one." Edwin slammed his hand down on the lip of the shelf. Something *cracked* and fell to the floor. The sound of papers rushing down filled Lukxa's ears. "*Ah-ha.* What do we have here?"

Lukxa sat up on his haunches, only three desks away from the men. Edwin pulled the long, thin, ledger from the small gap between the bookshelf and the desk.

"Is that the ledger?" Charles asked, peering over Edwin's shoulder.

Edwin looked around the back area. "I do believe it—"

"Good evening, gentleman. Can I assist you in finding whatever it is you're looking for in *my* office?" All the heads in the room whipped around to find Councilor Shad in the doorway, a bright oil lantern in hand. The light illuminated Charles and Edwins' faces as the councilor raised it high, stepping into the room.

Lukxa fell backward on his hands and hoped the beams didn't reach as far as to caress his face. His core trembled as Lukxa settled himself in a position much like a crab.

Charles blubbered. "Oh, Councilor Shad, yes, um. We've found what it is we were sent for—"

"Who is it that sent you?" Shad's voice was ice as he spoke. His words pierced the two men.

They scrambled over their words before Edwin finally spoke up himself. "Oh, you weren't told? I'll let h—them." He let out a sharp breath. "Our boss needs to make revisions to their numbers in the book. Realized there was a mistake so they sent us to come and grab the ledger for them."

Charles nodded his head along frantically.

Lukxa worried the man would break his neck at that pace. It would leave the castle down one guard. Though, Charles was corrupt. So it would not be much of a loss.

Lukxa crept backward in the shadows, now two desk lengths removed from where Charles and Edwin stood. His new position gave him a better point in which to keep his eyes on Councilor Shad and the two men whilst remaining hidden.

"The revision period ended *three weeks ago*. All revisions must be passed by *me*, and I require faces and receipts. I'm incredibly careful with anything concerning *my books*. *Also*, it's long after closing. You shouldn't even be in here." Shad hissed strode deeper into the room, extending his free hand. "You either give me the ledger or put it on my desk. Those are your only options. And you can tell your *boss* that they can come during my office hours and make the revisions with *me*." Lukxa could see the green in Shad's green eyes practically glowing. "I would *love* to know who ordered this."

That *doesn't seem natural.*

The two men swore. Charles' hands patted at his side.

What is he doing? Looking for a weapon?

Lukxa readied himself to jump in if needed.

"That's not a good idea. I suggest you leave. You've no idea the things in this room I have access to that could dismember you before you could make a step toward me." Councilor Shad repeated, his voice dripping with threat.

The two men growled and dropped the ledger onto the desk. The pair quickly left the office. Shad had stepped free from their path, then turned and watched them leave. Not long after Lukxa heard the doors to the library open and sink closed.

Shad took several quick steps and then the lantern swung in his direction, blinding Lukxa. "I take it you're here to check the discrepancy in numbers we heard this afternoon, Sir Lukxa?" Councilor Shad turned his eyes and found Lukxa as he spoke.

Lukxa's hands slipped out from under him, landing him solidly on his back. He *groaned* before standing and dusting himself off. "The minutes I was lent by Councilor Sypher had differing information. I wanted to be sure."

"Yes, I'm aware." Shad *clicked* his tongue. "So this was the true reason you wanted one of my keys, to snoop in my office rather than the third floor?"

"No, I am helping Hollis with her own research. I thought I would double check the ledgers in the process."

"Yes, research in treating the *Tablin flu*." Shad laughed and walked behind his desk, hung the oil lantern by a hook built on top of it, and set about reading the ledger. Lukxa wasn't fond of the open mouthed grin that stretched across Shad's face.

Lukxa followed up behind him, reading the numbers and dates as Shad did.

"Just look at them." Councilor Shad's hands *smacked* against the papers, the pads of his fingers wrinkling the pages. "They had the gall to try and cut the reported numbers in *half* during the meeting." Shad clicked his tongue as he straightened his spine, still reading. "I cannot exactly say who butchered the numbers. Sypher has to know. He could have written them down wrong, or some page boy may have gotten *his* numbers wrong. You would think that fifteen-hundred gold going missing would raise flags. But thus far, noticing the discrepancies has not happened with anyone. And Still! *Still I do not have enough evidenc*e. All of this can be excused away."

"Evidence for what, councilor?" Lukxa asked, standing up to match.

Councilor Shad's head turned slowly to scowl at him, face amused. "I'm *the keeper*. I keep my eyes on everything and I know *everything* that happens inside this castle."

Curiosity picked at his mind. "Everything?" Lukxa's feeling lent itself to fear as Shad's gaze darkened.

"Oh, yes. Don't think I do not know what's going on." Shad's voice sang. He scooped up the ledger and put it in a satchel at his hip that Lukxa had failed to notice sooner.

"Then tell me," Lukxa called what he hoped was a bluff. It would not have been too hard for Shad to notice that Lukxa was tracking the numbers, but to claim to know *everything* was a stretch Lukxa wasn't willing, nor could afford, to give leniency on. If Shad had ever been approached by those on the council that had hired Lukxa, he was done for.

Hollis came into view, bouncing on her heels and hanging her hands on the side door frame, a stack of books in her free hand. "I can't find any books that might work for fixing my mag—oh, hello Councilor Shad."

Lukxa watched as the councilor smiled at Hollis as she entered the room. "Yes, good evening, Healer Hollis. We seem to be running into each other quite often today." He sounded happy to see her.

An uncomfortable feeling pitched in his stomach.

"If I remember, you found me twice. I wouldn't count finding someone the same as running into them by chance." Hollis quickly deposited the stack of books she carried on a random desk and leaned against the edge.

"You've got me there. I assume you're both here to research the money laundering to pay off the physicians brought in to heal Prince Dagen? It's an absolute train-wreck that no one was able to find out that it was a Tablin flu sooner." Councilor Shad's voice rose in frustration. He scoffed and looked Lukxa dead in the eyes with a wide, and disgusted face. "Really, I *still* cannot believe the gall of some people. I do not know why they'd be editing the ledgers this poorly."

Lukxa shook his head in quick agreement. He would let Shad think what he wanted to about the whole situation and feed no information to it. "I noticed the odd numbers before I left to find Hollis." Lukxa would say that and be done with it.

Shad *hummed* before turning his attentions away from Lukxa to his shelves. "Healer, you said that you're missing some books. What can I help you find?" Shad looked back at Hollis, straightening his spine like a bird preening itself to a potential mate—*oh*, Lukxa really didn't like that thought.

Hollis gave a half-hearted smile in return. "I'm wanting books on. . . how to use a more natural method for healing the Tablin flu. Being that Prince Dagen has likely never been treated with the Tablin sight, I want to try and heal his body in a manner that is more likely to be received." She sucked in her lower lip, chewing it for a brief moment.

She was lying.

"I see. You're wanting to first treat him *without* magic. Interesting. Are there adverse side-effects to treating one with magic?" Shad cocked his hip and tapped some fingers against his chin.

Hollis paled, pursing her lips, likely to keep them from flapping like a fish. "Well, *councilor*, not really, but sometimes reweaving a person takes time. The body can reverse some of the effects of my healing, which would mean more healing sessions would be required. But if I can find out if the Tablin flu was ever healed with medicinal means, it would just be. . . *easier?*" Her voice almost squeaked out the last few words.

Goodness, she was a *terrible* liar. It was a wonder that she had even—

"I guess I can see the merit in that. His body may be more receptive to doses of medication alongside the healing, rather than relying on your magical healing alone. You're supplementing to get the best results. Combining both modern medicine and ancient healing. Such a marvel." Councilor Shad grinned. "If you're wanting books on Tablin medicine for treating the Tablin flu as Captain Lukxa told me, you'll want to check the archives. They're on the top floor, which Sir Lukxa has a key to. The archives themselves are hidden away, though. Being that they are filled with precious copies, we keepers try and *keep* them in good condition." Shad smiled and walked toward Lukxa and Hollis. "Hollis, dear, you'll need some gloves."

CHAPTER EIGHTEEN

HOLLIS

Shad's hands enveloped Hollis', gripping the base of each of her fingers, measuring the length of them. Once he'd seemingly studied every curve of her hand, he walked out of sight into what Hollis guessed was a closet for several moments. Not a long enough stretch of time that gave Hollis the feeling that she could talk to Sir Lukxa about this situation, just enough time to be put on edge.

Councilor Shad finally returned with two pairs of brown leather gloves.

"These should fit you nicely." Councilor Shad gestured for her hand. "Captain, being that you will entertain yourself with the ledger, I've decided you aren't in need of gloves. No hard feelings."

Hollis slowly stretched her hands out toward the councilor. Councilor Shad pulled her closer to where he stood. Throughout their few interactions she hadn't yet pinned an age on the man. He couldn't have been much older than herself or Sir Lukxa, though. His face, while defined, held no wrinkles or obvious signs of aging. Perhaps he was six and twenty? Seven and twenty? Hollis would be shocked to learn if he were any older than that.

Councilor Shad wasn't the youngest-looking person on the council, she noted. Hollis guessed that Councilor Collin held the title as oldest, while one of the two girls from Rex held the youngest. A range that spanned maybe forty years?

Cologne wafted about Councilor Shad's person. An ambery scent. He wasn't dressed in his uniforms at this hour of night. Instead, he wore a loose-fitting wool high neck which was tucked into a pair of *well*-fitting black pants and secured with a black belt with gold details. His mousy curled hair was tousled—not in an unkempt manner, but she wouldn't have expected it from the man she saw earlier in the day. His glasses still sat upon his face, the one consistent fashion choice.

Councilor Shad held her hand and slowly fit the glove around her. "I do not need any of the oils from your hands getting on the gloves *at all*." Councilor Shad met her gaze, emerald eyes piercing into her own. They complemented each other, his green to her maroon.

The attention he paid her was almost enough to pull a blush to her cheeks, were it not for the fact that every time they spoke Councilor Shad acted like Hollis was a specimen to be thoroughly examined.

Hollis tilted her head. "I understand."

Sir Lukxa said nothing throughout the encounter. He simply stood by her side, like a scary dog reminding others that he'd bite for his owner. Not that she owned Sir Lukxa. She'd be happy to sic him on someone on her behalf though.

Councilor Shad pulled a cloth from goodness knows where and wiped down the handle of her cane. Once finished, he nodded and strode toward the door behind his desk. "Now, I do not think I will have to tell you this, but be sure not to touch *anything* other than books with the gloves. I do not want grime or oil or dirt transferring to the pages I've worked so hard to keep intact past their lifetime. Your cane, of course, is the exception to the rule." Councilor Shad spoke over his shoulder at her as all three of them climbed the stairs tucked away in the back of his office.

"Of course, Councilor. I wouldn't dare." Hollis returned the councilor's bright smile and trudged upward after Sir Lukxa. Hopefully they walked toward the third floor and not some secret torture chamber.

The thin stairway was poorly lit. They had to step in one at a time to climb them. There were slits that lined the wall, they allowed light from the central room to lend some sort of illumination their path. And there were the few candles that Councilor Shad and Sir Lukxa held as they ascended. The glow of their light trailing backward to Hollis, who was the last of the group to start up the stairs.

The castle was impossible in its design. The keeps' office had looked to be a small office tucked into a wall until she entered it and found what must have been twenty desks, four rows of five, filling the room and forming an aisle toward a large desk in the back—Councilor Shad's desk. The walls inside the office had then further been filled with shelves of all kinds, some with drawers and others open. And finally, a secret stairway built into the back wall that trailed around the room upward.

Hollis wouldn't have been able to come up with a design such as this if she spent her entire life thinking about it.

Her lungs burned as they reached the top of the neverending, winding staircase.

Breath escaped her lungs as she took several measured steps forward. The third floor of the library was magnificent. The rails that formed a circle around the center of the room were bent back in such a way that no one from the bottom floor would be able to see up to where they were.

The second floor seemingly blocked the third from existence when standing at the bottom. Hollis assumed if she didn't curl herself forward over the edge, it wouldn't even look like there was another floor to the room at all. She wasn't sure how that worked, but it was impressive nevertheless.

The floors were lined in a dense cream carpet and filled with shelves and tables alike. Facing upward, Hollis was blinded as another flash of lightning filled the library. The glass ceiling was almost within throwing distance. How it seemed so close but still remained so impassively far away still was beyond her.

A chill ran down her spine.

Thunder rattled a few of the tables.

Hairs on the back of her neck stood on edge. Her eyes grew wide as another flash filled her vision, burning into her mind the fractured line of light.

Councilor Shad laughed. "Do not worry yourself about the windows. The give and shake in the glass is what keeps everything safe. If it were rigid and unmoving, it would be more likely to shatter."

Hollis turned to see him trailing away from where she stood. "I wasn't worried, councilor. But I almost am now," she responded, doing her best to keep up with the man as he continued his relentless pace across the top floor.

Sir Lukxa seemed to keep his position of walking between herself and the councilor equally spaced. Did the knight think he could have sights on both of them at the same time to keep her from getting too lost? *Courteous.* Tucked under Sir Lukxa's arm was the ledger and a small stack of papers. She saw him lift a pen from a nearby table they passed, but wasn't sure where he'd hidden it on his person quite yet.

Another shiver overtook her body. Hollis hadn't changed into any warm layers since lunch. She felt tricked by the afternoon heat that came—though she wouldn't have called it *heat*. More a light dusting of warmth. The thin remaining hairs on her legs she must have missed when shaving stood on edge. At the moment, she was thankful for the thin, albeit useless, covering they gave her goosebumped skin.

The three of them eventually arrived at a small bookshelf. The pale, ashen wood seemed ready to crumble at the lightest touch.

Hollis wished she could see it, *truly* see it. The grain was unique, and it seemed so *old*. She loved touching old things with her sight. Figuring out where an object called home, how long it had been since it'd been taken from its place.

She shook her head, sending her hair flying everywhere. Her sight would return—*it had to*—and when it did, she'd get the answers she wanted.

Councilor Shad tucked himself beside the shelf and gave a light push on something behind its right side.

The shelf *groaned* as it slowly shifted away from its position on the wall, raising *upward*.

Her mouth fell open.

"I know. It's a clever hiding place. I wish I could take it apart, but being that it's generations old, I would hate to be the one that broke it and couldn't put it back together." Councilor Shad sighed, watching as the shelf steadily rose into the air until it left a door-sized opening in the wall. Councilor Shad stepped backward, now right beside Hollis. Sir Lukxa stood to her other side.

A small cloud of dust rained down upon them as it stopped, burning at her eyes. She blinked and made to rub at them with her free hand.

Councilor Shad held her hand tight. "Oh, please don't. You'll get facial oils on the gloves. Sir Lukxa, you do not have gloves to put on. Wipe Hollis' face for her." Councilor Shad barked the order.

Hollis whipped her head around, trying to figure out which direction Sir Lukxa stood in. Her feet shuffled awkwardly as Councilor Shad let go of her hand.

A pair of warm hands encased her face and lightly tilted her head in a direction she assumed was toward Sir Lukxa. His calloused grip rubbed at her face, starting at her forehead. He tousled her hair for good measure, sending more dust right into her nose. How she didn't sneeze her brain out her nose was beyond her.

His thumbs pressed against her eyelids, rubbing them lightly. Tears pooled along her lash line.

"Blink a few times." Sir Lukxa's voice was low, his breath ghosting over her cheeks.

Hollis did her best to follow Sir Lukxa's orders. His thumbs tugged at her waterline when her eyes opened. She saw his face right in front of hers, far too close. She could invade his space—that was fine. But him appearing so close before her was enough to catch her off her guard. What was he—

He blew hard into her eyes.

The cold air shocked her and she let out a noise of surprise as her balance suddenly failed her. Sir Lukxa's arms found her waist and steadied her.

"What was that for?" Hollis all but shrieked. Using her ungloved forearms, she rubbed at her eyes and blinked, finally able to see once more. "Why couldn't I have done this before?"

"I'm sorry, I was trying to get the dust out easier. Likely should have warned you." Sir Lukxa gave her a sheepish grin that told her that he *wouldn't* have warned her.

"If you two are done, I've gathered a few books for you to read through, Healer Hollis. There's a table in here you can use, and I've lit a lantern. Sir Lukxa, you can sit out there and continue your comparisons of the ledger. I'm sorry to tell you but no gloves means no entry." Councilor Shad stood in the secret doorway, his eyes fixated on Hollis.

"Shout if you need me, Hollis," Sir Lukxa whispered, a hand clamped on her shoulder.

She returned his whisper. "Sir Lukxa I'll be fine, I'm sure."

He gave her a skeptical look. "Promise me you'll shout—*scream*, if anything. . . untoward happens."

She returned his nod. "I'll make Councilor Shad's ears bleed if anything should happen that I don't approve of."

Satisfied with her answer, Sir Lukxa took a step back and then made his way to the closest table to the peculiar entrance to the archives. "Councilor, I'll be sitting right out here with the ledger."

Councilor Shad spoke nothing in return as he waved Hollis inside the room. True to his word, a stack of books was already gathered up in his grip.

Hollis had expected the air inside the archives to be suffocatingly stale. Frozen in time like the books it seemingly held.

Pleasantly, she was proved wrong. The air wasn't the freshest breath her lungs had ever taken in, but it wasn't terrible. The room smelled of old paper and leather. Perhaps a hint of the burning oil in the lantern?

It was glorious. The light *crackling* from the lantern filled the room with an ambiance that Hollis didn't think could be rivaled.

Subtle movement trailed about the air, circling it in a manner that wouldn't allow it to grow stale and musty.

Councilor Shad tapped his fingers against a small table to her right, not far from the entrance of the archive. "Considering I've read almost every book in our library's collection, I think *these* will be the ones that are most useful to you. I've taken the liberty of writing my assistant a note. He will see it come morning and if he thinks of any other books to be of use to you, you'll be notified." Councilor Shad smiled and sat at the small table with a book of his own.

Hollis spoke her thanks and continued to trail the shelves that she could see. The room itself contained several towering shelves, filled with books, seemingly stretching on forever.

Hollis could see no stress upon the spines of the books from being packed together so tight. Each row contained as many books that fit comfortably. The shelves themselves were a dark wood, which matched the overall darkness in the room. The only light came from the opened door and the lantern that Councilor Shad brought.

The desire to grab the light and go running along the shelves to discover how large the room really was grew deep in her mind.

Councilor Shad's voice broke her concentration. "As you can tell, we take the preservation of books quite seriously here. The organizational system is a mess, however. If you think of any subject you'd like to read, let me know and I'll find a book that covers it. I don't need you getting lost in here." His face was flat as he turned a page.

Hollis returned to the table and sat down across from him. Four books sat on her half of the table. Books he'd pulled for her.

As his words registered, Hollis laughed. "You mean to tell me that you haven't organized this place yourself? No systematic organization standards you all follow?" That made the room seem all the more interesting. The possibility of unknown reads at her fingertips was fascinating. Books that may not have been read by Tablin eyes for generations.

The thought crushed her.

Councilor Shad grinned, his teeth catching the light of the lantern. "No, the books are always kept in the position in which they were first deposited in the archive. Sadly, we haven't had any books added in years, the last ones being decades old donations of Omillian work. Some interesting subjects in there. Sadly my understanding of the language isn't as strong as I would like it to be. With no one to practice with, it rusts and becomes obsolete." He turned another page.

"And these books?" Hollis gestured to the stack he had handed to her, tapping the one placed at the very top.

His lips flattened. He held his place in his book with a finger and looked up at her. "Yes, *those* books were taken from Tablin some time ago. I do not know if they were from the original battles, but they aren't from the most recent wars either. Likely from a time when the Catolian continent was split into two ruling clans and not the handful of nations it is now. But was this tome given as a gift to someone in Catol, taken, or found? A book's history is almost as interesting as the book itself, wouldn't you say?"

She nodded and opened the book in front of her. The writing was an old dialect of Tablin that wasn't too far from the modern version she knew. A few words across the texts were hard to understand, but for the most part, she gathered information just fine.

"What made you pick these books?" She skimmed through the pages, doing her best to be careful with what she was sure was priceless materials. One torn page and Councilor Shad would likely rip her head clean off— once she was outside the Archive.

The pages seemed old and worn as she trailed a gloved hand down the material. Perhaps not quite the same paper as the blank sheets for her notes.

But paper nevertheless, bound in a tightly woven cloth.

Councilor Shad grabbed the second book with his free hand from the pile and tilted it back and forth. "From what I remember, these books touch on the basic principles of healing illnesses. Much like my Omilian, Tablin is not a language I'm the most familiar with. My assistant manages to read both languages and has translated a good bit for me."

She cocked her head to the side, rocking on her heels. "You just said you didn't have anyone to practice with?"

His brows raised high on his forehead, an expression of mirth. "Being able to read something and *speak* it are completely different. While not far apart, it's enough. I'm not sure he would be all that willing to converse in a mostly dead language anyway." He turned back to the book he was reading and deposited the Tablin book back into her pile.

"So you can read and understand Tablin, but not Omil?"

He nodded, trailing a leather clad finger down the page before flipping to a new one.

"What—"

"I think your time would be best spent reading, Healer Hollis, rather than investigating me. You can do that some other time, perhaps over a cup of tea?" Councilor Shad grinned and continued reading. Which was fine because everytime this man grinned or smiled or *anything* at her it sent a wave of heat—and annoyance—through her.

Hollis felt that if he had met her flustered gaze, that it would only encourage his behavior toward her.

She took his advice to heart and kept reading.

Halfway to closing the third book in her pile she was skimming through, something caught her attentions.

"Healing with the sight comes from weaving. Reweaving threads is a delicate balance between tension, smoothing, and setting things to their right state. One cannot properly heal a body without considering the state it was in before illness began. Setting strings too rightly may result in the body being unsure of how

to properly operate. Leaving threads frayed can allow the original illness to re-manifest itself. Failing to consider order may result in chaos.

"There are numerous other ways to come into contact with the makeup of a person."

Hollis mulled the thought over in her mind.

Numerous manners in which to contact someone's threads? What other ways could I come into contact with someone's threads?

She drummed her fingers against each other, afraid of what Councilor Shad would do if he saw her touch anything else whilst wearing the gloves.

An idea planted itself in her mind.

Stupid, foolish, insane.

But *possible.*

"I think I have got what I need for the night. I'm growing quite tired, and I'm sure you are too, Councilor Shad. I hope you'll be all right putting these books away?" Hollis stood from the chair and ripped the gloves free from her hands and tossed them on the bit of table between her and Councilor Shad's book piles.

"Of course, have a good night, Lady Hollis. I'll see you come morning." Councilor Shad smiled but made no effort to rise and bid her goodnight. Not that she minded. No, he stayed seated right where he was and turned another page in his book.

As Hollis stepped outside the archives, the world was once more filled with the sound of rain. It poured against the glass ceiling much harder than it had when she'd first arrived.

Sir Lukxa was slumped over his table, his back raising steadily as he slept.

Jostling his shoulder had him upright in a moment. "Are you finished, Sir Lukxa?"

Sir Lukxa took forever to respond, slowly blinking himself awake. "Yes, quite. I will return the ledger in the morning. I do not quite trust it sitting in the office overnight. Were you able to find anything of use, Hollis?" He asked as he stood and gathered up his things.

She rather liked how he looked with the darkness of sleep ringing his eyes and flashes of light above them. It illuminated his hair and further deepened his eyes.

Sir Lukxa quirked his brows. "Hollis?"

Hollis grinned and rushed toward him until she was close enough to whisper in his ear. "Oh, Sir Lukxa, I have such a *wonderful* idea."

CHAPTER NINTEEN

HOLLIS

Hollis restrained herself from flapping her arms as she spoke. "I'm going to kiss you." The fireplace she stood by did nothing to warm her. Its heat was undetectable by her mind. All she could feel in the moment was pins and needles running along her flesh.

Prince Dagen's dark eyes widened, his jaw going slack. "I'm sorry?" His voice cracked as he spoke. The plush pillows he leaned back against seemed to deflate as his head whipped around.

"*What?*" Sir Lukxa parroted the shocked expression and tone Prince Dagen put on. His hands did that thing where he clenched them then stretched his fingers out a few times over. He stood on the other side of the bed from Hollis, putting Prince Dagen, and this bed, between them. The low lighting in the room furthered the dark glare set in Sir Lukxa's eyes.

Hollis quickly spoke up and walked closer to the bed before more words could come out of either of their mouths. "I was researching some stolen books on Tablin magic in the archives and came across the most interesting passage. It got me wondering if there were any other ways I could sense magic aside from normal. I can smell the curse, and I can internally feel my connection to the weave of the world." She took in a large breath to fuel the last bit of her explanation. "So, if I kissed you I should theoretically be able to *taste* the curse and interact with it that way."

Hollis' vision went a bit hazy as she took several smaller breaths to refill her lungs after such a speech.

The thick stench of the curse wafted in the room. Its miasma coated her lungs the closer to Prince Dagen she got.

Prince Dagen wet his lips, blinking several times before he managed to speak. "Why do you need to taste my curse to deal with it?" His voice was still pitched high, lending it the tone of embarrassment. The fact was fueled by the bright red in his cheeks.

Oh, she needed an answer to that question. Hollis fumbled over her first few words of explanation. "It's simple, really. I'm just wanting to—"

"Hollis is unable to access her magic." Sir Lukxa glared at her. It seemed he *didn't* want to keep her secret from the prince any longer.

Her head leaned toward her shoulder.

Well. . . that solved the issue.

The prince fell into another coughing fit, lasting several moments of growing awkwardness between the three occupants of the room—or perhaps it was just her?

Prince Dagen continued to sputter as he spoke. "What do you mean, Lukxa? Why doesn't she have her magic?"

Hollis waved her hand in front of her face. Prince Dagen should have asked her that question rather than jumping straight to the other man in the room. "It's a temporary problem brought on by a slight bit of illness myself. Don't worry."

"An illness? Could I catch this illness if you kiss me? Could my body handle being cursed *and* sick?" Prince Dagen's face was pinched tight with worry.

She shook her head. "There would be no manner in which you could catch this illness, Prince Dagen. I promise." Her fingers twisted around each other.

Prince Dagen turned his gaze from herself to Sir Lukxa.

Sir Lukxa sighed before he shrugged his shoulders until they were practically even with the thin line his lips had become. "I trust her."

"Seemingly against your better judgment." Prince Dagen spoke plainly. "I have never kissed someone in my life and this is to be my first experience?"

Hollis grabbed up her skirt and crawled on her knees to sit on the bed beside the prince. The thick blankets felt magical on her skin. She'd have to ask Sir Lukxa to get a set like this. "Neither of us shall count this as a first kiss. Have no fears, there's nothing romantic about this at all. Besides, you should feel grateful that someone would be willing to entertain the idea of pressing their mouth against yours when all you do is cough and vomit and sit in this. . . filth."

Horror filled Prince Dagen's face. "I am a *prince*!"

Before any other words could come out of the prince's mouth, she held his cheeks and pulled him up to meet her. Prince Dagen's fingers gripped her shoulders, pulling out some of her hair in the process. His muffled protests were smothered as she pressed her mouth firmly against his.

She released him, his breath cutting her face.

"I actually need access to your mouth, prince, if I'm to try and taste any magic." Hollis repositioned herself, straddling one of his legs with her own and threading her fingers in his hair. "Don't enjoy this too much—or at all, really."

The prince turned to Sir Lukxa. She followed Prince Dagen's gaze and found Sir Lukxa giving him a begrudging small shake of his head as he swallowed. Then, the prince turned back to face her, brows tensed up with a nervous look as he leaned his head toward her and closed his eyes.

Hollis pressed her mouth against his once more, his lips parting to give her access to his mouth.

All she could taste was the smoke and anix. It covered the roof of her mouth, filled her nose. But there was something underneath it.

She pulled his face harder against her own, her fingers tangling in his hair, not at all taking a moment to mind how his fingers clawed into her shoulder blade or how his legs shook the longer she had her mouth on his.

There was something *there*—close enough that she could almost see it.

Indigo threads began twisting around her mind, strangling a pale yellow chord with specks of red. They took shape the deeper she dug.

The prince's grip on her shoulders went slack. His hands fell against her hips.

"Hollis, he needs to breathe." Sir Lukxa's hands replaced the prince's on her shoulders, tugging backward with more strength than the prince had managed.

Hollis shrugged Sir Lukxa off. "I've almost got it. Just a few more moments." She blinked a few times, trying to clear the darkness that seeped into her mind.

"You cannot cure him by sucking the life out of him." Sir Lukxa's was venom through his teeth.

Hollis spared a look over her shoulder at him. Sir Lukxa's eyes were molten as he glared down at her, his lips pulled into a flat line.

"I'd hardly consider this sucking. Oh, that sounds horrible. Be quiet, you." She refused to think about the prince's blackened gums as she pressed her mouth against his once more.

A small, pulsating blackness sat still amid the smoke deep in Prince Dagen's chest. Hollis coaxed it closer, her own magic making a connection with the prince's weave of threads.

The moment the curse was within reach, Hollis' magic consumed the darkness, ripped it from his body and pulled it into her own. It twisted in her throat as she tried to swallow it. Screaming against her stomach and lungs. Her body heaved, trying to purge itself of the wickedness that did not belong to her.

Her spine gave out, she slumped forward, landing directly atop Prince Dagen. His ribs stabbed at her middle.

If Hollis had her magic, she wouldn't have to take the curse into herself. She'd slowly untangle it from a person's being and let it dissolve away into nothingness.

This felt far from nothingness.

She felt Sir Lukxa's hands on her shoulders again, ripping her off of the prince. The movement sent the room spinning in circles about her, a black haze covering most of her vision. The darkness threatened to spill from her. It scratched against her throat and insides, screaming in need of its host. Hollis rolled, landing on her knees beside the bed.

"I need something—" Her stomach lurched with the words, a thin trail of black escaping her mouth. She sucked it back with a sharp breath and pressed her hands against her sticky lips.

"What do you need?" Sir Lukxa's hands gripped tight at her shoulders, almost shaking her. Panic rooted itself deep in his pale eyes. His jaw shook.

Her mind spun. What would she need? Combat this darkness with what?

It hit her. An obvious answer. "Something clean, pure."

"Like what? Can you be any more specific?" Sir Lukxa's pale eyes now wide in shock and alarm.

Nothing came to mind. No coy answer to please someone, only smoke.

Perhaps that was an idea, smoother smoke with smoke.

"The dried eucalyptus from your room"—her body wretched—"bring it here and burn it."

Sir Lukxa nodded his head and left the room.

Hollis slumped along the foot of the bed, her body curling in on itself.

"What did you do? I can almost fully breathe again." The prince coughed behind her once more. She looked out the corner of her eye to see Prince Dagen's chest heaving. His brown eyes were still glazed, a touch of concern filling them as he took in the sight of her. "Hollis. Your skin is turning gray—"

Sir Lukxa rushed back into the room and stuck the bundle of dried herbs into the fireplace and pulled it out as quickly as it caught ablaze. "Now what?" His eyes darted between her own, occasionally drifting down to her clenched mouth. The Captain bit his own lips.

She reached out a hand.

Sir Lukxa closed the distance between them in an instant and set the thick stems in her palm, not yet releasing his grip on them. "What are you going to do with this?" The flames consumed the herbs, burning closer to their hands, filling the room with its scent.

The smoke sputtered from her mouth, doing its best to escape her. She pressed her lips tighter and drew in as big a breath as she could manage through her nose.

"Hollis?" Sir Lukxa asked, voice pitched.

Gripping the dried stems tighter, she dropped her jaw and shoved the smoldering springs into her mouth before the wickedness within could escape.

"What are you doing?" Sir Lukxa yelled, pulling back on the bundle.

The dry sprig *snapped* in his hands, leaving a majority of it within her grasp as Sir Lukxa fell a few steps backward.

Hollis crushed the rest of it in her hands and continued to pile the burning plant into her mouth before the captain or Prince Dagen could reach her.

Darkness screamed and fought back against the smoke and magic that surrounded it. Blisters formed along the roof of her mouth and throat as she swallowed the ashes. Her teeth singed her tongue as she tried cooling them.

Her body slid off the bed, the impact of her elbows landing on the floor sent shockwaves through her body as it curled in on itself. Convulsions threatened to overtake her. The muscles around her middle heaved. Acid climbed her throat. She swallowed it back down and breathed deeply through her nose.

She just had to wait.

This had to work.

A shrill ringing filled her ears, building until it smothered all other sounds. It screamed in agony and hatred.

And then, *nothing*.

Altogether her body relaxed and her chest slid down against the ground. "Hollis?" She couldn't tell who spoke her name.

Sounds blended around in her mind. Colors and shapes, sounds and thoughts, all spinning, crashing against her skull.

Her throat bobbed. "I need to vomit."

Sir Lukxa grabbed at her waist, hoisting her up from the ground and against his lap as he had the night in his baths. His fingers dug into her shoulder. A bucket sat at his side.

Hollis gripped the edges of iron and let the sludge pool out of her mouth. It filled every bit of her mouth and coated her teeth. She couldn't breathe as it poured from her.

Black filled the bucket. Her shoulders heaved as the last remnants of the curse left her. She could see the blackness wisping in the air. It struggled to reach further than the lip of the pot, obviously reaching toward the prince before it puttered out.

"You've cured me." Prince Dagen's voice was filled with an unbelieving laugh.

The prince sat at his full height. Color flooded in his face and hands. Oiled hair and the thinness of his frame still created a stark contrast, but he glowed.

Hollis let out a broken scoff. "No, no I gave us *time*. . . I couldn't hope to remove all of the curse."

The darkness within Prince Dagen had been so intense, rooted so *deeply* inside of him that she wasn't sure if it would ever have ended were she to sink herself into it.

It was a wonder Prince Dagen still lived and breathed.

Tears welled in her eyes, a sour feeling under her tongue. A terrible feeling. To know the extent of something so horrible and unfixable. Hollis hoped her feelings of pity and sorrow didn't translate to her face as she continued to speak. "This curse will keep growing within you until it has consumed your being. I can't get rid of it like this." *I couldn't hope to even try.*

Prince Dagen's face fell. "So, how will you truly heal me?"

She wiped her mouth with the back of her hands, grimacing at the ashes that rubbed off. "I haven't figured that out yet."

CHAPTER TWENTY

LUKXA

L ukxa stood where Hollis had stripped naked the few days prior, putting a majority of his weight on one leg as he cocked his hip.

"So," Lukxa drew out the word. "What's the reason you all wanted to see me?" He made a vague gesture with his right hand before he let it flop back down at his side.

Lukxa had been dreading this meeting since he deciphered the coded note his first night back in the castle with Hollis. He masked the feelings of dread with unimpressive boredom and annoyance. Keeping his chin slightly tucked, his face flat and relaxed.

The occupants in the half-empty council room turned to face each other. Bending heads toward one another as they spoke in hushed words. It was dark enough Lukxa couldn't fully make out everyone's features from underneath the heavy cloaks they wore. Enough light filled the room that Lukxa knew his own uncloaked features were clearly visible, while they remained hidden.

But not hidden enough as they should have been. Lukxa knew their faces, knew their voices. Or most of them. There were seldom a few bodies in this syndicate that were unknown to him. But Lukxa would shed light on their faces soon enough. Present them to the world with crimes that would leave them unable to further harm himself or Prince Dagen.

Or Hollis.

A voice deeper spoke up. "We simply want to hear reassurance from you about your mission ourselves. Not through our mutual friend."

Lukxa swallowed, hard, then fixed a glare on his face. "I'm not sure what else you need to hear, Councilor Collin. Our plan is still the same. Same as it has always been." He put on an air of indifference with his tone. Keeping it aloof, slightly condescending if possible.

Councilor Sophy let a sharp laugh burst from her chest. "I'm not even sure *you* know what the plan is anymore. First was pushing it back until you were more settled into your position as captain—*which we got you.*" She gestured to herself and Councilor Cane, who wore a similarly off-put expression. "Then it was too close to the king and queen falling ill and dying. And now, *now* it's just too close to Prince Dagen's coronation for comfort. *Our* comfort." Her voice took on a husked growl at the end.

Lukxa *clicked* his tongue. "I know—"

Another voice cut him off. "No, child. I do not think you do." That was a voice he did not know a face for. He assumed by their regal accent that the man belonged to a Dukedom that vied for power in the throne. Whoever the man was likely thought he had more power than he did. Figured the council would let him rule as king, when, in fact, the members of the council sitting in this room fought to dissolve the crown entirely.

Lukxa kept his eyes trained in the middle of the group. A sharp exhale through his nose. "I've finally retrieved an *actual* Tablinian healer. You know all the other physicians *you* brought in couldn't convey that you *actually* cared about the prince. It was sloppy work. Several other councilors made mention that it felt weird to hire such nobody healers in order to keep the secret that Dagen was sick." Lukxa's mind throbbed as he tried thinking of the other healers that had passed through the castle walls.

"And how exactly is some bumbling Tablinian healer going to help our cause? What if she manages to heal Dagen, *hmm*? Did you think of that?" Collin's condescending tone had Lukxa wanting to tear the man's throat out.

He had to think of a way to answer that quickly. Lukxa could not afford anyone ripping Hollis away from the castle. Not when she was finally able to make some progress toward actually helping Dagen.

"I've been bedding her." Lukxa swallowed and ran his tongue over his teeth. It wasn't technically a falsity. "I spent the two weeks you gave me to retrieve one last healer holed up in her house, bending her around my finger." Several persons in the room let out different sounds of astonishment or horror. Lukxa swore he heard someone bring up how she looked wretched when stripped naked in front of the council.

"Yes," Councilor Collin drawled on. "You say that, but there's a chance she could actually figure out what's going on. What would happen should she seek a private audience with any other councilor?"

"Councilor Shad looked like he wanted a turn with her. Practically foamed at the mouth." Councilor Sophy snickered again, a hand covering her mouth. "Add some knowledge to his world."

Councilor Cane followed Sophy's suit. "Perhaps lending her to Shad would finally bring him to see the light."

Lukxa tucked that piece of information in the back of his head, right beside the note of Collin wanting to throw him out of the council meeting the day Lukxa brought Hollis in. "I think you're overlooking one major point. Hollis is *Tablin*. Her disdain for the crown runs deep as mine. The monarchy blazed our homes, remember?" A scoff broke free of his lips as he raked a hand across his scalp and settled his palm to lay flat on the crown of his head. "I don't think Hollis is in want for any other. . . entertainment. Besides, I'm paying her to play healer. She isn't here to cure Dagen." Lukxa waved his hand. "Once my. . . deed is done, blame can be placed upon Hollis and Tablin as a whole for the death of Prince Dagen. You get to wage your war and take the throne."

Everyone seemed to nod and *hum* amongst themselves. Lukxa tilted his gaze up to stare through the glass ceiling. His feet tapped against the ornate marble floor. His shoulder cried at having his arm bent and extended so far above him. He dropped it and stuffed his hands into his pants pocket.

Acid in his stomach forced its way up his throat. Bile burned his tongue as he swallowed it back down, hoping he had not made too much noise. Lukxa hated this room. Hated the chill and ornate features. Hated that it was such an obvious place to meet.

Hated that within the heart of Catol such rot planned ruin and damnation.

"All right." Councilor Cane clapped his hands, silencing the room. "We'll allow her to remain here for now. We would hate for you to lose such a precious outlet of your. . . energy. But, remember your purpose here in these walls. Now get going, *Captain Lukxa*. You've got big plans to enact."

"It's been ages since I left my rooms. Oh, this is wonderful." Prince Dagen ran his frail hand along the hedge of a round-shaped bush. Dagen and himself had snuck in the castle gardens only a matter of moments ago and already Lukxa's ward had brought up the joy of 'freedom' seven times.

Dagen's '*official return*' to the castle from finishing school had yet to take place. Secrecy in their movements was a must. Pomp and circumstance was needed at the arrival of a *healthy* Prince Dagen. That was still a week away.

But Lukxa could only keep the prince cooped up in the royal bedchambers for so long on a nice day now that Dagen was feeling marginally better.

As soon as Dagen had the window to his room opened, he begged Lukxa to secret him away to the garden. Then Dagen had showcased his ability to get out of bed, touch his toes, and held a plank for several minutes. Lukxa had quickly been convinced the revitalized prince could handle a secret mission to smell some flowers and feel unfiltered sunshine in full.

Though, Lukxa shuddered at the thought of *secreting away* with the Crowned Prince of Catol. The poor use of language would not be repeated in his mind.

The pair had taken all the precautions they could to hide Dagen's identity from any possible wandering castle staff. Lukxa shoved at least three layers of clothing over Dagen's person. The top layer being that of a page boy's uniform. And atop Dagen's head, hiding the wheat-color of his hair, was a drab beige hat.

Dagen looked nothing like a prince in this moment.

There was no weight upon his shoulders of upholding a kingdom. Nor the stress of a wicked council after his throat.

The late morning sun began to lend her heat to the enclosed portion of the garden they meandered about in, not enough to allow Dagen to remove any of the layers that swathed him. The bulk of the layers on his body paled in comparison to the stature his frame used to be before the illness ate away at his being.

Dagen never sat still a moment in his life. Ever since Lukxa had taken the position of his right hand two years ago the two trained relentlessly— and for Dagen, it had paid off in strong muscles and a will like no others.

In Lukxa's four years spent as Captain of the Royal Guard—the last two where he also served as an honorary councilor and Dagen's right hand— Lukxa and Dagen had trained often. Only stopping once the illness came and the facade of finishing school came about. They could not even train in secret with Dagen's frail constitution that only seemed to grow worse.

A cough drew his attentions back to the world at hand.

Dagen's body heaved a few times before stilling. His frail hand tightly gripped the cane Lukxa had swiped from the physician's wing. Dagen hobbled over to a small stone bench nestled between towering yew and lilac bushes.

How the gardeners managed to keep the blooms alive past their expectancy was a secret hidden from all. The castle gardens were immaculate.

Light filtered through the leaves from surrounding trees and danced upon Prince Dagen's figure.

If Lukxa were a painter, he would call the scene perfect. A downtrodden man—*prince*—looking on at his cane with disdain, yet holding onto a glimmer of hope as the light around him shone on a body that slowly grew stronger.

Perhaps if Lukxa had not been sold to the knights academy, if Catol had not waged war against Omil, he would have studied the arts?

Or perhaps the wistfulness of capturing beauty could only be done in part because of the turmoil he had seen in his life.

Lukxa took a small step toward Prince Dagen, squaring his shoulders and spine, hands tucked behind his back, to speak with confidence. "You will be feeling better the more Healer Hollis works with you." Lukxa was not ready to extinguish the hope that had newly burned in Dagen's eyes. There was a time for reality and a time for encouragement. He yearned that the words he spoke were laden with truth and truth alone.

"Do you think I'll be well enough to take part in the tournament? I don't think I could take hearing of more salacious rumors with every event I miss. But missing my *own* birthday ceremony—that would take the cake, wouldn't it?" Dagen kept a smile on his lips but failed to push it high enough to reach his eyes in any fashion. Now his face looked ready to break.

Hope could only burn so long, it would seem.

"Healer Hollis has informed me that she believes the goal to be something possible." Guilt prickled his stomach as he lied directly to Dagen's face. There would not be a chance Dagen would fight in the tourney.

"How is she faring since she healed me last night? You seem to have spoken with her just fine," Dagen asked.

Lukxa felt his jaw tighten as he recalled Hollis' trembling form after kissing Prince Dagen and throwing up black tar. He had hope that Dagen was cured at that moment. That Lukxa wouldn't have to experience the painful and almost jealous twist in his gut as Hollis purged the curse from Dagen's body once more. Seeing the embodiment of something so wicked was enough to set tremors in Lukxa's body.

Another emotion grew in the pit of his stomach with the growing fear. Lukxa didn't want to give name to the feeling of anger and resentment combined.

The moment they had left Dagen's chambers the night before, Hollis had all but collapsed against the wall. Lukxa carried her the entire way back to his apartments and forced several glasses of water down her throat before helping her brush her hair and teeth for the evening.

Thankfully, Hollis managed her other facilities on her own. There hadn't been much talking aside from his checking that she was all right in the moments before she fell asleep. He applied a bit of salve to her lips while she slept when he realized she had forgotten to do so. Lips which were cracked and blistered.

Her body showed no signs of wanting to wake this morning, which was fine considering his sudden meeting with the—

Shaking his head, Lukxa spoke more encouragement to the prince. "It was always in Hollis' realm of thought that you would be healed by your birthday. I would not doubt her words." Lukxa did not see it necessary to mention that she was contractually obligated to try and heal him by his birthday.

"Yes, but that was when she could. . . *see*." Dagen spun about to be sure that no one heard.

Growing up in a palace that had ears built into the walls lent superstition to the young man.

The gardens were private, one of the truly private places in the castle. The thick yew hedges and towering bushes and trees blocked outsiders from glancing in, and the knights surrounding outside the castle walls kept all outsiders where they belonged.

"Hollis is a capable healer. You saw how she did last night. She is well-known in the world of holistic medicine apparently. More so than I think she realizes. She has not stopped working on a plan to heal you since she got here." He would leave out the bits involved in which he had to drag her here

245

to the castle kicking and screaming. "Do you no longer trust my judgment?"

"You're not trying to kill me anymore. Are you?" Lukxa couldn't read the stillness in Dagen's eye.

Lukxa forced a grin on his face. "The inclination has not crept up on me. I would say you are safe." The reminder, no matter how filled with jest, always brought pangs of guilt and remorse.

"I'm safe from *you*, you mean?" Dagen returned Lukxa's smile, unaware of the tensity. "Then I'd say I trust you. No better person to trust than the one who holds your life in their hands. Now, I rest in Lady Hollis' as well."

"I would caution you, Prince, about referring to Hollis with the title *'lady.'* I am almost afraid she'll take the title to head and flaunt it over me the rest of her stay." The scene was clear in his mind.

Dagen's laugh burst from his chest, the strength of it shocked Lukxa back a step. "Goodness, I don't think that would be possible from my meetings with her. Lady Hollis seems the type of woman that could weave an insult meant for her destruction as a powerful accessory. Truly, she's bent for politics. I can see it now. *Lady Hollis of the Hozen Court.*" Dagen sprawled his hands outward, making a grand show. "Maybe I'll make her a councilor."

The grin on Dagen's face only grew wider as more bits of sun cast on his face between the coming clouds. "It's so nice to be outside."

Eight.

"It is. Is there anything more you would like to do while we are out here or are you content with spending your time on this bench?" Lukxa could not permit himself to take Prince Dagen anywhere outside of the garden, lest anyone see him and rumor spread of a weakened and fragile monarchy. But there was the hedge maze they could walk in, or the lily pond.

"I am tired. I think I just want to sit here now. I know—I was so excited to stretch my legs," Dagen laughed again, "but I am *so tired*. My heart is sludge in my chest, and my lungs made of iron." Dagen's voice took on a dramatic timbre. But the sorrow laced between Dagen's words stabbed Lukxa between the ribs.

Lukxa nodded along as Dagen spoke. "The air here is fresh enough. The garden still flourishes. Flora lines the walking paths and curls around little alcoves and benches. Everything still blooms no matter the *storms* we endured. The little blossoms were stronger than I would have given them credit for, Lukxa. Though, I had not had the chance to see them before the rain. Perhaps they were fuller?" Lukxa twisted his head to inspect the blossoms that surrounded them.

Dagen pulled a lilac stem to his face and sniffed it before releasing it back to the bush. "The most interesting thing is to think that I *own* this. This garden is no longer my parents. It's *mine*. And I don't know how to feel about that. It's tiring," Dagen breathed.

"That is all right, Dagen. We can rest a while. Take solace in the fact that it seems like all storms have passed through the area." Lukxa sat on a small iron bench within arms reach from where Dagen sat.

A breeze, weighed with floral perfume and scatters of sunshine, swept into the garden. Carried behind it was the last trace smell of petrichor. It would have snatched the hat on Dagen's head had he not grabbed it.

Dagen *tsked*. "You know what? All that rain shouldn't have bothered me so. My joints ached for days as it poured non stop outside my window." Dagen leaned back, letting his head fall with his body. "I don't want to wallow again. No, I refuse to. Tell me, how is sharing your bed with our Tablin friend? *Oh*, that rhymes." His brows shot up as he laughed at his own joke.

Lukxa balked. He had been spending most of this waking time outside of his apartments trying *not* to dwell over the fact he was sleeping in the same bed as Hollis. What had once been a practical decision in his mind had grown into something he craved as emotions for the woman swelled within him.

Lukxa did his best to steel himself, hoping the warmth he felt in his cheeks was from the sun, and not a violent bout of blushing. "I have a settee, you know."

"You can't fit on that." Dagen grinned, trapping his lips with his teeth. The sunshine seemed to glow every brighter on his face.

"She certainly can," Lukxa quipped back.

Dagen waved his hands in the air. "But she isn't fitting onto it, is she? You are far too much of a gentleman. *Honestly*, Lukxa. Answer me honestly. The only gossip that circulates these days is my falsified wrongdoings or that the entire continent of Tablin is going to kill us all. People act as if we don't have *trade agreements* with a majority of the Tablin countries. I want to hear something more interesting."

Lukxa tilted his head, trying not to shiver as the low tied hair tickled the back of his neck. "I didn't take you as one for rumors and dramatics." Oh. *Oh*, his hair had caught itself in his collar. Lukxa bit his lip and calmly reached back and pulled the long strands free from his shirt without squirming like a child.

Which reminded him of the fact that Hollis had asked to braid his hair in the middle of the night. She had sat up, likely still sleeping, and told him *his hair would be so pretty braided*. He'd had to hold her down with his legs to keep her from crawling up the bed toward him to make a bird's nest of him.

"Tell me," Dagen pushed at Lukxa's shoulder with the cane he had, bringing Lukxa back to reality.

Lukxa pushed Dagen's back and took up his own seat on the far side of the same bench. "Is that a royal order? Do I need to get some paper, a pen, and your seal to make it official?" He coughed and spoke in a stuffy voice. *"Prince Dagen declares that Captain of the Royal Guard Sir Lukxa Ryoo is hereby required to share the intimate details of his housing situation with Lady Healer Hollis Avayana."* He trailed off in a fit of laughter.

Dagen's head fell forward, a grin eating his face as he laughed, clutching his stomach. "They're *intimate details*, are they?"

"You are impossible." Though. . . Sharing a few details would not hurt. Dagen was Lukxa's friend. This was what friends—Lukxa blushed, thinking once more about Hollis and his bed and, oh he had to stop—

this is what friends did. They talked. "She has been sleeping at the bottom of my bed, she sticks her frozen feet up my shirt in the morning, and she's—she is fine. Pleasant. No complaints." Lukxa would not mention the night where she slept wrapped up tightly in his arms, the scent of gin lacing their mingled breath.

He turned to find Dagen's jaw hanging slack. "Hollis sleeps at the *bottom* end of your bed? Isn't that uncomfortable? I was hoping for something. . . *more.*" Dagen pinched his fingers together and shook his hands as he spoke.

Lukxa waved his hand, brushing him off. "The bed is more comfortable than the settee for either of us—her legs would dangle off the ends of it most likely. And I was not about to sleep on the settee. Sharing a sleeping space has been fine. There was a problem in the baths the other day—"

Dagen's face lit up as bright as his blond hair. "*This sounds like exciting news.* Keep going with that." Dagen shook his head almost violently as his eyes went wide with excitement.

Lukxa glared at him. "You truly have nothing better to ask of me?"

"This *is* the best I could ever ask. You're sleeping with a woman. Lukxa Ryoo. The man who worked too much for anyone to be in the picture." Dagen's tone was filled with awe.

Lukxa glared and pointed at him. "Do not spin this worse than it actually is, Dagen Alder Catol. You know I *have* romantic inclinations toward women. If you are going to tease my virginal status I could easily turn it back around on *you.*"

Dagen raised his brows and squinted his eyes as he looked Lukxa up and down. "I'm ten and nine, you're five and twenty." He held the numbers up on his fingers as he spoke. "Making fun of *me,*" Dagen gestured to himself. "Would be childish. Also—being chaste is *expected* of a crowned prince. No siring possible heirs that could slit me or my legitimate sons in the throat down the line. Now, continue what happened in your baths?" Dagen waved his hands in a *continue* motion.

Lukxa gave a dramatic sigh before he spoke. "Hollis was trying to undress to take a bath. While she was undressing her shoulder dislocated or *something*. I heard her cry and came to check on her. Helped her set her shoulder, got the highneck off of her, and let her alone to bathe." He stuck to the basic facts and spoke as plainly as possible.

Dagen steepled his fingers in front of his mouth, and then pointed at Lukxa. "Was this the same day she stripped naked in front of the council?" Dagen raised his brows halfway to his golden hairline.

A blush burned Lukxa's body as the image of Hollis' naked form came to mind once more. "*How* in the world did you hear about that?" The words shook as they exited his mouth.

Dagen's grin grew wider than Lukxa thought possible. "Don't worry, Lukxa, it's not common gossip. My source is secretive. How did *that* whole situation go over with our murderous friends?"

Lukxa knew there were only a few Council members who would willingly go to speak with the prince. And of that number, fewer that would willingly recall such details.

Lukxa would place his bets on Councilor Dem being the canary that squealed.

"She stripped naked in front of the council as a power move. How do you think that went? Let us change the subject. Your birthday. What do you want? Anything I can look for?"

Dagen shifted his gaze away from him, back into the garden around them. The light dulled in his eyes, which now focused forever away. Unfocused, or focused on something that was not there. "I. . . am a prince. I do not have wants, remember? I appreciate the gesture though, I do. I wouldn't mind not being sick anymore. . ."

It was not a fun feeling whatsoever. Watching the light dim in a friend's eye as he slumped backward in his spot.

Lukxa patted Dagen's knee. He caught sight of his watch in the process. "Let me know if you think of something." It was time to dim the light even further. He trapped his lips between his teeth before he spoke. "I'm afraid it's time for me to return you to your rooms so I can attend training."

He lent Dagen his arm to stand with. "I haven't been outside in so long." Dagen's voice broke at the end. "Can't I stay out a little longer?" His jaw trembled as his eyes glossed with the threat of tears. "*Please?*"

Lightning shot through Lukxa's heart. "I'm sorry, Dagen. Your official coming home is scheduled soon. You will be free to do what you wish then."

Dagen scoffed. "Provided I am healthy enough to enact my *freedom*. If I look anything like the shell I am now, the council will keep me under lock and key. I'm no longer in the mood to be in the garden, so *I am choosing to go back inside myself.*" Dagen ground his jaw tight and used Lukxa's arm, and his cane, to rise to his feet.

It took Dagen several moments to steady himself upon being upright. His face had taken a pale hue, pupils blown wide—consuming the brown iris in black.

A cool breeze trailed through the garden, pulling a shiver from Dagen's frame. "I'm steady. Let's go. I want to lay down." His voice was low and quiet. Sounding fragile.

The two trailed down the cobbled circular stones that made up the garden paths. The stepping stones occasionally gave way slightly as they *squished* with the sound of rain the ground had yet to drink in. Distant sounds carried through the small path they trailed. Chatter and laughter. Birds singing. Bells tolling.

Dagen stopped his hobbling, pulling Lukxa to a sudden halt beside him. "I want lilac cordial and cake, with chocolate strawberries. I want to eat that again."

Distant memories of singing celebratory songs and the taste of fruit wine gathered in Lukxa's mind. Followed by the faint remembering of healthy monarchs.

Lukxa swallowed. "If that is what you wish. I will make it happen." Lukxa continued onward.

Dagen did not follow. He stood still between the rustling branches of an aspen tree. His face calm and regal as he tilted his chin to meet Lukxa's gaze. "Lukxa. . . You and Hollis seem lovely together. Moving fluidly, complementing each other. I recommend looking deeper into that."

Heat gripped at Lukxa's stomach and throat. "I think if I were to look any deeper I would *drown*."

CHAPTER TWENTY-ONE

LUKXA

The sun beat hard upon Lukxa's neck once more on this day. With the sun finally shining again, the rain behind them, Lukxa was able to secure a time-slot on the outdoor training field faster than the indoor rooms were going to be available.

Finally he could burn the energy and tension that pulsed under his skin.

The training yard—which was a large plot of packed dirt, sectioned off by a wooden fence and small wooden platform—was filled with thirty-some moving bodies. Half of Lukxa's knights did their sword drills without flaw, the other. . . spoke for themselves in a lack of ability. Those who fell behind in skill would be an embarrassment to his name at the tournament if they didn't strive toward improvement.

Perhaps it was time to switch things up?

Lukxa paced along the dirt training field. Walking along the large wooden fence. Moving around gave Lukxa the ability to watch his men from all angles. No one would be quite able to pin where his eyes landed on—or rather *who* they did. He was an invisible force hovering about them in a sense.

Someone jogged up toward him. Lukxa turned to find a young page approaching. "Captain Lukxa, Councilor Dem is itching to use the field. He said he knows you've still some time left, but he said—and this is him not me. . ." The young page waved at now reddening face. ". . . *Your men act like they could use some whooping* from his own group. Councilor Dem laughed as he said it, so maybe that isn't mean, um, but still your time—"

Lukxa pulled a small electrum silver piece from his pocket and gave it to the flushed and sweating boy—who was still fanning his face. "Tell Councilor Dem that his message was received. Thank you."

The young page nodded before dashing back inside the castle, sticking close to the fence so as to not be made acquaintance with someone's wooden sword.

"Listen up." Lukxa's voice easily carried over the entire field and silenced everyone. "I want you to pair off with someone who has more experience than you. Use this time to learn something new. Working with someone slightly less experienced can help drill in what you already know, and help others improve. We have got half an hour left on the field, so make it count. If we go over, Councilor Dem has offered to let his *personal* guard train with us. I do not think any of you want that." Lukxa's gaze trailed up the castle walls, settling his gaze on the window of his apartments.

Hollis had slept through Lukxa's readying himself for his morning rounds meeting and had still been sleeping as he returned from his walk with Dagen to again ready himself for the three hours of training. Lukxa had done stretches near his fireplace, drank a couple cups of water, and ate a slice of bread from the small loaf he had purchased along with the rest of Hollis' requests.

She had slept soundly the night before. Not moving around or stealing his blankets—he liked his blankets very much. But even when she committed blanket theft, Hollis was a soft, warm presence in his bed. Not that he would admit that aloud to anyone, including Dagen and his never-ending prodding.

A twinge of guilt grew at the base of his skull, souring his throat and stomach as thoughts he did not want to acknowledge surfaced.

You are using her as bait, are you not? Using her to push the hands of those who would willfully slaughter her.

No.

Lukxa counted backward from twenty. Grounding himself as he took in the world around himself. The light breeze that went through the training yard, the smell of dirt and sweat. How blue the sky was—how beautiful it was after never-ending gray skies.

Lukxa *would* be able to save Hollis and Dagen from the fate he was paid to bring them.

He had to save them.

The exact moment Lukxa first felt ill with his orders was blurry in his mind. He remembered slowly ruminating over his actions, feeling the weight of the coins that lined his pocket, and the praise he had been given for *being so dedicated to helping purge Catol—and the rest of the continent—of such wickedness.*

That praise helped fuel his pride and intense hatred for the crown that ordered the eradication of his people.

But after the death of the king and queen, his feelings lessened. They had been the ones, alongside the council, to wage war on Omil. Prince Dagen had no ties to such actions. Slitting his throat felt far from the correct thing to do.

Still, Lukxa had tried.

He continued trailing along the fence, counting numbers backward as needed when the thoughts of betrayal and guilt grew heavy.

"Flur, your grip is too tight in your top hand. Relax it slightly," Lukxa called out. The young knight made the adjustment and struck at her opponent again. "That is better."

Corrections were slowly shouted across the field from experienced fighters and himself. Each time one was spoken an encouraged nod would be given in response. Thankfully, Lukxa's new recruits were eager to learn today.

A small cry rang out just before Lukxa had the chance to call them all to stop for the day. He snapped his attentions back to the field to see a young knight clutching his upper arm. Lukxa resisted the urge to run a hand down his face and scream as he walked over.

"All right everyone, this is a small accident. Not something to gawk and waste time over." Lukxa extended a hand to the young knight.

The injured knight's face twisted as he held his arm out toward Lukxa. Travis was ten and seven, if Lukxa recalled correctly. Late in joining because of a lack of sponsorship into knighthood. But the young man had taken quickly to life in the castle. Did well during drills. *Usually.*

The cut on Travis' arm wasn't deep; Lukxa doubted that he could even reach most of his fingertip inside the cut. A small trail of blood ran down the sleeve of the boy's arm. Lukxa continued to poke around the injury.

"Can you feel this?" Lukxa studied the young knight's face.

"Yes, sir." Travis' brown eyes reddened as unshed tears formed. The muscles in his face pulled tighter the more Lukxa poked and prodded. It was an unfortunate part of checking the level of injury. Seeing how much pain a wound inflicted. Travis was doing well dealing with it all things considered.

"Good news—you will live. And it should be healed enough by the festival and tournament. Go see a nurse to get it cleaned up." Lukxa turned his attention to the knight Travis was training with as the latter ran off. "Could you not have missed?"

"I wouldn't have had to try and miss if the boy wasn't distracted," Harin said, wiping the edge of his sword free from the bits of blood it had stolen from Travis' arm.

Lukxa let out a sigh and ran a hand down his face. "Travis does need to learn."

"Dodging is an important skill," Harin spoke in a sing-song voice.

"Very." Lukxa looked back to his apartment's window and found a person standing behind the panes. He stumbled before righting himself. Hopefully, no one had seen his blunder.

Hollis was fully dressed and staring intently down at the field. She waved at him, her face too far for him to make an expression from. He held up a finger toward her, signaling he would be back to his apartments in a few minutes.

Lukxa cleared his throat, took a minute to steady his nerves, then pivoted to face his men. "All right, good work. Take the rest of the day off, everyone. We do not need any more injuries from anyone overworking themselves. If you have rounds tonight, though, make sure that you are keeping a *vigilant eye*. You do not want to be caught slacking off on. . . surprise check-ins." Lukxa grinned at a few of the older knights, a silent extension of permission to scare the life out of a few of the younger knights on rounds—if they could catch them unaware. Dodging was far from the only important skill that needed refining by these knights.

Lukxa waited for a handful of the knights in the area to leave before vacating himself.

Lingering gave Lukxa the chance to cool his body off before reentering the heated castle. He spotted several groupings of knights and other castle workers mingling scattered about the main courtyard. Nods and pleasantries were exchanged as Lukxa made his way to one of the servants' entrances on the far side of the castle to enter by the kitchens.

The wooden door stood cracked as he approached. The smell of yeast and cured meats wafted out the door.

Lukxa's stomach growled as he pushed open the kitchen door and stepped inside. He looked around the room, trying to spot a familiar face.

"Hey, *Sorin!*" Lukxa called out, a large smile growing on his face. "Do you think I can pawn off a small plate?"

Sorin, a cook who was around Lukxa's age, turned around, a joking scowl on his face.

"I can't exactly tell the captain of the guard no. I could try and tell a friend no, but I don't think it'd end in my favor." The man barked a laugh before putting together a plate of some bread, cheeses, and meats. Lukxa snuck a handful of grapes as he slunk out of the kitchens and to his apartments.

Lukxa snacked as he walked back to his rooms. The meats and cheeses filled the void in his stomach that always formed after training. The grapes refreshed his mouth after.

By the time he reached his wing, the plate was empty.

The door opened with a simple turn of the knob. He shoved down the tiny bubble of irritation. After several evenings of her begging him to leave her a key, he had given in. But seemingly she failed to use it. Lukxa's efforts to keep Hollis safe could only go so far. She had to employ *some* common sense herself. "You ought to lock the door when I'm not here."

As soon as he shut the door behind him the scent of floral perfume danced over his skin.

"Why go through the trouble? If someone waltzes in with the intention to hurt me, I'll spring one of the many traps you have set in this room. I've found thirty of them—I'm sure I've only scratched the surface."

"You have several more to find. Though, it may be in your best interest to *not* go searching for them." The guilt of her losing a finger or an eye already weighed on him. Hollis was smart, she had been able to recognize the tellings of traps without springing them. Perhaps she would be fine in the end? So long as she did not try to pick up the bed.

Hollis flapped her arms at her side. "We'll see. If you're done running around for the day, Lukxa, I need to purge the prince again. If we're to keep up the appearance that he's being healed by me, I actually need to do so." She *popped* her lips, giving him a wide-eyed expression.

Lukxa nodded his head in response, pushing through the stone that sunk in his stomach.

CHAPTER TWENTY-TWO

HOLLIS

P rince Dagen hadn't wasted a single second as Hollis entered the royal bedchamber with Sir Lukxa. "I assume that you're here to break my curse down more?" He closed the book he'd been reading, setting it on his bedside table as Hollis and Lukxa approached.

"*Smart boy*. Being that I've already removed it once, your body should accept my magic much easier. It won't take as long to remove another chunk." Hollis gestured to Sir Lukxa, who pulled a chair up beside the prince's bed along with a fresh chamber pot.

"Have you figured out your plan for *after* this? When or if someone from the *clinic* wants to see you heal me? Tricking the council was one matter, but I don't think we considered anyone else." Prince Dagen had been thinking; she appreciated a man who could plan for the future. Then again, his whole life was spent training him to rule a kingdom.

Hollis hadn't taken any potential snooping about into consideration. Unlike Prince Dagen and Sir Lukxa, she was a person of the moment and the moment alone. The idea that she would again be brought to Prince Dagen's rooms in the presence of other people—let alone healers—hadn't quite crossed her mind. Frankly, her mind was too preoccupied with a million other thoughts.

"Not really." She ignored Sir Lukxa's almost pained grunt as she spoke. "I know that if I'm brought to see you, I'll be expected to act as if I have my magic. The castle healers may be more versed in Tablin healing. Just need to. . . I'll just make it up as I go—*practice as normal really*. When I'm finished, you'll breathe easier and rest your face more. Water your forehead before we come to look like sweat. Give a more realistic show. Just how we tricked the council before."

Dagen nodded his head rapidly, to the point Hollis expected it to fly off his shoulders. "Got it. Fake sick, fake better. If we have the forewarning, you can heal me honestly and I can truthfully breathe easy." Prince Dagen counted his tasks off on his fingers.

Hollis found the mannerisms of the prince childish, in a cute manner.

"Good." Hollis stood on her chair and reached up into the curtains of Dagen's bed and broke free a few sprigs of lavender that hung. He sat up more against his pillows, resting a hand on her knee to stabilize her as she worked a few more sprigs free.

"Will that work as well as the eucalyptus?" Prince Dagen's voice held a touch of concern.

Hollis shook her head. "I don't see why it wouldn't. Both herbs are used in purifying and cleansing." She wouldn't mention to either that eucalyptus brought one protection and lavender was a sign of distrust.

Hopefully, it would aid her body in not trusting the curse—to help her purge it from herself? That sounded good enough.

She hopped back to the floor and set the sprigs on the small bedside table. "Besides, there wasn't any more in Sir Lukxa's apartments. I'll have more ordered later if I can." Hollis hoped that she could get such a thing ordered to the castle quickly.

"Terribly sorry for the inconvenience," Sir Lukxa said. His voice dripped with sarcasm. The tone didn't match with the tension that had grown behind his eyes. He couldn't look at herself or Prince Dagen too long without his face contorting as though *he* were going to vomit.

Prince Dagen picked up the few lavender sprigs. "Could I just eat it? Fire free?" He twisted them around, studying each cluster of flowers.

How perfect—he'd asked just the question she'd been mulling over all morning.

Now, she got to sound smart in her crazy idea.

"The burning makes it work. Burns the darkness." Hollis cocked her head. "The curse is rooted deep within you. When I rip it free, my magic," she grabbed the candle on his bedside table and lit it, then settled the purple buds above the flames until they started to blacken and burn, "combined with the burning purifier, destroys the bonds the curse has on you. Not the plant itself." She held it towards Prince Dagen's mouth. "By all means, you can try."

A grin stretched on her face as Prince Dagen's eyes widened at the smoking flower inching closer to his face. Perfuming the air with the scent of floral ash.

A hand landed on her shoulder. She caught Sir Lukxa's eye. "Perhaps another time, when the council would not be questioning his burned mouth?"

She held Sir Lukxa's gaze longer, feeling the tension growing in his grip on her shoulder.

What was wrong with him?

"Well spoken, Captain." She shrugged Sir Lukxa's hand off of her shoulder. The contact was missed soon as it was gone. She blew out the fire that had caught and handed the sprigs back to Sir Lukxa. His face wore an expression twisted. His eyes held a glint of amusement, but his smile didn't quite reach his eyes. Lending itself to an interesting blend of amusement and disappointment. "I don't want this to be cinders when I need it. When I pull away, please do light it for me."

Sir Lukxa nodded his head, holding the lavender over the flame, but not close enough as to catch them ablaze. His eyes now trained on the little flame from the candle.

Prince Dagen's face grew green at his cheeks.

Hollis glared. "Again, don't enjoy this."

"Hard to enjoy the feeling of my insides being ripped apart." Prince Dagen swallowed.

"Good." The moment Hollis' lips met Prince Dagen's, the darkness curled around itself. It pressed deeper into the prince's being.

No matter how hard it tried to hide, she knew how to cull it. Her magic sought to destroy what was wrong and twisted inside of Prince Dagen. Her magic siphoned off another small piece of the darkness, encircling it in its entirety.

It screamed and fought to weave itself tighter into the threads of Prince Dagen's being. The darkness pulled away from her, slipping free from the grasp of her magic.

Hollis freed his mouth for a moment to suck in a sharp breath. Her throat bobbed, burning as a few wisps of darkness clawed against her insides. Did it want away from her magic or back to its host? It didn't matter. Her stomach spun with acid as she coughed, the wisps vanishing into the air.

"This is the most I've ever kissed a man and I puke every time," Hollis wheezed. She covered her mouth so more of the darkness couldn't escape. "This isn't setting a good tone of kissing in my mind—Lukxa be a good sir and kiss me when this is all over so I have a good frame of reference."

The captain made a disgruntled noise.

Hollis grabbed Dagen's face, which had taken a much greener hue as she spoke, and smashed their mouths together, ripping the section of curse back into herself. Again the darkness coated her mind and thoughts. Strips of light broke through as her magic pulled against the root of the curse.

Hollis released Prince Dagen's face with a gag. She quickly reached a hand back toward Sir Lukxa, who promptly handed her a flaming sprig of lavender. She took a steady breath through her nose before opening her mouth and shoving it into her mouth before any wisps of the curse could slip by her lips.

Ringing filled her ears as she chewed the burning flowers. The roof of her mouth bled, mixing copper with ash. Swallowing was the hardest part. There was no moisture to help move things down.

Hatred filled her heart and mind. Stained her vision with black.

You do not want to be doing this. You hate this child and everything he stands for. Wouldn't you rather see the crown that burned your family rot and wither away?

Prince Dagen coughed, a light dust of ashes spread across his coverings. His chest heaved as he took in deep breaths. A subtle smile grew on his lips.

Acid crept up her throat just in time for Sir Lukxa to present the cleaned chamber pot to her. Hollis vomited up the black sludge, happy to feel the bitterness and malice leave her body.

Sir Lukxa took the bucket from her hands and set it on the floor next to the bed. "Well done, Hollis." Sir Lukxa spoke. His voice scratched from his throat.

"I second that, Lady Hollis. You've gone through something so terrible on my behalf—twice now." Prince Dagen nodded his head toward her. His words came in short bursts as his chest heaved.

Hollis nodded in response. "You're welcome, my highness. But I'll leave you now. I must attend to the burns on my lips before they grow worse. Sir Lukxa, if you'll escort me back to your rooms."

A few pleasantries were exchanged before Sir Lukxa bid the prince a good evening and walked Hollis back to his chambers. She braced her weight between her cane and the bent arm Sir Lukxa offered her. Her body pulsed. Every step against the ground sent ripples of pain from heel to head.

Sir Lukxa unlocked his door and ushered her a few steps inside, just enough to let the door sink shut. He didn't move. His free hand held her own, which gripped his left arm. His eyes kept shifting about. She tried to find what it was he looked at.

After several beats of her heart, Sir Lukxa placed his hand on the side of her face and tilted it toward him. His lips were warm as he pressed a kiss to her temple. Her whole body shook as she turned to face him. His head was tilted down. His darkened gaze met her own for before a flush overtook his cheeks and he pulled his eyes away. "I hope that's fulfilment enough for your request, Hollis."

It seemed her magic was able to speed up the process of healing her insides. The blisters that lined the roof of her mouth vanished over the course of three days and her voice no longer sounded as cinders.

The library had transformed in the light of day. It'd taken her days of lounging around in bed to feel strong enough to leave Sir Lukxa's apartments.

Hollis was thankful that Councilor Shad agreed to watch over her in the library today while Sir Lukxa went off and trained with his knights. Hollis wouldn't be violating the council's orders that she wasn't to be alone in the castle outside of Sir Lukxa's apartments without an escort. The manner in which Councilor Shad conducted himself always left her mind spinning. Hollis wasn't sure what to expect from the man with each passing encounter they had.

The sun shone through the glass ceiling and cast a rainbow of colors against the ground in some areas. A fairytale brought to life before her eyes.

It was a shame she didn't fit the part.

Hollis pulled the ends of her sleeves over her hands, relishing in the warmth. She had mustered up the courage to wrap herself up into one of Sir Lukxa's warm highnecks and a pair of fitted black pants she'd packed and forgotten about. A generous layer of cream laid against her skin in the places the lavender burned. Her lips were covered in a salve to fight the cracking they threatened. If only her outsides healed as quick as the insides.

She was able to eat without pain again, though, *mostly*. She would take that.

"Healer Hollis, are you quite all right?" Councilor Shad asked, making

his way from his office to where she was walking to meet him amid the shelves on the first floor.

"Yes, quite." She glanced around them. Along with the bright colors and lights that filled the library in the day, there were bodies. Several people sat around tables hunched over books and papers. Hollis hadn't expected to see this many people inside the library.

"Of course. Let me get you fitted with gloves again and I will let you up. Sadly, my assistant hasn't come up with any other recommendations other than what I gave you the other day." Councilor Shad picked up her hand and pressed a kiss to her knuckles. The man's actions were enough to flatter her and tickle her insides. But Councilor Shad's flirtations were nothing in comparison to the way that Sir Lukxa made her feel with only a glance.

Hollis gave a slight bow of her head in response.

Councilor Shad released her hand after a few moments and met her gaze with a warm smile on his face. "I will have to stay down here in my office. Feel free to come to me with any questions you have, though." He made his way back to his office.

Inside his office she was able to put faces to the empty desks she had wandered past that night nearly a week ago. Furiously scribbling hands made quick work of any document. The scribes and whoever else worked under the careful watch of Councilor Shad certainly were certainly efficient. They read at a pace Hollis could only dream about and jotted down notes just as quickly.

The keeps' room carried the scent of ink and paper, much stronger than it had when night lingered and bodies did not.

Not a single occupant of the office watched them, not even as she'd walked past studying them.

Somehow, in the back of the room by Councilor Shad's desk, an air of privacy settled. The scratching of quills and rustling of paper faded into the back of her mind.

Councilor Shad's hands lay open in front of her. "Lend me your hands again."

She set her cane against his desk and let him take up her palms.

His skin held the same unusual heat they had every time she came into contact with him. Something *hummed* underneath his skin.

His fingers traced each bit of her hands, carefully pressing the fatty parts and pulling toward the tips of her fingers.

"You have not revealed anything, have you?" His voice was no louder than a whisper against the top of her head.

The hairs of the back of her neck rose. Her lips stretched into a thin line, cracking in the middle. She could feel the blood swelling in her mouth. "I have to admit I've no idea what it is that you're talking about, Councilor Shad."

What was he doing? Letting on like he knew what was happening with her. He very well could, but if he wasn't going to be blunt about it, she wouldn't give him a thread to pull on.

No, she couldn't spiral with her thoughts. Councilor Shad was digging to find information that he severely lacked.

Councilor Shad seemed to be a man of knowledge. It would grate upon him to feel as though he was lacking. Yes, that was what he was doing here. He had no business asking her such things for the sake of his own desire for knowledge.

She wouldn't be the one to alleviate his desire.

He leaned his head from side to side, his brown curled hair flopping each direction. "I will be back with a pair of gloves."

True to his word, he returned from wherever it was he disappeared to with a pair of gloves. Not the exact same set she'd worn previously, but a close match. He fitted her hands inside the glove and walked her over to the door leading to the top floor.

The stairs were no easier to climb this time than they had been nights ago. Councilor Shad kept pace with her, one of his hands holding a small candlestick, while the other hand enveloped hers as they went. His warmth was welcome as a shiver ran down her spine.

Hollis would never understand how people lived in colder climates.

The top floor, same as the bottom, was bathed in the light of day. Each ray of sunlight illuminated the things she hadn't noticed when darkness swathed the area.

Her eye spied a few other shelves that were maybe made of the same tree as the one Councilor Shad currently raised for her access to the archives. Wandering hands would figure if there was anything behind them *later*.

Councilor Shad motioned her inside. Once Hollis stepped past the threshold he plucked a small lantern from the inside wall, lit it, and handed it to her. Finally, he nodded and made his way back down stairs to his office.

Hollis' shoulders sagged, a rough huff slipping past her lips. Councilor Shad kept true to his word and left her alone up here. She should have suspicions about the ordeal, but currently she was too thankful to question it. Being left alone with all these books was a dream.

The light was weak in the lantern; Hollis doubted the fire inside the glass would survive if she opened the door to feed it more air. *No chance of burning the archives down at least. If that's what he was afraid of.*

The air inside the room smelled lightly of cloves. The spice lingered with every step she took. It lent a feeling of warmth, even if it was all in her head.

The archives felt. . . comfortable. A silent room, save the *tapping* of her cane and the occasional *crack* and *pop* from the lantern. The dimness of the room only added to the sense of comfort.

All together, the current setting reminded her of saying up far past her curfew, reading in her room or hidden away in the library of her home village. Her parents never minded much her habit of losing herself in a book. Of course, it made working in her family's shop all the more difficult, with a mind bogged down with fatigue.

After depositing her cane at a random table, Hollis began to trail the stacks of books. While every space in the castle seemed to transform between night and day, this room seemingly stayed the same.

The impossible castle had a few consistencies it would seem.

Leather covered spines slowly leaned as she trailed a finger along them down the rows, waiting until one would stick out to her. Of course she read the spines, but that hardly mattered.

She couldn't remember the way back to the table.

"It would seem the archives are much larger than I thought." Rows of tomes stretched out in every direction, a labyrinth of leather. "Well, Hollis, you're seemingly lost amongst a stack of books. How delightful." She plucked a random tome and propped it against her arm to read. "I do hope the wool of my sleeve is enough to keep Councilor Shad from murdering me for holding this book."

She couldn't read the text inside; it was written in characters she didn't fully understand. Seemingly a system of sharp lines and rounded circles of varying completion. It was close in nature to the modern Tablin writing system, but different enough she just couldn't understand it.

"So long as you do not tell him, I don't think you have to worry about losing your head, Tablin Healer."

Hollis *screeched.* She pulled the book flat to her chest and swung her arm that held the lantern in a wide arc as she scrambled to find a body to place the voice. Her heart hammered against her ribs.

The lantern caught the opening of a small alcove the more steps she took forward. It revealed a seated man surrounded by stacks of books piled up on the floor.

The man was no older than Councilor Shad or Sir Lukxa. He wore the same dressings as the other bodies inside Councilor Shad's office. A light cloak, dark pants, black shoes.

He must be one of Councilor Shad's—

He spoke again. "Do promise me that, in exchange for keeping your transgression a secret, you won't go telling Councilor Shad how you discovered me up here? I'm supposed to be cataloging books on the second floor." The man ran his tongue over his teeth and *hummed.* "Yes, that's a rather good deal, healer. I think he'd simply murder me if he discovered I was putting books on the floor. To be fair, I only use the newer, more stable ones for the base of my towers." The sitting man smiled as he continued reading, flipping an aged page.

Hollis laughed. The unease in her stomach began to settle. He was hiding away from work in every book-lover's dream. She nodded her head. "I guess we have a deal, then." Her voice sounded slightly on edge, slightly breathless as her heart struggled to slow.

He faced her, a glint deep in his eyes.

As he nodded his head alongside her, the light showed off that he had a head of shaggy cut dark hair; Hollis couldn't make out its true color as he stayed swathed in shadow despite her small light. His eyes were a mix of amber and rust, that much she could see.

She thought she recognized him, but no memories came to mind in which he fit.

The man gestured a hand at her. "What are you searching for? I might be able to procure a proper book for you." His smile never left his face as he turned his gaze back to the books before him.

What was the best way to answer this? Of course, when she thought before she spoke things always went poorly.

The compulsion to speak the truth grew uncomfortable in her skull. "I'm. . . looking for books on different methods of Tablin healing." The pressure lessened. "Historic books were a rarity when I studied, and now that I've the chance to read them, I'd like to enjoy them fully." Not a fully spoken lie on her part. She'd mainly built her sentence on the truth. She did want to know more about Tablin healing methods, and she did enjoy them. She needed to know how to cure Prince Dagen without her magic.

No real damage done in omitting that. She smiled to herself, feeling rather proud.

He closed his book against his chest and tapped his feet on the ground. "I guess I would need to know more than that. We've a handful of books on

Tablin healing, a few of which you read the other night." Her eyes widened in shock. "Oh, goodness, I've *scared* you. I put books back in their place. So, because I do that, I know not to bring you those books." He narrowed his gaze, a smile growing on his lips. "Tell me if I'm wrong, it seemed like you pulled an idea or two from one of them?"

"Are you in here all the time?" She diverted from his question.

It would be interesting if he was always tucked away in here. A little book creature, living on a shelf in the archive. She'd enjoy that job. Perhaps she'd missed her proper calling.

He laughed and turned his attentions back to her. "I'm in here all the time I can be. Of course, there are times when I'm caught here in times I should not be. Now being one of them. I need to work on my hiding skills." His laugh and voice were warm as he spoke. The tone of his words betrayed an accent, subtle, hardly woven through his lips.

The book tucked in her arm grew heavy. Hollis shifted its weight on her hip as the man stood and walked a few paced closer to her.

The lantern cast onto his face stronger than it had before, highlighting his flat nose and wide lips. She couldn't solidly pin the coloring of his skin until she could see him somewhere with more natural light, but his complexion seemed similar enough to Sir Lukxa's. Hollis had decided that he was Omil, through and through. But while looking Sir Lukxa in the eye caused her to crane her neck, she was just shy of eye-level with this man.

"I'll take this, don't worry. Another one for my piles. And I will trade you these." He plucked the heavy tome from her arms as if it weighed nothing, set it down, and handed her a few smaller books.

He settled himself back into his tight alcove and seemed to disappear from her sight beneath the stacks.

"Thank you." Hollis did her best to find a way back to the table.

She walked forward, down from the alcove, and not the way she'd taken earlier. There were more shelves to explore on the way out.

Ringing sounded in her ears, high-pitched screeching. Her body sagged

forward against her cane as she stumbled.

Perhaps she needed to pause and breathe.

Decidingly doing so, Hollis checked the shelves around her. Not many books lined the area. In fact, Hollis could only count about thirty books on the seven shelves within sight.

"Sad, you're here all alone." She set her cane against a shelf and grazed her hand over the covers.

A leather-bound journal was her hand's final destination. Hollis plucked up the journal, shaking the dust free from it. Hollis set down her current stack of books and flipped through the journal.

She didn't pay attention to the words written, but she could tell it was written in some form of Tablin. Possibly Omilian?

Shrugging, she added the journal to her little stack and continued on.

Not longer than a quarter of an hour later, Hollis was tucked into the chair and worked her way through the various books the man had given her. Another look inside the black leather journal showed that she would need to consult a translation guide. It was written in *Old* Tablin—a dialect she hardly knew.

A scoff broke past her lips as she shut the journal again. Hollis decided she would work on reading it later and stuck to the texts where the words were easily known.

Her stomach growled some time later. Several books lay open on the table, little notes written on scrap pieces of paper between them.

"It's time for lunch. Did Sir Lukxa tell me he was doing anything today after training? Am I supposed to. . . meet him, somewhere?" She ran through her memories of the afternoon, doing her best to pull the thoughts of Sir Lukxa's voice to mind. His face was clearly visible in her mind, but no solid words came from his mouth as it moved.

Instead, the memory of his lips pressing against her temple bloomed in her mind. Warm, perfectly moisturized.

How she was able to get any concentrating done this afternoon was beyond her.

"I need to be more specific the next time I ask him to kiss me," she muttered.

Gathering up the books and notes in her arm, Hollis made her way back to the alcove where the man had been in, only to find him—and his large stack of books—gone. Stepping into the small space revealed no traces anyone had been there. He was good at covering his tracks.

Considering she had no idea where the books in her arms went, she simply placed them back in the far corner of the alcove. She hoped they would make their way back to their rightful place.

Hollis' hand lingered on the thin journal written in an Old Tablin dialect that she needed more time to translate. No, she tucked that one into her bag and prayed that Councilor Shad wouldn't check her person for any stolen goods. Though, he never said she *couldn't* take any books.

At the entrance of the archive she managed to get the door to raise and let her out. With the lantern extinguished and placed back on the hook, she tried to figure out how to lower the door.

"I'll take care of the door."

Hollis let out a shrill *screech* and jumped. Her heart hammered in her chest as painful fits of coughing took over her ability to breathe.

The man quickly patted Hollis' shoulders as she faced him. His brows were knit with worry as he leaned his head toward her. "I'm terribly sorry for scaring you like that." Outside of the archive Hollis realized the man smelled of moss and rain, along with the leather and ink that the archive held. She could see in the clear light of the library that the man was in fact Omil, sharing several more features with Sir Lukxa than Hollis had realized.

Hollis took a step back from him. "It's all right. . . I startle easily." She gave him a weak grin as her little coughing fit subsided.

He cocked his head to the side. "If you insist that you're all right." The strange man's voice sounded from behind her.

Hollis looked back and saw him waving his hands at her to step back

from the archives.

She obeyed and took further steps away from the threshold, letting the Omilian man close the door in whatever magical way it operated. "Remember, do *not* tell the councilor I was here stacking up books." He pressed a finger against his smile as the secret door sank in front of him.

When she entered Councilor Shad's office, hands freed from her gloves, he turned and greeted her with a smile. "I hope that you were able to glean something needed?"

She nodded. "Yes, I was. A few interesting books caught my eye, but I made sure to put them back from where I got them. No need to worry."

"I am glad you were able to find something. I know the shelves can be a bit disorganized at times. I'm sorry no one was up there to help you, but you seem to know what you're doing."

Hollis debated on asking if there were other ways in and out of the archive or telling Councilor Shad of the man tucked away hiding from his work in favor of reading.

Her promise lingered in her mind, staying her lips. She wouldn't tattle on her helper.

Clearly he belonged there if he knew of it and had earlier permissions, even if he wasn't supposed to be there at the moment. Any words describing him couldn't form in her mind to tell the councilor either.

No, she wouldn't mention anything.

She handed Councilor Shad her gloves, smiled, and left the library. Journal tucked into her bag. Promise intact.

CHAPTER TWENTY-THREE

LUKXA

Lukxa set his pen down atop of the papers lying in front of him. Lines of names on one, supplies another, and goodness knows what else was hiding in the piles on the small stretch of desk between himself and Councilor Dem.

"I shock myself every year with the amount of paperwork needed for this tournament." Dem's voice carried a laugh that filled his small office.

The Eargile offices were generally quite a bit smaller than the offices inside the castle given to the councilors from Rex and Hozen. Due in part to the responsibilities the other prefectures carried—but no one held a larger office than Councilor Shad. And then the keeper's office was only shadowed by the size of the throne room.

Lukxa had a small space in the barracks that could be used to host any meetings that needed to be held as captain of the guard. Or, there was the option of the study in his own apartments.

"When there is much to plan, there is a paper for everything." Lukxa gathered his papers and tapped them on the table, evening out the stack.

"We have to be prepared when things go wrong, or right. At least my daily portion is done. Which reminds me—when are the other councilors arriving?" Lukxa asked, sitting back in his chair. He could not stop the grin that spread across his face.

It was hard to find moments one could fully enjoy during such chaos. Sitting down and talking with a friend was much needed. And what was coming, would be even more enjoyable. Lukxa refused to let the looming presence of the other councilor's bring down his mood.

The annual—and only *slightly* legal—placing of bets was a time honored tradition since Dem decided the Eargilean councilors needed something more *exciting* to keep their attentions on the winter tournament.

"I'd say we have another few minutes until they arrive." Dem coughed into his hand a few times. "Just enough time for me to ask how things are going with your *lovely* little healer. You're having her stay in your apartments, right? Not even in one of your guest rooms." Dem's eyebrows wiggled as he gave Lukxa a most suggestive face. "You get any more shows?" Dem grinned and gave him a face on top of that.

Lukxa choked on the spit in his mouth. No, he could compose himself. There was no reason that Hollis should be making him this flustered.

Dem burst at the seams with laughter. His hands clutching at his sides as he hunched over his desk. "I'm not sure what that means, Lukxa. Use your words, good sir." He finally straightened and ceased his laughter, tears streaming down his face that he rapidly wiped at. A few little chuckles escaped his dark lips as Dem made eye contact with Lukxa.

Lukxa gathered himself, shock still flooding his system. Finally he swallowed the spit in his mouth. "My primarily open schedule makes it ideal that she stay with me. *And* since the council ordered that she has to stay inside the castle walls, with me or another guard—at. *All.* Times." He attempted to push down the memories of her form. "I do not know why you would expect any more *shows*, Dem. Healer Hollis has been nothing but professional with myself *and* Prince Dagen." Lukxa wasn't sure why everyone honed in on the fact that they were sharing a room. Of course, only a select few people knew they were sharing a room in the first place.

Lukxa just. . . grew flustered at every reminder from anyone who did know.

It was a sound, tactical decision. Practically an order by the council.

Granted, he'd been the one saying she was to stay in his room in the first place.

It wasn't like having her stay with him was an insane idea either. The barracks often were overflowing and called for mixed rooms. Nothing ever happened that was untoward.

How was this any different in everyone's minds?

His stomach fluttered, as if he had swallowed butterflies whole. Now he finally understood the turn-of-phrase. The feeling spread warmth throughout his body. Lukxa knew if he didn't calm himself he would start blushing like a madman.

There was nothing behind it other than keeping her safe from whatever was happening inside the castle—something Lukxa could not bring up with anyone.

Lukxa caught Dem's boyish grin, tucked between the forming wrinkles on his face.

He cleared his throat, giving Dem a pointed glare. "I think. . . we should change the subject to something more useful." Lukxa bit the inside of his cheek.

Dem gave him a flat, mocking face in return. "All right, I'll stop teasing you. Tell me, how is Prince Dagen fairing? I heard it's some type of magical flu? Is his majesty recovering with Healer Hollis' treatments?"

Blood left Lukxa's face, lending light-headedness. How was Lukxa to respond? Why had he not thought to ask Hollis more about the condition that *he* himself would surely be asked about. He could speak on the truths he did know.

Oh goodness, he was becoming Hollis. Talking in half-truths and riddles and outright lying to suit his needs. He should stop sleeping with her; her brash tendencies and careless speaking were rubbing off on him.

He should stop saying he was *sleeping* with her.

"Um," Lukxa coughed to hopefully cover the sudden awkwardness he'd become. "Prince Dagen is faring much better than he had been. Healer Hollis' treatments seem to be most effective in treating the Tablin flu. I do not know much else in the way of healing. She mentioned that it would take several treatments to fully purge it from him, being that his body is not used to magical ailments or treatments. But she expects a full recovery by Prince Dagen's birthday." Hopefully that was enough information. Or was it too much?

Dem *hummed* and nodded his head as Lukxa spoke. A serious air of interest surrounded him. His eyes focused, mouth pursed. "I hope he is able to make a swift recovery. It'd be great for him to have the chance to rule as he was born." Dem then opened and shut his mouth a few times, hands raised as he looked like he wanted to say something. Lukxa tilted his head, urging Dem to speak.

Dem raised his hands as he continued to talk. "Each of us councilors, we hold the balance," he closed his grip, "but Prince Dagen *is* that balance. Without him to keep us all in line there's nothing for us to cling to." Dem appeared older as he spoke. Lukxa noticed the little pieces of silver amid a sea of black hair.

Lukxa leaned back in his chair. He had not expected such words from Dem. While Dem had always been able to motivate and encourage anyone he spoke with, Lukxa had never heard such heartfelt words. "You are right. And. . . I think that is the most eloquent thing you have ever said." Lukxa spoke the words with admiration.

Dem waves his hand in front of his face. "Oh, I've given some wonderful and mighty speeches, my friend. Ale fuels the imagination." Dem gave another round of laughter as the door to his office swung open.

Lukxa's heart stopped beating as he caught sight of the other two

Eargilian councilors. Both Dem and himself greeted Cane and Kleo as they strode into the office. It was several awkward moments of watching them have to sidestep the many chests of weapons that needed to be taken to the smith for sharpening. The rest of Dem's meeting room was filled with a few shelves of old manuals, history texts; the walls held a few tapestries of historical battles won in honor. In short, the office was an absolute mess.

The door had let in a rush of fresh air. It was a shame that the windows of this room were barred shut. The precaution was important for keeping any information inside safe.

It was a blessing that the windows had not been filled in with stone. Instead they were still allowed rays of sun to grace the floor and desk. That did not stop Lukxa's longing that a breeze would steal the stale feeling out of the room. Unfortunately, the momentary draft from the door shutting would have to be good enough.

The little bit of air stirred the scent of ages old sweat that seemingly bred in the cracks of the stone floor.

When was the last time Dem gave the room the deep cleaning it so greatly required? Or delegated someone trustworthy under him—hopefully not Lukxa himself—to do it, since no one wanted the mantle of fear that came with cleaning this room. No risking documents coming upon ruin due to half-hearted cleaning jobs by maids or thievery by possible threats.

"Hello, my fellow councilors. You're right on time!" Dem stood and gestured Cane and Kleo to sit in the only available chairs in the room. Both were located on either side of Lukxa. Dem clapped his hands before he continued speaking. "I received word on which knights from the academy are traveling here and which houses are sending men from their armies. We'll be able to schedule seating matches today and afterward we can place our bets. Provided none of you have any last minute additions from our own rankings here?"

"None from me, nor Councilor Cane." Kleo shook her head and crossed her arms over her middle.

"Wonderful," Dem responded. "Let's get to building then."

Kleo sighed, seeming a hair away from running a hand down her golden face as she glanced between the few chairs Dem's office had left to offer. "Shouldn't we place our bets first and foremost so we can't possibly set our chosen picks up for an advantage without anyone knowing?"

Dem shook his finger in a joking manner toward her face. "But that is half the fun. Trying to slip in favoritism and victory."

Kleo pushed his hand away as she sat in the seat farthest from where Lukxa sat. "No offense, Councilor Dem, but I believe in winning with honor. I do not want my first tournament to leave me feeling like a cheat."

Lukxa forgot that at times. Kleo had joined the council before spring. How quickly Lukxa had forgotten her predecessor. King Trist and Queen Susan's passing had been fresh on the hearts of everyone then. Prince Dagen hadn't been old enough to have a seat on the Council—not even the honorary one he currently held now.

"It seems I've brought a somberness to you, Sir Lukxa. I apologize." Kleo bent her head toward him. Lukxa was not sure if she meant her apology or not. He didn't know where to place Kleo in the grand scheme of things. Which side she sat on. If she were ever a part of the meetings in overturning the crown. Lukxa was none the wiser. There were several people who were unnamed that followed the select few on the council's decision of a coup and war.

"Don't worry too much, Kleo. Nothing bothers our good Sir Lukxa." Cane spoke with a tone that bordered on mocking. Lukxa knew better, though—Cane fully meant to mock. The man thought himself the next general of the country, as good as a king.

If only Lukxa could tell Dem of these things. But there was so much uncertainty of what would come, and how Lukxa would be treated in the process if he revealed this plot.

Lukxa had to be clean from this. Had to be in a position where he could protect Dagen—and Hollis.

"All right, we shall place our bets now, and then we'll go from there. We've got a full day ahead of us," Kleo responded, her voice flat.

That was something Lukxa appreciated about her. Kleo was prepared to take care of whatever business was asked of her, and she did it in time without complaint—because she didn't complain. She gave what she ever so lovingly referred to as '*suggestions for making the process easier.*' She was an efficient worker when the situation called for it, and took her personal time in stride. Kleo was a major voice that every worker in the castle had a 'work-life-balance', as she said.

Lukxa agreed. He very much enjoyed his time spent *not* having to work.

"If you're so worried you'll be called a cheat, Kleo, give us your pick first. Who do you think will rank third overall in our lovely tournament?" Dem held out a pen with the lists of knights who were registered to partake. The same list Dem and Lukxa had taken the last three hours organizing.

Kleo plucked the list and took a minute to browse the names, giving the other men in the room a glare when they coughed or seemed to hurry her. "My bets are on. . . Nath Penen. He's done remarkably in all his classes in the academy to date, and beyond that, he's got grit. He's on top for a reason." She quickly handed the list back to Dem who leafed through it in half the time Kleo had.

"I think I'll take Patrick Brook. He comes from a strong family and has kept up his work as heir while in knighthood here. Lukxa," Dem handed Lukxa the list, "it's a good thing we're betting on third place. We can't all put money on you finishing first, Lukxa." Dem laughed as he leaned back in his seat, pointing a finger at Cane, and the two joked together.

Kleo seemed unimpressed with the other men's merriment, the glare she gave them seemed chilling. "I still do not know why we are allowed to compete. It doesn't seem fair to everyone else with Sir Lukxa—"

Lukxa *clicked* his tongue. "I'm not competing this year, actually. No worries there."

Shock ran across Dem's face. "What? Why? I thought you wrote your name down earlier?"

"You need to learn how to read." Lukxa pointed at Dem. "I am simply tired of winning." Lukxa had become Hollis indeed. He read through the list for show, already knowing who he was going to select. "I place my bets on Wilfrin Evest."

"Picking someone from your own guard. How innovative." Cane scoffed as he snatched the list, almost leaving small cuts on Lukxa's fingers. "I'll take an underdog this year. Charles Snyder. He's done well under my guard as of late. I can see him getting quite far in the grand scheme of things."

Lukxa blinked. "Charles Snyder. . . Edwin's cousin?"

Cane narrowed his eyes at Lukxa, his mouth parted. "Yes. I'm surprised you remember Edwin, Lukxa. He left your program for papers quite some time ago. I know, I teased you for picking one of your own men and I turned around and did the same. Charles simply needed some extra direction. I think he's headed on a good path now." Cane nodded his head as he held his hands out, palms up. "Like how a dog needs a good master to guide and train it. Yes, he's become quite a good pup," he finished, satisfied with his explanation as he resettled himself in his chair and set the list on the wooden desk that Dem sat behind.

The blood in Lukxa's veins chilled. He allowed the cold feeling to dissipate before starting to wander through his thoughts.

A solid thread wove into his mind. The ledger discrepancies—an unknown account with money being poured into it. Nothing that Lukxa did gained him the access needed to dig into who was behind it.

Perhaps Cane's selection of Charles as his knight and what he just spoke of training and dogs could be useful. Lukxa could speak with Councilor Shad in approaching Cane's personal accounts and gaining information about the transferring funds.

Another realization rose to the surface.

If Cane was more connected to the issues with the ledger, that would be the crime Lukxa could bring to light—which would then further reveal the fact that Cane had spent months stockpiling weapons. A fact Councilor Sypher kept off record. Lukxa formulated his plan now. He would not even have to be the one to bring up the weapons, only point Councilor Shad in the right direction to look.

Yes. This would be the final piece Lukxa had needed in order to keep Cane locked up and away from Dagen.

And if an accident happened whilst Cane was incarcerated, that would just be. . . a shame.

The smell of ink and leather was suffocating in the Councilor Shad's office. Lukxa stood patiently on the other side of the councilor's desk as Shad dropped a rather thick book on the surface. It landed with a hard *smack* against the wooden top.

Councilor Shad stood hunched over his desk as he flipped through the book. "Do you know what year Charles joined the ranks as castle staff?" His thin fingers trailed across and down every name listed on the pages. His other hand shook through his hair. How the councilor was able to read them so quickly was beyond Lukxa's comprehension.

Lukxa traced through his memories. "Charles would have joined. . . two years ago, maybe four?"

Shad *clicked* his tongue. "I need a more solid number, I do not wish to be searching through the record books hours on end."

Lukxa closed his eyes and thought. "Four years? Not long after me." He snapped his fingers. "And because I remember he joined the same year that several other recruits broke their ankles trying to scale the outer walls as a competition."

Shad gave him a blindingly fake smile before flipping forward several *large* scores into the book. "Morbid way to remember. I appreciate it."

From what Lukxa could read, the book was filled with a list of names—

which captain each squire and knight was assigned to. Shad jumped forward another few pages. Lukxa's name was now on the top corner of the page, and the next. He quickly put faces to the names that flowed beneath them.

Wilfrin, Trevor, Lucy, Issac. The list went on.

"I knew you were the keeper of records, keeper of everything, but this level of detail is not something I knew you had." Lukxa marveled at the details on each page. He caught quick glimpses at birthdays, eye color, hometown, even weight at recruitment.

The financial ledger had a similar style of detailed keeping when he had read it. Precise numbers, names, descriptions, the value of inflation at the time.

Which reminded Lukxa of the leather satchel that hung at his side, in which sat the ledger he had yet to return to Councilor Shad. Hopefully he would not fume when Lukxa returned it before leaving.

"Quite." Shad pressed his glasses back up his nose as he read. The councilor seemed stressed as he raked his hair back and out of his face. Soon, the name at the top changed to Councilor Cane's. "It is important to have detailed records so that one cannot be fooled if someone claims to be someone they assuredly *aren't.*" Shad looked at Lukxa over his glasses, his green eyes narrowed. "You are quite certain Councilor Cane said that he now had Charles as his. . . *dog?* I don't remember changing the records to add him in Cane's group. I remember scratching him off of *your* list." Shad *hummed* as he read.

Lukxa coughed into his hand. "Yes, I am. He made it quite clear what his thoughts were on *dog* ownership." What a ridiculous thought, to treat knights like dogs. It was no way to train someone, no way to build confidence or instill a sense of loyalty to one's country and crown.

Perhaps that was the purpose of it?

Shad leaned back against his chair, trailing his hand through his hair and rubbing at his temple. He blinked several times before gesturing to the text in front of him. "According to my records, Councilor Cane took Charles under him nine months ago." He blew out a stream of air and then ran his tongue over his teeth, his brows raised. "I've no idea why Cane would send him to procure the financial ledger. It's a decent thing *you* stole it before they got in again." Shad's gaze turned on Lukxa, one eyebrow now cocked.

What did that expression mean? Was the councilor questioning Lukxa's audacity? Was he reading that right?

Lukxa turned to the side of the room and studied the clerks' desks. "I thought it better I take it—"

"*No.*" The sharpness in his voice jerks Lukxa's head back toward him. Councilor Shad's eyes were piercing behind his frames. "It would have been better if *I* had been able to take the ledger back to my chambers so I could further study it." His words were venom dripping from his lips. "I know you were doing what you thought best, Captain Lukxa. But it was a *stupid* decision. When it was gone I thought they broke into my office again. So, I haven't left this room at night since." Shad crossed his arms across his chest and glared down his nose at Lukxa.

Lukxa's spine stiffened, blood pooling in his legs causing a tingling sensation up to his spine, and a dizziness in his head.. "They broke in *again*?"

"A few nights after we went to the archives together with Healer Hollis." Councilor Shad sighed and quickly made to lock the door to his empty office. "It might have been the two from the other night or someone else. I'd already installed a *different* type of lock on this door. Whoever it was got quite a *shock* when they tried breaking in. I haven't caught who tried, I doubt they will again in this fashion." Shad slowly made his return back to his desk. He let his hands trail over the edges of the desks he walked past down the aisle. His fingers drummed along the tops.

Lukxa didn't want to question the grin that grew on the councilor's face, so he mustered up a response. "Sounds interesting, Councilor."

"Yes, quite so. But locks can only stop so much force, Captain Lukxa. Evidence is needed to do anything more." Shad's jaw grew tense.

Lukxa knew that feeling of uncertainty all too intimately. It was the reason behind the numerous traps in his apartments. "I am worried about Councilor Cane's financial decisions," he spoke. Lukxa needed to push Shad to go digging even more into Cane. If Shad could discover the inaccuracies beyond just the Hozen tax discrepancy, he could do so much good in removing councilors from power.

Shad narrowed his gaze. "Why do you say that?" He straightened himself and shook his head slightly.

Lukxa shifted on his feet, his hand holding tight to the strap of this satchel. He pulled his mouth side to side. "There could only be one legitimate reason that Councilor Cane would want the ledger *after* the reports from the last council meeting went out. Cane has to be changing records of his own purchases. I think several councilors have. While mathematics isn't my strong suit, I think numbers have been off since the king and queen passed."

Councilor Shad chewed his lip. "This is exactly what I get when I allow someone else to manage the ledgers for me. *Fraud.* Thank you for bringing this to my attentions, Lukxa. You've helped me a great deal. I now have a potentially full circle of people using their budgets incorrectly. Would you happen to have any idea where Councilor Cane would be storing whatever extra purchases you claim he's been making? *Legitimate* proof that this isn't copy error?"

Lukxa shifted his weight between his legs. "Quite possibly in the southern store shed."

"The shed that is not to be used?" Shad raised his eyebrows and tucked chin to chest. "Really. Just. . . that easy. They're hiding things in a place they aren't supposed to be—I'm working with children." Shad threw his hands up in the air, his expression wide and flabbergasted. "*Go.* I will have this sorted out soon. If I need more assistance, I know where to find you." Shad then rubbed his hands along his face a few times.

Lukxa nodded his head and turned to leave the room.

Oh, "Lukxa before I forget." The expression Councilor Shad gave him would have chilled Lukxa to the bone if it weren't for the fact that they were equals. "Have you decided to finally *return* to me my ledger?"

Lukxa reached his hand into the satchel at his side and pulled the financial records free. His face twisted as he handed it out. "Again, I do think it is safer with me in my apartments. But I understand that it is your task to care of it, so I will return it to you—"

Shad strode up and took the ledger from him before returning behind his desk. "Thank you. Returning my property to me seemed like such a big task." He glared. "Just because you are our guard captain doesn't mean that everything and anything is safer with you. I have ways of keeping my books safe. The ledger is my responsibility—"

Lukxa cut him off to explain himself. "Yes, but—"

Shad leaned forward over his desk, his hands planted firmly on the surface. "I am not fond of you interrupting me in my own office and your taking of my things, Captain Lukxa. Your notes on Charles and Cane working together are useful, along with presenting that Sypher is likely helping several councilors change their budgets. It would have taken some time for me to discover that considering I had freed myself from the tedious task. You have my thanks. . . and my dismissal. *Good night.*"

CHAPTER TWENTY-FOUR

HOLLIS

The pages of the black leather journal sliced the tips of Hollis'
fingers. Again.

Hollis hated how thin and sharp each page was. The journal
simply protested at her reading of it. It would be a decently quick read. It
couldn't have been filled with more than eighty pages.

She did her best to mind the small dribbles of blood that let from the
superficial wounds. Now Hollis understood the odd stains along the edges
of the book. This journal took as much as it gave to whoever discovered it.
She was now added to this book's collection and would be another hand in
its history when she returned it to the archive.

That was, if she didn't burn it instead.

The old script on the pages refused to make any sense in her mind.
Even what she could translate in her head lacked the context to make sense.
At least she was able to understand that the writer had delved *deep* into the
realm of curses, but anything past that. . .

She leaned back against the chair that called Sir Lukxa's small study
home. The journal quickly tossed onto the desk in front of her.

Darker use of Tablin magic was far from common where she had grown up. As a child, her parents kept her sheltered from it best they could. Of course, they'd told her about the small sects of people who wanted to strike back at the Catolian crown for what they'd done during their wars with Tablin.

Then, as Hollis grew older and worked to heal alongside them, she'd seen what curses could do to a person—she'd even dismantled a few smaller hexes herself. But her parents had spared her the details she found within the pages of this journal.

A bit of cold air came in from the windows to her left. Hollis allowed her body to slump in the chair, melting away as far as she could without becoming a puddle on the floor.

Fire shot up her spine. It straightened her posture. "Goodness, I can't be this broken inside that I'm not even allowed to be a puddle of wallowing." Hollis stood from the chair, cracking both her knees in the process. "Oh *boohoo*, I'm standing now. Happy?" She righted her black skirt and carefully stepped over to the colorful bookshelf that sat against the far wall of the study area.

While the selection of books here in Sir Lukxa's apartments wasn't as useful as the archive, that didn't mean it wasn't deserving of a perusal. She kept meaning to, especially in the long hours she was kept inside his apartments. Every time she stood to make her way over to the shelves, something pulled her attentions away.

"Who knows, maybe I'll find something interesting?" Hollis dragged her fingers along the spines of the books.

"Or, maybe if you move your hand a few books to the right, you'll lose a finger?"

Hollis turned to find Sir Lukxa entering the room. He slid his jacket off his body and hung it on the small coat rack beside the door, which also held her bag. Next he pulled off his over-sweater and tossed it on the floor by his dresser in a heap. A servant would be by tomorrow to collect the washing.

Hollis' clothes had joined his pile. The maid that did the collecting always had a blush on her face when she entered the room.

"Lose a finger? That could have been a fun adventure," Hollis snorted.

Sir Lukxa laughed and joined her in front of the bookshelf. "Perhaps I'm merely jesting." He leaned closer to her.

The aftermath of light training he'd done perfumed his collar. Not fragrant enough to repulse her, but sweat lingered. He was likely to bathe soon, which meant that he would soon smell of sandalwood and amber. She enjoyed his scent either way. Fresh or worn.

Hollis laughed and jabbed at Lukxa's shoulder. "Just how many more traps am I going to find? Perhaps I should poke around until I do lose a finger? Are there things of such value lying about in your apartments that you would risk the life and limb of others?"

"I would advise against testing me in that."

She studied his darkened expression. The way his pupils expanded as his head tilted down to reach her level. Even the gravel in his voice.

"Now, what are you wanting, dear Healer?" He dropped his head closer to her ear and whispered.

"I. . ." she swallowed. A newfound heat in her stomach pulled her throat tight. Her words came out pinched. "*Found* a journal in the archives. A book of curses as far as I can tell. It's written in an old Tablin dialect that I can't fully translate. I wasn't sure if I'd find anything of interest in your shelves that could help or inspire me." Hollis rubbed her hands together, shifting from leg to leg as Lukxa straightened his spine. He now stood a foot or so away from herself. Sad.

He cocked his head and narrowed his gaze. "Hollis, I do not like how you said *I found*." He mimicked her tone, though he spoke in a *far* higher pitch than Hollis did. "I will not question you, though. Rather not hear something I wish I had not." Sir Lukxa grumbled the last few words and scanned his shelves, tracing a finger in the air over different titles.

Relief melted through her marrow. Glad that Sir Lukxa wasn't going to pry into the matter of her thieving. . . again. She wouldn't have wanted to talk much about her trip in the archive as she might slip that she met some random, mysterious person tucked away up there. "So, you think you have something that can help me?"

His face softened again, replacing the darkness that had covered his brow. "I do not think I do. . . but it never hurts to double-check. Perhaps I can take a shot at the journal and help you out."

A hand flew to her chest in shock. "You know Old Tablin?" She tilted her head toward him as she spoke, genuine curiosity laced in her words.

Lukxa laughed. She liked when he did that. His head always tilted backward, he smiled with his teeth. He was beautiful.

"Goodness, no. But the Omil language shares roots with Tablin. I would bet there is some crossover. Together perhaps we can read a whole book." The aura about him warmed again, inviting her to take a step closer to his person.

She chewed her lip. "How much Omilite do you remember?" This was exciting. Learning more about the captain was an adventure Hollis happily embarked on.

His tongue ran over his teeth, pale eyes seeming forever away. "I was not brought to Catol until my tenth year. The war had started to run its course and as an act of. . . *mercy* from Catol, they allowed any children under the age of five and ten to be given up. My parents thought it the best choice to give me up. They thought I would have the possibility of *life* here rather than the inevitable death I would face in Omil. I presume they are long dead with all the rest of the country. Not like Omil was all that large and powerful to begin with."

He turned his attention back to her. The words that next rolled from his lips were similar to Tablin, but only enough for her to notice the similarities—

The word *beautiful*. It was slightly different from the Tablin word, but he definitely used it. Unless it carried a different use in the Omil tongue. He finished speaking, his posture having relaxed. He now stood with a cocked hip, a hand placed upon it as he leaned over her.

"What did you call beautiful?"

Sir Lukxa's eyes widened, a light flush gracing his cheeks. "*You.*" He spoke just above a whisper. "I called you beautiful. *And* a menace."

Heat bloomed up her neck as she took a small shuffle back. "You didn't even try to hide what you said? I only caught one word. *Lying is an option.*" Her stomach spun into her chest. Emotions swirled up inside her.

Perhaps she hadn't misread any of Sir Lukxa's mannerisms or words.

Sir Lukxa smiled and scratched a hand across his scalp, leaning his head into the crook of his arm. "Why would I lie about something I said in earnest? I think you're beautiful. I would feel remorse in hiding that fact from you." He dropped his arm and pointed at her. "But do take note—I called you a menace."

Her mind spun faster than she could weave her thoughts. "Everyone calls me a menace to my face and my back. No one really says anything like. . . *beautiful* to me and means it after knowing me. It's not like it isn't true; I know that I'm pretty." Hollis thought back to their evening shared over a glass of gin.

How his eyes had consumed her very being with every sip they took. How his calloused fingertips traced over her skin while she was half-asleep, tied up in his arms.

The light kiss he'd pressed to her temple when she'd asked.

How she noticed he had little freckles on his nose in the mess hall when they'd first introduced her to some of the general castle populace.

Sir Lukxa's smile grew. His left hand cupped her jaw, thumb lightly rubbing her cheek. "I'm happy to do so. You, Hollis Avayana, are a beautiful menace. You're chaotic, brash, a chronic liar, and so many things that all encompass who you are. And I'll say it again: one of those things is beauty. Ethereal. Plucked from the night sky itself."

"Okay, that's enough." Hollis slipped away from him, face burning.

His hand grazed her shoulder a moment as if to hold her there with him.

"It's not as if calling you beautiful is a confession of my undying affections for you." Sir Lukxa followed her to the desk and loomed over the chair she perched herself in. Hollis wiggled deeper into it to make sure there was no extra room for him to sit beside her and continue to heat her skin.

Sir Lukxa came up behind the chair and leaned over it. Then he reached out and took the journal up from the desk, opening it so they could both read. "Where are your translation notes?" His breath ghosted over her ear.

A shiver ran down her spine. "I did them in my head. I wasn't going to dig around in your desk and, say, *lose a finger*." It was her turn to mock his voice and tone. She gave him a stuffy sounding voice that was deep and grim.

He let out a harsh sigh and set the journal down. Then he practically climbed over her shoulder to pull open the middle right drawer of his desk. "In here," he gestured, "you'll find fountain pens, the ink to refill them as needed, and paper. I will not say as to which of the other drawers are laden with traps." Sir Lukxa pulled a few sheets free and placed them on the desk, which already held an assortment of pens and jars of ink.

Hollis transcribed her notes. She translated as many sentences as she felt was necessary, noting down words that tripped her up. As she worked, Sir Lukxa rummaged around in his kitchenette. The sound of water cut through the silence, followed by the even louder sound of Sir Lukxa gulping down several glasses of water. Next, food bags rustled—interrupting her tranquil workflow with him munching on something.

Hollis mainly focused on the pages with words that seemed as though they would fit Prince Dagen's curse. Notes of symptoms caused, and potential reasonings that such a curse would take effect.

Sir Lukxa flopped down on the chair across from his desk, one of his legs hooked over the arm of the chair. He braced himself up in it as if he were posing in a rather *entertaining* painting.

Several, *several* pages later, the journal flopped closed as she finished transcribing everything she thought was important. She then picked it up and shook the journal toward Lukxa. "Are you ready to read this through?"

Sir Lukxa had exhaustion settling in his face.

Hollis gestured to the seat at the desk as she stood. "Here, you can sit in your big fancy chair now. I'm going to eat a snack myself. As *loudly* as I can."

Sir Lukxa took the chair, journal and her notes in hand and set about reading.

She glared at him before making her way into the kitchenette. Her loaf of clover bread sat open on the counter. After buttering a slice, she slowly ate it. Chewing each bite as slowly as she could before swallowing, taking a sip of water, and repeating the process.

Hollis figured it best not to interrupt his work, unsure of what his current hot and cold mood could hold. Not that she feared any violent retaliation from the hands that swiftly turned the pages.

Quarter of an hour burned down a candle when Sir Lukxa shut the book, and pen he'd picked up from somewhere, down on the table by her notes. "It seems I was correct in my earlier musings. I can pick up more words than you can, but I am far from perfect. You will have to make due with context clues if you are wanting to read this to completion. I did my best to flip through and jot things down." He tossed the journal down on the desk. "This book is vile."

Stones sank in her stomach. "You wrote *in* the book?" Hollis scrambled back toward the desk and flipped the pages.

"Being that we do not have much time on our hands, yes. I have wronged both you and the evil book of curses. My notes are in the margins where you can easily find them." With that he stood and turned about the room. She heard the faucet run and fill a glass twice, or two glasses once. How could the man drink so much water?

The pages cried out to her, ink smudged against the text from Sir Lukxa's fine script; thankfully, it hadn't covered any of the existing text.

Despite the horrors of him *writing in a book*, Hollis was impressed with how efficiently he'd managed to note things. He seemingly skipped paragraphs where the information must have been deemed irrelevant by him.

Nothing should be irrelevant in a book, though. It's here, so it has to mean something.

Context clues only got her so far with those skimmed paragraphs.

A third of the way through the journal was a small translation note beside her own. She would have translated it as *ward*, someone to watch over and protect. It would seem that Sir Lukxa had translated it as a protection placed on something general—non-specific. Her fingers drummed against the table.

"Can you tell me how you came to translate this?" she asked. "The rest of this sentence doesn't make sense translated like this."

Sir Lukxa downed *another* glass of water that held in his hand—the man was going to be using the bathroom all night at this pace—and set it upon the counter before coming to stand beside her. One of his hands rested on the back of her chair while the other gripped the arm rest. He leaned over her again.

Goodness, he smelled divine. She would melt in this chair and simply cease to be.

He had to know what he was doing to her.

"It reads closer in meaning to the Omil word *barrier* than it does anything else. Does not really sound like a curse to me."

Hollis shook her head. "You're right, it doesn't. In my mind the rest of the phrase makes sense with the meaning of this word being ward as in child? *Place the* child *under protection for the sake of longevity and unwanted influences.*"

"I see what you're doing. I think you are mistranslating this." He pointed to her notes. "This word would be read *Putting into place a* barrier *for the sake of longevity of unwanted influences* in this context. It is about keeping something *out* rather than keeping someone safe. It essentially means the same thing. The semantics may not be worth arguing about." Sir Lukxa straightened and turned his face down to meet her gaze.

Hollis blinked a few times and mimed her thoughts before uttering them aloud. "What if it's a barrier to keep other *magical* influences out?

Something that. . . would hinder my magic?" Her body did a slight shake as she spoke. A little jolt. "A ward keeping magic out so an inflicted curse wouldn't be able to be lifted!" She jostled in her seat.

"Or. . ." Sir Lukxa cocked his head and leaned closer over her shoulder to read the journal again. "Something placed onto you specifically to block your magic in its entirety. You told me that the feelings of suppression had not lifted when you joined us for training outside." He turned to meet her gaze, his face only inches away from her own.

Hollis swallowed. A sudden nervousness overtaking her and drying her throat. "But I didn't want to stray far from the castle walls." Hollis hadn't wanted to leave the castle since she arrived. It felt safe, somehow. Though she didn't enjoy the moments where she had to parade about with Sir Lukxa to add to their story of being long friends. Constantly lunching with strangers was draining, especially when she had to remember so many little details in case someone asked her a question about Sir Lukxa or his time training in some forsaken academy.

"If it was something placed on the castle itself, wouldn't you have regained your sight once you left the walls?"

"I haven't left the castle *grounds* at all, no. I've been in the training yard. That may count as outside enough, considering I didn't lose my sight until I crossed into the main building?" She blinked. "Whose translative argument are you rooting for now? Mine or yours, because *I* suggested that the word would be ward as in person, not ward as in building. So if it's placed on a person—"

Sir Lukxa shook his head. "I do not think that matters at this moment—"

Hollis grabbed at his hands and shook them. "Yes, it does. I want to know if I'm right!"

Sir Lukxa pulled himself free, digging his thumbs into his palms. "A barrier being placed on *you*. Your magic is being blocked by a barrier placed on you?" His voice rose in pitch as he spoke. "Not as a ward of protection, but a ward protecting. . . *from?*"

Hollis grabbed the journal reread the passage, doing her best to make the old scribbles make sense. "If that's true, then this would be an old *spell?* Not a curse. One of the first spells rooted outside of what the weave of magic allows. Unless we are completely wrong. Which is possible."

History spun in her mind, pulling at every detail she'd learned about the split from Tablin sight to Omil magic. It seemed this may be one of the first rooted places.

"If we can figure out how this spell is placed, we can reverse it in the same fashion. It wouldn't matter if it was placed on you, or say the castle." Sir Lukxa's voice rose in pitch, sounding quite eager.

Excitement that coursed through her, warming her face. Her fingers wiggled as she bit her lip.

The magic deep within her stomach *hummed.* She could imagine the threads under the tips of her fingers and just within sight. All that was left to do was read the passage until her eyes bled with understanding.

Sir Lukxa grabbed the journal from her and made quick work on the rest of the words written on the page, starting at the top and moving down toward their epiphany word. He made little notes in the journal as he went, ignoring Hollis' sounds of scorn and anger with each stroke of his pen.

"All right." He drew out the word as he twirled his pen. "I think I've done what I can. Tell me if you need anything else translated. I suggest that you try whatever it is we uncover until something works?"

Hollis wrapped her arms around her middle. With each conversation she and Sir Lukxa had through the evening, her magic practically *purred* against her middle. "That's as good an idea as I could come up with. Try things until something works." She watched each word he wrote with baited breath, forgetting to inhale every few moments.

"I have done what I can for the time being. While you go over my notes, I am going to wash up. I am quite sure you're tired of me smelling as I do." Sir Lukxa patted his hand against the back of the chair she sat in.

"I enjoy how you smell, but yes, go wash up and let me have the space I

need to think." Hollis caught his bashful smile from the corner of her eye as he pulled away and walked into the bathroom.

Pen set in hand, Hollis made notes based on his translations best she could. A few words had her giving different guesses; the grammatical structure was nowhere to be found, and her mind hurt from thinking.

The water in Sir Lukxa's baths ran. She could hear when Sir Lukxa threw his belt and scabbard on the floor. Hear the light *splash*es and groans as he slid into the tub.

Her self-control couldn't stop her from imagining what he looked like in that moment.

His arms braced against the edge of the tub, head leaned back. Of course his hair would be untied in her imagination. Hollis wasn't sure how she would picture his legs. They'd either be bent inside the walls of the tub, or he would have one leg extended out over the lip, dripping water onto the floor from his foot.

Hollis tucked chin to chest as she pushed the impure thoughts out of her mind.

Oh, how she wanted to linger.

She set back to working on Sir Lukxa's translation notes. Making adjustments to her own notes and correcting them when needed.

Slowly, as the sounds of Sir Lukxa washing filled the room, she worked through the pages of the journal again. Skipping through bits that seemed irrelevant to the both of them.

The door to the apartments *clicked* and opened; it sent a ray of light along the floor. Hollis pushed the journal across the desk and grabbed at whatever was next to the chair and stood to face the intruder.

The world grew dark at the edges of her vision.

Perhaps she'd stood *too* quickly.

"By the fields, Healer Hollis—are you all right?" Councilor Shad's fear-laced voice cut through the spinning darkness as she half-fell, half-sat, against the chair. Thankful, she hadn't collapsed to the floor.

A groan built in her throat before she could speak. "I'm fine. You know, *knocking* is a wonderful way to let someone know that you're wanting entry to their room, Councilor Shad." Hollis' vision brightened after a few moments of blinking. When she could focus once more, she found Councilor Shad had nestled himself in tight and trapped her between himself and the desk. His face far too close for comfort. His hips were pressed against hers.

She pulled her head back. "Can I help you?"

Councilor Shad's hands pressed against the sides of her face. He turned her head this way and that. "Interesting. You acted like you were going to pass out, but you appear to be fine now."

Hollis brushed his hands away from her and pushed lightly on his chest until he took a step backward. "It's just a thing that happens if I stand too quickly. Now, is there a reason you're here?"

Freed from his caging, Hollis sat on the settee.

"Here as in, in this room, or pinning you to the chair?" Councilor Shad gave her a lopsided grin. "I am simply checking in to see if you found anything of interest inside the archives tonight." He sat beside her on the settee. The scent of leather and dried ink lingered in his place.

Hollis wouldn't reach for the journal; that would only serve to draw attention to it. Her eyes kept trained on the councilor. "Enough, yes. I may return a few more times."

She hoped he would leave. His sudden presence tied her stomach into knots.

"You do know the festival takes place quite soon, correct? Do you have any thoughts on how you're going to finish healing Prince Dagen? He seems to be doing better, but something about the whole situation feels. . . *off*." Councilor Shad's gaze pierced her. "And I think if I do not give you enough time to speak, you will flounder around with your words and lies and *finally* tell me the truth."

"I am doing my absolute best to be sure that Prince Dagen is perfectly cured from his ailments by the weeks end." Hollis had no idea if she'd be able to manage that or not, but giving herself a week's buffer between now and the coronation sounded like a good idea. It seemed doable. If she could get this journal translated or find a way to get her magic back.

There was no guarantee that this journal had anything of use to her, though. Two weeks was all that stood between her leaving this castle a free woman or hung. Sir Lukxa had promised that she would be taken care of, and she wanted to believe him. But the glare she'd received from some of the councilors at her healing session with Prince Dagen screamed that, if she didn't heal the prince, she wouldn't leave the castle alive. Or perhaps they were because they thought she *was* in fact healing him?

"What are these notes—"

The bathroom door swung open and hit against the wall. Sir Lukxa stood in the doorway, water dripping from his hair down his *bare chest.*

By the—

"Sir Lukxa, it seems you've misplaced your clothes." Councilor Shad spoke, a catch in his throat.

Hollis couldn't tear her eyes away from Sir Lukxa. He stood with nothing but a towel wrapped low around his middle. His hair was free, and water dripped from where the strands ended halfway on his chest down to the lip of the towel. The dip of his hips formed a deep *V* before the cloth hid him away from her sight..

"It appears I forgot a change of clothes. Councilor, I was not expecting you. Were you, Hollis?" Lukxa ran a hand through his hair, slicking it back against his head.

"No, I wasn't—"

"My apologies, Captain Lukxa. I merely wished to discuss Healer Hollis' progress." Councilor Shad placed a hand over his heart. "It seems you've both found a common interest in translative work." Councilor Shad stood and reached out to pluck a piece of paper from Hollis' pile of notes.

And then his hands found the journal.

She tried to take the papers back. "I would appreciate if you wouldn't—"

"Where in the world did you get this journal? It's unlike anything I've seen."

Blood ran out of her face. Hadn't he told her that there was not a book in the archive unknown to him? "I was gifted it recently. Someone thought I'd find it interesting."

Sir Lukxa strode closer, still only clad in his towel. He stuck a hand out toward Councilor Shad. "I know you've an interest in all things related to books—especially older books, but it is quite impolite to *snatch* things from people." The scent of his soap was thick in the air, which had become heavy laden with the humidity from the washroom. "Or do you not remember our earlier conversation?"

"Yes, much like you *snatched* my ledgers the other night. I am merely observing an interesting artifact." Councilor Shad stood and side stepped Sir Lukxa as he flipped the pages of the journal open, keeping a level gaze with Sir Lukxa. "This journal would not be too great of interest to me. I cannot read whatever language this is in—either some Tablin language or Omil. Perhaps even some other northern language?" Councilor Shad flipped a few pages forward. "I would have handed it to you, but you're still soaking wet, Captain. Oh *goodness*, one of you *wrote in it!*" Councilor Shad's eyes went wide with horror.

Hollis balked, unable to watch as Councilor Shad read Sir Lukxa's notes. Her eyes wandered back to Sir Lukxa. His skin glistened.

He was standing so close to her. So close. . . in nothing but a towel.

At least there were no puddles they'd have to mop up later.

He took another step toward her. The scent of his soap and oil coated her mind.

Focus, Hollis, there are more pressing issues at hand. Like the fact that Councilor Shad is going to figure out what you're doing.

Hollis shook her head, shaking out the impure thoughts that wanted to ruin her mind. "Councilor, I would appreciate it if you would return my journal to me." Hollis stood and grabbed at it. Again, Councilor Shad dodged her and continued reading.

"These notes you wrote are written in Standard Catolian, which I can read just fine. You seem to be writing an awful lot of notes of *curses* in your margins, Healer Hollis. Why is that?" Councilor Shad took another small step backward. The green in his eyes struck her. It was a frozen glare.

"Councilor, if you would return my notes to me, please?" Hollis further reached her hands, doing her best to mask the trembling that lay under the surface of her skin.

"Or, perhaps Captain Lukxa can put some clothes on and you both can explain this right now before I go to the rest of the council and tell them that you're planning on cursing someone." Councilor Shad's voice held strong, his eyes narrowing into a glare. He snapped the journal closed and held it tight against his chest.

Sir Lukxa's jaw ground shut. The muscles lining his mouth swelled with tension. With a sharp exhale through his nose, Sir Lukxa walked over to his dresser, grabbed some clothes from the drawers and stepped behind his dressing screen. The towel was quickly tossed over the edge.

Hollis could see his outline on the screen as he dressed.

"Goodness, you do not have to act so bitter, Captain Lukxa. It's not far from a modest request that you clothe yourself when others are in your room." Councilor Shad quipped and set himself upon the far edge of the settee in the study. He crossed one leg over another and leaned back on a bent arm, and propped his face in his hand. "I refuse to have anything to do with naked men."

The moment Sir Lukxa was fully clothed he rejoined them in the study, his harsh steps almost rattling the objects on his desk. He settled himself on the settee between Hollis and Councilor Shad.

Several moments passed and no one spoke. Councilor Shad tapped his fingers against his arm. Soon after, he quirked a brow. "Are either of you going to speak or are you silently formulating a plan to curse me?"

Panic clawed at her stomach, sending ripples of pain to her back. She bit her lip and tried to think of a way to fix the situation. She was versed in spitting out whatever foolishness came to mind in the moment. That required something to come to mind. And nothing did. "We are not planning to curse anyone. We're trying to figure out how to lift one," Hollis answered.

The moments of silence stretched again.

"You're trying to. . . *lift* one?" Councilor Shad steepled his hands at his mouth, thinking. His browns knit together. "Are you implying that Prince Dagen is not ill, but *cursed*? It would be the only logical explanation."

"Councilor Shad, as much as it pains me to say this, yes." Sir Lukxa sighed and shook out his hair, sending little droplets of water everywhere. "Healer Hollis has confided that Prince Dagen is being cursed. She has been able to manage the effects, but we haven't quite found a manner in which to break it completely. That is what we have been doing in the library. We spoke the truth—Hollis is seeking alternative treatment methods. And we are close." Sir Lukxa's face held raw emotion. His eyes were wide, jaw quivered, and she could see him squeezing his hands.

Councilor Shad cocked his head and pushed up his glasses. "Close enough to a cure that you didn't think to tell the Council what was *really* happening? We asked you what you thought. Did you not know then what you were thinking?" Disappointment and disbelief filled Councilor Shad's voice.

Sir Lukxa let out a shaky breath. "Shad, we do not think it wise to inform anyone else on the Council of this matter."

"Because of the laundering of funds and Cane's obsession with keeping extra weapons in stock? I cannot believe that. I refuse to believe—"

Hollis felt no guilt in interrupting Councilor Shad's ramblings. "The refusal to believe something without giving proper thought is folly."

Councilor Shad scoffed, a sour face. "And who exactly would you like to pin this blame on? *Hmm*? You imply it is someone on the council due to mismanaged funding."

Sir Lukxa raised a hand as he leaned forward to explain. "We believe Councilor Collin and Cane may—"

"Oh yes, Captain Lukxa, we can all agree that Councilor Collin is an outright jerk, but that doesn't mean he's behind all of this. And like I said, Cane is obsessed with being over prepared for any disaster." Councilor Shad glared at Sir Lukxa. "You need better proof than this to claim someone on the council is trying to curse our last remaining monarch. The person we currently live our lives to serve."

"I agree, Councilor, but I side with Sir Lukxa. Councilor Collin seemed a bit too dimwitted to pull this off on his own. But that doesn't mean he isn't tied to the happenings with Councilor Cane. Which then implies that other councilors could be working together in more sinister actions." Hollis ran a hand down her leg, finding a stray droplet of water resting on her thigh. "Don't you think it's at all odd how many healers it's taken to find this out? How upset Councilor Collin was when I said *I know what's wrong!*" She threw her hands up in frustration. The movement did nothing to help burn the energy that built in her muscles.

This night was quickly becoming uncomfortable in many fashions. Her mind swam with the different twists and turns. There was no telling what Councilor Shad would do if they couldn't convince him of the prince's curse.

"I'm inclined to have you both imprisoned for this, but seeing as the only thing I've found is a few scraps of paper with random scribblings and your raving ideas—no. *No,* I do think that's enough actually. In fact I *will.* I'm going to Councilor Dem *right now.* You pointed me toward Councilor Collin, and Cane, and Sypher to cover your own tracks! Make yourself seem like a *good guy* when in reality you're *one of them.*" Councilor Shad barked his works and tossed Hollis' notes on the table and made for the door.

Hollis shot up, stumbling. "No, please! You don't understand—we aren't cursing Prince Dagen!" She stumbled forward trying to reach Councilor Shad before he could get to the door. "We aren't involved with this." Her voice tumbled out of her mouth.

Councilor Shad turned back to face them, eyes wide with rage. "No, I'm not having any of this—"

Sir Lukxa shot up from his spot and swung his fist into Councilor Shad's jaw. The resounding *crack* of struck flesh filled Hollis' ears, followed by Councilor Shad's body crumpling.

Sir Lukxa caught the man's head before it could bounce on the hardwood floors.

The room froze. Hollis stood in shock, watching as Sir Lukxa checked Councilor Shad's breathing and pulse.

Hollis' jaw quivered as her fingers crept to her lips. She couldn't believe she saw that. Refused to believe it. There was nothing in the world that could make her mind accept that Sir Lukxa would punch someone across the face and send them to the floor.

"I do believe this can buy us some time." Sir Lukxa met her gaze with a solemn darkness across his face. "There is nothing I would not risk in order to protect what I need to. You get your magic back—*now*. Think of something. Anything. I bet the answer is in that book. We are so close I can taste it." He nodded his head as he spoke. "I'm going to drag him into Prince Dagen's room. Then, I'll explain everything to Prince Dagen." Sir Lukxa grabbed Councilor Shad's limp arms and hoisted the unconscious man onto his back.

Hollis raced him to the door and unlocked it, her hands shaking. "What if I can't get it back by the time he wakes up?" Her vision shook as she found Sir Luxka's pale eyes boring into hers.

"I believe in you. Besides, if you don't have your sight, I'll knock Shad out again. I'll be back to check on you soon. Lock the door behind me this time. If you can't remember where the key I gave you is, there is a spare in the fourth drawer of my dresser, beneath my underthings. Open the drawer two-thirds of the way open to keep a knife from popping up and slicing your hand."

And then he was gone. Hollis quickly shut and locked the door behind him. The wood scratched against her fingers as she fumbled with the lock.

Her breathing came in fast, short bursts. Everything around her spun as she made her way back to the desk.

CHAPTER TWENTY-FIVE

HOLLIS

Nerves blistered down her spine, spreading to each limb of her body. Hollis felt a fool. The bright pages of translated words contrasted greatly with that of the old journal that smelled of worn leather.

She no longer had a week to break Dagen's curse. She had *tonight*. That was it.

And then, she had to heal Councilor Shad himself. The damage inflicted by Sir Lukxa's fist sounded terrible—she'd likely have to treat *his* fist! She had three patients now and no sight to cure them.

The settee cushioned her landing as Hollis flung herself upon it. Dramatically throwing her arms over her face.

She straightened. A brilliant idea struck her.

Maybe she could allow Sir Lukxa to keep punching Councilor Shad in the face over the next two weeks while she worked? That would give her enough time to think through these notes and then some. She could cure the entire kingdom of every illness and be back to wake the councilor with a cup of tea whilst she fixed the damage done to his mind.

Hollis shook her head, hair nearly stabbing her in the eyes as it flew about her face. The pile of thoughts was distracting her from what she needed to be doing right now: translation and restoration. Her magic would be returned to her tonight.

Sir Lukxa could deal with the councilor. She would deal with the pile of paper and magic on the desk.

The directions on the pages swirled together as she translated. Nothing made sense, but she had to *make* it make sense. Time was running out.

She grabbed the pen from the table and held it close to her nose. "I had more time and now I've lost it. *Why* do things have to be so difficult?" The tremors from her hand shook the pen about as she rambled. "Sir Lukxa is holding the second hand of a clock counting down on my fate and I am sitting here studying some old script that forms no connections in my mind. . . and I'm talking to a *pen*." She tossed it back on the desk and allowed herself to flop back into her seat.

Fingers continued to twiddle about.

"I don't have time for this. Why give my attentions to some creepy journal? I need to think of a better plan." She pushed herself up from the chair and did her best not to trip as she ran to his kitchenette.

"Find something, Hollis. *Something*." She rummaged through every drawer and cabinet her fingers came across, pressing each one at odd points to see if it triggered some secret opening.

The tea drawer was filled to the brim. Nothing particularly useful jumped out at her. Silverware was polished and neatly organized under the cupboard that stored the few plates and bowls the captain owned.

"Let's see if you've anything useful in here, Sir Lukxa." A sharp scent sent her backward a step. The liquor cabinet's astringent odor cleared her mind of the scrambling thoughts. "Goodness, I hate that."

There were only a few bottles tucked inside. Memories from the shared night of drinking gin came back as she gripped the bottle in her hand. Each ridge bent into the skin of her palm. The bottle felt much lighter than she remembered it being. The gin found a new home on the counter next to the small sink area. The words Sir Lukxa had spoken to her beauty settled deep in her.

Had two weeks passed already since that moment?

She eagerly awaited the *after* in all of this. Finding a time where she could breathe and explore the range of her emotions tied to the man.

A wax sealed bottle of wine joined the gin on the counter, and soon three other glass decanters until one labelless bottle remained. She pulled the cork and sniffed it. *Vanilla.* Spiced vanilla warmed her senses.

"Rum. *Rum.*" She spun the bottle between her hands. "What can I do with this? Of all the things here, you're *sweet* in nature. Sugar-cane based, sugar likes people, people like sugar. Why were we drinking gin when Sir Lukxa had this vanilla spiced rum? It would have been far more pleasant to drink. *No,* back on track. Keep thinking, Hollis. You'll find something. What can I do with this?" Holding the rum fast she paced the length of the room. "Sugar moves people, alcohol slows the mind and opens it to all to influence." Her foot smacked into her leather shoe, sending it flying toward the bathroom door. It landed with a wet *smack* against a puddle on the floor.

Leather and rum. Leather and rum.

"If you want to be safe, why don't you pour some. . . rum steeped with leather around the door frames."

"What does the rum do?"

"Doors are. . . happy when drunk? They stay tight-lipped, unlike people. So they'll keep any unwanted magic creature from venturing in."

The bottle started to slip through her fingers. Hollis quickly tightened her grip. Her fingers becoming as claws against the glass. She could feel the tension in her fingernails as she held it fast. "No, no I *made that up.* Besides, that's for keeping things *out.* I want in. What would I do with a drunk door to even let me in? *Sober it up?* How would one sober a door?" She turned back toward the counter. She set the rum down. "How does one sober up. One sobers by drinking something else. Drunk then sober; closed then open. No, first, drunk. I need something leather—no, a pot first."

Hollis ripped open the drawer that held a few small pots and pans. The largest of which was in the far back of the cubby. She pulled all offending objects in her way off the shelf and *ever so carefully* deposited them on the floor. "I do hope Sir Lukxa won't kill me for the mess I'm making."

The pot *smacked* against the stove as she slammed it down before reopening the bottle of rum and dumping it inside, save a large sip she took for herself.

It burned down her throat and cleared her nose. "Oh, why did I do that? Oh, oh—by everything *good, that's horrible*." She bounced between her legs as she fanned at her mouth and dangling tongue.

"Leather next; I need leather." There wasn't a chance she was going to use her own shoes for this. Borrowing from Sir Lukxa seemed the only option at large.

She dug around the bottom drawer in his dresser, which he had noted only held things he didn't much use anymore. Practically an invitation for Hollis to take what she'd like.

A leather knife sheath without the blade fit inside made itself known to her. Grommets shone in the light, blinding her a moment. It had the leather she needed and was an item that Sir Lukxa didn't much care about. She could cut out the metal bits. Unless they wouldn't harm her concoction?

"Think, metal. What would metal do here? Shiny, hard, cold, grommets keep things together. But too much togetherness may mean that I would keep whatever is holding my magic back, intact. So it can work for the drunkenness, but. . . I need to keep metal out of whatever I use for the sobering. Goodness, all his pans have metal—no, *no*. He has something clay. I felt it. Doesn't matter, drunk first." The leather sheath quickly found itself submerged in the simmering pot of rum. It bounced around against the walls before settling into a pattern of slowly turning around.

"Perfect. *Drunk.* Sober now, sober next. What sobers? Water sobers; not well enough, coffee sobers, but I hate it. It's irritating, and I can't have an irritated door. . . tea, *tea*, I need tea. This man has tea." She scanned through the tea drawer again, studying each container. Pulling out boxes and tins alike, tossing them wherever she pleased.

"Herbal, herbal, herbal, her—this is why this man is *so calm!*" She threw a small bit of a floral tea against the ground, spilling chamomile buds across the floor. A few caught wet spots by the floor of the washroom and tinged them a pale yellow. Her body wavered. "I need to calm down, but I can't calm on my own. Why can't he be here to keep me calm?"

Hollis sank to her knees, the sounds of the roaring boil of rum and the metal grommets hitting the sides of the tall walled pot bouncing about in her mind. She froze against the floor.

Breathe, Hollis. You could do things before you had a handsome face helping you along. Just do *as you always have.*

She swallowed hard and drew in a steadying breath. "I can do this." Pushing off the ground, she quickly scanned through the teas once again. "You gave me something when I was hungover. It was a black tea, *strong.* You didn't pull it from this drawer through—" She slammed it shut. "—you got it from the same place you got me the salve." He'd pulled it from a cabinet nestled against the wall of the kitchenette.

A blue tin painted with gold swirls. It took more effort to pop off the top than she would have expected, but when she did, the inside revealed the black tea leaves and little blue flowers.

The tin found a home next to the stove as she retrieved the clay pot and filled it with water before dumping more than a fair share of tea into it. Her bones refused to move and she stood to watch the pot boil.

The night wind scratched against her skin. It dug deep into her marrow. Both the rum and tea sat in pitchers placed on either side of her bare feet as she stood on the small stone ledge outside Sir Lukxa's apartment window.

The tips of her toes held her up on the lip of stone as her heels dangled over the side of the fall. She wished she'd decided to use the servants door on the ground floor of the castle rather than risk life and limb standing in a ledge several stories off the ground.

No, there isn't any time. Besides, You have conquered this window before. The only difference is that now you can't hold onto the wall.

Standing on the window sill was the closest she could be without her feet coming an inch within the castle walls. She had to be *outside* coming in. Needed to act quickly.

Hollis released her grip on the window frame.

Her knees *cracked* as she bent to grab the pitcher she'd filled with the steaming rum and set on the inside of the frame. The glass handle settled into her grip with ease as she balanced, keeping her eyes trained forward, locked onto the bookshelf. That was her spot, she couldn't tear her eyes away from it. She would have preferred spying the bed if it were nicely in sight, or the door, but neither were to be found where she was.

The wind pushed against her spine, she imagined a bundle of blue threads keeping her upright.

"Thank you. Now, let's drink."

Steaming rum ran down the right window sill, collecting on the stones and wooden frames near her feet. Pitcher now in her left hand, she poured it down the walls again, being mindful not to taint the tea with any splashings of rum.

"Just have to get the top and bottom of you now. Nice and drunk you will be." Reaching high as she could, Hollis threw the pitched rum against the top of the window sill.

A small cry broke free from her lips as the hot rum splashed down against her, leaving red singed marks against her skin. The aroma of rum dizzied her mind. It ran across her front and dripped into the room. Her feet itched as the liquid pooled around her. If she wasn't careful, she'd slip. And with her luck, she'd fall backward toward the ground. She gripped the groves of the stone wall with her free hand, not breaking past the edge of the window and into Sir Lukxa's rooms. The stone scraped her nails.

Hollis took a steadying breath. Let it go in a mist of air. "I'll give you time to soak that up." She wouldn't let there be a chance of the 'doorway' not being drunk enough to sober after.

Her balance tettered as the winds blew harsher and whipped her hair and clothes around her person.

"Just to be safe." Hollis took a deep breath and poured the rest of the pitcher over herself. It had cooled, slightly, but still held great warmth. She shook her head and blinked the rum off of her lashes.

Her arm extended backward as she dropped the first pitcher to the ground, waiting to hear it shatter against the stone below. Several moments passed, lending itself to a long fall.

Hands now free, she rubbed at her face.

Hopefully the rum had done its job.

The tea had cooled significantly as it sat on the still, not enough that it didn't scald as she splashed it against the stones and rocks. She dipped her hands into the pitcher and rubbed the tea into the window frame and the wall.

Sobering required force.

The sky roared, deafening her to any surrounding sounds. Tea mixed with the rum on the gale, intoxicating her mind and bringing a sharpness to reality. She dropped the second pitcher. The wind caught it instantly smashing it to pieces against the stone wall of the castle.

"You've kept me out, my *magic* out." The wood of the window threatened to break the skin of her fingers as she reached inside and gripped tightly to it.

The gust fought her grip, pulling her backward toward the ledge.

Liquid pooled and burned against her feet, her toes unable to find full, solid purchase for more than the tips.

Her mind heard the faint *click* of a lock and mumbled words.

Hollis gripped all the harder at the stones, feeling them rip at the tips of her fingers. "Now you're sober so you will *let. Me. In.*" She could see that the inside of Sir Lukxa's apartments were perfectly still. Nothing flew about or tumbled on the ground. No suggestion of the magic that threatened her life.

Pulling herself forward, Hollis screamed. Her throat burned as her body fought against the wind. She needed inside the room.

One foot forward, the wind grew harsher.

Thunder rumbled as the tempest tried to rip her back.

Hollis thrust an arm forward. Tried to find a grasp on anything she could. Wall, curtain, window frame. Anything grounding.

The door to the apartments opened. Sir Lukxa slipped around the door and froze as their gazes met. *"Hollis!"* He rushed toward her. Fear etched itself on every inch of his skin. Sir Lukxa slid along the floors as he scrambled toward her. Finally within reach, he gripped her soaked wrist and pulled her down to the ground against him.

Her knees and arms landed on either side of his body against the wooden floor. Impact sent a course of needled pain through her. Her fingers spread to find Sir Lukxa's body. Cold fingers found warm flesh. Her eyes rolled back into her skull.

Waves of nausea crashed up her throat as air plunged it down.

"What are you doing—what were you *thinking?* You are soaked." Sir Lukxa's voice pushed rapid breaths against her ears. His hands grabbed at her figure, assessing her.

Her arm fanned about over his chest, hands tracing the skin of his neck, the emerald threads of his being. Every thread was known to her.

Sir Lukxa's heart hammered in his chest, her own following his rhythm.

Her voice caught in her throat. Hot tears that had welled in her eyes dripped down her face, then fell to Sir Lukxa's chest. "I can feel." She pressed her face into his chest. "I can, I can *feel you.*"

CHAPTER TWENTY-SIX

LUKXA

Lukxa balanced his weight between his legs, shifting slightly under Hollis' ire. "It seems I struck Councilor Shad much harder than I had aimed for." Lukxa had been standing under it for an immeasurable amount of time in his mind.

Hollis had taken her time walking down to Dagen's chambers, pausing to marvel at every little thing with her newly acquired sight.

Lukxa could not blame Hollis for her slow pace.

He had watched on in the hall, breathlessly, as Hollis bent the moonlight in the air and upon the floor to her *will* with the twist of a finger.

He had forgotten the weight her magic carried.

Hollis sat on the floors of Dagen's room with Councilor Shad's unconscious head resting on her lap. Her fingers lightly traced around his face, plucking with her middle finger and thumb at random points. He imagined her holding a needle and thread, the Councilor's face a work of embroidery. She was slowly stitching him back together.

"It's not that you hit him harder than you thought, it's that he isn't a trained knight. He's a glorified librarian! The threads in his face are tattered, all bundled and close to snapping. Congratulations, you broke his jaw." Hollis smiled up at Lukxa, a glint in her eyes. "It was a clever move. Hopefully you can restrain him to a. . . lesser degree while I work on disentangling the curse from Prince Dagen's person."

"Yes, while the two of you continue talking as if I'm not here. What's going on?" Dagen yawned and rubbed his eyes as he squirmed from his spot on the giant bed. Dagen had his eyes glued onto Hollis since the moment he'd realized her magic was back, studying the deft ways she moved her hands.

Hmph—Lukxa could almost be jealous. Dagen wore a far more eager and exciting expression now than when Lukxa had dragged Councilor Shad's unconscious body into Dagen's room. Of course, Dagen had forgiven the imposition once he realized what was happening.

We must not let the rest of the council know. It would spell disaster for all three of us, Dagen had said.

Lukxa agreed with the sentiment.

Hollis glanced up at Lukxa, which brought him out of the past and back into the present. Oh, yes. Dagen had asked a question. "Sir Lukxa didn't tell you? Our dear Sir Lukxa decided that fists talk better than mouths. Respectable." Hollis laughed as she continued her stitching or weaving over Shad's skin.

"I had already told Prince Dagen that bit of information, Hollis." Lukxa bit his lips. He did feel slightly bad at the injuries caused. In the dim candlelight of the room he could clearly see the bruises that marred the councilor's face. As Hollis wove her hands, they slowly faded beneath his skin, morphing from black to purple, finishing from a sickening yellow to pale red. Leaving Shad with only a minorly irritated spot on his left cheek.

Hollis held Shad's head up, lightly twisting it about to see his face from all angles. A light blush coated her cheeks as she studied the councilor's face closer, she trapped her lips between teeth. "His body will have a much easier time fully recovering like this."

Dagen nodded his head. "So you get the body in a position where it's equipped to care for itself rather than completely healing it."

Hollis gave Dagen a glowing smile. "Sometimes, yes." In this moment, Hollis appeared to thrive on teaching and explaining her magic to such an eager listener. She continued speaking, doing a few more pokes around Councilor Shad's nose. "This way he'll still feel the sting of Sir Lukxa's fist on his jaw." *There it was.* Her little pursed smile of victory. Pride swelled in his chest as he smiled. Her expressions were lively.

Hollis rested Shad's head on the wooden floor with care and made her way to stand beside Lukxa.

As she picked up Lukxa's hand, it sent a burning sting up his arm. He *hissed* as she twisted his wrist.

Hollis *clicked* her tongue in response. "Nothing seems to be broken. Your hand is in better shape than Councilor Shad's face. I'm half tempted to leave it this way, you know. But, you did this for my honor—"

Lukxa interrupted. "To keep him from ruining the only way to save Dagen's life—"

Hollis continued speaking, nonplussed. "My honor means so much to me, I'll heal this free of charge."

Lukxa hung his head, hiding the flush that crept up behind his ears. He had truly spent too much time with Hollis. He had taken to making rash decisions, like punching his fellow councilor in the jaw rather than reasoning with him.

It *was* nice to do things in a simple manner for once.

Hollis' fingers wove over his hand. Within moments, the burning pain stopped. No longer could he feel the throbbing in his knuckles. Hollis released his hand, allowing him to stretch his fingers and move his wrist about. It was perfect.

A retching sound came from the direction of Councilor Shad. "*Oh*, my head. What did you do to me?" He blinked several times and pushed himself off of the floor. He continued retching as he slowly got to his knees.

Lukxa bit his tongue before he found the right words to speak. "Sorry, Councilor Shad. You were going to do something you would regret."

With great effort, Shad managed to get himself upright.

Lukxa watched Hollis puff her cheeks and lock her gaze onto the ceiling. "Hollis, I thought you said he would be fine?"

She blew out the air stored in her mouth. "I said his *jaw* would be fine. You still punched him hard enough he fell unconscious. I can't fix the gross feeling that comes with it." She puffed out her cheeks and teetered on the balls of her feet. "Anywho, Councilor. While you were out, I, rather conveniently, managed to get my magic back. An odd bit of magic seemed to have either been placed on me—or maybe the castle itself—to ward off outside magic." She tucked her bottom lip between her teeth. "But now you'll be able to see first hand the curse laid upon the prince—and my removal of it."

Shad let out rough scoff. "That proves *nothing*. You both could be covering your tracks and—"

"*Councilor!*" Dagen's voice filled the room. Far from an angry cry, no. Simply the charge of royalty that came in his voice. "It is *true*. The fact was hidden from you due to a great plot that's been formed in these walls these years past. Tonight marks our second step in overcoming it." Dagen sat straighter in his bed. Even though the bones of his shoulders protruded from his skin, though his eyes were cast in shadows, he looked once more as a prince should.

Lukxa could see the glow beneath his skin, the upward tilt of his jaw. Dagen commanded power.

"Second—what would the first step have been?" Councilor Shad took a more solid step toward the bed.

Dagen snickered. "You'd love to know."

Lukxa's insides burned as he recalled Hollis' medicinal kisses with Dagen. "*That doesn't matter right now.*" He resisted the urge to glare at Dagen for that little comment. "It's time to finally rid Dagen of this curse and ready him for the crown."

As soon as Councilor Shad was able to stand without seeing stars, Hollis sent him and Lukxa scrambling secretly around the castle for different supplies, namely a blood orange, a wooden bowl, and a *'something gold with a pearl in it.'*

When the two had arrived back into Dagen's chambers a quarter of an hour later, Hollis had extinguished almost every candle in the room, save the ones by the door and two by the bed. She quickly took the supplies from their arms and carried them to Dagen's bed, drew closed the gauzy curtains, and refused to allow Lukxa or Councilor Shad to be any closer than ten paces away from the bed.

It was not long before the flickering candlelight bounced from wall to wall. Burning lower and lower. The light flittered about in the cream gauzy curtains that surrounded Prince Dagen's bed. It was interesting, seeing the room bathed in moonlight.

Quite some time had passed since Lukxa was last here in the evening. Or at least, when he felt a stillness inside his bones that would allow him to take a moment to breathe in the atmosphere.

Lukxa ducked past a low-hanging bundle of flowers, lilacs and wisteria as he paced the room.

A cold breeze swept in the closer he stood to the bed. Not exceeding the ten pace limit Hollis had set.

The chill made it impossible for Lukxa to sit longer than a few moments in his chair next to where Councilor Shad brooded.

Instead, Lukxa kept pacing back and forth, looking between the councilor and the two whispering figures outlined on the drawn curtains from Prince Dagen's bed.

He wished he could see past the offending material to visualize what

was going on. The degree of separation from Dagen bordered on discomfort. There was something unnerving about being right next to him, without being able to see him whatsoever. Even the words that escaped were muffled.

Being right there, yet feeling so far away from the ability to step in should anything go wrong.

That was wrong, he needed to trust the woman. There was no reason to think anything *would* go wrong. She hadn't given him any reasons not to trust her.

But a small piece of himself did not in the moment.

Lukxa hated that.

Shad wore a pinched expression, likely trying his best to figure out what Hollis was doing with Prince Dagen. The scholar in Shad was relentless— and, while Lukxa hadn't been on the receiving end of his scrutinizing glare, Hollis seemed to be sick of it. She'd told the man if he took another step toward her that she'd undo the healing to his face. Lukxa understood Shad's determination to watch the healing. Lukxa wanted to be closer to where Hollis and Dagen sat.

Even with the moonlight, it was difficult to see past the gauzy fabric that swayed in the breeze.

A shiver ran up Lukxa's spine. Hollis had taken to opening the windows to freeze them all to death it would seem.

The faint sounds of night life floated in the air. Laughing, the occasional noise of cattle, and nature itself.

Tingling spread up from his fingers, but shaking out his arms dispelled the feeling.

It quickly returned, creeping up his skin.

Close to an hour had passed since he had pulled Hollis from falling out his window, marking the start of the prickling sensation. And it had been intensified further by her then healing his hand.

Residual magic?

The air about her being changed the moment she stood on her own earlier. Her spine straightened, her arms carried a slight bend, and even her hair seemed to float on a nonexistent breeze.

It was his turn to scoff. He had become so poetic in describing her.

Lukxa could not imagine the experience of losing something so much a part of one's self with the promise of it being right within reach. He was happy that Hollis had it back. There were plenty of things ripped from his own being that held no such promise of return.

Curiosity grew, rooting deeper in his mind as the slow moments of time passed. Hollis spoke of his people learning to access the weave of the world as Tablins could. Being able to bend nature to their own will.

What would my will have nature accomplish?

A scoff came through the drawn curtains from Hollis.

In the half-hour since they had arrived, Hollis had repositioned herself and Dagen multiple times, her hands moving precisely about in the air. Prince Dagen seemed perfectly fine, Lukxa could occasionally hear a few labored breaths and words less fitting coming from the mouth of the crown.

Whispered words floated closer to them from the hem of the curtains.

"What do you think she is doing to him in there? I do not like this whole blind trust thing. It's unnerving, not knowing something." Shad asked, his own voice hushed as he stood to join Lukxa.

"I can knock you out again so you do not have to watch and wait." Lukxa wasn't sure how to react quite yet concerning the Councilor's flipped attitude.

"It's simple." Shad kept Lukxa's gaze. "I trust Prince Dagen."

Lukxa averted his gaze and straightened himself as the two outlined figures moved. He would guess they were sitting on their knees, facing each other. Figuring out which silhouette was who was simple.

Hollis repositioned herself and Dagen again. She now sat with her back to the window on the left side of the bed, while Dagen sat opposite to her, illuminated by the starlight. Their detailed features were obscured by the fabric, he could still see the brilliant green hue of Hollis' hair.

Hollis lifted her hands and swirled them about in the air around Dagen's body. The more Lukxa watched the movements became clearer. It was as if she was sewing and weaving in the air. Her fingers pinched and pulled in a conducting movement.

Something squeezed against Lukxa's lungs and middle. He turned to better look out the corner of his eye to see if Councilor Shad had any reaction. Shad wrapped his arms around his stomach, his face still impassively watching Hollis' movements. After a few moments, Shad opened and shut a few times.

The pressure vanished.

Lukxa's head snapped back to the bed. Dagen and Hollis sat still. Neither body moved an inch.

The silence in the room began to throb against his skull.

Dagen's voice crept out past the gauze. Lukxa couldn't make out the words, just as he hadn't the others spoken between them. Then the word *please* stuck out—not a begging notion, but a soft asking.

An asking of what?

Hollis' hands lifted and cradled Prince Dagen's head and neck before pulling him close to herself. Their heads bent and joined in the middle, muddling their shadows together.

"What is she doing?" Shad's voice rose in pitch and confusion—along with notes of horror.

No sounds came from the bed. Their figures sat still as Hollis' hands held Dagen's face close against her own. Lukxa thought he saw a twitch of movement from Dagen's arms.

Lukxa spun to face Shad, suddenly uncomfortable with the feeling that grew in his own gut. "Before Hollis had complete access to her own magic, she was able to lessen the curse by drawing it into herself and purging it." Lukxa watched on as Councilor Shad turned his blushing face toward the door. "Which involved her. . . *kissing*, Prince Dagen."

Lukxa turned his attentions back as the figures pulled apart.

"There is nothing of malice left inside of you. And I don't feel the sudden need to vomit all over your floors." Hollis' raised voice flitted through the soft cream panels.

Dagen's hands rose to her hips. It felt like an intimate moment.

Again Lukxa leaned foot to foot as he watched the pair, suddenly unable to pull his eyes away.

"How nice to know what your lips actually feel like when my insides aren't being ripped apart, Healer Hollis." Dagen's voice sounded strong, ringing with a force and power Lukxa had not heard in months.

Her laugh filled the room, sharp and clear. "How lucky you are to know such a thing that others do not. Very nice indeed, Prince." Her figure cradled his head once more, bending it down and pressing a kiss to the crown of his head. "I pronounce that you are healed, my majesty."

The curtains flew open as Hollis stood on her knees, hands gripping the sides. "You can see him now." She made to climb off the bed, and Lukxa rushed over and offered a hand to her.

Hollis met his gaze. "Thank you, Sir Lukxa." Her smile was warm, but the strength in which she gripped his hand showed something amiss.

"Are you—"

"Not now." She whispered while using his shoulder as a stabilizer to climb off the bed. Her eyes shook as she shuffled on her feet until she stood solidly.

Councilor Shad approached. "How are you feeling, my prince?" He gave a slight bow of his head as he approached the foot of the bed. Shad's face was glowing with excitement. His mouth stretched wide in a smile as he looked over every inch of him.

Lukxa turned to finally look at Dagen. While the prince's face was still slightly sunken, there was a warmth to his skin, a strength in his eyes.

"Better than I have in ages." Dagen lifted his arms and admired his hands. "I can *breathe*. I forgot what it felt like to take a full breath." He laughed, twisting his torso around.

Lukxa found Dagen's laughter contagious.

A lump formed in Lukxa's throat, catching his laughter. His eyes stung. Lukxa blinked several times, slowly shaking his head to alleviate the sour burning of a cry that stretched from his throat to beneath his tongue.

Councilor Shad turned and walked to the edge of the bed, a position in which Shad could see all of them clearly. "I think I can say, rightfully so, that Prince Dagen is fully healed. Meaning you were either telling the truth in that you were not the ones to curse him, or. . ." Shad's face was twisted with a range of emotions. His brows scrunched, then raised, his eyes refusing to stay in one spot. Finally it stayed in a neutral position, completely deflated.

"Councilor," Dagen started, "I've no reason not to trust Healer Hollis and Captain Lukxa. Lukxa is my closest friend and has been nothing but truthful with me. I know he wouldn't do *this*."

Shad's lips drew thin. "Then, tell us, Healer Hollis, what type of curse *was* plaguing Prince Dagen?"

Lukxa turned to find that Hollis had a touch green in the face. "It seems that someone placed a curse of *ill-will* upon the Prince." Hollis' voice came out controlled, steady. And while she looked ready to vomit, the strength in her eyes was a marvel.

"I thought you didn't know much about curses?" Lukxa found himself asking.

She nodded her head. "That's only true to a degree." She tilted her head. "I've healed a few when I worked with my parents. They tried their best to keep me free of the dark magic. And, while I couldn't figure it out without my sight—with it I can see anything and everything. I can break down whatever it is I wish. Ailments call their name, as this curse calls its name. I wish it'd call its caster," Hollis muttered.

"What exactly is a curse of ill-will, Healer Hollis?" Shad's fingers drummed along his middle and mouthed words. He looked rather much like he wished for a pen and paper.

Hollis drew her lips into a tight smile before speaking. "Simply put, the more ill-will wished on a person, the sicker they become."

A silence washed over the room. No one spoke as a breeze rippled the curtains, creating a light *scratching* sound.

"So," Lukxa found himself finally cutting in, "if someone cast this on a well-liked person they would not fall sick? The curse would not hold?"

"Exactly," Hollis spoke.

Lukxa trailed his gaze to the bed.

Dagen's face was unreadable as his eyes fixated on a point beyond all their heads. "So what you're saying is, people think I'm horrible?" The words fell flat. "And because they think that *so deeply and intensely*, I almost died. That is what you have said, correct?" Dagen's voice shook as he finished speaking. Lukxa could see the quiver set in Dagen's jaw. How Dagen squeezed his eyes shut and drew in a deep breath with his nose in some attempt to steel himself.

Hollis trapped her bottom lip between her teeth. "So. . . what I'm saying is that. . . Yes, in order for the curse to hold and harm someone there has to be a large collective sense of hatred towards them. No small amount could render a person this ill." She stumbled over her words. Her right hand rose and rubbed across her face and through her hair, shaking the fluffy pieces around in the air. Under the cover of her palm, her face showed how exhausted she was. Her eyes carried so much sorrow as she too took a deep breath before she dropped her hands. A still expression upon her face.

Dagen's face paled. "I guess that would make sense. Can it come back if that. . . dislike, isn't changed?" His throat bobbed, a slight retch coming from his mouth.

Hollis shook her head. "I've woven your threads back *tight*. Nothing should be able to lay claim to you for a while. Someone would need direct physical contact with you in order to do anything."

Lukxa walked over to the opposite side from where Shad stood and rested a hand on the bed. "Do not take it too greatly to heart, Prince.

This tells us the rumors were not only for discrediting your right to rule, but spread to tarnish your character in order for the curse to take hold— far from the baseless gossip sold in desire of coin as we had thought." Dagen scoffed. Lukxa quickly reached forward and took one of the prince's hands in his own. "Knowing this gives us the knowledge on how to best overturn those rumors. To rebuild your reputation. Once you're king, we will no longer turn them a blind eye as the council has ruled. *You* will be able to show everyone how strong a leader you are. You will disprove every false thing said about you."

The look on Councilor Shad's face lent itself to guilt. He had been one of the main voices in favor of the palace ignoring the malicious gossip spread to the papers from claimed "inside sources".

"Your words ring true, friend." Dagen ran a hand down his face. "I will be healthy enough to go in front of the people and show them my strength." Dagen relaxed back against his pillows, his face melting into a mix of something downtrodden and tired.

Hollis let out a sharp cough. "I would like to go to back to sleep now. So, if you'd excuse me." Hollis gave a small salute with two fingers and hobbled toward the door.

Hollis' hand was bone-white as it gripped the handle of her cane. It very well may have been a trick of the light, but he did not want to dismiss the possibility of it belonging to something more. Lukxa would be sure to find a sweet treat for her once he returned to his apartments—if she did not manage to find one herself first.

"Yes." Dagen laughed. "I think rest is in order this night. While I feel so much better, the weight of mountains grows upon my eyes and I do not believe I can keep them open much longer. Both of you, leave my room as you will. I'm going to lay down. Do not expect responses if you attempt to speak with me. Goodnight." Dagen gave a little flourished bow with his arm before he tucked himself back under his sheets, his eyes still open.

"We will reconvene in the morning with the rest of the council." Lukxa gestured Councilor Shad towards the door where Hollis stood. Lukxa waited for Shad's movements before moving himself.

Shad started to walk, head bowed toward Lukxa. "I do not think we should mention the curse to them quite yet. You were right to keep that to yourselves." Shad's whisper hardly graced Lukxa's ear. He would chide the man for speaking so quietly later. "When we announce Prince Dagen is healed we shall simply state the truth—that Hollis was able to use. . . the power of the moon to fully heal Prince Dagen?" Shad asked as he twirled his thumbs around each other.

Lukxa twisted up his lips. Shad's idea sounded more far-fetched than he would normally like.

But Lukxa did not see himself coming up with a better answer.

In fact, Lukxa would have to answer to *another* group as to why Dagen breathed easier and smiled like a radiant sun during his official *coming home* ceremony from "finishing school."

Lukxa let out a sigh. "That is what is best. Considering we do not have solid evidence yet on who did this and we are unable to rule out *anyone*."

Hollis tapped her foot by the door. Both her hands rested on her cane. Her posture leaned back and forth in a delicate sway.

"Healer Hollis," Prince Dagen called out.

"Yes?" She let her head fall back to look at him, her hair falling over her shoulder. Lukxa followed her gaze back to Dagen, who sat up in his bed once more.

A faint flush overtook Dagen's face. "Thank you, again. You know. . ." Dagen wet his lips. "Your magic has been persecuted by my family and my people for ages. And you used it to save my life. There isn't a way to compensate for your actions." Dagen dipped his head in a low bow.

"Prince Dagen, do not worry yourself with such things. I serve the crown of the shining sun and the man who will wear it." Hollis placed her right hand over her heart as she gave Dagen a solemn smile.

"You can go ahead to the room, Hollis. I'll follow you there shortly."

Lukxa waved her away.

Hollis nodded and slipped out the door.

"I'll see you in the morning, Prince." Shad gave Dagen a bow before turning to face Lukxa. "Again, thank you for setting me straight." Shad pointed his finger a hair away from Lukxa's nose, a snarl upon his lips. "But do not ever strike me in the face again, Captain." Shad bowed his head one final time before making his own exit.

And then it was just Dagen and Lukxa in the room.

"She's remarkable, isn't she?" Dagen spoke. He still lay curled up on his bed, picking at pieces of fluff from his covers.

Lukxa gave a small bark of laughter. "I would certainly say so. But when you stop to think about it, she is just as remarkable as every Tablin with the sight. Does that make her less remarkable and more. . . normal?" He pushed his hands into the pockets of his pants. The feeling of his arms sagging was nice. It gave his shoulders the chance to relax.

Dagen *hummed.* "I guess you're right?"

Lukxa gave Dagen a thin smile. "I think you just have a crush on her—"

"Oh, no. *No,* I don't. No." Dagen's face burned as he threw his head back against his pillow. "I'm grateful and she's beautiful, but I don't think I could have an actual relationship with her. She's far too wild to be queen. And I think every time I'd kiss her I would have residual, phantom pain in my stomach. Hollis is quite stunning and needs someone to match. . . Perhaps she and Councilor Shad would make a good pair? They have the sort of personality that I think blends nicely together. Her chaos to his. . . research?" Dagen lifted his head, a sly smile growing on his face. "Or even you *yourself.*"

Lukxa scoffed. "Are you saying I should get together with Councilor Shad?" He raised a brow, enjoying the moment of teasing.

"Goodness no," Dagen sat up. "*You* and *Hollis.* I've said it before, in a manner, and I'll repeat it now. I think you'd make a handsome pair. You seem to bring out the best in each other. Aesthetically you work well. And you've been sleeping in the same bed the past several weeks." Dagen wiggled his eyebrows.

Lukxa did his best not to let a flush overtake his face, though it burned at the collar of his shirt.

The idea wasn't horrible. And he knew the thoughts that swam around in his mind concerning himself and Hollis. But there was work that needed to be done. A reputation to be salvaged and remade, a council to weed like an overrun garden—

And the woman who had just *healed the prince from a curse* was sick-looking and alone in his room. "I should go make sure Hollis got to the room safely." A panicked edge crept into his voice.

"Oh sure, leave to make sure she is safe and do not stay to protect my own—I see how it is." Dagen yawned. Lukxa wondered if it was faked. "Anyway, I want to sleep." Dagen waved him off with a smile.

"I am only a few doors away," Lukxa said, hand on the doorknob.

"Yes, a few doors away with a beautiful woman in your bed. I feel ever so safe." Dagen ran a hand through his hair. "I'll see you in the morning." He further cocooned himself into the covers and stared out the window.

The hall was silent as he pulled the prince's door shut. It *clicked* as the door met frame and he locked it. Lukxa walked down the hall, the sword at his side dancing at his hip.

"Captain Lukxa." Councilor Shad stood just in from the bend that would put Lukxa back into the hall of his own room. "I want to talk with you."

Lukxa swallowed. "Go ahead." He came to a stop a foot away from the councilor.

Shad sized Lukxa up and down. "A few years ago some councilors. . . prodded me about my position of loyalty to the crown. Not in obvious terms, but it wouldn't have taken the genius I am to figure out what they were after. I didn't think much of it, mainly a test of my own loyalty. Through the years there have been moments that have caught my attention."

Lukxa interrupted him. "Can you get more to the point, Shad?"

Shad *huffed*. "I want you to be honest with me." He held Lukxa's gaze, his green irises seeming to glow. "What was your reason in becoming Captain?"

A tingling washed down Lukxa's neck, pulling at his throat. "I—I was hired for a specific purpose." Lukxa swallowed and faced away from Shad.

"So, you know for certain that there is a group that is actively seeking to harm Prince Dagen?"

"There is not a shadow of doubt in my mind." His mouth went dry.

Shad nodded, *humming*. "I see. Was Hollis hired for the same reason?"

Lukxa's gut twisted. "No. No, I sought her out. On my own." The light in the hallway seemed to dim. It felt relieving to speak of such things, to be honest. Being vulnerable was dangerous, but so freeing. "She does not know of my previous. . . *involvement*, either. I hope that she will not know."

Shad quirked a brow. "It may be in your best interest to tell her of such a thing. If any of this were brought to light—"

"Who?" Lukxa cut him off, holding up a hand. "Who would tell her of this?"

"Word spreads, Lukxa." Shad took a step forward, brows furrowed. "What if someone on the council who is involved, or any other manner of person you seem to be speaking about, were to approach her? Her confidence in you would shatter." Shad raised his arm as he spoke, and when he finished he let it flop at his side. "It's best to make things about yourself known by your own lips than those that would wish harm."

His words hit Lukxa square in the chest.

If someone were to reveal this information to Hollis, it would likely ruin any trust Hollis had in Lukxa. Though, perhaps his earnest attempts at curing Dagen would give more evidence toward him caring?

Would Hollis trust Lukxa enough to still desire being with him if she were to learn of his truth from any mouth other than his own?

Lukxa pushed past Councilor Shad and jogged the rest of the way to his apartments.

Voices sounded on the other side of his door. Heated voices.

He pushed the door open, finding Councilor Dem and a few other knights tugged at Hollis, who stood in nothing but a maroon shirt and underwear.

"What's going on?" Lukxa rushed into the room.

Dem turned to face him. "There's been an accident."

CHAPTER TWENTY-SEVEN

HOLLIS

pparently there was no time to find one's pants in the middle of an emergency.

Hollis' legs struggled to keep up with the fast pace the knights dragging her and councilors set.

She wished her cane was in her hand. When Hollis had arrived back in Sir Lukxa's apartments, she tossed the wooden thing into the study out of frustration and changed with reckless abandonment. She figured that Sir Lukxa was taking his sweet time talking with Dagen.

Now, her heart screamed and pounded against her ribcage, begging for mercy she couldn't give.

This pain and embarrassment was earned.

"What happened?" Sir Lukxa's voice wasn't far behind herself and the group that dragged her forward. He'd arrived at his apartments just as she was being dragged out of it by Councilor Dem and his knights.

The knight that dragged her barked at Sir Lukxa to run faster as he rounded another corner. Hollis' vision spun, her feet bumbling as she continued down the hall.

"I said, *what happened?*" Sir Lukxa snapped, his voice raised.

The knight finally spoke, shouting backward at a level that made her ears want to bleed. "We aren't entirely sure, Captain Lukxa. Councilor Muse was supposed to have dinner with Councilor Collin. When she didn't show up, he sent a page and they found her bleeding out on the floors of her apartments. We currently have groups searching the castle for the assailant." The knight ended up spittling on her as he shouted.

She wanted to vomit.

"How could this have happened?" Sir Lukxa's voice sounded closer. It seemed he had almost caught up to the group.

Hollis spared a look back, pleased to see a pair of her pants in his hands. He must have stayed behind to find them. The thought was warming—and chilling at the same time, as he likely had a nice view of her undergarments currently.

Despite the chaos, Sir Lukxa and Councilor Dem's knights seemed not to show a drop of emotion on their faces. They were the example of calm in a storm. Uniforms perfectly pressed, hair taken care of, attitudes calming to those around them. Hollis was feeling better already.

She scoffed.

"Is this truly the fastest you're able to walk, child?" Councilor Dem asked from the front of the group.

Embarrassment heated her cheeks.

Her ankle rolled beneath her, ripping a cry from her throat as she fell. Sir Lukxa's arms were around her, lifting her into the air as he held her to his chest.

"That's far from the proper manner in which to bring someone along with you." Sir Lukxa chided the knight as he held Hollis fast in his arms like a princess. "And there is no need to ask insulting questions, Dem. Hollis isn't a trained knight, and beyond that, she isn't feeling the best." His voice was deep and vibrated her against his chest.

Sir Lukxa's hands held fast to her shoulder and thighs—reminding

herself even more of her undressed state.

Hollis called up ahead. "Can I please *clothe* myself?" Blood pounded in her ears.

"Afraid not!" Dem called back. "There will be time when we reach the clinic."

Hollis used a hand to tug the shirt down, attempting to cover her undergarments. "What's the difference between *here time* and *there time*? I'd rather not show up in my underthings." She could spy the warming pink on Sir Lukxa's cheeks. Watched the knot in his throat bob as he swallowed, coinciding with another tightening of his grip on her bare legs.

"I'd rather we get you there and help Councilor Muse than worry about the notion of modesty. Besides, if you remember, the whole of the council has seen you in far less," Councilor Dem shot back.

Her lungs froze, her face recoiling.

That stung.

Several of the knight's heads turned and watched her as they ran, a few whistled and snickered. Hollis didn't want to decipher the lewd expressions they wore. She could see more than she would like in their threads. Their tensed nether threads lent a violating feeling in her gut.

She readjusted herself in Sir Lukxa's arms. She plucked her pants from his grasp and did her best to thread her legs through the openings as he ran down the hall.

"Just. . . Hold on, Hollis." Sir Lukxa moved her around in his arms, almost flinging her over his shoulder as he struggled to keep a steady pace. Finally, he paused one moment and he settled her with her forearms braced against his shoulders. Lukxa grabbed the waist of her pants, which she'd managed to get her feet through and part way up her legs, and *yanked* them up until she was fully clothed.

The strength in which Sir Lukxa held her up via the waistband was sure to wedge her clothes awkwardly in the creases of her body. But, Hollis wouldn't complain to him.

As soon as she was clothed, Sir Lukxa took off running. He quickly rejoined the group.

"Your strength is something to be marveled at, Sir Lukxa." Councilor Shad laughed and came into view behind them. He cut around a corner in the hall. His laugh was far from humorous. "Where are we running to?"

"Councilor Muse was attacked," Lukxa responded. His words heaved. Hollis saw Councilor Shad falter before he continued running.

She held tight to Sir Lukxa's body, doing her best not to cry out as he continued jostling her while he ran.

The group spun around another corner of the hall, Hollis almost lost her stomach, and dipped into a smaller passage that was heavily laden with moisture. Hollis hadn't taken this passage of the castle before. She didn't recognize the countless doors they passed, nor the paintings that flickered in the candlelight. It smelled different, too, lived in but somehow still pleasant.

Another few moments of running and being jostled around in Sir Lukxa's arms and they were in what Councilor Dem called the *high rank clinic*. A private room that only a few persons could be treated in. Hollis assumed the list was narrowed to several high ranking officers, the councilors, and royal family.

The iron-rich scent of blood slunk out the green doors.

Sir Lukxa set her on her feet, which were still bare and froze to the floor, as the rest of the knights made their way inside the clinic. Hollis took the moment to properly fasten her pants and right herself in the garment before entering alongside Councilor Shad.

Her lips curled up as she freed her creases from the tightly wedged pants.

The clinic was quiet, save the *tapping* of feet as nurses rushed around a bed. None of them stopped working; someone always hovered over a still body.

Hollis approached, watching the expressions of every council member as they stood around in the room. All of them were in varying states of dress. Some still wore their uniform, while others were in casual wear or sleeping clothes.

At least she wouldn't have been the most underdressed if she hadn't arrived in pants.

Now standing closer, Hollis could hear the whispers passing between lips, see the shifting gazes, the furrowed brows. A healer spoke with Councilor Dem at the back of the room, her ginger hair frazzled as she continuously ran her hand through it.

Hollis turned her attention back to Councilor Muse.

She suddenly understood the silence.

Several stab wounds marred her chest. Her once peachy lips had taken on a dangerously blue tint sitting on her sunken face. Atop the weeping stab wounds was a pile of white powder—clumping powder, Hollis would assume.

Hollis turned to lock eyes with the lead healer at the back of the room. She seemed relieved to see Hollis.

Councilor Dem cleared his throat "I'm going to escort Healer Penny to the store room to fetch supplies." He pointed his hand at every body in the room. His face wore a stern expression, his eyes wide, brows raised. "*No one* is to leave. I still haven't heard back on if we've caught whoever did this. We need to remain alert and on guard."

Healer Penny spoke next. "I'm leaving Nurse Hunter and Healer Hollis in charge during my absence."

Quick goodbyes were said as Councilor Dem left with Healer Penny and two other knights. They all reeked of blood as they stepped past Hollis.

Their absence left them five knights. *Eight*, if the two other Councilors from Eargile and Sir Lukxa were counted.

Hollis focused her gaze as she approached the bed, side stepping the puddles of blood on the floor.

The rails on the bed stuck to Hollis' hands as she gripped the cold metal in her hands.

The threads in Muse's body were snapped in several places. Some cords of life stayed woven from the strength of one, tense, fiber.

Every system in her body was snapping and shutting down.

Recovery from something like this was unlikely.

"Do you think you can heal her?"

Hollis whipped her head around, pulled back into the world around her. A few councilors had moved away from the bed where Muse was lying and now sat in chairs on the far side of the room. A few knights stood between the councilors and the rest of the occupants to give them a wall of privacy.

The tired councilors, who had been rubbing at their eyes, suddenly stared at Hollis.

"Can you heal her—completely?" Councilor Sophy snapped a pale finger as she spoke. Her words were shaky and clipped. She stood not far from Hollis with one arm wrapped tightly around her middle, the other still bent in the air from snapping. Tears welled in her amber eyes, which she rapidly blinked away.

Hollis shook her head. "I can try. But Tablin magic can't do everything. I cannot promise to meet expectations which may be set too high." The stares of everyone in the room bore into her skin, digging down to her marrow.

"Do that then. *Try.*" Councilor Sophy sucked in her lips. She quickly steepled her hands over her mouth. After a few moments of silence, she walked over to the group where the rest of the councilors sat and found herself a spot on the wall between the darker Councilor Aphi and pale Councilor Sypher.

Councilor Collin met her gaze with a tense expression. His muscled figure loomed over her.

Was he in pain? Councilor Muse was supposed to meet him for dinner.

Councilor Collin ran a hand down his face, holding his palm over his mouth. His head shook before he raised his eyes to meet Hollis' gaze. "I don't think all the gold in the world could amount to heal her. There simply isn't enough."

Hollis could see an odd tension building on his face. She blinked several times, her mouth flapping much like a fish before she found the words to speak. "*What are you saying?* I. . . I do not need money to save someone from dying like this."

Her heart skipped a beat as Councilor Collin closed the distance between them.

Councilor Collin's hand clamped down on her shoulder as he whispered in her ear. "I'm simply stating that perhaps there is nothing that could allow you to heal her." He raised his brows while tilting his head downward. "Is there something that would make it. . . difficult for you to heal her? You deserve a large payment for something like this."

What lay under his words? She didn't want to spend the time thinking through what he was trying to offer her.

"I don't have to think of a large number required for me to *save* her." Hollis pushed him back, and a knight stepped between them. Councilor Collin held his hands up, an exasperated tension to his brow. He blew out a breath before sitting down on one of the other few beds in the clinic, wrinkling the pristine white sheets.

Hollis turned her attentions back to the rest of the council. "Do I have *your* permissions to work?"

"No." A person spoke behind her. "Healer Penny left you in charge, Healer Hollis. You don't need permission to run what is currently *your clinic*," Nurse Hunter said. He gave a sharp nod of his head, his expression calm but determined.

Hollis returned the gesture and found the nurses had stepped back to give her space to work. Every face was tense as she approached the side of the bed. The healers' eyes analyzed every movement she made as if to anticipate what would come next.

Hollis walked to the side of the bed and stretched out her hands. One of the nurses poured an orange disinfectant over Hollis' skin. It ran over Hollis' hands, sinking into every line of skin, doing nothing to aid the numbing cold she felt surrounding her being.

Hollis ran her hands over Muse's wounds and wiped away at the white clumping powder. It caked up beneath her fingernails; the sensation set Hollis on edge. Another small, terrible, thing that added to the weight that grew in her stomach. The smell of the wounds did nothing to help. If Hollis had any food in her stomach she would have vomited it upon the floor when she entered.

But she could do this. Could handle the feeling of sick.

If she was going to save Councilor Muse, Hollis had to get the bleeding woman into a stable condition quickly. The best course of action was to heal from the outside in. Show the body that it didn't need to focus as heavily on the end of her limbs, giving it the ability to focus on the center of her being where a blade had cleaved.

A steadying breath grounded Hollis and visualized herself as sturdy as the marbled floor.

Hollis opened her eyes and set back to investigating Councilor Muse's wounds.

They hadn't even cauterized or stitched the councilor closed yet.

Hollis stuck a finger into the wound, realizing why such actions hadn't taken place yet. The wounds were deeper than Hollis' finger could reach.

She stepped back a moment, clutching the edge of the blood-soaked bed. A few steady breaths were needed.

In, out. In, out.

All right. She could do this.

Hollis stepped back to the bed, her hips pressed against the metal siding. She wiped the blood and clumping powder free from her hands and she once more pulled at the threads of Councilor Muse's body. She would have to work carefully to sew from the deepest part of the wound up, lest she neglect a bleed.

Each thread Hollis plucked at pulsed strong at the end of her arms and legs and thrummed at Hollis' touch. Slowly, she gripped a thread at the base of one of the councilor's clammy fingers. Hollis gently rolled it between her own fingers as she stretched it up her arm to reconnect at Councilor Muse's elbow, giving it enough slack and length to reconnect and weave back together.

Hollis repeated the process for each finger on Councilor Muse's hand, stretching it to the elbow until all five fingers had reconnected at the joint. She wove them all together, careful not to tug more than she needed, lest she snap a thread and be forced to repeat the process with what was left intact.

She took pause, mulling through her options. There was the possibility that she could reintroduce new threads to the councilor's being. Threads from something pure and organic that still yet *lived*. But that took time.

The threads in Muse's arms slipped against the tips of Hollis' fingers, frayed and ready to break if tugged too hard.

Hollis tried working the healthy threads from Muse's legs up her arms to give slack for the ones fraying in her middle and neck. No matter how she grabbed or tugged, the threads wouldn't budge.

A better angle was needed for this.

"Excuse me." Hollis lightly pushed a nurse back from the bed as she then swung her right leg up onto the cot and then pulled the rest of her body upward onto it.

A few murmured words went out in the room, but Hollis paid them no mind. She needed to focus only on the body in front of her. She did her best not to put any of her weight onto Councilor Muse.

Settled, Hollis reached a hand back, dragging her fingers from Councilor Muse's shins to her middle, slowly tugging the threads along the way. The thread's purple color was slowly fading in the middle of Councilor Muse's body.

The world felt heavy on Hollis' shoulders.

Pain shot through her head as she rubbed the threads together, willing them to rejoin. The tapestry of the woman was starting to unfurl in her mind. Small threads uncoiled and unraveled further and further away from her struggling heart. Something stable was needed.

Stable, stable. What's stable in this room? The steel is stable, but it's holding us up. One wrong pull and we'd be on the ground and I'd cry myself to sleep in a jail cell. The bed itself? No, it has give, too much give to be stable. Holding the bed. . . sheets? Sheets hold us when we sleep, keeping our bodies warm and held.

"Someone, I need a set of sheets. Tear them into wide strips, no thinner than three inches." Hollis' voice had taken a rough sounding texture.

As the sound of ripping fabric filled her ears, Hollis worked to slow the bleeding inside the woman's body.

"I've got a strip for you." Nurse Hunter's voice broke through the silence Hollis had created in her mind.

"Thank you." Hollis stretched out a hand.

Her hands were sticky and laced with blood. A stark contrast to the perfectly white linen.

It was so sticky. . . and thick. She rubbed her fingers together. The blood pulled between her fingers as she stretched them.

Acid churned in her stomach. This was so much blood.

No. Hollis shook her head. *I can deal with that later. Focus on the now.*

Hollis blocked out the world around her best she could until the only noise that remained was the subtle pulse of blood in her own ears.

Setting the strips of fabric against the councilor's chest, Hollis felt for any little loose threads from the makeup of the linen sheet itself. Threads behind threads.

Slowly, the white woven design made itself known, and she pulled the natural threads free, and wove them into Councilor Muse's middle. Her body clung to the support offered by the material.

The white threads from the sheet slowly took on a rich violet hue as Hollis pressed and twisted the threads together. Merging Councilor Muse's body with the support of the fabric.

Slowly, Hollis moved the threads upward and brought in new pieces of fabric as needed.

The actions reminded Hollis of spinning yarn, adding more flock to the wheel to be tightly spun for thread.

The natural violet threads in Councilor Muse's body began to relax, the tension sliding downward and out of her body.

Hollis continued moving in that rhythm. Occasionally a nurse would wipe at Hollis' face with a towel or offer more strips of fabric.

Soon, the wounds were sealed.

Hollis ran her arm across her face, wiping on her own at the sweat that had the gall to drip down her brow. "If Councilor Muse has the will to recover, she shall."

As Hollis finished speaking the world came to life around her. Sounds of people talking bounced around in her head. There were several pairs of hands on Hollis' body as she climbed off the bed. Several nurses rubbed and scraped at her blood-soaked skin.

Hollis' spine screamed in agony after being hunched so long. Her legs wobbled as she walked toward Sir Lukxa, who held his arms open for her. She held fast to his forearms as his own hands supported her weight.

"Councilors," Councilor Dem spoke, stepping further into the room to allow a new barrage of knights to stand at the front of the room. "I am recommending that all of you return to your apartments. You'll each have a group of knights guarding you. With any luck, we'll find who did this in time for a few hours of sleep." Councilor Dem ran a dark and scarred hand down his face. "Lukxa, I'm sorry, I will need you with me. Along with you three." Councilor Dem pointed to a few knights and ordered the rest of them to follow the councilors back to their apartments.

"Yes, sir." Sir Lukxa nodded back at Councilor Dem. "Wilfrin, I am placing you in charge of watching over Healer Hollis in my apartments." He handed Hollis off to Wilfrin, who offered his own arm for Hollis to hold onto.

"Lady Healer Hollis," Wilfrin spoke softly.

Hollis was pleased that Wilfrin would be escorting her back to Sir Lukxa's apartments and keeping guard. She was familiar with the knight. He seemed trustworthy.

The chaos that followed the emptying of the clinic was maddening. So many voices and threads.

Pain shot up her leg as someone's heavy boot made contact with her toes.

"Here, Lady Hollis." Wilfrin's voice was harsh against her ears as his arms suddenly wrapped around her waist. He awkwardly picked her up from her middle and pushed past the last few people, who gave them reasonably rude remarks.

Her ribs screamed in protest against the pressure, threatening to *crack* out of place and stab her lungs. She could feel the blood on her shirt and pants clinging to her skin.

"Put me down, please." The words squeezed out of her lips.

Wilfrin dropped her. "Sorry, I didn't want you getting stepped on again. Sir Lukxa would have my head if his woman got hurt." His voice was laced with a tense fear.

Hollis blinked. "I'm sorry, what?" Her face exploded with warmth.

She could ignore the blood that covered her person, she needed more information on what this man just said.

Wilfrin waved a hand in front of his face. "Don't worry, we're all more than fine with this. In fact, all of his knights have agreed that it's great he's finally settling down. And with a healer? How lucky!" His boyish face lit up with glee as he shook her hands before gesturing her inside Sir Lukxa's apartments. "You stay here by the door while I do a sweep of the room. Don't worry, I won't lose a finger. I'm one of Captain Lukxa's trusted knights, so I know where all the traps are." Wilfrin gave another grin before he started looking around every bend and cranny of the Captain's rooms.

It took Wilfrin several moments to open every drawer and cabinet that weren't rigged with traps. Hollis wanted to tear her hair out watching the man work at such a slow pace.

Hollis couldn't take the waiting any longer. "Why do people think Sir Lukxa and myself—"

Wilfrin cut her off. "*Don't worry*, you do not have to hide it any more. Everyone in his company knows that you're both sharing a room. And Captain Lukxa is the kind of man who would only share a room with his wife—well, aside from a fellow knight, but you understand." Wilfrin's eyes went wide as his hands flew up and shook wildly in the air. "Not that he's ever *slept* with any of the knights! I don't want you to think I'm trying to sully his name. Rest assured, though, we all have your back." He gave her another wide smile and nodded his head.

Hollis couldn't tell if all the blood in her body rushed to heat her cheeks, or sank to her feet.

Wilfrin clapped his hands together, dusting them off. "All right, the room is safe. I'll step outside so you can rest." He gave Hollis an awkward sort of side-hug and left the room.

Hollis couldn't move. Absolutely frozen.

"His entire company thinks we're secretly *married*? I don't hate the idea, but, goodness." Her hands flew to her mouth.

Oh, her hands were *still* covered in blood. And now it was up her nose. That wasn't sanitary.

Hollis gagged as she rushed to the wash room and turned the tap at the sink to scrub at her face.

Once every trace of blood was gone from her person, Hollis threw the sullied clothes into the fireplace and changed into a freshly cleaned pair.

Exhaustion weighed deep in her marrow. She practically had to crawl to the bed from the fireplace. The covers felt like a dream as she swaddled herself up.

"Married to Lukxa. . . that sounds nice."

CHAPTER TWENTY-EIGHT

LUKXA

The night had drawn on and Lukxa felt as though it would never end. Councilor Shad's words from earlier circled his thoughts with every step he had taken. Every moment of searching for the assailant, hoping that Hollis was all right, all Lukxa could think about was being honest with her. Telling her the truth concerning the things he had almost done, had been *so willing* to do.

Lukxa shoved open the door to his apartments and swiftly closed it behind himself before he spun to locate Hollis.

He let out a shuddered breath.

Hollis lay on their bed, head raised with slow blinking eyes. "You're back sooner than I thought you'd be." A yawn broke onto her face. The light the fireplace provided and a few still burning candles cast a gentle glow on Hollis' face.

The room smelled faintly of blood and burned fabric.

Lukxa walked further into the room, removing his belt and sword to leave by the dresser. "Are you feeling better than you were earlier?"

Hollis nodded in response. "Yes. It was. . . quite something to remove the curse in full. But far easier than sucking it out of him." She let out a soft laugh as she nuzzled back down onto the bed. "I had worn it down so much the past several days that it didn't give me much of a fight when I untangled it from Prince Dagen's person. And now, the sun *will* shine on his crown."

Hollis' sentiments warmed his core. He had chosen well on who to heal Dagen.

Lukxa twisted his hands around each other and moved toward the bed. "Hollis, there is something I need to talk to you about." His face warmed as her eyes widened, a small smile crept onto her face.

Hollis cocked her head. "All right." Red crept up her face. She held her bottom lip with her teeth.

It almost froze him in his steps. There was a hope about her face that Lukxa knew he was going to dash.

He stepped just past her and sat down in the middle of the bed, legs hung over the side. She sat up and settled herself beside him. Her hand rested just shy of his own.

Lukxa knew what he wanted to say, but did not know how to start. His words were frequently interrupted by pauses. "I do not want this knowledge to come to you by another source. My hope is that in telling you this information myself, that it will be easier for you to comprehend."

Her eyes squinted and she tilted her head. "I don't understand—what?"

Lukxa licked his lips, then drew in a large breath. He was going to confess. "I did not rightfully earn the position of Captain of the Royal Guard. I was bought and sold into the castle guard for reasons far from pure. As a scapegoat." He paused, gauging her reaction.

Hollis kept a still face. The fire in the hearth *crackled* and *popped* as silence drew on.

He continued. "When I was brought to Catol as a child. . . I had a great hatred in my heart. A hatred that refused to falter. When I was in the knights' academy, I was approached by a group who *refined* my anger. Intensified it to the point that when they asked me to take the position of captain to assassinate the Crowned Prince, I agreed." His actions seemed so egregious to his current state of mind.

Now, he could never imagine the hatred he had being targeted toward Dagen. Partially his parents and the council as a whole, but not Dagen.

Hollis' breath hitched, spine straightened as she pulled her hand away. "*What?*" Her words nothing more than a broken whisper. "Then you knew Prince Dagen was being cursed this whole time?"

"*No,*" he raised his hand in front of his chest and shook his head so quickly that his hair whipped around. "No. By the time that took place I was already working with Dagen to weed out those who were trying to end the royal family." The words tumbled out of his mouth faster than his mind could keep up. "I suspect the reason he was cursed was because I stilled my blade far longer than the group liked."

"The *council* you mean." Her face grew tense. "That is why you were distrustful of them. Because you were once a part of their scheming?" The skin near her cheeks and eyes grew red. Her jaw trembled.

"Yes. *Some* of them." Lukxa turned his face away, unable to withstand the pangs of guilt building inside him. "I have been unable to be truthful with anyone outside of Dagen—and Councilor Shad, with this information because I was not entirely sure of who all was connected with the council in this. I could not bring myself to tell you this news either. I had hoped that you would not know the corruption I had. . . sold myself into." His voice trailed off at the end.

"Who?" Hollis' voice was soft. "Who all on the council was involved? I was *alone* with several of them so many times and you never thought to let me know that I could have been in danger?" Her voice came out strained from the base of her throat. It graveled in his ears.

He deserved this pointed anger.

"I do believe you were always in the presence of someone trusted. It is one of the reasons I wanted you always by my side." He avoided the rest of her question. "We found who attacked Councilor Muse tonight.

And it is good news."

"Really?" Hollis straightened her spine, leaning toward him once more.

"Yes," Lukxa responded. "Healer Penny told us when Councilor Muse woke up, a long while after you left. . . Muse said Councilor Collin. . . attacked her." Sir Lukxa worried his lips with his tongue. The words stabbed at his chest. "Councilor Muse said she had discovered Councilor Collin was embezzling funds, much like the rest of us. When she confronted Collin, he refused to agree on coming clean to everyone else. He stabbed Muse to keep her from telling anyone—which is a shame because Councilor Shad and I already knew. With Councilor Collin's crimes being brought to life, and Councilor Shad bringing up the charges of Councilor Sypher changing the records, they're *caught*. A majority of the ones causing the issues have. Been. *Caught*." A fractured smile formed on Sir Lukxa's face as a shred of light glowed in his eyes. "I'm finally free, Hollis."

Lukxa swallowed like he couldn't breathe. Starving for air. He turned to face her on the bed, left knee bent onto the bed. "Collin is going to be interrogated. He cannot say anything about me and my part in the attempted assassination of Dagen. Now as it will seem like anything he says is him trying to save his own skin—if he tries to involve any of the other councilors, they will all deny it and it is *just*," his breath shook out of him. He closed his eyes, licking his lips. "I am *free*." His whispered words shook as he dropped his face.

Tears gathered in his eyes. He quickly wiped at them, laughing at himself.

Hollis bit her lower lip. "That. . . is a lot to take in, all at once." Her voice was still and soft. She blinked. Lukxa spotted the tears welling in her own eyes, slowly dripping down her face. "I'm sorry. You went through so much it seems." Her voice cracked.

"I did," he nodded.

Lukxa quickly stood from the bed, wiping at his face with his sleeves.

Hollis watched him as he stood. Her lower lip was dropped from the top, wet from her musing, eyes glossy from tears. The way her head was turned, causing her hair to fall so perfectly.

These thoughts should not persist in his mind after the wickedness uttered from his mouth. He had gone along with the idea of bringing a Tablin healer in for the purpose of creating a war between Catol and Tablin.

Hollis' life was to be a sacrifice so the council could get their war—and he had helped. Even while he fought to expose the council, his mind still played a part.

He needed to leave. "I can imagine that your sense of trust in me is fractured at the moment. I understand that you may need some space. I am going to patrol the area. Maybe I will return before morning but who knows?" He practically ran to his dresser and reattached his belt and sword before turning to the door of his apartments.

His heart attempted to carve its shape deep into his ribs.

Hollis scrambled from the bed, a hand raised. "Lukxa!"

He was out the door. Locked it behind him and ran down the hall.

CHAPTER TWENTY-NINE

HOLLIS

No thunder rolled against the stone walls of Sir Lukxa's washroom this night.

Bubbles of soap danced along Hollis' hand as she swayed in the tub. The evening was full of draining surprises with no chance of rest. While sleep called to her, the thoughts that ran through her mind kept herself from finding rest.

"Prince Dagen is healed now. The main scary part is finished. As soon as the coronation is over, I can finally go home. If I. . . want to leave? Do I want to leave?" She pulled her legs to her chest.

Wilfrin's earlier comments about herself and the captain continued weaving in and out of her mind. Swirling through every other thought she had, stealing her attention. While the statement of herself and Captain Lukxa being in a relationship caught her off guard, it didn't feel *bad*. Hollis found her time with Sir Lukxa quite enjoyable. He meshed with her antics perfectly. They worked together flawlessly.

Hollis wouldn't mind furthering their relationship.

Before that could even be possible she needed to wrap her mind around the fact Lukxa had told her all of those terrible things and then ran off like a scared duck before she could think to say anything in response.

How was she supposed to react to the news that Lukxa had first tried to assassinate Prince Dagen? He no longer held the thoughts in brilliant attitude and was actively fighting against them.

But he had still *had* them.

The same thoughts Hollis' hated hearing. That revenge was justified against those who took no part. Prince Dagen had no involvement in the wars against Omil or Tablin, yet he was used, as much as Lukxa was, to create more conflict.

Words of blame people used over and over again.

She lifted a bubble on the tip of her finger, watching the iridescent hue shift in the candlelight. The threads of the bubbles tickled her fingers. The desire to pull at them and see what would happen grew, but so did the desire to simply melt.

The door to the apartments opened and swiftly closed, the lock *clicking* quietly.

"Lukxa?"

She'd left the washroom door cracked to alleviate any worries Sir Lukxa would have upon his return about her bathing alone on such a draining night.

Steps wandered around the room before approaching the bathroom.

The bubbles slid down her hand and arm. They enveloped her with the scent of sandalwood and the floral oil she'd taken from Prince Dagen's room. It was a pleasant combination and made her happy.

The door pushed fully open. It let a burst of cold air into the bathroom.

She sank into the warm water and glared toward the cold door. "I'm fine—"

The man from the archives stood in the doorway. "Hello again, Lady Hollis. I must say, you solved this problem in a much different manner than I had anticipated." He cocked his hip against the doorframe. He waved his hand in the air in front of his chest. "It would be a pleasure to meet you if it weren't for the fact you keep messing up my plans. Though I guess you did just do me a great service."

She further recognized the man before her. Finally, memories and faces came flooding back.

The man from outside the castle when she first arrived.

He stood swathed entirely in black clothes—it brought out the creaminess of his skin, and the predatory hunger simmering behind his amber eyes. If she looked hard enough she could see the darkness of his clothes wisping in the air.

The steaming water of her bath became needles against her skin. Her throat bobbed, eyes drying as they refused to close.

"What are you talking about?" Hollis hunched her shoulders and narrowed her gaze on the man.

He'd yet to move from the doorway, lazing on the wooden frame.

She took a solid breath through her nose. There was no room to cower in fear—not that she felt afraid. She subtly sank a slight bit more to cover her chest with the bubbles of the bath.

Modesty and fear were different.

He pushed off of the doorframe and slunk toward the tub. He grabbed the little wooden stool she'd dragged over by the tub and sat. One leg crossed over the other in a neat pose. The scent of moss and rain settled over Sir Lukxa's sandalwood soap, suffocating it under the water.

She leaned away from him, a hand holding the lip of the far side of the tub.

The man broke the silence with a small laugh before speaking. "Settle down. In the spirit of transparency, I wasn't all that upset by you breaking my curse. You regained your sight and broke it *easily*." He punctuated the words with a flick of his hands. "I'm so impressed with you. Which isn't something I say often *or* lightly." A smile grew on the man's face as he leaned his arms against the edge of the tub.

Hollis did her best not to move in response, but darkness reeled off of him and wrapped around her throat. She felt hungry for air. Couldn't take a breath deep enough.

"What do you want?" Her voice shook slightly. Her insides threatened to upheave themselves as she inhaled the darkness. Emotions hammered in her chest. Wanting to burst forth.

Why did she feel such fear? What reeled from this man that made her insides want to crawl down the drain and hide?

"*You*—but beyond that, I want to *learn* from you. To see what you'll do and how you'll do it." He dropped his head to lean on his arms. "I want to see if you're truly worthy of my attentions. You see, at first I thought you were a thorn in my side, but then I realized you could be so much more. How you could teach me everything I lack." He flicked at the bubbles that gathered near her right knee. They flew into the air and quickly fell on the floor behind her. He repeated the action several times. Each *flick* driving the sense of fear further into her gut.

What would Lukxa do in this situation? His actions were far more likely to be less chaotic and brash, and less likely to get herself killed without her sight.

No.

Courage. She could defend herself. She had her sight *back*. Nothing could back her into a corner like this.

Brash, chaotic, hopefully won't get me killed.

Hollis shot a hand out of the water and wrapped her fingers around his silk clothed throat. Her knuckles *popped* as she tightened her grip. It felt good to hold the man in such a manner. The feelings were chaotic. Her insides screamed, her *magic* screamed.

He grinned down at her, furthering her anger.

She spoke as low and graveled as she could, an attempt to channel the threatening tones she'd heard in her life. "Let me save you the worry—you do not have my attentions and I will teach you *nothing*. I suggest you leave before Sir Lukxa finds you here. *Or* before I decide to unwind you thread by thread." Bravery was something she could pull off at this moment. The anxiety that tried to climb her throat, drying it, scratching it, were swallowed down best she could.

Hollis ground her teeth together as she tightened her grip. The light stubble against the man's otherwise clean shaven jaw and face dug into her hand.

He grinned wider, speaking hoarsely as her hand was gripped around his throat. "You can't *unwind* me. You cannot even see my threads. Something I'd be happy to teach you when you prove yourself fully to me."

What?

Hollis narrowed her eyes again, searching the rest of his body.

Her eyes burned. She squeezed them shut before opening them and focusing harder on the man's face and chest.

The muscles in her jaw trembled, it rattled her teeth.

Her hands couldn't find his threads either, no matter how she changed her grip on his throat, which bobbed with broken laughter.

A quick scan of the room around her proved that the threads of everything else still stood. Her grip went slack, hand sliding to rest upon his clavicle.

"Now don't give up just yet." He slapped his hand atop her own and tightened her fingers around his throat once more as he sat up, "I'll give you a few moments to see if you can discover them. I've hidden them quite well. I admit, it's a bit of an unfair challenge. But, Hollis, you seem to be quite adept at getting out of tricky situations." He tightened his grip on her hand, increasing the pressure around his own neck. A wicked grin split his face.

Try as she might, she couldn't see past whatever the man had done to conceal the threads of his being.

A part of her swelled with interest.

She had never seen such a thing. Aside from when she'd lost her sight, nothing had been able to hide from her. Not the shrew family hiding in the grocer's store room, not the tension that built in the earth beneath her home in every storm. Hollis could always *see* and realize.

353

"I can feel that. *Curiosity.*" He spoke each part of the word with emphasis, his eyes wide. "Such a beautiful feeling. The pursuit of knowledge is a wonderful skill to have. I think you would sit nicely at my side."

She didn't like the sound of that. Her words managed to flow unmangled through her still clattering teeth. "What?"

The man pushed her hand away and straightened himself. Water ran down his neck, fading into the darkness of his clothes. He ran his hand in the waters path and then flicked it from his hand. "Catol slaughtered Omil—my people—my *family*—because we learned how to use magic and wouldn't share the secret. You yourself are not but three generations removed at most from the burnings." He clicked his tongue and ran his eyes over the room before they settled back on her. "I cannot destroy an entire kingdom as their armies did mine. But I can *upheave* it. I can deliver *judgment*. Planting the idea in the council's mind to curse Prince Dagen in the stead of the captain finishing his task gave me *ample* opportunity to do so."

The skin of her hands itched as if she could still feel the stubble of his throat against her palm. She rubbed her hands together under the water, trying to rid herself of the feeling.

This man's words were an attempt to twist her mind and thinking. Hollis wouldn't sink into his words. "Just because wrong was done to us doesn't mean we have the right to commit further wrongs."

He cocked his head and grinned a slivered moon at her. "I've learned so much from you. I mean, I *sealed* your magic and you still managed to partially cure Dagen from my curse. So. *Apparently*, I'm not quite knowledgeable enough yet. I want to learn more about what magic can do. I have to. The ghosts of my people cannot rest until they are joined by the entire royal family of Catol and a majority of her people." He tilted his head to the other side, giving her a quizzical squint. "Should we not hold the evil-doers responsible? You see, I was hired by the very same people who swore to protect this kingdom to get rid of the monarchy. It was a brilliant plan on her part—really. Catol breeds destruction. From the inside out, it *implodes*. I'm merely saving us all time and making sure that the rest of the world comes out all right after."

The man's words were nonsense.

Hollis had heard this type of talk several times over, mainly from those who couldn't forgive what they couldn't forget. She raised her chin and pushed down her own anger toward the man. "The majority of people who committed the crimes against *both our peoples,* against the people of Tablin and Omil and so many other countries, are dead or old enough that they can harm no longer." She took a deep breath through her nose. "Why would we commit the same crimes against those who were not involved? There would be no point. It would be a vicious cycle." The water around her grew cold. Bumps rippled down her skin and shivers set in her bones.

"That's why I'm going to break the cycle."

"The cycle can be broken without further retaliation." It was hard to keep her voice steady. Anger still roared within her. So many emotions from this night twisted in her gut. Hollis wanted to scream and shout and slap this man across the face until it was recognizable no longer.

"When Muse brought me here, I realized the cycle was far from finished, Hollis." He flourished his hands about in the air. "The filth of Catol *churns itself.* We have to be the ones to stop it. Dagen can't, he'll grow to be a part of the problem."

Hollis' stomach sank. "What do you mean, Muse?" She was going to vomit.

His face lit up as he laughed. His hot breath ghosted over her skin. "Oh, you didn't *know?*" His voice was filled with mockery. "Shocking. I'm your dear Sir Lukxa's replacement. Finishing what he couldn't even start, except I'm taking it a step further. Why stop at murdering the prince when I can eventually rid the country of an entire ruling Council? Thank you for saving Muse. While I do not necessarily need her anymore, it is nice to have another pawn on the board of chess, no? Sacrifice can come further down along the road." His grin stretched ear to ear.

Sound refused to form on Hollis' tongue. Her mouth made half-attempts at forming words.

He reached a hand out and cupped her jaw, holding it with such care as the pads of his fingers trailed over her skin.

"Why are you telling me this?" The words spilled from her lips.

"Because." He leaned down to mingle his breath with her own. His eyes focused on her mouth. "I need you to know everything you can to best see how you react. How can you optimally teach me if you're lacking in information? It's simple. And because I was quite tired of lingering in your shadow. I'm tired of making you forget who I am everytime we interact inside the castle walls. That's why I'm here." He let out a breathy laugh before he released her face and slowly leaned back and upright.

Hollis' stomach sank.

The door to the apartments opened again. Both their attentions turned to the bathroom door.

The man had a twinge of surprise on his face. "Oh dear, my time is up." He raised a hand, it glowed a dark purple.

His hand quickly wrapped at the base of her neck, her body stiffened. His grip tightened until her spine fully straightened.

She couldn't breathe. Her vision spun, darkening at the edges.

His words crashed in her ears. "You won't speak a word of this interaction to anyone, in any fashion. Written, verbal, telepathically—nothing of this will enter another soul's mind. I will give you this, however. There is more than one way to kill a king." The world around her thrummed as his hand traced delicately up her neck, his face drawing closer to hers. "A few days, I'll give you a bit of time to rest. *That* you can tell our dearest *Knight Captain Lukxa Ryoo* as he'll likely accompany you when you are forced to flee—sadly. Lukxa seems to push you on nicely. You two do react nicely together. How rude of me never to introduce myself properly when we've met *so many times*. You may address me as Nok when we speak. And I do hope you'll use my name. I am eager to hear it from your mouth, Lady Hollis. Now, *silence falls."* His lips pressed against her temple, cold and warm at the same time—a terrible paradox.

"Oh, I would appreciate it if you would bathe in something other than Sir Lukxa's and the prince's scents. It's unbecoming of you. Maybe I should have some proper soaps delivered to you." Nok's hand left her throat. Her body slid deep into the tub, her mouth only just above the water as her body trembled and shook.

He stepped toward the far wall of the washroom.

With the sweep of his hand all the candles in the room extinguished and plunged the room into darkness.

The bathroom door swung open, and all at once, the candles relit themselves.

"Hollis!" Lukxa came into view. His eyes wide as he rushed over to her. "What happened?"

His hands plunged into the water and gripped her slides, hoisting her upward until she was in a seated position.

Hollis opened her mouth to tell Lukxa what had happened. A burning pain silenced her. "I—" she would have to lie. "I dozed off." She swallowed. "I don't think I ate enough and the bath water was. . . hot."

"You have to be careful." Lukxa's voice was soft in her ears. Calming.

She leaned forward over the edge of the tub and set her head against his shoulder, dripping water from her hair down his back.

"I didn't want you to leave earlier." Her trembling arms raised and wrapped around his shoulder. "Please don't leave me alone in this forsaken castle again."

Lukxa's swallow was audible. His hands slowly curled around her body, pulling her closer to his own in a tight embrace. "I cannot promise that you'll never be alone in these walls again, but I will do my best to make sure that I am by your side." He tucked his face into the crook of her neck.

Hollis mirrored the action. She drew in a deep breath of his scent. Lukxa smelled of the woods, of freshly laundered clothes, of warmth and safety.

"Do you need help drying off?" His voice grew softer than she could imagine it ever could.

"I'll manage, thank you. Help me out, though?" Her jaw trembled as she spoke. She couldn't trust her legs to carry her weight outside of the tub.

Lukxa counted to three before he lifted her into the air. The cold air chilled her body, raising every hair along her flesh. He quickly set her upon the floor and wrapped her in a towel. "I need to wash up myself, do excuse me." No inch of Lukxa's skin was freed from the blush that consumed him.

He turned and walked to the sink where he gathered up his jar of teeth cleaning powder and a thin brush.

Hollis dried herself and joined Lukxa in finishing her evening tasks of brushing and oiling her hair, and then cleaning her own teeth.

Lukxa spoke to her again as they reentered the main portion of his apartments. "Hollis, I know we spoke earlier of what you would do once all of this was finished, and I do not want to push the topic at this moment, but I do look forward to working with you more. If that's something you wish?" Sir Lukxa's face softened as the morning sky began to warm behind him. The words tumbled from his mouth.

Hollis had never seen him so flustered.

Her heart pounded against her chest and climbed up her throat. Her stomach flipped and flopped as a shaky smile grew over her face.

Nok's words came crashing back. *You two do react nicely together.*

Hollis swallowed and tried to push the thoughts down. "Perhaps that is something I wish for. But, first, if we are to get any sleep this night—or morning as it is now, we ought to now." She gestured to the window in his study behind him, he followed her gaze and nodded as dawn broke across his face.

"Yes, you are quite right. You know, this is a celebratory evening. You do not have to sleep at the foot of the bed. Not any longer." Lukxa gave her another smile, adding to the soft smiles he kept giving her this evening.

They did nothing to settle around the prickling of her nerves.

She noticed when he slipped into bed beside her, how his body threatened to fit and mold so comfortably against hers—the tips of his fingers resting lightly against the fabric of her shirt, but not close enough to touch her spine. She couldn't find comfort in him.

Her skin burned as she slept in the light of the rising sun.

CHAPTER THIRTY

LUKXA

"We have finalized the lodging that all the knights traveling for the tournament need. All of the inns have rooms set aside for merchants, officials, and anyone else of a higher ranking title who may not be staying within the castle or any of the duchy in the area. All the functions have been organized and finalized. Representatives from Eargile will arrive sometime this evening, and I heard a few snow storms held them up. Let's see. . ." Lukxa trailed off, reading through the last few notes on his report.

The preparations the past several days had kept him busy, but did nothing to dampen the feeling of freedom he felt.

Almost nothing.

He tossed the papers onto the desk in front of him.

Hollis had been on edge since they caught Collin a week ago. She was constantly packing and repacking her things. She'd even tried her hand at packing his own things. Anytime he tried speaking to her about the matter of her endless worrying, she simply brushed him off and made light of how she just wanted to be prepared to ride the death train back to Hozen.

Perhaps he had pushed her a bit too far with his talks of future arrangements?

He couldn't deny his feelings that had been growing between them.

The desire to give them the space to grow and see if they were real or simply formed because she had come and saved himself and the crown.

Lukxa blew out a stream of air and leaned back in his chair. Trailing his eyes about the room brought no sense of comfort. The office of the royal family was stunning. The painted ceiling of lush green fields with different smiling creatures dancing, singing, making merry, stared down at him.

The walls leading up to the grand ceiling were coated in ornate paper of gold, silver, and bronze tree branches that wove together, leafing and flowering at set points. A few pale, gold-brushed, wooden shelves decorated the spaces on either side of a window. Filled with books and little treasures. Golden globes and figures, knights, spyglasses.

"Hello? Am I finally allowed to participate this year?" Dagen interrupted, signing off on another piece of paper in front of him. Another from the stack of Dukedoms and other families wanting to gain permissions to enter the castle. "I missed it last year. And you and Hollis keep giving me different answers." Dagen sat with his back to a grand, round stained window. The light flooding in painted his hair in a litany of colors.

Lukxa picked up his papers once more, allowing them to bend around his hand. "Prince, we've had this conversation. *Several times* by now" Lukxa was almost getting sick of Dagen's constant asking.

"That was when I was sick. I'm not sick anymore. Haven't been for an entire week." Dagen gestured to himself, showing off his very much 'no sick body' as he kept referring to it by. "I rode back into the castle on a grand carriage, sitting with an open window, smiling and waving. I would have kissed babies if it were allowed."

Lukxa gave Dagen his best impression of a mockingly stern expression before smiling. "You'll be sitting where your parents did, announcing the opening and close of the tourney. Any awards, *kissing babies*, whatever else is needed to help repair your reputation to the people. If it helps, you know I am not entering either. I will be right by your side. Maybe my beauty can help with your reputation."

Dagen gave a bitter scoff. "Yes, my *wonderful* reputation. I have a feeling it may take quite some time for me to polish what's been tarnished." He shook out his signing hand a few times, rolling his eyes as he did so. Dagen's wrist *cracked* a few times as it went.

"You have got time now, Dagen. Though your anger and disappointment are understandable. Next year's tournament will celebrate your first full year as king. Perhaps you will have a blushing bride to dedicate your victory to." Lukxa gave him a reassuring nod of his head.

Dagen scoffed. "If you say so. *Eugh*, I do not wish to live long in whatever the people think of me. I want Catol to see me as I am." He quickly signed the last piece of paper from the stack in front of him with a large, flourished signature, and set it aside to dry. The waiting pile to Dagen's left received a sharp glare.

Luxka nodded as he mentally refused to read another piece of paper this day. "I hope so. And that more last-minute work does not reveal itself to us." He went back on his words. "Though. . . if we were to come across more evidence against any of the councilors, I could deal with more paper. It would be a shame to miss something." Lukxa thumbed through the pile of papers pertaining to the case built against specific members on the Council.

Councilor Shad had been efficient in gathering testimony and evidence for Dagen and Lukxa to go through. The official charges would be brought after the coronation and tournament ended. Neither of them wanting to stain the events with what had transpired.

Reading through the papers had been a difficult feat. Every new page brought the burning anxiety of Lukxa discovering his own name thrown into the mix of damning evidence.

Especially hard was Muse's recollection of Collin attacking her. It had been brief, her words, but they were enough to warrant a deeper search of his chambers than the one that had been done when he was originally escorted back to ensure that the supposed attacker wasn't waiting for anyone in a room. Councilor Dem, Lukxa, and a few other knights had found the bloodied knife stashed deep in Muse's room. The rest of the set the thing belonged to was found in Collin's room.

Rather sloppy work.

The whole castle had woken in a tizzy at some point early that morning. The alarm of someone having been attacked, and then discovering through loose lips that a councilor had turned on another?

The rest of the council was red in the face as they attempted to keep the information as close to chest as possible. It wasn't long before gossip of the attack, and of Dagen's mysterious illness, made its way to the lips of the common people outside the castle walls.

"The gossipers and newsstands are going to love all of this," Lukxa drawled as he thumbed through another few pages.

"That may be good for me, Lukxa." Dagen said, leaning on his elbows and tapping his fingers together. "Yes, take the heat off of me, show me rising with my crown under the hand of a twisted council." He nodded his whole body as he spoke, egging himself on. "This is perfect. I should have sent someone with a letter to the papers in the city *days* ago. Get a good exclusive story out, have people clamoring to garner my attention at the tournament. You're right—I'll be far too busy to even think about participating." The glowing grin on his face was a pleasant sight when compared to the half-hearted, sickly smiles Lukxa had received recently.

And within a moment, that bright expression fell into something stale.

"Are you all right?" Lukxa asked, inclining his head toward his friend.

"Yes, I'm fine. Just. . . nothing. I'm fine." Dagen gained more and more strength by the day.

A week had passed since Hollis had lifted the curse upon his mind. It relieved Lukxa to see his charge walking freely without strain, though his body wasn't quite used to the freedom it had. Every now and again, Dagen's demeanor changed—like a flash of lightning. Lukxa could not tell if Dagen was waiting for the feelings of illness to return, or if he simply reminisced about them. Either way, Dagen refused to divulge what plagued him when those moments of somberness came.

Lukxa trusted that, in time, Dagen would open up about them.

Dagen propped his head up on his hand. "You know, fairy tales would dictate that I marry Hollis." He nodded his head as he spoke.

Lukxa's hand jerked, and he sliced his finger against the edge of the paper. He quickly stuck the bleeding finger in his mouth. "Fairy tales would have you marry the knight who saved you. I'm first in line for that wedding ring." This was a quick change of subjects. But as it was a far happier one, Lukxa was all right with the suddenness of it.

"No, no. It has to be Hollis." Dagen waved his hand about.

Lukxa snorted. "Do you have sudden intentions to marry her now, my prince?"

Dagen put on a mock-thinking face. "You know, perhaps I should. They say you never forget your first kiss."

"I didn't think you wanted to remember what her mouth felt like, considering it always came with the feeling of your insides being ripped apart?"

"Lukxa, I do not foresee myself forgetting what any of that felt like. Good or bad." Dagen flitted through a few more pages before setting them down on his desk and signing them.

The setting sun shone through the windows, backlighting the prince as he wrote.

For the first time in what seemed to be ages, Dagen wore his circlet. While there wasn't a strict need calling him to wear it, Lukxa presumed Dagen found some sense of comfort in having it settled neat against his brow. Reminding him that his official coronation would come as the sun rose.

Come morning, Dagen would be king.

A *knock* came from the ornate wooden door behind Lukxa. "Your Majesty, I've been sent up with your—and Captain Lukxa's—evening meals," a male voice sounded.

"Yes, bring it in," Dagen called. "I hadn't realized how hungry I was. How hungry *I've been*." He gave a half-hearted laugh as the door swung open.

In walked an Omil man with shaggy dark hair, dressed in pressed white shirt and dark pants. He pushed a small wheeled cart that held a few steaming plates, cups, and a pitcher.

It always took Lukxa aback to see someone that looked like him within the castle walls or Catol itself. It wasn't like it was a rare occurrence—hundreds of families surrendered their children to Catolian orphanages before the wars demolished everything in their path. Lukxa himself was taken into an Eargile home and shipped off to the academy when he came of age. That wasn't an uncommon fate for the extra children brought back from war.

The strange man kept his head bowed while he spoke. "Tonight's meal is a bit lighter in comparison to what they've been sending you the last few days, Prince Dagen. I assume they don't want you to be bogged down before tomorrow. If you require anything else, do let someone know and more will be brought." The server's accent was perfectly Catolian.

"Thank you. I will keep that in mind." Dagen responded, gesturing to the few empty spots on his desk.

The man quickly unloaded the meal in the sparse places and made to leave the room.

"Oh, before I forget, I was asked to relay a message to you," he spoke and stepped around the desk to Dagen's side when he'd gestured him closer. The man bent and covered his mouth as he whispered to Dagen.

Lukxa couldn't make out the words, but trusted he'd be told if necessary.

"I see. Thank you for relaying this information. Tell your sender that I understand."

"Consider it done, your Majesty." The man crossed an arm over his chest and gave a slight bow before putting the cart by the door and leaving.

"So, how much longer do you think it will be until Councilor Shad finishes his investigation into the Council embezzlement?" Lukxa asked, settling back into his chair on the opposite side of Dagen's desk, plate in hand.

Collin would be lucky he still breathed after everything he had done. Though he wasn't going down on his own. From what Lukxa heard of the interrogations, Collin had willingly outed several people inside and outside the council who had helped him with the embezzlement in return for a possible lighter sentence. Lukxa wasn't privy to the intimate details, but Shad told him that Sypher, Cane, and Sophy's names were all spoken with contempt in the investigation.

Though, no one breathed a word of the largest crime committed.

Lukxa wasn't privy to the list of people who were to be tried, but he knew it wasn't a short list. Yet it was a list in which every name lightened the load on his shoulder and the weight on his conscience.

Dagen's face smoothed over. "I don't think it matters when Councilor Shad wants to be done investigating into the matter. Everyone will be tried and sentenced tomorrow with what we have right now." Dagen stabbed at a small potato and ate it quickly before taking a sip of water.

"*Tomorrow?*" Lukxa could feel his confusion showing on his face. "Don't you think we should wait until we know where the money is going before we perform their hearing? Besides, you did not want to stain the festivities."

He tucked in on his own dinner, steamed and boiled potatoes paired with a small portion of meat and a hearty serving of leafy greens and vegetables. Perfectly pleasant, if only lacking a bit in the amount of food they were both given.

Dagen shook his head and leaned into his hand. "No. I've decided that if we draw out the whole process, it will feel like I'm slowly disbanding the Council for whatever reasons I can. If we bring to light all the issues, all at once, alongside Collin's attempted murder charges, it'll reflect better on my part as King. We do not have to know where the money was going to deal judgement on those who have done evil."

Lukxa's brows knit together, confusion settling in his stomach. "That doesn't sound like a phrase you would use."

"It's the truth, though. Why speak around it?" Dagen glanced up from his food, meeting his gaze. His brown eyes were cold. "You know as well as I do that this isn't something to deal with lightly. If we have enough to rule that they be dealt with, then dealt with they shall be." Another potato, another sip of water. "We don't need to waste time."

"I agree, but your words sound rather harsh."

Dagen blinked, his head shaking the slightest bit. "I do not know if I would count them as harsh, but then again, it was my life that an attempt was made on, not yours. I cannot extend mercy to everyone as I did you."

That stilled Lukxa's tongue.

It seemed Hollis wasn't the only one to speak rashly with him the last few days. She'd been tense whenever he spoke with her—no matter the topic.

Lukxa pushed the food on his plate about. "Your display of mercy is one I've never forgotten."

"I would hope not." The air in the office grew stagnant, no longer carrying the scent of the food or dried herbs and flowers. "Lukxa, you are one of my closest friends and a protector of our people. I charged you with upholding that. Protecting Catol is key." Dagen reached forward and picked up his glass of water, downing it in several, long swallows.

Then Dagen stood from his chair and stretched his back. It *cracked* several times as he twisted.

"That's true. Perhaps I've forgotten about some of the dangers that grow." It wasn't hard for Lukxa to slip into the mind of comfort.

Dagen *scoffed* and walked toward the round, stained glass window. "I do not blame you, Lukxa. It's hard to face the ugly in this world. But we have to so others can be spared of it."

"That's a rather mature statement, my prince. You're sounding more and more like your father."

Dagen's face turned toward Lukxa and glowed. It filled Lukxa with a sense of awe. "I hope to wear my father's crown with honor. But, in order to do so, I will need my beauty sleep. If I understand things correctly, I'm to be woken quite early to be bathed by the priests in the fountain as the moon sets, then bathed *again* in oils and perfumes, dressed, pampered—all manner of pleasant and unpleasant things." He quickly walked back to the desk and sat down. Then he shoveled the final bites of food from his plate in his mouth.

Lukxa raised his brows, tilting his head to the side. "Understandable, I do not envy you in this."

Dagen wiped at his mouth. "Perhaps you should take some effort in your appearance tomorrow, Captain Lukxa? I'm sure Lady Hollis wouldn't mind helping you bathe." Dagin shoved another bite of food in his mouth, chewing it with a knowing grin.

Lukxa almost choked on a carrot coin. "Oh, yes. I'm sure she'd find the task quite enjoyable."

Dagen smirked., "Yes, she would, wouldn't she? Why not give her an enjoyable task for once?"

Lukxa laughed. "All right, that's enough."

"I could make it a royal decree if you'd like? Or perhaps as a reward for her service to her country I could arrange that the two of you be wed. Yes, my first decree, marrying off my closest friend."

"Please don't."

"Oh, don't you worry," Dagen smiled. "I have something for you tomorrow."

CHAPTER THiRTY-ONE

HOLLiS

Morning came with Hollis being woken by Lukxa rummaging about his rooms for his dress uniforms. The sun hadn't even risen yet, and Lukxa was making a cacophony of noise.

"I do not understand how I misplace them every time I need them." Lukxa huffed and stalked to the wooden hope chest he had said was armed with a trap that would take Hollis' hand off if she wasn't careful.

"I'm not sure what to tell you. It's not like I took them." Hollis leaned back into her pillow at the top of the bed, doing her best not to vomit. Her stomach wrought itself without pause since her interaction with Nok.

Another shudder washed over her.

An entire week of darting her eyes everywhere she went searching for traces of his magic. Signs that Nok was going to strike herself, Lukxa, or Prince Dagen.

Even Prince Dagen seemed to notice the slightly odd feeling in the air. Everytime she had spoken with the prince since she'd cured him of the curse his eyes seemed forever away. His responses were curt and to the point.

Perhaps Prince Dagen was simply overwhelmed and tired. Much like herself.

"I heard you were fitted for a gown these last few days. Do you like it?" Sir Lukxa asked as he seemed to find something worthy in the chest to bring light to his eyes. He promptly slung it over his shoulder and moved onto the next search location in the area. His study.

Hollis *groaned*. "Yes, I was shocked at how quickly they were able to produce a dress. It's lovely." She hadn't remembered the last time she was so pampered. It was an enjoyable feeling. Almost enough to rid her of the sinking feeling that everything was going to be upheaved upon her head.

No, no it was far worse than the sinking feeling. Every fiber of her being *cried* out, willing her to shrink herself as small as she could become and hide away in a tree or rock the rest of her life.

Hollis had entertained the idea nights before. Imagining herself surviving off of flowers and nuts. Making friends with little rabbits and cats. It had been what she wanted once. To be free as dandelion fluff.

The idea wasn't worth losing her companionship with Sir Lukxa, or whatever more it was becoming.

And she had a mortgage.

There was no escaping without Sir Lukxa. And she wouldn't be able to convince him that they needed to leave until it was too late.

Lukxa walked back to his dressing area. Several new items hung over his shoulder. "I take it that the dress is hidden somewhere here in my rooms—or will it be brought to you?"

This was the part of the dress she wasn't fond of. "Yes, the nature of the garment requires that someone come and. . . sew me into it." She mumbled the last words into her pillow.

The seamstresses were convinced that the best way to secure the dress with how quickly they had to make it was by *sewing* Hollis into it.

Hollis hated the idea. But she would comply to wear such a beautiful dress. "Someone should be by soon. We've still a few hours until everything is starting, right?" She rubbed at her eyes and yawned. Her jaw *popped* a few times.

The sun hadn't even crested the mountains. Tradition dictated that Prince Dagen be crowned with the morning sun shining upon the crown.

With the coming dawn he would be a *king*.

Lukxa laughed. It was warm and light. "A few hours before things start does not mean a few hours until we have to be ready."

Hollis kicked her feet under the covers and buried her face into the pillow. "Please, Lukxa, I want to sleep." She turned her face to look at him and found his back was to her. Hollis hoped that he would answer by being quiet in his movements and letting her return to the land of dreams.

Lukxa stood frozen in his machinations. "When did you start to speak my name without a title?" His voice was no more than a whisper as he peered over his shoulder at her, a light blush on his face.

Hollis bit the inside of her cheek. "Is it still a problem for me to address you as such?" She could feel heat simmering up her own neck.

Lukxa's eyes widened slightly. "*No.*" His voice sounded breathless. Lukxa quickly blinked and turned back to finding his formal clothes.

"I give up." Hollis righted herself upon the bed. Sleep was not going to return to her with the conversations at hand.

Pushing off of the bed, she made her way to the kitchenette and poured herself a glass of water.

The threads of the glass pressed lightly against her skin as she drank from it.

Throat now cleared, her voice sounded crisp. "You're carrying in some ceremonial sword? Scepter? *Thing?* Right? Very official, quite amazing." Hollis took another long sip of water, relishing in how it cleared her mouth and throat of sleep.

"Yes, I have a few official things on my plate as Dagen's right-hand and as the Captain of the Royal Guard. I'll be overseeing the tournament in many fashions, making sure all the healers on site are prepared, smashing the hopes and dreams of anyone coming for my job."

She joined in his laughter. "Glad to know you're keeping your job safe." *It won't be for long.* "I hear there's to be a ball to close the evening?" That seemed the most likely time for Nok to start whatever upheaval he was planning. "I wonder how everything will go?"

"What are you meaning?" Sir Lukxa redressed himself in his dress uniforms.

She turned her gaze back into the kitchenette. "Well. . ." How could she phrase things without her throat closing up as it had the past week? She tapped her foot. "We're still unsure of who cursed Prince Dagen. What if they show up tonight and do something?"

"At an event celebrated by bringing in almost every knight in the kingdom? I would think it unlikely. You've dispelled the curse. Dagen is free of it. Collin is going to be locked away, as are other members of the Council who have been found guilty. I doubt whoever placed the curse is waiting around to see what happens. They likely got paid and ran off with the money."

Hollis heard metal fidgeting and assumed it safe to face back into the heart of the room.

When had Lukxa stopped changing behind the screen?

She drew in a long breath. Lukxa was stunning in his dress uniforms. A fitted ensemble of indigo, white, and gold. The high neck of the undershirt showed off the lines of his jaw. Over it lay a jacket decorated with several pins and medals. He'd tied his hair at the top of his head, and the shiny locks still cascaded down to the base of his shoulders. Strapped to his side was his ruby encrusted sword.

"Were you able to officially tie any council members to the cursing?"

Sir Lukxa sucked in his lips. "Not exactly. We're moving forward with the trials as is. They will happen today with whatever evidence and information we have." Lukxa stretched his neck in a circle, *cracking* several joints in the process. "It is likely that we may never know who placed the curse unless we get a council member to reveal that. And no one is going to talk because it will only make problems worse for everyone. Dagen has ordered me to let it go. We have what we need, we are not going to push for anything more than that." Lukxa didn't sound too pleased at the notion. Hollis wouldn't be either.

Then again, she knew who was behind all of this.

Councilor Muse had made a swift and speedy recovery thanks to Hollis' aid. And Nok was lingering about in the castle waiting for Hollis to teach him something. She hated the idea of being observed like a specimen. She was a person.

Nok had appeared a few times, posing as castle staff to bring people Hollis was around little missives or whatever. The seamstresses, kitchen staff bringing her meals, he even poised as the servant who came to pick up hers and Sir Lukxa's clothes for laundering.

Nok was insane. Claiming to want her by his side? What sort of fantasy was he living in? Life wasn't some sort of novel where a villain could get the girl and what he wanted.

No.

"By the way, Hollis." Lukxa's voice jerked her out of her musings. He held her gaze as she glanced up. "I have something for you tonight, after everything is over." He smiled.

Her spine straightened. "What is it?" Oh, she enjoyed getting gifts. But would Lukxa even have time to give her a gift? Would it be something she could easily carry with her once she left the castle?

She likely had until after the tournament finished in a few days. But which day would he strike in it? The day the jousters were crowned and given a rose to present to a lover? The hour that the sword-fighting ceased? Where would Hollis be when he launched whatever he was scheming?

"There's more than one way to kill a king."

Lukxa laughed. "I can not tell you now. That would ruin the whole point of a present."

A knock sounded at the door. "Lady Hollis, we're here to prepare you." The seamstress Hollis had worked with the past few days tried the handle.

"Just a moment," Sir Lukxa called, making his way over and unlocking the door.

"It's a pleasure, Captain," the older woman said as she pushed past him, quickly followed by two other seamstresses who carried Hollis' dress and a bag.

"Of course, Mirella. Make yourself at home. I'll be taking my leave. Hollis, I'll see you after the coronation. We can talk more then." He smiled and left, shutting the door behind him.

"Now that he's gone, it's time to get you into this beautiful dress." Mirella, the head seamstress, waved Hollis forward. "Go ahead and take off your over clothes, no need to be shy." Mirella was a middle-aged woman, Hollis would guess. Her dark hair melded beautifully with her ebony skin.

Hollis did as commanded and was positioned by the seamstress in the middle of the room, wearing only her undergarments.

"It's sad we cannot do anything with your hair," one of the younger girls with auburn hair mumbled. "It'd be so pretty braided." The young auburn haired girl then set to applying various powders on Hollis' face with a brush while the others unpacked the parts of her dress on the bed.

Hollis laughed, doing her best not to sound too disappointed or nervous. "Don't worry too much about adorning me." She wished her hair was a bit longer so they could do some sort of fanciful braid or updo. But they tended to pull at her scalp and cause her head to throb. Wrapped braids, though. She missed those greatly. And they'd never hurt her head.

"Nonsense, you're a guest of honor in the castle. I cannot believe you've been here for weeks! We could have prepared a grander dress. Not that your gown isn't grand already. I'm quite happy with my work," Mirella said, and held the dress forward to let Hollis step into it.

The silken layers slid up Hollis' middle. She stretched out her arms, allowing one of the seamstresses to fit the sleeves of the dress up to the bodice for sewing. Hopefully the sleeves wouldn't trap her arms. It would not be in the best interest of anyone if she wasn't able to move properly. They quite reminded her of the sleeves a bishop would have on their garments. Billowed in the length, but cuffed at the bottom.

Her eyes trailed to the bed as she was slowly sewn into the dress.

Hollis had taken the liberty of packing her bags with clothes and some money, keeping everything organized in case anything should happen. Beside her own sack was one she had packed for Sir Lukxa. She'd done her best to take items he wouldn't realize had moved but that'd still fit and prove useful to him in the long run—if they had to go somewhere for a long time without access to supplies.

Her mind had come up with several different, extravagant, situations that the pair of them could be thrown into.

There was no affording the stressful overthinking and wondering of when something would happen. Having a handful of things packed away and ready if they should need was enough to help still her mind from wandering too far.

A burning scraped along her side. Hollis jumped and let out a hiss of pain. The scrape of the needle pulled her attentions back to the matter at hand and the warming sky outside the window.

"Oh, sorry dear. But you're just about finished. Let me know if you want any adjustments made." Mirella said, turning Hollis' figure toward the golden mirror in Lukxa's room.

Delicate layers of silk floated down from her waist, sitting a hair above the floor. The midnight fabric was traced with golden lines. The bodice fit snugly against her frame, a soft lace outlined her chest extending up to swath her neck before the dress sank into the sleeves that sat cuffed at her wrist with little pearl buttons. It was beautiful.

"I believe you'll match the Captain in this. You make a handsome pair." One of the other younger seamstresses giggled. She had a lighter brown shade of hair, complementing her reddish-brown skin. The girl then approached Hollis with a small pink glass bottle of perfume and sprayed it around Hollis' body.

White flowers and sandalwood.

Hollis loved the combination. The scents reminded her of Lukxa's soap and the flower garden she had toiled over back in Quinlin.

They were beautifully melded together.

Heat flooded her cheeks. Hollis nodded, a shy smile creeping onto her face. She felt like a princess. "Thank you, and thank you for this dress. I know you didn't have much time to prepare it—"

"If I can speak frankly, the pattern is a classic. One of my favorites." Mirella picked invisible lint from the sleeves. "And it was a good exercise in teaching how to construct a fitted dress. Many dresses we work on in the castle aren't fitted to a person per say, but general sizes. Nice to work on such a pretty thing again." She patted Hollis' side as she continued checking the seam allowances.

"You look wonderful. Are you sure we can't convince you to do anything to your hair?" The youngest girl, skin matching Mirella's, spoke. She helped tie Hollis' shoes onto her feet. Her emerald toned walking boots weren't the first pick of the seamstresses, but Hollis was picky about what went on her feet. And the shoes were comfortable and fashionable enough to match the dress.

"Girls, we do have a few other people to attend to this morning." Mirella circled her hand, gesturing to the mess of pins and threads. "Let's get cleaned up and *out* of Lady Hollis' hair."

She bequeathed the seamstresses an appreciative smile. "Thank you for the beautiful dress everyone."

Hollis stood as they finished packing their things. She stood long after they left. Simply there in the middle of the room. Staring at the door.

It suddenly opened. "Lady Hollis, I'm here to escort you to the coronation." Wilfrin was dressed in a set of uniforms similar to Sir Lukxa's, though Wilfrin's weren't near as glorious.

"Wonderful." Hollis addressed Wilfrin first before she grabbed her cane by the door and left the room.

She and Wilfrin took a brisk pace down the halls, passing servants and corridor alike. The castle buzzed with life in a manner she hadn't seen before. Maids dusted every possible surface—even the ones that never gathered dust—servants rushed through the halls with linens tucked tightly in their arms, and people dressed in fineries wandered about.

Nok's face stood grinning out of the corner of her eye in a side corridor. Hollis froze and whipped her head back only to be pushed forward by Wilfrin. "No time to wander around, we truly don't want to be late."

Hollis' heart began to race. She bit her lip and kept walking. Her heart skipped another beat as Nok's face appeared in the next corridor, and the next—each time a step closer to the junction.

Each time she saw his face her body tattered. The desire to run and hide in a hole grew stronger. The wickedness and malice that came from his figure smothered any sense of hope she'd built up in her heart.

No. No, that was what he wanted her to feel. What his magic influenced her body to do.

She steered her vision forward. His image was a petty trick intended to frighten. She would not give it the power to do so.

The grand doors of the Throne Room loomed down the final hallway, open. She could hear people bustling about, making idle chatter.

One hall left to pass in front of. You can do this Hollis. That's the plan. Keep walking, Hollis.

Nok stood there, shoes lined with the edge of the carpet, a grin stretched across his face.

Wilfrin turned and gave Hollis a bright smile. "We're here. In one piece. I was told your spot is reserved in the pews toward the front. I can't sit with you I'm afraid. You should be able to see myself and Sir Lukxa at any given time."

"Why tell me that—"

"He's worried about you." Wilfrin's brows knit together as he looked her over once more before entering the tall doors.

"This is exciting." Nok's breath burned her neck, but he disappeared before she could turn her head.

No, *no.* He was messing with her.

He couldn't do anything in front of so many people.

A step inside the throne room showered her in the opulences the rest of the castle was not afforded.

Velvet curtains lined the windows that made up a majority of the walls. Gilded pedestals that stood between the embroidered curtains, each holding up pearled vases. Incense burned at other intermittent points of the room, bringing a deep wooded scent to the room.

It weighed her shoulders toward the floor. Tears filled her vision, her body lurching as she walked down the aisle, struggling to breath.

No, not the scent of the woods. *Fear.*

Voices clamored over each other, all talking of the future of the country, the rumors of what happened inside the castle walls a week ago.

The desire of power for oneself.

Hollis shook her mind free of it.

The first hint of morning light danced at the edge of the windows in the room.

She straightened her spine and made her way toward the front of the room, finding a bit of free space on the edge of a pew that sat beside the windows.

Hopefully the sun would warm the room as it continued to rise. Even though the space was filled with bodies, the air was frozen with anticipation.

The different threads wound together in a dizzying display. So many variations and colors pushed against her skull. Hollis did her best to settle them down in her mind, as if putting a haze over them to see the physical details better.

"Everyone, please be seated," an old priest intoned. Hollis jumped at his

voice; she hadn't seen his entrance. His face was covered in wrinkles and a glimmer twinkled from his eyes.

Hollis sat pinned to the edge of the bench by a few older women who flapped their handheld fans wildly, which did nothing to help the chill that settled deep into her marrow.

It wasn't long before the priest finished rambling on about the glory of reigning and keeping peace over all. A short history lesson was added in at different points, subtle stabs taken at each prefecture for their history of fighting over the throne that, according to the priest, belonged to Catol.

The doors at the back of the hall where Hollis had entered *cracked* open. They sent a burst of air down the aisle as they swung open.

Everyone in the room stood and craned their heads backward to the grand doors.

The councilors processed in first, Councilor Dem leading the pack, a crown held high in his hands. Councilor Collin surprisingly was trailing behind them at the end of the line, though he seemed worse for wear.

Her stomach dropped when she first saw him, but understood that some pretenses needed to be kept. That had to be the reason the man was walking in with all the other councilor's Lukxa said had committed terrible crimes against the crown. A warning would have been nice.

Hollis assumed Lukxa wasn't aware of it.

Councilor Dem bowed, handed the crown into the hands of the priest, and continued on. The council all lined the front of the room as if they were witnesses in a wedding.

Lukxa strode down the aisle next. His uniforms had somehow become even more stunning on his person since she had seen him last. A large sword lay flat against his two hands, which held it outward in front of him as he walked. It was a magnificent blade, and a sharpened one at that.

Hollis focused on him, taking in the sight of his emerald woven threads. His body was beautifully woven.

Each step Lukxa took toward the priest was steady and sure. No wavering or faltering in his manner.

His eyes locked with hers and grew brighter, a smile fighting to take place on his trained face. She gave a slight nod of her head and the meekest of smiles she could offer without being obvious to everyone surrounding them.

As Lukxa walked past her she could smell the rich sandalwood oil from his hair. And white flowers—

No. Not oil.

He was wearing the same perfume as her.

Hollis' eyes grew wide as the sun, and her face was as hot to match.

"Who brings the sword that has brought peace in this land?" the priest called.

"I, Sir Lukxa Ryoo, Captain of the Royal Catolian Guard, have brought forward the Sword of Peace, forged in destruction to bring it no more." If Hollis wasn't in love with his voice already, this moment would have been the one she fell for it.

The confidence in which Lukxa spoke brought a sense of pride to the room. Lukxa then took his place on the right side of the older man.

The doors opened once more.

Whispers and gasps alike filled the room as everyone's eyes went wide.

Prince Dagen was a golden sight to behold. Gone was the sickly boy wasting away in his bed. He had been replaced by a striking man of twenty years with the strength to match.

His garments were completely white with golden trim, while a ruby cape with golden embroidered suns on his shoulders dragged on the floor behind him. Set on his head was a rosen circlet, the finer details obscured. The scepter he carried looked to weigh an unreasonable amount despite being thin and long. It reached his shoulders, woven in gold what appeared to be four branches of a tree, emerald leaves sitting at the top holding tight to a giant pearl or opal.

As he approached the altar, tiny whispers fluttered in the air.

Questions of this being the same prince that every rumor abounded by, confirmation that he was late King Trist's son, and a number of words Hollis couldn't decipher.

"All may be seated." The priest's voice boomed through the large hall.

A large *clatter* sounded from overhead.

Hollis craned her head up and suddenly realized there was seating *above* her head in the arched balconies that framed the painted ceilings.

"We have gathered here today to witness the sun rising on the crown anew. Prince Dagen Alder Catol, you have come into the age in which this crown shall be placed upon your head. You shall uphold it upon your body as you uphold the people of Catol. Looking upon everything that is just with pride, and everything that is foul with disdain. Today, you swear upon the sun that you will let this crown shine for her people as a beacon of light beckoning in the future." The old priest took a step back, allowing Lukxa to fill in his place.

Lukxa raised the blade and rested it over Prince Dagen's left shoulder. "Prince Dagen Alder Catol, you have grown in the teachings of Catol, have been nurtured by her love and compassion. Do you vow with this sword, forged in destruction to bring it no more?"

"I vow to keep peace in the heart of Catol." Dagen's voice sounded strong, filling the room easily.

The sword moved to rest above his head. "Do you vow to wield your power in a manner that is befitting the strength of Eargile, the wisdom of Rex, and the growth of Hozen as the ruler of Catol?"

"I vow to uphold the values of the people as my own." The gathered crowd stirred with every word he spoke. Nothing would be said here, but Hollis could tell everyone had thoughts of their own about Prince Dagen's words.

Finally, the sword settled onto his right shoulder. "The final vow we ask you swear by is the greatest of all. Do you vow to hold the needs of Catol above your own, nurturing her as she nurtured you to this moment in your life, forsaking self for other?"

Dagen stood, rising up with the blade still upon his shoulder. "I will raise her needs above mine own as I raise the sword with my body. So do I swear." His voice was solid and warm. It easily filled the room with a confidence and sense of finality.

Lukxa quickly drew the sword back and extended the blade's handle to Prince Dagen, who readily took it up in his right hand. Scepter held tightly in his left hand.

Sunlight steadily filled the top of the room, casting bands of golden hues.

The priest moved forward once more to stand beside Lukxa. "The vows of the sun have been taken as morning light obeys their command. As your circlet is removed, do not forget the weight it gave you. It taught you how to carry and right yourself in order to keep it upright and steady in preparation for the crown, whose weight may be more to bear than expected."

Lukxa's hands gently took up the circlet from Prince Dagen's head and walked backward toward Councilor Shad. The pieces of flaxen hair around Prince Dagen's face fell in waves as he twisted his head. The rest of his golden curls sat tied just between the blades of his shoulder.

The air went still as the ornate crown, which now shone brightly in the morning sun, was lowered onto Prince Dagen's bowed head.

Lukxa's voice sounded in a loud cry. "All hail the father of our land, King Dagen Alder Catol. May the sun forever shine upon your reign!"

Dagen straightened himself and turned to face the crowd, the scepter and sword firmly grasped in his hands and the crown standing brilliantly upon his head.

The room exploded in voices, everyone standing on their feet.

Hollis joined in the cry from her seat. "*May the sun forever shine upon your reign, King Dagen!*" Once more tears pooled in her eyes, but for a far different reason. Pride filled her.

She clutched at her chest, fingers tangling in the flowy fabric of her bodice. Her heart sang.

The ceremony was beautiful. Everything had been perfect. Even with all the councilors who would ruin it if they could. Perhaps their reason in attending was to see that there was no manner in which they could have tarnished the crown?

Dagen gave a subtle nod of his head to the people in the room. "As I vowed, I will uphold the honor and peace in Catol to the best of my abilities. Starting at this very moment. Judgment must be enacted."

The noise of the crowd vanished as everyone stood frozen.

Hollis could feel the fear return, settling deeper into the room, smothering all scent and sound.

She blinked, the once happy tears falling from her eyes.

Dagen continued. "As I approached the age of beginning my reign, and Catol rested in the hands of the Council, a miasma spread. Conspiracy to tarnish my reign flourished in the mouths of those who should never have bred it. My first act as king is to bring to trial Councilor Collin, for his misdeeds against the people of Catol and the attempted murder of Councilor Muse."

A few knights who had been standing guard along the walls of the room seized Collin and dragged him to stand before Prince—*King*—Dagen and forced him to his knees.

More whispers floated in the air, too many words for her to process. Her ears grew fuzzy as all the sound around her grew faint.

"*Silence.*" Dagen's voice was commanding, but far from harsh. It commanded power easily. "It is unprecedented to hold such a trial on the very day of coronation, but there are actions that need to be brought to light. Right now the light of Catol shines strong. So it is fitting it use it in an effort to eradicate any and all darkness."

Quiet washed over the crowd. "Councilor Collin, for your misdeeds against the people of Catol with the embezzlement of funds meant to benefit the people you serve and your attempts to cover such actions by your violence against a fellow Councilor, from this moment on, the name of Hozen is wiped from the Council. The line ends with *you*. You have disgraced your position to this kingdom and to your family. What say you to this?" Dagen's facial expressions lent themself to curiosity, his pitch bending.

And then Dagen's face went perfectly still. Smooth as a river stone.

Collin fumbled his words a few moments before he seemed to find the strength to speak. "I find what you've said to be true, your majesty. I acted in greed. But please, have mercy upon my family. Do not take this title from my sons. I alone sought to end another's life. I alone stole funds from the people who needed them most. Have compassion on those who have done no wrong." Collin clasped his hands, lacing his fingers together. Tears and snot ran down his twisted face as he begged.

Dagen scoffed, casting his hand forward to the rest of the room. "What mercy did you have for the sons and daughters of Catol? The Council has ruled and found that your heart is lacking. Your title and lands will be given to one who is able to uphold the values Hozen proudly bears for her mother Catol. Your coffers will be given to replenish what was taken. You, Collin, shall be held to the full extent of our laws. Now, shall you walk out of this room with your head held high in the hopes of regaining the trust of the people, or shall you be carried out in mockery?" Hollis had never heard this tone from Dagen before.

While it held tones of ridicule and scorn, it was almost frightening, even if the words themself were exactly what she wanted to hear.

Collin was being punished for his heinous crimes, but yet lived.

Perhaps his fate of a stripped family title and repossessed funds were worse than imprisonment or death.

"I shall exit with the small shred of honor I have left for my family." Collin stumbled over his words and scrambled out of the throne room, two guards following closely behind him.

Hollis stood frozen as several other members of the council and Dukedoms of the land were called forward.

Councilor Sypher and Councilor Cane were banished from the council

for their own embezzlement, they were to return to their homes with nothing to their names. Several dukes' and duchess' were found guilty of treason and conspiracy for murder.

Judgment fitting their crimes was excised upon each of their heads. None quite as severe as Collin's, but all shameful in their own right.

It was not long before a solid group of the crowd had vanished. Punishment and shame attached to their names. All condemned in their own rights.

Soon, there were only six councilor's left standing at the front of the room alongside Dagen were Muse, Shad, Sophy, Dem, and another two whose names Hollis couldn't pull to the front of her mind.

And of course, Lukxa, who stood by with an expression of calm horror in his eyes.

Dagen smiled and raised his hands slightly. "Now, before the celebrations begin, there is one more motion I need to bring forward. One of great importance. Sir Lukxa, Lady Hollis, come and kneel before me."

Her body stiffened as she stood, not knowing how she was able to find the strength to move.

Carefully she approached King Dagen. His gaze pierced her as a tense smile grew on his face. The sun pelted down upon her as she knelt beside Sir Lukxa. She restrained herself from asking what was happening.

Dagen's voice whispered in their ears. "I told you I had something special for you."

"I'm afraid that some more concerning news has come to light." Councilor Muse stepped forward. Her auburn hair pulled back tight against her scalp. "In our searching through Councilor Collin's journals and ledgers, we found some information that all the remaining councilors agree is troubling." Muse's mouth pulled into a flat line.

Hollis studied each councilor's face. Each one was devoid of emotion. All their threads were hidden from her.

What was happening?

"Another sentencing is to be carried out. One I regret in having to deliver." Dagen's voice lost all warmth and life, replaced with a frigid pain.

Hollis turned and narrowed her gaze on Dagen's face, trying to see if any remnants of illness or curse had clung to him.

She blinked a few times, trying better to focus.

Her head cocked to the side.

Where are his threads?

The tension in her jaw grew. A sourness stabbing beneath her tongue.

"Dem, what's going on?" Sir Lukxa's figure was wavering.

Councilor Dem faced away as Sir Lukxa attempted to stand, only to be forced back to his knees by the scepter in Dagen's hand. Knights came up behind them and gripped Hollis' and Lukxa's arms. The flow of blood was cut off from Hollis' hands.

"Of course, you didn't think we would not uncover the fact that you tried to assassinate Prince Dagen? Treason of the highest kind—you and the Tablin woman will face your sentencing right alongside your friend, dear Councilor Collin," Councilor Sophy responded, her fingers trailing against the blade of her own ruby encrusted sword.

"*Healer* Hollis, it is by your hand that the past several months our king fell ill, to the point of death." Councilor Muse spoke, each word carrying more weight to add to Hollis' crumbling resolve. Muse rubbed her hands over her middle where the scars of the wounds Hollis healed sat. Muse's lips moved, '*Thank you*' she mouthed.

Hollis was going to vomit. She couldn't stop her gagging and dry heaving. Her back spazzed, the pain in her head so great that she couldn't see.

The knight that held her shook Hollis hard. It snapped her body out of its retching.

"Now." Dagen took a small step forward, hesitant. "Captain Lukxa, you have been found to be working with a Tablin magician in the efforts to poison myself and end the reign of Catol all in the name of revenge. Your charade of being the last savior in this country has been revealed."

Dagen cleared his throat as shouts of shock and horror filled the room. "The punishment for your crime is *death* as you would have delivered it. You've been given the grace to witness the sun one last time. As she climbs full in the sky, you shall be delivered unto death. My heart is broken for the loss of a friendship I believed to be true, but I vowed as king to uphold the needs of Catol before my own. However. . . I do not need a friend who would so mercilessly *take*." A rage laden between his breaths.

There were no threads surrounding Dagen. No fiber of his being was made known to Hollis.

Her throat closed, and she couldn't swallow the fear that built in her mind. The room spun about until her gaze fixed upon a silhouette lined in sun from the far shadows in the room.

Nok emerged, smiling from where he walked out of the shadows and into the broad light of day. No one seemed to notice him other than Hollis. He gave a sly glance side to side, tilting his head as he went.

Nok's teeth clenched tight to hold back the laughter she could see bobbing in his throat. Slowly he lifted a finger to his lips and the world faded into dull buzzing.

Nok's hand moved from his mouth to the ornate vase standing proud on a pedestal beside the grand throne. His slender fingers traced the rim, he sucked in his lips. Then he gave it a delicate push with a singular finger, sending shards scattering across the floor.

The knights startled and faced each other, confusion written in the wide-eyed expression they wore.

Smoke and anix coated Hollis' mind.

Magic.

Vase after vase crashed, one after another down the grand room. A roaring wind flooded into the hall and flapped the thick velvet curtains.

The room roared with magic as Nok raised his arms and unleashed an array of chaos the room gladly descended into.

Remaining courtiers, knights and servants alike screamed as the grand windows shattered inward, raining glass upon them all. Shards from the vases and glass cut through the air and the hands that gripped Hollis' arms disappeared. She fell forward, curled up on the ground.

Hollis did her best to keep her eyes open, she searched the room for Nok, but could not find him.

King Dagen took a step backward, his ruby cape flying behind him as he held the sharpened ceremonial sword backward. The blade caught beams of sunlight and blinded her.

Hollis' teeth ground together, an angry cry stuck in her throat. She clutched at her head. Blood throbbed against her skull.

Nok's laughter filled her buzzing mind. "This, Hollis, is where you *run*."

THE END

ACKNOWLEDGMENTS

I'm typing this page last, after everything has been said and done. I'm sitting in my office chair waiting for my sisters to come hang out with me for the first time in months. So many people helped make this dream of publishing my debut book a reality. It is hard to believe that I'm finally finishing my debut novel, my third book, and publishing it for you all to read!

It's crucial to thank the people around you after such a large accomplishment. It's also crucial to take a moment to realize that you did this. So firstly, thanks to me, for having the grit and determination to get this book done and into your hands. You did the hard thing. You were brave when fear threatened to smother your creative light, and determined when you wanted to quit. You did this.

Thanks to my editing team! Without them, I couldn't have given you such a polished book. To Hannah Carter, for spending hours upon hours chatting about plot and characters with me. Without you, this book wouldn't be nearly as good as it is now. Everyone praise her, she (and Willow) made this book wonderful. Without her, it'd be 30k words shorter! So she gave you more Hollis and Lukxa fluff.

To Willow Whitehead, my Nightshade Publishing® Buddy. You helped me dream of this book and the little chaotic beans the characters are! Without you, I wouldn't be able to run this company or post things to social media spelled correctly. You're a wonderful friend.

To Hunt, for nurturing this idea with me as a joke and then pushing me to turn my silly idea into something bigger. I hope this was everything you dreamed this story could be. I want to make you proud. (And I'm excited for your book too! It'll be amazing; everyone read it when it's out!)

Next, Alexandra! Thank you so much for your feedback on the story and the encouragement you gave me. It means the world to me to have friends who truly care about me and my stories. I love being in your tribe.

Zilla, you were a wonderful help in keeping me on track! Our messages of encouragement and pushing each other got our books done. You did it!

To my loving husband, to whom the book is dedicated. Your love and support have allowed me to work on my craft. You push me to be a better writer, but also to *rest*. Without you, I likely would have gone crazy and never slept. Thank you for everything you've given me, and this book! Words cannot express how much I love you.

Thanks to my family, for all their encouragement and support. (Specifically Abigail, who was upset when she opened the proof and didn't see her name explicitly written out. You get to be special Kablabby.) I love you all so much and I hope that you actually never read this book, but because I know that you will, against my wishes, don't judge me.

A big thank you to the helpful members of my writers' group. Your encouragement and constant meetings were the spawn of many, many chaotic ideas.

To all my beta readers, those who read the rough versions of this book and still loved it. And, to all of you! Thank you for picking up my book and giving it a chance. I hope you enjoyed it! Your support allows me to keep writing and publishing stories. Something I dearly love to do.

To LolloCo! You brought my characters to life! Without you, there'd be no art, no pretties, and no beautiful drawings of my Catolian Trio. You truly brought this book to life! Here's to book two!

Finally, to God. Everything that has happened to me has led me to this moment. You gave me the desire to craft and create. And when I turned away from it, in fear and anxiety, you pushed me to create. To write. I should trust in you more.

Xanna Renae loves daydreaming about how to save her characters from the messes she puts them in. Currently she is giving life to the ideas inside her head from rural Missouri where she lives with her husband, Noah, and cat, Maestro. She has a bachelor of arts in Creative Writing from Southern New Hampshire University, where she graduated with highest honors.

When she isn't writing you can find her tucked away in her little bungalow reading, snuggling with her cat, or playing video games with her husband.

Find her online talking about writing, publishing, and life with chronic illnesses just about everywhere

@XannasBooks or on her website XannaRenae.com